# Love Overboard

Ada Barumé graduated with a politics degree from Cambridge University before moving to London to become a journalist, specialising in African news. With her debut novel she draws on her own experiences of being a young, black woman looking for fun, love and adventure. When she's not working, you'll find her agonising over what outfit to wear or searching for the nearest dancefloor.

# LOVE
## Overboard

### ADA BARUMÉ

avon.

Published by AVON
A division of HarperCollins*Publishers* Ltd
1 London Bridge Street
London SE1 9GF

www.harpercollins.co.uk

HarperCollins*Publishers*
Macken House, 39/40 Mayor Street Upper,
Dublin 1, D01 C9W8
Ireland

A Paperback Original 2024

1

Copyright © Ada Barumé 2024

Ada Baruméasserts the moral right to
be identified as the author of this work.

A catalogue record for this book is available from the British Library.

ISBN: 978-0-00-868630-7

This novel is entirely a work of fiction.
The names, characters and incidents portrayed in it are
the work of the author's imagination. Any resemblance to
actual persons, living or dead, events or localities is
entirely coincidental.

Set in Birka by HarperCollins*Publishers* India

Printed and bound in the UK using 100% Renewable Electricity at CPI
Group (UK) Ltd

*For all the brown girls who convinced themselves he didn't fancy you: he did.*

# Chapter One

Sofia hadn't been abroad in so long that she could not help but feel startled every time someone spoke to her in Italian. This particular someone was the receptionist at the maroon-carpeted, three-star hotel she was going to be spending the night in.

She looked up from her phone where she had been staring at the internet search results for 'bars and restaurants near me'. She was standing in the hotel lobby, brow furrowed and feeling out of her depth. Ironic really – her life was food, but she couldn't remember the last time she had gone out to eat or drink. 'Um sorry, I'm English,' she said apologetically.

The receptionist seemed to understand what she was apologising for. 'Did you need any recommendations? There are a lot of nice places nearby, maybe for food or a drink?' Her English was perfect, and Sofia felt oddly flattered that she had not immediately been identified as a 'Brit abroad'.

'Oh yes, I was actually trying to look up somewhere to . . .' Sofia fumbled with her phone as she walked to the reception desk and held the screen up for her to see. 'This place is quite near here. Is it any good?'

'Lovely for a glass of Aperol Spritz – I know that that is very popular with our British guests. It's right on the beach, so there is also a lovely view.' The woman looked younger up close and Sofia could see what looked like a love bite peeking above the collar of her white shirt. She couldn't help but wonder what it would be like to grow up in a place like this, a stone's throw from miles of beautiful beaches, days bathed in sun, evenings spent at beach bars, balmy late-night walks, kissing in the moonlight. It had been a while since Sofia had thought about anything resembling 'romance', and here she was lusting after the imagined life of this stranger in front of her, who looked like she was barely out of her teens. She reminded herself that she was not here for pleasure; she was here to work. Moonlit strolls along the beach were not for people like her. She didn't have the time for stuff like that.

'Perfect, I'm only looking for somewhere pretty to sit and enjoy the sunset. Thanks for your help.' The receptionist smiled, absent-mindedly rearranging her collar, and then started typing something. Sofia wandered out into the evening, down the road and towards the beach.

She found a small table in the corner with a beautiful view. A rugged coastline, terraces of white and terracotta villas, and beyond that swathes of marbled green and grey hills. Sofia wanted to just enjoy the view, but she couldn't shake that niggling feeling of anxiety that had been born in the pit of her stomach since she landed this new job. She knew that Mary had taken a chance on her, and she didn't want to let anyone down. More than that, she didn't want

2

to have to return to London with her tail between her legs and admit that her big adventure had been the 'foolish' career move her friends and old colleagues had warned her it would be.

She pulled out the recipe cards from her bag and began flipping through them. This was her chance to finally cook her own menu. She was excited and nervous as hell. She had planned the whole first three weeks – breakfast, lunch and dinner – each day with its own set of flavours. To try and be as efficient and seasonal as possible she was going to borrow an idea from her old restaurant: that some of the same ingredients would feature throughout the day. She might make pancakes with a pineapple compote for breakfast, and then lunch would be a poke bowl with pineapple instead of mango, and then dinner would be topped off with pineapple and rum pudding. This would make the meals feel thematic, but she hoped it wasn't too gimmicky. A culinary journey from sunrise to sunset – that's what she had pitched to Mary.

She was messing around with Wednesday's ingredients list. Would she be able to source blueberries when they stopped off in Capri? Berries in the Mediterranean in early summer? What was she thinking? She began flipping through her dog-eared notebook. She was sure she had done something similar with apricots instead.

She heard them before she saw them. *As you often can with Americans,* she thought, stealing a glance in their direction as they made it very clear to the waitress that they were only there 'for drinks'.

3

'How about that little table overlooking the beach?' The voice was distinctly low, and manly, she found herself noting.

He was the sort of man who was almost obnoxiously good-looking, and as is often the way with men like that, he seemed to be fully aware of it. His dark hair with just the right amount of curl, and the kind of lustre that only generational wealth can buy. Broad shoulders, a light stubble and deep tan. She thought that he looked like the leader of the pack, the chief Chad. The waitress blushed slightly as she walked the four men to the table near the window.

'*Grazie mille,*' said Chief Chad, in what sounded like disarmingly fluent Italian. As he looked up Sofia caught his gaze, and it was only then that she realised she'd been staring. His eyes were green. She felt embarrassed and looked away. She was just another blushing woman to him, and she couldn't bear to give him the satisfaction. There was something about the way he smirked at her that made her irrationally angry. It was something that was always there in men like him, the ones who waltzed through the world like they owned it. She was determined not to reinforce that belief, if she could help it.

This was her last night of freedom, and she wasn't about to let this random jock distract her from her recipe cards and the delicious Crodino she was drinking. She looked around the terrace and took a moment to think about where she was. It looked like somewhere straight out of a wanderlust Instagram story. The light was turning golden, a warm breeze drifting in from the sea. She looked out across the horizon. Soon she would be out there herself. Well, she would probably be holed up in a tiny, windowless kitchen for most of the day, but she would be at sea. It was all she could remember having wanted. She set down the jumble of cards on the table.

She had grown up by the sea, albeit the English coast, which was not really in the same league as the Amalfi variety, but still, the smell of salt in the air was comforting. When she had got her spot at Lochland Fleet's culinary school, she couldn't have known it would take her seven years to get back to the ocean. Three years in the Yorkshire Dales for school, another two in Oxford first as a commis chef and then as a chef de partie. London next, where she'd landed what she thought was her dream job, at Nakachwa, the trendiest Michelin-starred spot in the city. She was promoted to sous after just six months. It was unheard of and she suspected everyone had hated her for it.

For a second, she let her mind wander to those last few weeks at the restaurant, how tired, sad and pale she had been. How much she had dreaded setting foot in that pristine, beautiful kitchen, how hard she had had to work to never meet his eyes over the countertop.

Amid the blood and sweat and tears of the last eighteen months she had lost sight of what she really wanted. On those lonely night buses home, through the blinking lights of the dozing city, she would fantasise about the sea. The flat expanse of blue, the calmness and the chaos of waves meeting the shoreline. She shook her head, and away with it the memories of drizzly London. She was here now. She could feel the colours seeping back into her body, chasing out the sepia tones of a past life. Her skin turning browner, her curls catching the bronze of the sunshine. She drank in the last rays of mauve sunlight, letting out a deep sigh. She was ready.

Over at the table overlooking the beach, the Chads were laughing, far too loudly, thought Sofia.

'Well, I guess we won't see you until Thanksgiving?' one of them was saying.

'Aww, you going to miss me?' joked Chief Chad, smacking his friend on the back so hard that he began to splutter on his beer.

'He's only asking for his sister. He can't stand another six months of her asking after you,' interjected another.

Chief Chad threw back his head, laughing and revealing a pearly row of very American teeth. 'Listen, the girl is sweet. Honest to God, I think she's great, but I think I made myself quite clear.'

'Did you give her the "lone wolf" line?'

'Hell no, that's so ten years ago. I told her I was "emotionally unavailable".'

At this, all the men laughed raucously, whilst many of the other drinkers, who had up until now been enjoying a more subdued evening drink, volleyed disapproving glances in their direction.

Internally, Sofia raged. Why did men like him have to say things like that? Once upon a time 'emotionally unavailable' had been something that she and her friends had said, rallied around and shielded themselves with. It was the reason she was single – 'it's not you, babe, it's him!' That and her complete disregard for a work-life balance. Now here was Chief Chad using the line to cast off some poor girl he probably never had any interest in in the first place. What had been a balm turned into the hot poker of rejection.

More laughing, more drinking and then the shrill clatter of smashed glass. 'Oh shit, Connor. Watch out, man, these shoes have got to last me.' But Chief Chad was chuckling, dabbing at his wet shirt with a napkin. His eyes sparkled with good humour and Sofia found herself, once again, thinking about how green they were. Time for another drink. Sofia wandered over to the bar, elbows on the counter, trying to catch the eye of the waitress, who seemed to be the only person working that evening.

'*Scusi,*' she mumbled weakly.

'*Mi scusi, potrei avere altre due birre? E penso che potremmo aver bisogno di aiuto per le pulizie.*' That perfect Italian, still somehow American-sounding and too loud in her ear. She could feel him right behind her, standing too close. The waitress looked up, blushing again.

'*Il tuo italiano è impeccabile,*' she gushed. '*Naturalmente, farò venire qualcuno al vostro tavolo.*'

'*Grazie.*' The waitress scuttled off into a back room. Sofia sighed loudly. Apparently, she was doomed to have to witness the obnoxiousness of Chief Chad up close, and wait indefinitely for a drink.

'Sorry, I didn't mean to push in. I'll get you a drink to make up for it,' he intoned over her shoulder. She looked up, annoyed by his sudden faux chivalry.

'I'm fine, thanks, I can wait until you guys have wrapped up your little flirtation.' It came out sounding more bitter than she'd intended. He laughed and her rage resurfaced with a vengeance.

'British?' he asked. She hoped he wouldn't follow with an inane comment on how cute her accent was.

'Yes,' was all she said.

'Well, my experience with Brits has generally been that you guys need to learn how to take it easy sometimes. Look around, we're in one of the most beautiful places in the world, and you won't let a nice guy like me buy you a drink?' He was leaning even closer now, looking at her in a way that she assumed he thought was alluring, but was actually incredibly off-putting.

Sofia was not about to be beguiled by those green eyes. 'You think quite highly of yourself, I see.'

'Well when faced with a beautiful woman such as yourself, a guy has got to psych himself up.'

Sofia rolled her eyes. 'How many women have you called beautiful this evening?'

He laughed again, and despite herself Sofia cracked a smile.

'And she smiles, too! Only you, sweet cheeks, oh and that lovely little waitress who is having trouble finding the mop.' He ran his hand through his hair and held Sofia's gaze. She felt like the one-woman audience for a one-man show.

'Is that your signature move?' she asked.

'Buying a beautiful woman a drink?' He smirked. 'Kinda, yeah.'

'No the whole hand through the hair, intense eye contact thing, and enough with the "beautiful woman" schtick.' She thought she caught a glimpse of him looking something akin to wounded and it thrilled her. He quickly composed himself.

'Even the wet shirt isn't doing it for you?'

'Ahh yes, nothing gets the girls going like a beer-soaked polo.'

Right then the waitress came back, much to Sofia's relief. She wasn't sure how long she could keep up the witty comebacks; she hadn't flirted with a man for months. She wasn't even sure that's what she was doing, but wasn't that what strangers did at bars?

The waitress pulled two draught beers, and placed them on the counter, quickly lowering her eyes when she caught that sparkle of green.

'So what are you drinking?' He wasn't looking at her; he was still smiling at the waitress.

'Um, I think it's called a Crodino.'

The waitress finally seemed to notice Sofia.

'*Si, Aperol senza alcool?*' she said as she busied herself with an orange and a tall glass.

'Yes, the Aperol one, thank you.' Before she could get her card out, Chief Chad swiped his.

'I could have got that myself, thank you.'

'Well, I mean it's not like you need to worry about me

trying to get you drunk and take advantage. I didn't even know there was such a thing as alcohol-free Aperol.' That smirk again. 'You're really not out to have a good time, are you?'

Any feelings of warming to him rapidly evaporated. Sofia was angry. What did this guy know about her life? She was getting ready to quite literally embark on a new, terrifying, and exhilarating chapter in her life, she didn't need a hangover right now.

'I'd really like to enjoy my drink in peace if you don't mind, so I am going to go back to my table now and if you and your boys could keep it down I think everyone else in this bar would really appreciate that too.'

For a moment he looked stunned. He turned to pick up his beers and gave her a slow once-over. 'Such a waste when a beautiful woman like you turns out to be so uptight. You need to learn to live a little.'

She didn't really even think about it. It all happened so quickly she could hardly believe she had pulled it off. As the Chad was speaking the waitress had gingerly put the bright orange drink on the counter. Next thing Sofia knew, it had made its way into her hand and then promptly all over the once cream polo standing in front of her. For a second she felt embarrassed, and then newly empowered. She put the glass firmly back onto the counter and turned to walk away, her heart beating wildly in her chest.

'I knew you had a thing for the wet shirt!' he called after her. She ignored him, gathering her things from the table.

'Jack, bro, what the hell happened up there?' She could hear the boys laughing even more loudly than before.

As she walked out the bar she made sure not to look over at his table.

# Chapter Two

Seven minutes before her alarm was set to go off, Sofia woke up with a start. The room around her was grey with morning mist, and the smell of the sea drifting through the open window put a smile on her face. Today was the day. Six weeks ago she had responded to a Facebook post on the 'Yachties of the Med' page and now she was only a few hundred metres from the *Lady Ixchel* herself. She had expected to feel more nervous, but her girlish excitement was getting the better of her as she hurriedly pulled a T-shirt over her head and hopped around the small room with one leg in a pair of jeans.

In the bathroom she looked at her reflection in the mirror. She should have got a haircut before she left London, or maybe even cornrows. Her fringe was already beginning to frizz from the humidity and her long tight curls would need to be secured with dozens of pins every morning to fit into those silly little hairnets. She couldn't help but admire the colour that had returned to her face, even the pinkish tint on the tops of her shoulders. In London her brown skin had been fading into a worrying shade of grey; now she was looking like herself again, although she realised with a start that she couldn't remember the last time she had, in fact, looked like herself. Was this 'beautiful woman' staring back at her really what she was supposed to look like? It was amazing what a couple of good nights' sleep and the lack of an impending sense of dread about the day ahead could do for a person.

*Beautiful woman.* Just then she remembered why the phrase was swirling around her head and the events of the previous evening came back to her, accompanied by a healthy dose of cringe. She wasn't entirely sure where the drinks-swirling version of herself had come from, and she was worried about what she might do next, but she also sort of admired her. The Sofia who didn't suffer fools, the Sofia who stood up for herself and didn't wither in front of men who, even she had to admit, were unsettlingly handsome. God knows she'd had her fill of handsome fools.

She decided a tight bun would be the best look to contain the frizz. She wet her hands, then her hair, and methodically dragged her brush towards the back of her head, applying gel liberally. When she was done she stood back to admire her handiwork. It was important to make a good first impression, even if she suspected she wouldn't be keeping up with laying her edges under a chef's hat.

Breakfast was continental, a mystifying array of hams, cheeses, fruits, yoghurts and cereals laid out on a large white tableclothed counter running down one side of the room. On the other was a panel of large floor-to-ceiling windows looking out over the harbour. It was a surprisingly grand room for the calibre of hotel, as if someone had decided to scrimp on the quality of the bedding in order to add another few centimetres to the ceiling height.

Sofia went for a grapefruit, one of the yoghurts and a drizzle of honey. She wasn't sure how often she'd get access to fresh fruit on board, so she was going to make the most of it.

Thirty minutes later she stood at the reception, settling up her bill with her packed bag beside her. She found herself disappointed that the pretty young receptionist had been replaced by a rather curt man who looked like he could be her father. Maybe the young woman had been out with her lover and didn't have to work today. Once again Sofia caught herself daydreaming, and had to drag herself back down to earth. The romance of this place was getting to her and she needed to get her head in the game.

Walking down to the marina with her wheelie case, Sofia felt ecstatic but in her absent-mindedness, while pulling the bag onto the pontoon, she lost her footing. She was almost overcome by the dreadful moment just after you are blissfully upright and just before you can accept the fall, but in the spike of panic she felt a hand grab her shoulder and pull her up straight.

'Whoa, careful.' He was about the same height as her, young and very dark-skinned, something that was exceedingly notable in the middle of this rural, and mostly white, Italian seaside town. Sofia smiled in relief, at being saved from an unplanned dip into the harbour, and at that

14

sort of singular joy of meeting another black person when there aren't that many of you around.

'Oh my God, thank you so, *so* much,' she gushed. 'I am so embarrassed. I wasn't really paying attention to where I was stepping.'

The man bent down and dislodged the wheel of her case from a gap between a gnarly-looking length of rope and the pontoon. 'My name is Declan,' he said returning her smile, straightening himself up and offering her his other hand to shake.

She shook his hand enthusiastically. 'You're from the UK, huh?'

'South London born and bred,' he said with a grin.

'I used to live in Peckham,' she replied. 'Just up from Queens Road.'

'Oh yeah, my aunty lives around there. I moved around a bit, but spent most of my time in Croydon.'

It was the sort of familiarity that made Sofia feel a bit giddy, and that she was sure followed black Londoners everywhere. Despite the fact that she had only recently taken on that title.

'Oh sorry, um, I'm Sofia.' She was feeling flustered and as the adrenaline slowly drained from her body it was replaced by the oppressive sense that she really needed to be somewhere.

'I actually . . . this is really rude, but I am kind of in a rush.' She checked her watch. The crew's very first meeting was starting in ten minutes.

'So am I actually,' said Declan. 'I'm going this way.'

15

He pointed to the far end of the marina.

'So am I actually!' she parroted, and both of them chuckled – a little nervously on his part, Sofia thought.

'I might need some supervision,' she joked. Declan leant over to take her bag and she waved him away. She didn't want to make a habit of being a damsel in need of saving. 'It's fine, I've got it,' she said, and then, because she'd sounded a bit dismissive and the flicker of wounded puppy dog that flashed across his face broke her heart: 'Thank you though.' Just like that the unclouded cheer returned to his face.

'Ladies first,' he said, lowering his head in a theatrical bow. Sofia rolled her eyes, doffed a make-believe cap and strode ahead.

The *Lady Ixchel* was much bigger than she'd imagined. Even though she had been sent the physical measurements of the boat, from where she was stood the yacht seemed ridiculously huge. On the deck, she thought she could make out Mary, and it wasn't until Declan yelled, 'Captain Mary!' from beside her and the woman waved back that she clocked that this friendly stranger might not be one for very long.

'Wait, are you working on the *Lady Shelly* as well?'

Declan's eyes lit up. 'Yeah! It's my first ever season. Are you one of the stewardesses? This is going to be so fun.'

Sofia cringed at his assumption, but decided to be kind. 'Actually, I'm the chef . . . but I'll give you the benefit of the doubt and assume that you weren't jumping to conclusions because I'm a woman.'

Declan, to his credit, looked embarrassed and lowered his eyes. 'I'm so sorry, Sofia; it was unfair for me to assume that.' His earnestness melted her heart and she found herself wanting to give him a hug.

Instead, in an awkward tone that verged on matronly, she said, 'It's OK, Declan, just make sure it doesn't happen again.' He looked up, caught her eye and they both burst into a fit of giggles.

'This is going to be so fun, man,' he said, shaking his head and smiling to himself as he took her bag and made his way to the slipway. She thought about protesting, but once she caught sight of the rickety-looking ladder, she thought better of it.

# Chapter Three

Once on the deck Sofia took a moment to gaze out at the ocean, as Declan enthusiastically greeted Captain Mary. The boundless ripples shimmered in the mid-morning sun, shooting out silver shards of light. Sofia let out a deep sigh. She already felt right at home.

'Sofia, it's nice to meet you in person.' Captain Mary was a taller woman than Sofia had realised in their video interviews, with the kind of transatlantic accent that comes from a life on the move. She reached out her hand and shook Sofia's firmly. It was hard to work out exactly how old she was, but Sofia reckoned somewhere between forty-five and sixty. The lines around her eyes had been resolutely carved by years of exposure to the sun and sea air, and by the need to meet each new rotation of unruly yachting crew with a friendly smile and an abundance of patience.

'Captain Mary, it's an honour to finally be aboard the *Lady Ixchel*. She really is a beauty,' Sofia said honestly. Captain Mary glowed with pride at her praise.

'She really is, even if I do say so myself. Let me give you and Declan a tour, before the rest of the crew arrives.'

'Great, I'm really looking forward to getting familiar

with my new kitchen.'

Captain Mary gave her a bemused look. 'Perhaps you should wait until you see it before you get too excited.' Her tone was flat and a little stern but there was a sparkle of humour in her eyes. 'Follow me.'

Captain Mary led the pair into what she called the horizon lounge. Living up to its name, large square windows lined three sides of the room, offering a wealth of views in all directions. There were too many places to sit, Sofia thought. A chaise longue to her left, a dining table circled by ten chairs to her right; one, two, three sofas dotted around and a gathering of armchairs by the gold-veined marble bar. Everything was dark wood and the upholstery in various shades of green velvet.

'Wow,' was all Declan could say, as he slowly rotated on the spot, eyes wide.

'So this is really Petra's domain. She's in charge of hospitality, which mostly includes making cocktails all day,' Captain Mary explained. 'I believe she sometimes extends that skill set to serve the crew . . . on special occasions.'

Declan leant in and whispered in Sofia's ear, 'For the legendary crew parties.' He winked at her as Captain Mary continued explaining the hierarchy of the boat. At the top of the pyramid was Captain Mary herself. Then came Petra who was acting up in the combined role of purser and head stewardess; the head chef – that was Sofia; chief engineer – a man called Stuart; and the first officer. Below them was a second stewardess and a deckhand, the aptly named Declan, who would answer to each of their superiors respectively.

'So you'll be answering to Jack. It'll be his first tour as first officer.' This was directed at Declan, and Sofia thought she could detect a hint of pride in Captain Mary's voice. 'He should be here any minute.' She looked at her watch and frowned. 'Ten minutes late, not getting off to the best start are we, Jacky,' she mumbled under her breath.

Next, they were taken down the stairs and shown the main saloon. More velvet, this time a deep blue; more polished wood; even more places to sit.

'So how many guests will there be this time around?' asked Declan.

Captain Mary shot him a look. 'Well, as per the briefing document you should have received last week, we will be joined by Miss Amelia Cox and her partner Brian McGregor for this six-week leg of the season.'

'Wait up, you mean Milly Cox, from *The True Course of Love*? No way!'

Captain Mary was trying to look disapproving. Declan had clearly not taken the time to read the carefully put together crew manual, but his enthusiasm was infectious. Sofia found herself chuckling softly.

'Yes, Declan, the very one,' the captain said dryly.

All this space, and all this staff, just for two people – it seemed a little excessive to Sofia, but then, she supposed, that was the point.

'And right here is the kitchen.' The three of them

had left the main lounge and ducked through a very narrow, and very low-ceilinged hallway. Captain Mary had stopped next to an equally narrow white door. All the luxury had been used up upstairs. There was nothing plush about the scrubby oatmeal carpet they were now standing on.

Sofia turned the handle, which was disconcertingly sticky. She did try not to let out a gasp, but she failed. 'Oh,' was all she could say, as her eyes scanned over the small space, taking stock. Four burners, a deep fryer, two countertop spaces, a microwave and only one oven. She had had more to work with in her London studio flat – at least she'd had a separate grill.

'I did warn you,' said Captain Mary, who was already turning to lead Declan down the hallway. The expansive kitchen at Nakachwa flashed into Sofia's mind, the rows and rows of spotless counter space, the huge fridges, the sharpest knives. She tried to compose herself. There was no looking back and she would have to make do. She determined that separate grill or no separate grill she would not let her menu suffer.

She closed the door, took a deep breath and followed the sound of voices. Declan and Mary seemed to have found some company. She was a rookie (or *green*, she supposed, in yacht-speak), but she'd done enough research to know that she was now firmly in staff quarters. They must be in the mess – the main communal area for the staff on the boat.

'Sofia is around here somewhere. She's the chef.'

21

Declan was speaking to someone excitedly.

Sofia opened the door to find five people sitting around a large table and Captain Mary standing at its head.

'Ah there she is. Do take a seat, Sofia. This is Petra, that's Stuart the engineer, Tabitha our stewardess, Declan of course, and Jack Carter – our first officer.'

Sofia turned from one face to the next, trying to look both suitably professional and approachable, before landing on a devastatingly familiar smirk and a pair of startlingly green eyes.

Her mind went blank.

'It's, um, lovely to meet everyone,' she managed after a beat, and then even less convincingly, 'I'm really looking forward to working with you all.'

# Chapter Four

Sofia slid into the spare seat next to Declan at the table, feeling flustered and suddenly forgetting what normal people are supposed to do with their gaze. She decided to fix it resolutely on Captain Mary.

'First of all I'd like to thank you all for being here. We have a challenging season ahead, as two of our crew are acting up for the first time. Petra and Jack, I have no doubt you will both rise to the occasion. And for our chef Sofia and our new deckhand, it will be both of their first times working on a boat. Tabitha too is joining us for the first time, although she has worked a couple of seasons in the Caribbean. So welcome to the madhouse!'

Sofia smiled at Petra, who did not return it. Declan held up his palm, and then thought better of waving and put his hand down. 'Can't wait to get stuck in. It's an honour to be here.' He grinned.

'Hi, everybody,' said Tabitha weakly. She was another Brit, petite with hair that was somewhere between brown and blonde. She had a pretty face but it was clear she wasn't feeling her best. *That is why you don't want a hangover on the first day,* thought Sofia, with a tinge of smugness.

A wry chuckle from Jack, but Petra seemed concerned.

'Sorry, Captain, I wasn't aware we had two . . .' she shot a look at Tabitha '. . . almost three greenies onboard. What happened to Toby?' Petra had a thick Australian accent. Sofia wondered how she'd ended up on this boat on the other side of the world.

'Toby is getting married actually.' By way of clarification Captain Mary turned to Sofia and Declan and said, 'Toby was our old deckhand, but the yachtie life isn't for everyone, especially those who want to settle down.'

'Not everyone is cut out for a lonely life out on the open seas, hey, Captain.' Sofia dared to glance over at Jack as he spoke. Though he sounded as bolshie and self-assured as he had last night, he looked different. His hair was combed back from his face, he'd shaved and his uniform made him seem older.

'I don't know if it counts as a lonely life if you have a girl in every port, Jack,' quipped Petra. Captain Mary chuckled at that, and Sofia noted a warmth in her eyes as she smiled at Jack. *The effect of his charm extended to women of all ages,* thought Sofia, resisting the urge to roll her eyes.

'So as you all know we are operating with a skeleton crew for this charter, as there are only two guests, although might I remind you they are, as all our guests are, VIPs, so it cannot "feel" as if we're offering anything less than an all-inclusive service.'

Petra nodded in agreement, glancing again at Tabitha, who was now sweating profusely.

24

'For those of you newcomers who enjoy the job you might be interested to know that I am looking to take on two new permanent staff to join me and First Officer Carter for the rest of the season.' This was news to Sofia. She'd been told that this was a six-week gig, that might extend to a second charter, but a whole season? She hadn't realised that was on the table, and that the prospect excited her.

'Petra, if you could show Tabitha and Sofia to their quarters? Jack and I will need to steal Declan for a more detailed tour.' Declan bounded to his feet, knocking the table in his excitement and spilling the remainder of a half-drunk glass of water down Sofia's light blue T-shirt.

'Oh no, sorry, Sofia, I didn't mean to . . .' Declan reached for a napkin and went to dab at her before he seemed to realise he would have to touch her chest.

'It's OK, Declan, it's only water.' Petra's words were kind, but Sofia could see she was mentally resigning herself to all the work she was going to have to do to get this virgin crew up to scratch.

Sofia had taken over dabbing at the thin cotton so she was looking down when she suddenly felt a presence looming over her.

She looked up at Jack, with an eyebrow raised. The embarrassment and surprise she had felt earlier had evaporated, and in its place a quiet sense of dread had settled. She was going to have to put up with this guy for at least the next six weeks.

'Don't worry, I've found that cotton dries pretty

quickly in this weather,' he said with a mocking smile.

'Yes, I have heard that sunshine and wind have that effect.' He laughed lightly, but it seemed forced. Maybe he wasn't used to being met with anything other than a giggle and a blush.

'And anyway,' he continued, 'you're lucky that it's water. Drinks like, say, Aperol stain pretty badly.' She held his gaze for a moment, daring him to say more. To her surprise he was the first to look away, his eyes following Captain Mary as she left the room. When he looked back, a sort of distance clouded his gaze, and Sofia felt his retreat.

'I've been terribly rude,' he said flatly. 'I'm first Officer Jack Carter. It is very nice to meet you.' He held out his hand, and she shook it, noticing how rough his hands were.

'Sofia Harlow, but you can call me Chef Harlow.' She had meant it as a joke, in an attempt to lift what had suddenly become an uncomfortably heavy mood. There was no flicker of humour in his face, which he had set into an impervious mask.

'Well, Chef Harlow, I'll see you around.'

'I suspect you will.'

He walked off, following in the direction of the captain. Sofia was irritated. Jack was one of those men who insisted on setting the tone. When he wanted to banter, everyone was expected to laugh along, but the moment she tried returning the volley he got sulky. She was only ever allowed to be on the back foot.

'Sofia, can you come with me.' It was Petra, and it wasn't a question. 'And bring your things. I'm going to take you to your room.'

As they walked down the hall Petra reeled off a list of things that Sofia would really have liked to write down. The main takeaway though was 'preference sheets'.

'They're your gospel. Always *always* look at your preference sheets. I know a lot of chefs come in here with a lot of fancy ideas about their menus.' This last word she said scathingly, and Sofia began to gnaw anxiously at her thumbnail. 'But the guest is king, or queen in this case. Have you had a good look at Ms Cox's preferences?'

'Yes, she said she enjoyed "fine dining", wants to avoid heavy carbohydrates and loves seafood.'

Petra didn't seem convinced. 'Really? Ms Milly Cox always struck me as more of a burger and fries kind of girl.'

'So you've watched the show then?' Sofia hadn't pegged Petra for the reality TV type.

'I mean, I'm not like a fan.' Was that a hint of defensiveness? 'But it's kind of hard to avoid, and if I'm being totally honest—' they were standing in the narrow hallway, and their proximity had chiselled away at Petra's spikier edges '—I actually have a bit of a thing for Brian,' she said with a grin that lit up her whole face.

Sofia sensed that as soon as the words had left Petra's mouth she regretted them. Sofia needed to get her back on side. Petra was someone you wanted to have in your corner. She could feel the coldness sinking into the small space between them, and she wasn't about to let that happen again.

'You know what, so do I,' declared Sofia, and to her pleasant surprise, Petra giggled, her no-nonsense facade cracking to reveal something a little girlish.

'Who knows, maybe I'm just jealous, or just nervous about meeting him in real life?' Petra's voice had gone up in pitch and she kept tucking a strand of her blonde hair behind one ear as she spoke. 'Obviously, it goes without saying that there is ZERO crew-guest fraternisation allowed.' Her voice was verging on breathless.

'Obviously,' parroted Sofia, happy to have cracked the case of Petra's excitement, 'but it doesn't hurt to look eh?'

Petra looked Sofia dead in the eye. 'You know, I think we're going to be friends.'

Sofia blushed at the directness, her Britishness getting the better of her. 'I'd like that,' she said, unable to hold Petra's gaze.

'Well then enough gossiping. I'm supposed to be showing you to your room, and then I have literally a million things to do on this boat before the guests arrive tomorrow.' She opened the door. 'And I don't want to make a bad first impression on Brian.' She gave Sofia a knowing look, her eyebrows raised playfully.

The room was even smaller than the kitchen. A set of bunk beds jotted out from the back wall and the remaining floor space was mostly taken up by one tiny bedside table and a chair. Everything was beige. A pile of nylon-heavy looking clothing was neatly folded on top of the pristine sheets.

'Cosy,' said Sofia unconvincingly, and Petra bristled.

'Well I know this is all new to you but you're actually the only one who even has a room to yourself. Usually you'd have to share.'

'No, no, it's lovely, thank you.' Sofia couldn't seem to stop putting her foot in it. She needed to reign it in with the wisecracks and knuckle down. She was the chef, not the damn jester.

'The bathroom is that door there, and those are a few uniforms.' Petra pointed to the stack on the bed. Sofia picked up what turned out to be a cream polo neck with a navy trim.

'Is this a . . . skort?' Sofia gingerly held up the matching bottom half.

'That's right.' Petra was standing with her hands on her hips. 'Don't worry you only really have to wear that when you're interacting with the guests, which for you is pretty much only on the first day.'

Sofia sat down on the bottom bunk. There was barely enough room for two people to stand.

'I need to go work out what's wrong with Tabitha. She better not be goddam seasick – we haven't even left the dock.' Petra turned to leave.

'OK, do you know when my ingredients will be arriving?' Sofia imagined a pile of scallops, rotting in the midday sun somewhere on the marina.

'I'd ask Jack. The deckhands usually bring all supplies on board.' She looked like she was going to say something

29

else on the matter and then decided against it. 'Dinner is at eight. We'd usually eat after the guests but seeing as it's just us tonight, we can eat at a civilised hour.'

'Oh great, what are we having?'

Petra stared at her a moment and then burst out laughing. Sofia grinned.

'Yeah OK, fine, that's kind of funny. See you later, Chef.'

As Petra closed the door behind her, Sofia congratulated herself on a joke well delivered. Maybe she and Petra could be friends, she thought. Usually women like Petra intimidated Sofia. She admired, and envied, the honesty in their brusqueness, the seeming lack of self-consciousness that comes with being 'no nonsense'. The surety with which they can decide what they do and do not like. Sofia often found it hard to distinguish between actually liking someone and enjoying someone liking her. She supposed that made her a people-pleaser, but she was determined to change that. With a friend like Petra at her side maybe she could learn a thing or two.

What better way to test her new alter ego than to track down Jack and get her new kitchen set up for dinner.

# Chapter Five

She found him on the top deck chatting to Declan. It bugged her that they seemed to be getting along very well. As she approached, she could see them partaking in all the requisite backslapping and laughing that usually indicated men were 'being friendly'.

'Sorry to interrupt,' she said to the back of Jack's head. He swung around and offered up an easy grin. His sulky mood from earlier had seemingly vanished.

'No at all – what can I do for you, Chef Harlow?'

'I'm trying to locate my ingredients.'

'Ah yes, perfect timing – the delivery truck just arrived. Dec and I were about to head down and bring everything up.'

'*Dec*', she thought, *this guy moves fast.*

'Do you need a hand?' The boys exchanged a look, and Sofia felt immediately irritated. It was frustrating how quickly Jack seemed to inspire that in her.

'It's all pretty heavy stuff,' said Declan with what seemed like genuine concern.

'Maybe leave it to the brawn. Beauty has its place, Sofia, and it's not lugging crates across the dock.' He raised one devastatingly perfect eyebrow, and Sofia was

31

determined not to blush. Without Captain Mary in the room, Jack had reverted to his flirty bar chat. It was just as infuriating as ever.

'Chef Harlow,' she corrected. 'And I don't know when the last time you worked a ten-hour shift in a professional kitchen was, but let me assure you that there is a lot of "brawn" required.'

Declan laughed. 'Well, Jack, that told you!'

With his eyes still fixed on Sofia, Jack responded dryly, 'You better watch how you talk to your superiors, Dec, or else I'll have to make you walk the plank for mutiny.'

Sofia was the first to look away this time. 'So where is this van then?'

Jack was already walking down the steps to the lower level. 'Right this way, Chef,' he called over his shoulder.

'After you, milady.' Declan took a deep bow.

Sofia rolled her eyes, her mood lightened by Declan's antics, and the pair of them followed Jack off the boat and onto the dock.

About fifteen minutes later Sofia was deeply regretful. She'd made a stand against her better judgement. She had known it even as she was speaking to Jack on the deck, but now the lactic sting in her arms and legs, the ever more acute pain in her lower back and the sweat dripping down her forehead were concrete confirmation.

She was used to hauling a five-kilogram bag of onions down from a high shelf, but this was different. This was enough food for the whole crew and two guests for the next five days until they could dock and onboard more.

She was only on her second trip between the truck and the kitchen. Jack had lapped her twice, and she could feel the satisfaction radiating off of him each time he passed.

It was Declan who came to her rescue. 'Maybe you should start unpacking everything from the crates while we bring in the rest of it.' She could have kissed him. The back of her shirt was wet through and she could feel her blood pumping. She put down an icebox of closed oysters on the counter.

'I think that's a good idea. I'm going to need to jenga this kitchen into working order.' Declan gave her a knowing smile and slipped back out of the room.

She opened her fridge and took a deep breath. The empty shelves stared back at her. It might be small but it was her kitchen. She was head chef, her own boss, with no one to answer to. Granted, she also didn't have anyone answering to her, a skeleton crew meant no sous, so she would have to do all her own prep. But before that she had the fridge to organise.

At Nakachwa, with its huge walk-in fridge, she had found it calming to methodically arrange the ingredients in the cool, dimly lit space. It had always been her favourite part of the morning. The restaurant specialised in East African cuisine. The joint owners were Ethiopian and Ugandan respectively, Peter and Joy. It was named after their daughter. Or maybe the daughter was named after the restaurant – it was never clarified.

Despite being half Rwandan she had never been to Africa. But in that fridge, she could get a glimpse into the taste of the place. Mangosteens, papayas, the sweetest little bananas she had ever tasted, pawpaw, starfruits, matoke, manioc. All these flavours brought her a little closer to herself and gave her the confidence to experiment with new produce. She had a plan for what she wanted to cook of course, but she had to remain open to substitutions, to journey alongside the food. Everywhere had its own flavours. It was part of what excited her about this job, to discover the tastes of her travels and put them on a plate.

In her new fridge there would be artichokes, asparagus, radishes, pomegranates and the season's first strawberries. Early May in Italy was the perfect time for brassicas, so there were kales and cabbages to be crammed in as well.

Sofia was so engrossed, she didn't notice Jack come into the kitchen, as small as it was, and she jumped when she turned to find him standing behind her. He seemed to have developed a habit of doing that.

'Jesus,' she exclaimed, clapping a hand to her palpitating heart. 'You like sneaking up on people huh?'

He chuckled. 'Where did you want me to put the lobsters?' There were four of them and they were disconcertingly alive, sauntering along the bottom of a large plastic tub filled with water.

'How are you just holding that? It must be so heavy,' she mused, and then immediately regretted saying it. He beamed with smugness.

'Well you know, doing this job, it's better than any workout.' He set the tub down.

'I don't really have the time—' she gestured around her '—or the space, for your preening.'

'A thank you would suffice,' he snapped. She was taken aback by the sudden venom in his voice. 'I changed my schedule, you know, to bring in all this stuff first, so you could arrange your little kitchen in plenty of time.' His tone tipped into a sneer.

'I'm just trying to do my job. I'd appreciate it if you could do yours without requiring my undying gratitude,' she said coldly.

There was a long pause. Jack seemed to be talking himself down from saying something else. 'I'll get out of your hair then,' was what he settled on, before walking out. He didn't look back.

# Chapter Six

Sofia decided on pasta for the crew's first dinner. She wanted a gentle warm-up in the kitchen and, well, Italy.

She lay a luscious bunch of cavolo nero on the counter. She chopped eight plump cloves of garlic, shredded the dark, spongy leaves and then started on the guanciale, cutting the lump of fat into small nubs and throwing them into a smoking hot pan. She watched them shrink as they hit the aluminium, oozing with grease. The pork was laid to one side, and in went the garlic and cavolo nero, until the leaves had wilted, glossed with a film of fat. She boiled a large vat of pasta, heavily salted the water and grated the parmesan. When everything had cooked, it all went in with the pasta, along with a big dollop of crème fraiche.

Before she called Petra in to help serve it up, she took a moment to admire her work, dipping a fork into the skillet and swirling the creamy pasta around its prongs. It had been so long since she had cooked an entire meal for someone. Not just chopped the onions, or made the roux, or seared the fillet. She had been part of a machine, a highly efficient one to be sure, but nevertheless a cog among cogs. Now she was the whole operation. Each dish, her very own masterpiece.

'Petra, can I get a little help?' She was still getting the hang of her radio, and she felt goofy using it, like a kid playing make-believe.

A harsh crackle and then: 'Heading right down now.' Mere moments later Petra was standing on the opposite side of the counter. 'Smells bloody delicious,' she said. Sofia offered her a mouthful. She chewed appreciatively, her eyes widening. 'Damn, is that bacon?'

'Guanciale.'

'I have no idea what that is, but I want more.'

Sofia ducked her head to hide her blush at the compliment and hurried herself serving up. Petra dutifully picked up the first three plates and disappeared out the door.

'The masses are starving,' she called over her shoulder as the door slammed.

Sofia made up another four plates and radioed in after waiting a couple of minutes, with no sign of Petra.

'Err, Petra, I think I'm going to need a hand with the final plates.'

'No need, our poor little Tabby cat will not be eating anything tonight.'

Sofia thought she could hear laughing in the background.

Then the voice of Captain Mary came through. 'What Petra meant to say is that Tabitha is having some trouble finding her sea legs and has had to retire for the evening.'

When Sofia walked into the main saloon, where the crew were allowed to eat only before the guests arrived, the boys were already eating. 'I don't think you've met Stuart?' Captain Mary gestured to a nervous-looking man as she laid down the final three plates.

Stuart was startlingly blonde for a man of his age, although she had to admit she wasn't entirely sure what that age was. He had pale grey eyes and a patchy arrangement of facial hair that didn't quite converge at the tip of his chin. He was not an unattractive-looking man, but he was an odd-looking one. She smiled in his direction. 'I'm Sofia.'

He hastily wiped his mouth, which was spattered with flecks of crème fraiche, and swallowed emphatically. 'Yeah, um Stuart, like the captain said, I'm the engineer,' he said, the last syllable rumbling from his throat in a strong Scottish accent.

'Pleasure,' said Sofia with a bright smile. 'Hope you're liking the food.'

He flushed, and the pink spread from his cheeks all the way down his neck, and all the way up to his hairline. 'Sorry, I wanted to wait, but I was starving.'

'No worries, I was warned by Petra.' She hadn't thought it was possible for the man to get any redder, but at the mention of Petra's name, he sunk into an even deeper shade of scarlet. Sofia understood – the head stewardess seemed to intimidate everyone. Sofia sat down and joined the rest of the table in their ravenous swallowing, feeling a pang of pride that her food was being so thoroughly enjoyed. She looked around the table and caught the eye of Jack, who was slurping a length of spaghetti. He winked at her.

'Great stuff, Chef Harlow.' She was disconcerted by the sincerity, and the cheeky tone. The hot and cold of their interactions was unsettling and she resolved he was doing it on purpose.

She was mulling over a retort when Captain Mary spoke. 'Good work today, everyone. I feel like we've got ourselves in a suitable position ahead of tomorrow, and a special thanks to Petra for stepping up to the plate and covering for Tabitha, as well as getting on top of her own duties.'

'What's wrong with Tabitha anyway?' This came from Declan, who had already scraped his plate clean.

'Turns out she's only worked on docked boats, and she's seasick.' Jack chuckled. 'Honestly, Captain, where do you find these people?'

Almost immediately it was clear to everyone around the table that he had crossed a line. The rowdy table went completely silent.

Sofia had yet to see the captain be anything other than friendly, in a professional, measured sort of way that Sofia admired. When she responded, her tone was still measured, but there was a coldness to it that oozed with authority. 'I go to great lengths to carefully select a crew that I believe will work well together, and whose skills and experience complement each other to give our guests the best experience on board.'

Jack, too, seemed to grasp that he had stepped out of line. Sofia noticed the withdrawing in his eyes she had seen earlier, and he replied in an equally steady tone. 'Of course, Captain, I meant no offence.'

'I appreciate that, Officer Carter.' The formality of the exchange had chilled the atmosphere around the table, and the rest of the meal was eaten mostly in silence, with the occasional polite question offered up to the room.

'So has anyone been to Italy before?' said Petra cheerfully. Responses were varied and the slightly strained amicability was palpable.

'I'll clear the plates,' said Declan when everyone was done, probably sounding the least enthusiastic she'd heard him all day, and Sofia stood up a little too quickly to help him.

Back in the kitchen, the pair of them silently scraped the plates and Declan began to fill the large sink with soapy water.

'Don't worry about those. I can do them in the morning; you must be exhausted after today,' Sofia said.

Declan put on the rubber gloves and took the plates from her hands anyway.

'I'll wash, you dry?' he suggested. It was such a domestic scene that Sofia felt a pang of homesickness.

'OK, deal.'

As they got to work, Sofia's curiosity got the better of her. 'So how did a black guy from Croydon end up working on luxury yachts then?'

Declan chuckled. 'That's such a fair question. Not many Nigerian deckhands about huh?'

'I mean I haven't been in the game very long, but I'd

assume not.'

'I actually started off on sailing yachts, went on this holiday to the South Coast with this friend from school and his family, and they were like "boat people", you know?'

'White?' said Sofia dryly, and Declan chuckled again.

'Yeah, how did you guess? Anyway, I sort of fell in love with it. I was gutted to leave after a week, so I googled "sailing clubs" and managed to persuade my parents to drive me to Portsmouth every weekend to go out on trips.'

'I grew up around there,' said Sofia, as she polished the cutlery.

'Oh for real? So you're a proper country girl then?'

'At heart, yeah I guess. I haven't ever really been on a boat like this though, like a yacht or whatever, but I've always been a bit in love with the idea of being "at sea", you know?'

Declan nodded thoughtfully. 'Yeah, I know exactly what you mean.' They worked in silence for a minute or so. A familiarity settled around them as they continued with their respective jobs, quiet and comfortable.

'So anyway,' said Declan, as he seemed to continue out loud the train of thought he had been riding in his head during the brief silence. 'I graduated from Durham last year and my parents really wanted me to get a job straight away, so I did this grad scheme thing, and I *hated* it.' He drained the sink and began peeling off the yellow gloves. 'So, I quit in January, and they were so mad, but like I started sailing again and met this guy who had just got back from a charter in the South of France, and it sounded sick, so he gave me Captain Mary's details.' He leant back against the counter and looked at Sofia with a grin. 'And the rest is history, as they say.'

'What did you study?'

'Economics,' he said with in a tone that verged on disgust.

Sofia laughed. 'God, that sounds dreadful,' she conceded.

'It was.'

She started to put everything away.

'And how did you end up here then?' Declan asked.

'Oh you know, same kind of deal really, quit my job and ran away to the circus.' She had expected a laugh, but when he didn't say anything, she looked over to him and he was smiling kindly, waiting for her to say more.

'I umm, was kind of burned out I guess, and not very happy and um, I had this weird thing with a colleague there who um . . .' She trailed off, suddenly shy and wary of dragging her baggage into this new chapter of her life.

'It's OK,' said Declan, sensing he had asked an innocuous question that could not be met with an innocuous response. 'You don't have to talk about it if you don't want to.'

Sofia was touched by his sensitivity. 'Thanks, it's not like a big deal. I just don't like to dwell or whatever.'

Declan's grin banished the heaviness from the small room. 'Well if you ever do want to talk, you know where I am,' he said cheerily. 'Thanks so much for dinner – that cabbage stuff was mad tasty.'

'Cavolo nero.'

He mimed a chef's kiss. 'Anyway, I think it's time for me to go to bed.'

'Yes, you're probably right. Thanks for your help.'

'Yes, Chef!' He saluted and left the kitchen.

As Sofia walked back to her cabin, she could hear some muffled voices coming from the crew's mess. She contemplated poking her head around the door but then thought better of it. The call to her pillow was too seductive.

That night she slept deeply, dreaming of fruit tarts and delicate mountains of fresh crustaceans.

# *Chapter Seven*

When Sofia awoke, the cabin was pitch-black but she could feel the boat coming to life. Outside her door, purposeful footsteps hurried past and she could hear a faint whirring from somewhere below her.

Sofia was not historically a morning person, but today she leapt out of her bunk and marvelled at how much energy she had. She put on the white chef's uniform she had laid out the night before and pulled her hair back into a small, tight bun. She had prep to do. The guests were to arrive mid-afternoon but she was expected to have an afternoon snack ready and then their first three-course meal on the table by 8 p.m. There was no time to lose.

Past the crew mess, down the hall, Sofia practically skipped to the kitchen. She was so wrapped up in her own glee that she jumped when she crossed the room to find a figure bent over into her fridge. It was Jack.

'Um, can I help you?' She crossed her arms, trying to manage the sensation of adrenaline turning to liquid rage as it coursed through her body.

'Just feeling a little peckish,' he said in a ludicrously stilted British accent as he stood up straight and smirked

44

at her. Her eyes flew to the half-eaten strawberry in his hand.

'Are those the strawberries for my tarts?'

He looked at his fingers and feigned surprise. 'I suppose so? But I've only had a few.'

Sofia liked to think of herself as a reasonable person. Generally, she excelled under pressure – she wouldn't have gotten to where she was if she didn't – and historically she was not someone who jumped to anger. But there was something about this man. She leant back on her heels and straightened her back, taking a second to give Jack a slow once-over. He looked rough, and she thought she could smell something like despair radiating off his skin. His hair was unwashed. He was hungover.

When she met his eyes again, they were brimming with disdain and when she spoke, there was venom in her voice. 'I don't know if this job is some sort of joke to you, and frankly I don't care if you want to sabotage this opportunity that Captain Mary has given you by getting wasted and welcoming the VIPs with a, quite literally, stinking hangover. . .' She wrinkled her nose and for a moment she was taken aback by the ease of her cruelty. Then she remembered the tarts, how she had practised them in her small studio back in London. She had sliced each strawberry, delicately laying down the heart-shaped slivers with tweezers in a concentric spiral on top of a custard base.

'But I will not have you and your unchecked arrogance ruin this for me. I am not just winging it, and I've worked damn hard to get where I am. Those are not a hangover snack; they are Sabrosa cultivars and they can only be harvested in early May in Southern Italy.' She took a deep breath. She was shaking and her voice had cracked on that last word. For one horrifying moment, she thought she might cry. 'And they were for a tart.' This last part she said quietly, like the wind had been knocked out of her and she couldn't hold his gaze any longer.

There was silence. Sofia picked at the skin around her thumbnail. 'I don't know what your problem is.' Jack's voice was measured. 'But it's clear that you have made up your mind about me. I think it would be best if we avoided each other from now on.'

Sofia's head shot up. 'You're literally standing in *my* kitchen right now.' She sounded like a petulant child, and she hated herself for being the one who couldn't keep their cool.

Another deep breath.

Jack held up his hands either side of his face in a gesture of surrender. 'I am leaving right now, Chef. Stick to the bottom half of the boat. I'll be staying out of your hair on the top deck.' He strode out of the kitchen.

Sofia was left standing in the middle of the kitchen staring at the open fridge. She took a tentative look inside. She caught sight of the imperceptibly diminished punnet of strawberries and she felt a small nugget of shame settle in the pit of her stomach. Still, he shouldn't have been raiding her kitchen, and maybe he would have eaten them all if she hadn't caught him. He was right about one thing:

it would be better for both of them if they avoided each other. She couldn't remember ever having had so many bad interactions with one person in such close proximity in her entire life, and she'd worked under the infamous Lochland Fleet.

For the next four hours Sofia chopped, whisked, simmered and baked like her life depended on it. She had an extravagant first meal planned. Pan-seared scallops to start. Then a classic lobster with a twist she'd learnt at Nakachwa, swapping out the white wine for palm wine, which she'd smuggled over in her own suitcase. For dessert, the strawberry tart. Those would be served with a small scoop of samphire sorbet, tying it in with the two seafood dishes. That was the plan but as it stood the sorbet was overly crystalline and, with only half an hour to go before the guests arrived, Sofia was beginning to panic.

Right on cue, Petra poked her head around the door. She was flushed. 'T-minus twenty-eight minutes. Time to prep the welcome snack,' she said, vanishing just as suddenly.

The pale green slush would have to wait. It was time to put together a charcuterie board. Sofia was nervous about the cheese pastry puffs she had prepped, remembering Petra's warning about preference sheets, 'no carbs' ringing loudly in her ear as she took them out of the oven. But Brian had made no such proclamation and she challenged any sane person to reject cheesy pastry when presented with it.

Exactly twenty-eight minutes later, Petra was back.

'They're not here yet, and no one can get hold of them.' She was clearly agitated, constantly checking her phone. She held the radio up to her mouth. 'Any signs?'

Jack's voice crackled through – 'not yet' – and Sofia bristled at the sound of it.

Petra checked her watch. Sofia was surprised by how stressed she seemed. It was only three minutes past four.

'I'm sure they're on their way,' she offered.

'I just don't get why people can't be on time.' To Sofia's disbelief, Petra sounded almost nervous. Sofia sensed there was more going on here.

'You're a professional, Petra – no celebrity crush is going to jeopardise that.'

Petra looked over at her, pausing to decide whether or not to deny the true source of her anxiety. She decided against it and smiled shyly. 'Yeah I know you're right. It's just Captain Mary really has no time for stuff like that and it's a lot of pressure for my first time as head stewardess.' It was reassuring to be reminded that even women like Petra were occasionally plagued with self-doubt.

'You're doing a great job. You've got this whole boat running to the minute.'

Petra tucked her hair behind her ear, as if resolving to get herself together. 'You're right, even the food is ready to go, and that literally never happens. You're really on top of this. Thanks.'

Now it was Sofia's turn to awkwardly take the compliment. 'London kitchen training, I guess.' She shrugged.

'Michelin training, more like. Do yourself justice, Sofia – we're really lucky to have someone as talented as you in our kitchen.'

'Thanks.' The two women exchanged the sort of look that left them both determined to prove the other's faith in them right.

'They're here.' The sound of the radio startled them both.

'OK, everybody, let's get this show on the road.' Petra was in army general mode as she walked out of the kitchen, gesturing for Sofia to follow.

# Chapter Eight

They stood in parallel rows on the deck, Petra and Sofia facing Jack, Stuart and Declan. Sofia thought the girls versus boys setup was a little trite but she didn't say anything. She adjusted the collar of her polo shirt and tried not to dwell on how self-conscious she felt in an outfit that seemed better suited to a netball match than a professional meet-and-greet.

As the captain led the couple across the deck, the whole crew took the opportunity to get a good look. Milly Cox's proportions were perfect but she looked like she had been miniaturised. Her hair was a startling shade of red that Sofia felt could not really have been captured on camera. It fell in a straight sheen to the tops of her shoulders either side of an immaculate middle parting. She wore white from head (large rectangular sunglasses that covered most of her freckled face) to toe (a pair of precariously high strappy, heeled sandals). Brian by contrast stood at least a foot taller than Milly, and was dressed entirely in black. It was the outfit of a man who was reluctant to stand out, but still wanted you to know he'd thought about what he was wearing. Black short-sleeved linen shirt worn open over a black tank top and paired with linen trousers and black flip-flops, which on closer inspection seemed to be made of leather. She wondered idly if Milly had chosen the outfit for him.

The captain introduced each crew member in turn, with the exception of Tabitha who was apparently still throwing up somewhere below where they were standing.

'It's absolutely stunning,' said Milly, an Essex twang curtailing the 'g' from the end of her sentence. She was standing at the edge of the deck and looking back towards the boat. 'Can you believe it, Brian, home sweet home for the next six weeks.' She squealed with delight as Brian strode over and planted a kiss on her lips. The captain averted her eyes respectfully, but after a moment of silence in which the two of them remained lip-locked, she had to clear her throat.

'Would you like a tour of the rest of the yacht? Petra can show you to your suite, and Declan, could you take their bags down as well?'

'If you'd like to follow me,' said Petra, smiling over at Brian. Milly snapped a selfie and then stared critically at the screen as she examined herself. 'Come on, baby, this nice lady is going to show us our rooms now.' Sofia noticed Petra blush and then quickly collect herself.

'I'm sure you'll both be very pleased with the amenities.' Petra caught Brian's eye and tucked a flyaway strand of hair behind her ear.

Declan busied himself with the mountain of Louis Vuitton–emblazoned luggage as Petra led the couple away. The captain walked off, leaving Jack and Sofia standing awkwardly on deck.

Sofia thought he might just ignore her. She found herself simultaneously hoping for and dreading the idea.

'All prepped for today, Chef?' Was he suggesting she didn't have everything under control? Maybe he was just making small talk? Or sincerely checking in? She scanned his face for a clue about what he might really mean, but his expression was inscrutable.

'Yes, everything is ready to go.' She tried to mimic his tone and give nothing away, in case she revealed how much he had unsettled her with a simple question.

'Glad to hear it,' he said flatly, and with that he walked off towards the upper deck. Sofia stared at his retreating back, bemused, before getting a hold of herself. She didn't have time to stand around and overthink; the tour would be done soon and the guests would be expecting their snack in the main saloon. She headed back down below deck.

On her way to the kitchen she bumped into a flustered-looking Petra.

'Everything OK?' Sofia asked cheerfully.

'No, I've left the guests to unpack and just had a chat with Captain M, and she thinks we should leave Tabitha behind.'

'Oof, that bad?' Sofia was sympathetic. She had worried about the sturdiness of her own sea legs before accepting the job; she would have been heartbroken to have been kicked off the boat, betrayed by her own body.

'She said it's my call, and I really don't know what to do, but whatever I decide, I have to do it soon.' Sofia was reminded then that this was Petra's first time as head stewardess. It was easy to forget, when she radiated such confidence. She remembered what it had been like, back at Nakachwa, when she'd first started as sous, the weight of the expectation that you would just suddenly make all the right calls. The sense that you might let down somebody who had taken a chance on you. Sofia knew all too well what that could do to a person.

'Whatever you decide, Petra, you'll make it work. If your gut is saying something useful, listen, but I know it can be hard to block out the noise if you're feeling panicky.' Petra looked up and smiled at Sofia.

'You're very thoughtful,' she said, already seeming calmer.

Sofia let out a dry chuckle. 'It's advice learnt the hard way.'

'Well thanks for getting it the hard way and giving it the easy way.'

'You're welcome.' Sofia had forgotten how lovely that first flush of friendship was. It had been a while since she had enjoyed the comfort of it at work, and she was grateful for it.

Petra closed her eyes for a moment and when she opened them, Sofia saw a look of resignation. 'She has to go.' She was decided. 'It is one thing to have to steward this boat on my own, it is quite another to have to do it on top of playing nurse and babysitter. We just don't have time for her to get a prescription sorted and that over-the-counter stuff never works.'

Sofia nodded reassuringly. She felt bad for Tabitha, but she wasn't about to put her neck on the line for her. 'Sounds like good reasoning to me.'

'Thanks, Sofia, I'm really glad to have you on the team.'

She hadn't realised how much she'd needed to hear those words until that moment. As Petra marched off to find Tabitha, Sofia's eyes welled up with gratitude and she hastily swiped a tear from her eye. Her sentimentality would have to wait. She had an afternoon snack to present.

When she entered the main saloon with a large chopping board of cheeses, charcuterie and savoury pastries, Brian could hardly wait until she'd placed them on top of the bar.

'I'm bloody starving,' he said, systematically hoovering up one, two, three parmesan puffs in quick succession.

Sofia watched him with satisfaction. 'Welcome aboard. I'm very much looking forward to cooking for you both.'

'You're very pretty.' This came from Milly, who had looked up from her phone and was walking over. 'I bet you've got gorgeous hair. Shame it's all tied up.'

Sofia laughed nervously. 'Oh, thanks, I kind of have to, hairnets in the kitchen and all that.'

Milly was still staring at her intently. Sofia felt like she was being appraised by some sort of knowledgeable dog breeder, or an antiques specialist, each angle of her face being evaluated.

'Isn't she pretty, Brian? Doesn't seem right for you to be trapped down in the kitchen.' Brian looked anxious, as if a trap had been set and he was trying to work out how to avoid it.

'You have very nice . . .' he paused, looking panicked '. . . teeth.' He froze as Milly glanced over at him. When she smiled, he smiled back, relieved.

'She does, doesn't she,' said Milly. 'Do you want a selfie?'

Sofia had never been a big fan of *The True Course of Love*. She found the format degrading and often cringed at how exposed people were in front of the cameras. But she was not about to out herself as a non-believer.

'Um yeah, are you sure?' But Milly already had an arm around her shoulders, pulling Sofia toward her as she grinned, astonishingly naturally, into the outstretched lens.

'OMG, cute. You look great,' said Milly although Sofia thought that the picture was distinctly unflattering. Milly actually did look good though, and Sofia supposed that was probably the point.

'Anyway, I had better head back down. Pleasure to meet you both. I'll have dinner on the table at eight.'

'Thanks . . . um . . .' Milly was engrossed in her phone again, pinching and swiping. It was Brian who spoke.

'Sofia.'

'Thanks, Sofia, these nibbles are mega tasty.'

Back in the kitchen, Sofia made final preparations for

dinner. Eyeing up the lobsters in the tank up against a giant saucepan felt a little cruel.

A voice came through on her radio. 'Anchors up in fifteen minutes.' It was Captain Mary. The lobsters would be enjoying a stay of execution. She wanted to be up on deck.

As she walked to the stairs she passed an open door. Inside was a sorry sight. Tabitha was crying as she stuffed her belongings into a suitcase. After just two days of being confined to her cabin she looked an unnatural shade of grey, bags framing her eyes, and her hair developing a sheen of grease at the roots.

'Hey, sorry to see you go. I hope you feel a bit better soon.'

Tabitha sniffled. She wouldn't meet Sofia's eyes. 'Yeah, thanks. Bon voyage, I guess.'

There was nothing more Sofia could say or do to help Tabitha. She made her way up to the top deck.

From her vantage point she could see Milly and Brian below. It seemed they were trying to recreate the *Titanic* pose at the bow of the boat.

Declan walked over to where Sofia was standing. 'It's so weird to meet them in real life,' he said, joining her to peer over the railing.

'I don't think I really believe that they're in love,' Sofia said assuredly. She thought of herself as someone who was pretty good at reading people.

'Nah sure they are. You can't fake that stuff.' They were stood side by side but Declan kept glancing over at

Sofia as he spoke.

'How old are you, Declan?' He looked a little surprised by the question.

'Um twenty-two, why?'

Sofia was only five years older, but she felt she had learnt a lot about what people could and couldn't fake in that time.

'Just wondering,' she said, unwilling to offer any sort of unsolicited advice that would invariably sound patronising.

Petra came and joined them. 'There she goes.' She was pointing at a figure with a suitcase on the marina. It was Tabitha. 'I can't believe I'm the head stewardess, and the only stewardess. Hardly feels like a promotion if I'm just doing everyone's job at once.' Her tone was exasperated but she looked relieved. 'I hope she finds another job soon – something on dry land.'

'Anchors up, Dec.' Jack's voice came through the radio, and Declan jogged off.

As the boat manoeuvred its way out of the dock, Sofia felt a deep sense of calm and, for the first time in months, she knew she was doing the right thing.

# Chapter Nine

Back in the kitchen, everything seemed to be happening at once. Pots boiled over, pastry charred and sauces curdled. On a couple of occasions, Declan poked his head through the door and was immediately instructed to take that pot off the heat, or chop some herbs before being shooed out again. Somehow by 8 p.m., the starters were ready to go. Pan-seared scallops with a parmesan crumb, samphire sprig and pancetta-infused reduction. Declan was deeply confused by the mound of uneaten strips of cooked bacon.

'Let me get this straight, you cook the bacon but then you only serve the, like, bacon juice?'

Sofia was growing impatient with his idle chatter. 'Reduction, yes.' She was bent over one of the dishes, rearranging the samphire this way and that. Finally when she was happy with it, she stepped back to admire the plates, wiping her hands on her filthy apron with satisfaction.

She remembered how to smile, offering one to Declan in the form of an apology for her short-temperedness over the past three hours. 'But don't worry, I'll be making use of them for the crew dinner later.'

Declan grinned. He had been enlisted to help serve the meal, now that they were a stewardess down.

'Ding,' she said. She hadn't been given a bell. 'Service.'

'Is that my cue?' He beamed.

Sofia laughed. Declan was unshakably cheery. He couldn't know how grateful she really was for his good humour.

'Something funny?' he asked, confused, as he picked up the plates.

'Nothing. Thanks, Declan.'

With a frown of concentration on his face, he left the kitchen, dishes in hand.

The next two courses went out right on time and when Petra came back into the kitchen with spotless plates, Sofia glowed with pride.

She had worried that her time at Nakachwa might have ruined cooking for her entirely. She was grateful that making great food for people still filled her with joy.

After the last of the dishes had been washed up, Sofia got started on the crew meal, a Cajun-style gumbo with the leftover seafood. As nice as it was to put together her best dishes for the guests, she also cherished making the meal that she would be sharing.

She was met with five hungry faces that turned to her expectantly when she came into the crew mess with the first round of plates.

'Sofia, that smells even better than what I took up to Brian and Milly.' Declan was licking his lips as she set the food down in front of him.

'It'll be our little secret,' she said, winking at him.

'So, are you like a seafood chef then?' It was Jack. Sofia bristled.

'Well, no, I've had a pretty broad range of training.' She sounded more defensive than she'd intended, and once again a chill descended over the table.

Declan, ever the diplomat, broke the silence. 'I guess it makes sense.' He was covering his mouth with his hand, then he gestured around the room. 'When in Rome!'

'Actually, geographically speaking, it might be more accurate to say "when in Naples".' At Stuart's valiant attempt at a joke, the table laughed politely. Sofia noticed that Petra seemed genuinely amused, giggling a beat or so longer than anyone else.

The chiming of cutlery on china only amplified the lack of conversation, and it felt like whole minutes passed before Captain Mary had a go at instilling some team spirit.

'I'd like to take the opportunity to thank Petra for today. As you may know, she had to make the difficult decision to send Tabitha home.'

'Will she be replaced?' Jack again. He seemed to feel comfortable questioning Captain Mary, even after yesterday's reprimand.

'Already in search of fresh blood, Jacky?' He and Petra exchanged a look Sofia couldn't quite decipher. It was tinged with familiarity. Jack winked at her, and Petra rolled her eyes.

'I would say that – I'd never dream of coming between

you and your new stewardess, but if I'm being honest, it's exactly the sort of thing I dream about.'

Sofia choked on her mouthful of gumbo, but everyone else was laughing, including the captain.

Petra patted him on the shoulder. 'Keep on dreaming, Jacky, and anyway it's very presumptuous of you to assume it'll be a girl.' She looked over at the captain.

'Woman,' corrected the captain firmly. 'But you're quite right, I haven't decided. I have a few candidates in mind, but I'll have to let you know in the coming days.'

'I'll give you a hand with the dishes,' offered Petra as Sofia started gathering them up.

In the kitchen Sofia's curiosity got the better of her. It was always easier to ask probing questions when you were stood side by side – and they were shoulder to shoulder, just as Sofia had been with Declan when he dared to delve into her past.

'So what's the deal with Jack and the captain? They seem kind of . . . close.'

Petra seemed unfazed. 'Oh yeah they go way back. I think she's his godmother or something.'

So he was a child of nepotism. She couldn't say she was entirely surprised.

'His family, the Carters, they're in books. I think his dad basically runs New York publishing.' Petra glanced at Sofia out the side of her eye. 'You're not the internet-stalking type then?'

'To be honest with you, this whole thing felt like a fever dream until I stepped on the boat. I couldn't quite

61

convince myself it was real, let alone think ahead.'

'What made you want to try yachting?'

'I think I felt stuck, and I wanted to get as far away from that feeling as possible. A boat – well, being at sea – it seemed like a good option.' She shrugged, and they continued washing up in silence for a moment.

'Similar to Jack then really,' said Petra.

Sofia scoffed. 'Hardly, my mum's a schoolteacher and my dad works for the local council, and I don't have godparents who can give me jobs on a whim.'

Petra laughed at her outburst. 'Easy, comrade, Jack didn't just become a first officer; he's been on boats for years.' She emptied the sink and began putting away cutlery. 'But we've had conversations "about choosing this life"—' she did air quotes as she said this '—and I remember him saying the same thing, about feeling stuck. I guess it's the next best thing after running away with the circus.'

Sofia was not pleased with being compared to Jack. She tried to conceal her irritation. 'So Captain Mary has been working with Jack for a long time?'

'Since he started, so almost ten years.' Petra lowered her voice, shifting her eyes from side to side, and Sofia knew she was about to get a juicy titbit. 'I probably shouldn't go spreading this around really but, since you asked, Captain Mary used to have a partner – Jean. This was before I met her, and I think they tried to have children, and it never happened for them. They split up just before I started working with her, and I think Jack has always been a sort of surrogate son.'

Sofia considered this information. It explained their dynamic, but she wasn't best pleased by the idea of Jack as the object of Captain Mary's misplaced maternal pride. She knew she shouldn't push it, but she found herself asking: 'What happened between Captain Mary and her wife?'

'I think just the usual. It was too hard, as she said, life at sea and all that. It's not exactly fertile ground for a functional relationship.'

'We're all doomed to die alone then?' Sofia's tone was light-hearted, but she felt the question settle somewhere uncomfortable in her consciousness.

'Speak for yourself, honey. I'm planning on bagging myself a footballer and never working another day in my life. This—' she waved her arms in the air '—it's inspiration, not just aspiration.'

Sofia laughed. 'Poor Milly better watch her back.'

'Exactly,' said Petra with a tone somewhere between sarcasm and sincerity, 'and with that, I'm off to bed!'

Her first night on the open seas, Sofia slept like a log, her dreams softly lapping at the edges of her mind, indistinguishable but calming, like the tide.

# Chapter Ten

It was a misty morning, but Sofia had the urge to go up on deck. It was still early, and she couldn't hear the telltale groans from the crew's neighbouring bunk beds, so she figured she was the first one up. Growing up near the beach, Sofia had always loved to be in the midst of a morning fog. It was like standing in the sky and the sea at the same time.

She made herself a terrible instant coffee and headed upstairs. All around the light was the colour of dried lavender, mauve frosted with grey. She took a deep breath and leant forward against the railings.

She closed her eyes, losing herself for a moment in the tingle of sea spray and absolute solitude. Or so she thought. In the quiet of the morning, she heard footsteps before she saw the figure emerge from the mist.

'Oh sorry.' It was Jack, dressed in green tartan pyjama bottoms and a heavy fleece that made him look boyish. 'I didn't think there would be anyone up here. You know it's, like, 5 a.m.?'

It was amazing how quickly her serenity evaporated. 'Yes, thanks for that information. I can tell the time.'

'How can you possibly be this bad-tempered already?

What is it you Brits say . . . "woke up on the wrong side of the bed, did you"?'

'That phony British accent is somehow extra grating before the sun has fully risen.' She was already nostalgic for her moment of peace only minutes before.

Jack was scrutinising her face quizzically. 'I just don't know what I've done to upset you.'

'It's not personal, don't worry. I've just met, and worked with, men like you before, and I know what to expect.'

He raised an eyebrow. 'And what exactly do you mean by "men like me"?'

'Rich white men who have fallen into jobs thanks to their parents' connections, who think that they can have, and discard, whatever they want.' Sofia felt she'd said too much, and once again she was even more angry with him for making her lose her cool.

'Listen, honey.' Coming from him the word 'honey' sounded jarring. His tone was hard, and she could see the anger mirrored back towards her. 'I don't know who broke your heart, but in this world you can't go around making that everyone else's problem. You have no idea who I am, and actually I think I'd like to keep it that way.' He stopped for breath. 'I believe, as per our agreement, the deck is my territory anyway, so if you'd kindly find your way back to your bunker kitchen, that'd be much appreciated.'

He gave her a cold smile, did a little bow, and held out his arm to motion for her to pass by him. She stormed across the deck, thundered down the stairs and collapsed back into her bunk, full of righteous anger. When it had passed, she replayed the scene in her head. On second viewing, she realised she had behaved like a petulant teenager. In keeping with the mood, she screamed into her pillow, took ten deep breaths, and decided to try and get up on the right side of the bed.

Sofia busied herself with breakfast, first for the crew, and then brunch for Milly and Brian. They had requested a 'lie-in' and she liked to imagine them lounging together in the absurdly big marble bathtub she'd glimpsed through a door left ajar. She made scrambled eggs and salmon on rye bread served with a scoop of black caviar.

As the plates made their way upstairs, Sofia was already prepping for their afternoon snack and thinking about the dinner menu. It was only her second day at sea and she found herself already looking forward to their stop-off in Capri, where she would get a day off from cooking. Work at the restaurant had been hard, but she'd had regular time off, and backup. Right now, she was immersed in her own little bubble, flitting around the small kitchen to find that hours had passed.

At four o'clock she enlisted Declan to help set up an elaborate afternoon tea in the horizon lounge, on the upper deck of the yacht. She had gone all out. Tiers of cucumber, crab, egg and cress sandwiches, cheese scones, sweet scones, pots of cream and jam, and jewel-toned macarons. Milly and Brian were in the corner of the room. They had barely noticed Sofia and Declan come in. Sofia wondered how long it had taken for them to become people who were accustomed to being around 'staff'. Only two years ago they had been relatively normal. She, a paralegal from Ramsey, and he, a mid-tier footballer from Bournemouth. Now they were lounging on a 154-foot yacht as a private chef and a deckhand laid out an extravagant, 'afternoon snack' that had taken several hours to prepare.

Milly was wearing her hair back in a tight bun, and when she finally looked up and saw Sofia, she squealed. 'Hey! Sofia, look, you inspired me.' She turned her head to the side and motioned to her updo.

'Looks, um, very nice.' Sofia was embarrassed by the interaction – maybe they weren't so clued up on the VIP-staff dynamic after all. Sofia had been under the impression that she would be expected to serve and smile, not provide style tips.

When Brian looked up, his eyes went straight to the food. 'Oh great, finally – I could eat a horse.'

*Finally,* Sofia thought, was a bit of an exaggeration. They had only eaten brunch at midday. As Brian made his way through the first tier of finger sandwiches, Declan poured out two glasses of champagne and brought one over to Milly. She downed the glass without looking up from her phone.

'Another please . . .' She looked up and smiled at him.

'D-Declan,' he stumbled, tripping a little over his own feet as he backed away.

'Thanks, Declan.'

Over by the bar he fumbled with the bottle. Sofia went over, taking it from his nervous grip. She poured another glass.

'She's very pretty huh,' Sofia said, teasing him. He looked down, embarrassed, and she immediately felt bad.

'It's not like that. I don't . . . it's just I've never, like, seen anyone from TV in real life before.' They were speaking in hushed tones, but Sofia was sure that Milly understood exactly what effect she had on people.

'Anyway . . .' Declan looked directly at Sofia. 'She's not my type.'

It occurred to her then that Declan might have misconstrued her friendliness for something more. She thought about admitting that she saw him more as a little brother and then she thought better of it. It would be enough to give the poor boy a complex, at his age. She knew you had to be delicate about rejection. Instead she decided to do the proper British thing and sweep it under the carpet, feigning ignorance.

'She's everyone's type, Declan,' she garbled, busying herself and looking away. 'And anyway, you've got more pressing things to think about than pretty girls. I'm sure you'll be needed back up on deck as soon as you're done here.' She couldn't look at him, so she didn't see the pang of disappointment cross his face.

'Yes, Chef! Let me know if you need any help clearing.' He walked off and she went over to hand Milly her glass.

'Just bring the whole bottle over, would you, hon?'

Sofia obliged, thinking back on the days that she too

would polish off a bottle of wine in a single sitting. She sometimes missed the numb warmth of it and then she would remember how the world took on a cooler edge afterwards. Walking back to the kitchen, she took the scenic route around the deck, marvelling at how bright the world looked these days.

# Chapter Eleven

For dinner, Sofia had settled on a simple caprese salad for starters. The tomatoes she had were at their peak ripeness, and she could no longer resist the allure of the buffalo mozzarella bathing in a tub of brine in her fridge. For the main course, she had a couple of seabass she was going to roast whole, and dessert would be apricots poached in sweet wine with rosemary syrup and a dollop of crème fraiche.

As had become the usual, Petra dropped in to ask about the menu, and Sofia thought she saw a frown briefly flit across her face at the mention of the main course.

'Whole seabass? Any chance you might be able to fillet them?'

Sofia felt herself getting defensive and tried to calm herself down. 'Well, in terms of the flavour profile, roasting it whole just really does preserve the taste of the fish.'

'You're the chef,' said Petra, looking relieved when her radio crackled and she was summoned upstairs. 'To table in forty-five minutes,' she called over her shoulder as she raced out of the kitchen.

Sofia was ready, the salads sitting on the counter when

Declan arrived, wearing what could only be described as a 'white pinny' around his waist.

'Well isn't that a charming look,' said Sofia, trying to suppress a giggle.

Declan looked as close to grumpy as she had ever seen him. Somehow it made him even more endearing, like a toddler threatening a tantrum. 'It was Petra's idea,' he mumbled sulkily. 'She said that I'm too clumsy and she can't spend all her time washing my uniform.'

Sofia gave him a teasing pat on the back. 'I think you look very cute.'

Declan cracked a smile, despite himself. 'Cute isn't exactly what I was going for, but from you I'll take it.'

She'd stepped right into that one, and she berated herself for not being more careful. It was Sofia's turn to be saved by the radio.

'Service in the main saloon please.'

'That's your cue,' she said to Declan, her back to him as she finished preparing the seabass.

Twenty-five minutes later he was back, salad plates empty, and waiting for the seabass.

'They said they really enjoyed the salad.'

'Oh, good, nothing beats a raw salad when the ingredients are that fresh.' Sofia beamed. 'Seabass is ready to go.'

'Eeeesh, would you look at the eyes on that.' Declan was staring at the plate she had handed him.

'Not you too – it's just a fish.'

'Can I give you some advice? Not trying to mansplain

or whatever.'

Sofia rolled her eyes. 'Advice is not the same as explaining something, Declan.'

'Right, yeah, OK so basically, I'd say, cut the head off.'

'You really think they'll be put off by seeing a fish head on their plate? Surely they know where the fillet comes from.' Declan shrugged, but Sofia was feeling defiant. 'If they say something, bring it back and I will replate it, without the head.'

'OK.' Declan stood there for a moment, opened his mouth to say something, and then promptly bit his tongue, turned on his heels and walked out.

Sofia pitted the apricots and put them in a pan, simmering with the dessert wine. She had expected to have the next twenty minutes at least to herself so she was caught by surprise when the kitchen door swung open again.

She turned to find Declan with his head bowed, holding the two plates, untouched.

Sofia felt a jolt of embarrassment. He had been right about the heads and she had been too stubborn to listen. 'They didn't like the heads then?' she said quietly, taking the plates from his hands and transferring the fish to a large chopping board.

'Um, well the thing is, Sofia—' He was cut off by Petra coming through behind him. The three of them were now squished into the small kitchen, and Sofia began to feel claustrophobic.

'Sofia, hey, so I need to have a word with you about the food.' Petra had taken on a matronly tone that Sofia hadn't heard before. She began to feel a sense of dread.

'Go on,' she said, although she really didn't want her to.

'So Amelia has made it clear to me that she has not been enjoying what she called "a relentless" amount of seafood, and that she doesn't really eat fish.'

Sofia was finding it hard to follow what Petra was saying, as the panic clouded her hearing and locked her jaw shut.

'She told me that she would rather have a meat-based menu from now on, and that she has been missing carbohydrates.'

Sofia found her voice. 'But her preference sheet literally said the opposite of that. Why is she only mentioning this now? Yesterday they loved the scallops and lobster.'

Petra and Declan exchanged a look, and then neither of them would quite meet her gaze.

'Well actually, they haven't been finishing the food.' Petra looked down at her hands. 'We've just been clearing the plates before we bring them back to the kitchen.'

Sofia's vision began to throb and she could feel her breathing quicken. The blood was too loud in her ears and she felt the prickle of tears. Suddenly Declan and Petra seemed and sounded very far away. She put her hands on the counter to steady herself.

In the distance she could just hear them. 'Is she OK?' Declan sounded worried.

'I think she's having a panic attack. Get her a glass of water.'

Petra brought over a small stool and lowered Sofia down. 'Deep breaths, Sofia. Listen to me, slow down your breathing, and lower your head between your legs.'

Sofia felt like she wasn't breathing at all; she thought of everything she had given up to be here, a promising career in London's top kitchens and the chance to follow in Joy's footsteps. Now she would probably get fired, and have to return to the grey city with her tail between her legs. She would have to accept that this had been a mistake, like so many people had told her it would be.

Declan handed her a glass of water. She took a sip, the cold liquid bringing her back to herself for a moment.

'Let's get her back to the cabin.' Petra helped her to her feet.

'But what about . . .'

'We can cover her for tonight.' Petra was in army sergeant mode, and Declan was ready to receive orders. The two of them led Sofia back to her room.

'It's going to be OK, Sofia. You didn't know, and that's my fault. I'm still getting the hang of this job too.' Petra was taking off her shoes, and Sofia leant into the comfort of her voice and the feeling of being looked after. She had stopped shaking, but she felt exhausted.

'What about dinner?' she mumbled weakly, curling herself up into a foetal position.

'Don't worry about that right now.'

Sofia was awash with gratitude. 'Thank you, Petra. I'm really sorry, and thanks for . . . for looking after me.'

Petra stood up. 'Yes well, enough of the soppy stuff for

tonight. I have a ship to run; you get some sleep.'

Sofia couldn't believe that she would be able to sleep that night with the anxiety still coursing through her veins. As soon as Petra softly shut her door, the darkness and the gentle bobbing lured her into a fitful sleep. She was transported back to the day, two months ago, when she accepted the job on board the *Lady Ixchel*. She had asked the head chef at Nakachwa, Joy, for a meeting; she had seemed like she was expecting it.

'Sit down, Sofia, how can I help?' Joy's voice was, as always, warm and deep. As she settled into the seat at her desk, she templed her slender fingers up to her chin. Her locks were piled in a crown on top of her head and with her back straight, she looked as regal as ever.

'I don't really know how to say this, but I'm handing in my notice.' Sofia took a deep breath and dared to meet Joy's dark eyes.

They were sympathetic, but also weighed down with something else. Disappointment, thought Sofia with a heavy heart.

'Right, I see.' A pause. 'And can I ask why?' Joy's brow was furrowed with concern.

Sofia could not admit to Joy, or maybe even to herself, that it was because of Simon, and in many ways it wasn't, not entirely. She didn't know how to say that she had lost herself, to work, to a man, to drink, to the city. So instead she said: 'I just think it's time for me to move on.'

'I'm not going to pretend I'm not sad to see you go, Sofia, and I really hope you are making the right decision. I saw a bright future for you here, but I have noticed that you've lost your focus, and maybe your drive.'

Joy leant forward and placed a hand over Sofia's, which were fidgeting in her lap. 'Look at me, Sofia.' She waited until Sofia dragged her eyes up. 'Don't let anyone dim your light, Sofia, and don't let any distractions get in the way of becoming who you want to be.'

Sofia had not been able to hold back the tears then. Joy had patted her on the shoulder before leaving her alone. In the dream, the tears began to pool at her feet, and then the room began to fill with water, salty water. Before long she was up to her waist, and the tears would not stop flowing. Eventually she was lying on her back, staring at the ceiling as the water kept rising, pushing her nose up against the plaster until she was completely submerged.

Sofia did not awake in a panic; instead she felt a weighty sense of calm. The cabin was rocking with the waves. She wiped away the single tear running down her cheek. She rolled over, shut her eyes once again and this time was welcomed by a deep, empty slumber.

# Chapter Twelve

Sofia woke up determined she would not let herself be disheartened. By 6 a.m. she was in the kitchen, flipping through her recipe cards and notebook, designing a whole new menu. The crew would be having lobster tonight and Milly and Brian would get their carb-heavy comfort food. She could adapt.

By the time Petra poked her head through the door at 7.30 a.m., Sofia was confident she had a plan to cover all the meals until they docked in Capri and she could get more supplies.

'Oh good, you're here. I was worried when I saw your cabin empty.'

'Yeah I was this close to throwing myself overboard last night.'

Petra looked at her with such genuine concern that she couldn't keep a straight face and cracked into a grin.

'Oh I see, well I'm glad you've recovered your sense of humour.' Petra chuckled, and then tentatively asked, 'Are you good to go?'

'Got a whole new menu, not a crustacean in sight!' Sofia could hear her voice was verging on the manic. She took a moment and composed herself. 'But on a serious note, Petra, thanks so much for last night, I really needed a friend, and it's . . .' she suddenly felt shy '. . . it's really lovely to know that I have someone on this job who has my back.'

'Don't mention it. We managed to cobble together a burger, and they bloody loved it.'

Sofia groaned. 'After all that, all they wanted was a burger?'

Petra slapped her on the back playfully. 'I told you that these VIPs never have the refined tastes they think they do!' With a wink she was off.

The next couple of days passed without incident, Sofia was getting back in touch with the simpler dishes in her repertoire, the things she would often cook for herself, or for friends: casseroles, pasta, steak frites, Wellington. She noticed that Brian no longer lunged at the sight of the afternoon snack and felt bad for having essentially starved him for two days. It can't have been easy to sustain all six foot four of him on a diet of cheese scones and finger sandwiches.

The crew meanwhile were feasting like kings – all the shellfish had to go somewhere. Sofia began to enjoy their dinners together. Once she tuned out Jack's cocky interjections, she found herself joking easily with the captain, Petra and Declan of course, and even Stuart.

'I honestly don't think I ever even knew what a fish out of batter looked like until I left Glasgow.' Stuart was regaling the table. It was late and he had produced a bottle of whisky from his cabin. It was the night before they would be docking in Capri, and everyone was looking forward to some time away from the guests.

'Don't you guys deep-fry Mars Bars?' Petra was flushed pink, and she was giggling a little too enthusiastically every time Stuart spoke, much to Sofia's amusement.

'Aye,' he said, 'I'll have to give you a masterclass in the fine cuisine of the deep fryer sometime,' he told Sofia. 'I'm sure Miss Amelia would love a bit of battered sausage.'

Sofia couldn't help but laugh, and the rest of the crew joined in. Petra was on the brink of tears. It seemed that a little Dutch, or perhaps Scotch, courage had brought Stuart out of his shell, and he seemed thrilled with his temporary role as court jester, blushing his deep shade of crimson every time he caught sight of Petra enjoying herself.

'Anybody for a top-up?' He passed the bottle around the table.

Sofia declined, as did Jack, she noticed, who had been strangely quiet all evening.

'Not much of a drinker, are you, Sofia?' Stuart noted.

Sofia hated this conversation, especially with other Brits, there was always an assumption that people had the right to know what had 'gone wrong' for you to make such a dramatic decision.

'Not really, I er, used to be.' And there it was. A concerned hush fell around the table, as though everyone was waiting for her to begin her AA testimony. 'Not like, you know, an alcoholic, but there was a lot of drinking at my old job and I just wanted to start afresh a bit, you know?'

The faces looking back at her didn't convince her that they did know, apart from Jack's, which was both sincere and devoid of pity. She found herself looking at him a little too long, and they both looked away suddenly after a moment.

'Fair enough,' was all Stuart could muster. 'Anybody else?'

'Pass it here.' Declan didn't seem like he needed any more, but Stuart was pleased to have a companion.

'That's my boy,' said Stuart cheerfully as he poured an alarmingly large measure into Declan's glass.

'Don't overdo it, Dec,' warned Jack. 'Remember that you and I will be taking the guests out on that boat trip tomorrow, so it's not entirely a rest day for us.'

'Aye, aye, Captain.' Declan drunkenly saluted Jack and then realised that Captain Mary was still sitting at the table and began to giggle uncontrollably.

'Well on that note, I think it is time for me to retire.' Captain Mary got up from her seat, smiling with good humour. 'Have a good evening, everybody. Jack and Declan, I will see in the morning to get the tender ready.'

'Night, Captain,' everyone replied in a primary-school-like chorus.

One by one, the rest of the crew excused themselves. First Jack, and then Declan. Sofia was left with Petra and Stuart. He was talking about his childhood, growing up in Scotland, what school was like. Sofia was interested in what he had to say, but at a certain point she began to feel like she was intruding on something. There was a shift in the energy of the room, and she felt it was time to go to bed.

'OK, guys, I'm off. Gotta be up early to make Milly and Brian's picnic lunch so . . .' Neither of them really seemed to notice she was still there.

'Oh yeah, night, Sofia, have a good one.' Stuart didn't even look up. He and Petra were sitting opposite each other, knee to knee. As she walked back to her cabin Sofia found herself wondering what it was about work that made people fancy each other. She had fallen into that trap before and suffered the consequences. Petra and Stuart, she hoped, were older and wiser – maybe they knew what they were doing. *She* certainly would not be making that mistake again. She made a note to herself to double down on her efforts to dissuade Declan and then her mind wandered to the subject of Jack. He'd been so sullen at dinner, maybe it wouldn't hurt to try and clear the air with him, if only to make things less awkward.

# Chapter Thirteen

Sofia was in the kitchen, chopping up a grapefruit for a citrus pavlova, when there was an urgent knock on the door. She checked her watch. It was only 8 a.m. – she had another hour until the guest breakfast needed serving.

'Come in?' She was expecting Petra, so she was caught off guard when she looked up to find Jack standing in front of her.

'Sorry, I know I am very much on your turf here.' He looked bashful, and Sofia was intrigued to hear what had brought him down here, into her lair. She raised an eyebrow, waiting for him to say more.

'I have a pretty big favour to ask you.' She had not expected this, but she was surprised to find that she was enjoying this change in their dynamic. It was nice for him to be on the back foot for once.

'Oh really?' She was a little too gleeful to sound cool and composed as she had wanted to.

'Dec is in a bad way . . . after the whisky . . . and I need someone to come with me on the boat trip later on. You wouldn't need to drive the boat or navigate or anything, I just need someone there to keep an eye on the guests, keep their glasses topped up, make sure they keep their life jackets on, that kind of thing.' It was fascinating to watch him ramble, because he was flustered. Sofia bathed in the smugness of his discomfort.

'Well as long as you don't require too much brawn, I reckon I can help.'

He gave her a shy smile, and Sofia felt a twinge of compassion towards him. He was clearly grateful. 'Thank you very much. You've really got me out of a sticky situation, and I'm sure Dec will be very appreciative too, once he can stand up without vomiting again.' He ran his hand through his hair, clearly relieved.

'It's the least I can do really, after he covered for me the other day when I um, well, I wasn't well and I couldn't get dinner ready. He and Petra really saved my arse . . .' She trailed off, and it was her turn to be humbled. Jack gave her a strange look that she couldn't decipher.

'Right yes, well, great, meet me up on deck after you've sent breakfast. I'll have to talk you through basic safety procedures. It's not very complicated – don't worry.'

There it was – once he had done his grovelling, the patronising tone was back. 'I think I'll be fine. I know you like to think that the only alternative to brawn is beauty, but there's also brains, and girls have those too!' She tapped her head sarcastically.

He let out an exasperated sigh. 'Yes, of course, sorry, I just meant it won't take long.'

Sofia turned back to her grapefruit. 'I'll see you around nine then?'

'Great, looking forward to it.'

83

She wasn't best pleased with the sarcasm dripping from his voice but she decided to let it go. They would be spending the whole day together on a small boat, no room for delineated territories, so she needed to practise exercising patience.

After Jack left, Sofia busied herself with breakfast: pancakes with summer berry compote. At 9.04 there was still no sign of Petra and Sofia was worried about the steaming mountain of freshly flipped batter going soggy.

'Petra, breakfast is ready.' She hadn't quite got the hang of the radio yet.

'This is the captain. Try channel six, over,' came the reply.

'Sorry, Captain, over.'

She tried the other channel, and just then Petra burst through the door, looking a little worse for wear.

'Long night, huh?' Sofia teased.

Petra groaned. 'Honestly I completely see why you don't drink anymore. Once you hit thirty hangovers are no joke.'

'Excuse me, I am twenty-seven, thank you very much.' Sofia rolled her eyes, but thrust a bottle towards Petra. 'Here have some of this coconut water. You need to rehydrate.'

Petra chugged down half the bottle and let out a long sigh. 'So you're only twenty-seven? That's crazy, I was so sure we were the same sort of age. I mean I'm thirty-two so not a million miles off.' She laughed at Sofia's deep frown. 'Not because you look old, my God, your skin is

84

incredible, just that you seem, I don't know, mature? Like you've seen some stuff, like you know who you are?'

Sofia let out an incredulous scoff. 'Hardly – sometimes it feels like I don't recognise myself at all, let alone *know* myself. I think it's fair to say that I've tried to reinvent myself a bit since stepping on this boat.'

Petra tilted her head to the side. 'Huh, well you're doing a great job, kid – very convincing.'

'OK, I'm not sure about "kid".' Sofia playfully swatted Petra with the tea towel in her hand. 'Enough of this chit-chatting; these pancakes are not going to serve themselves.'

'Damn they look good. Any chance of a couple of rejects going?' Sofia stepped to one side to reveal a pile of slightly misshapen ones on a plate behind her. 'You are an angel sent from heaven,' said Petra, blowing her a kiss before picking up the plates.

'I'm covering for Declan on the boat today, so help yourself. I have to go and get ready with Jack.'

'You and Jack? Together on a small boat all day? Are you sure that's a good idea? We're already a skeleton crew; the last thing we need is a homicide on our hands.' Petra was teasing, but Sofia felt herself blush profusely. She thought she had managed to keep their frosty relationship under wraps. She didn't want a reputation for not being able to keep things professional.

'Oh please, you think I haven't noticed how the pair of you can barely be in the same room? Well you know what they say, it's a very fine line between love and hate.'

Petra winked at her and before Sofia could protest, she was gone.

Sofia didn't have time to dwell on that comment. She had to change out of her chef's whites and get up on deck for her safety training. The thought of having to be instructed by Jack made her skin crawl but she would have to suck it up.

'Right on time, Chef Harlow.' Jack was inspecting the tender. 'Could you just check that all four of those life jackets over there are operational?'

Sofia walked over to the pile of orange nylon and picked them up awkwardly. She had no idea what exactly she was looking for.

Jack glanced over. 'Just make sure that the buckles are working and the straps are tight around each vest.'

'Yes, got it,' she snapped. She was not going to enjoy this: being in Jack's world, answering to him, it was the very definition of being on the back foot. Why had she agreed to this? To make a point about not being the damsel, but the knight? Had she really wanted to prove that she could come to Jack's rescue so badly that she had willingly gotten herself into this situation? She respected Petra but she was starting to think that her assessment of Sofia as somebody who was 'wise beyond her years' was way off.

After the life jackets, Sofia had to mop the floor of the dinghy and wipe down the seats. Jack was busy fiddling with the motor and the dials at the helm. Sofia was not convinced he was actually doing anything useful, and thought he was treating her as his dogsbody.

'So I'm doing all the real work and you just stare at the controls huh?' She was twisting murky water out of the mop head.

'Well I know you understand the chain of command, having worked in a "professional kitchen" as you like to keep reminding everyone, so it shouldn't come as a surprise to you that covering for Declan means that you have to do as I say.' He was smirking, clearly enjoying himself.

She decided to ignore the pointed comment about her last job. 'I thought you said I would just be "filling up glasses".'

'Once we're on the water sure, but we can't have Milly and Brian sitting on – what is it you Brits say – *manky* seats while you pour the champagne.'

'Of course not,' she said with a bright and unconvincing smile. Once they were done Jack talked her through the safety protocol; basically, don't fall in, and don't take your jacket off. Sofia rolled her eyes. She hardly needed to be here two hours early for him to tell her that.

'And you have the picnic hamper ready?'

Sofia nodded grumpily. Jack ignored it. He was in 'first officer mode' now. How quickly he could slip in and out of it, Sofia thought.

'I was thinking we could go around the north coast, towards the Grotta Azzurra, maybe pull into a little bay for the food and then head back mid-afternoon. They're spending the night on land at some fancy villa that Milly saw on Instagram, so we need to get back in time to dock *Lady Shelly* and get supplies on board before dark.'

'Sure, that all sounds good to me.' She decided she too could be civil and professional. She also had to be. 'I have a list for the supply run ready, and I'll bring the hamper up to the boat before we leave. I'd like to keep it refrigerated as long as possible.'

'That you very much, Chef Harlow. I'll see you in an hour.' He strode off and Sofia began to feel a little better about her chances of surviving the day.

She went back to her cabin and changed into the spare stewardess uniform. She admired herself in the mirror. The maroon skort and polo actually looked quite good on her, as she always did in shades of red. The top was a little tight. Tabitha had been very slight, but she felt presentable.

'Sofia, I need you on deck please.' She jumped as the radio came to life from where it was clipped to her waistband.

'Coming.' She checked her watch. Shit, she was five minutes late. She'd gotten distracted, but she'd have to think of a better excuse before she got to Jack. She couldn't bear to imagine what he would have to say about the damsel getting lost in her own reflection.

When she got up to the deck, Milly and Brian were already in the boat. Jack was clipping Milly into her life jacket, and she giggled as he tightened the strap around her waist. 'Easy Captain,' she said playfully.

Jack wasn't thrown like Declan had been. 'You better

88

behave yourself, Miss Cox, or else I'll have no choice but to throw you in at the deep end.'

'I don't think I'd mind taking a dip in the deep end with you, Captain Carter.'

Sofia watched them in disbelief, glancing over at Brian, who seemed completely unbothered by the interaction. He was gazing out at the sea.

'Ah hum.' Sofia cleared her throat to catch Jack's attention and bring this embarrassing episode to an end.

'Harlow, how nice of you to join us. 'He gave her an admiring once-over, and suddenly she felt like maybe she should have asked to borrow one of Petra's polos instead.

'Oooh yay, Sofia, you're coming! Love this colour on you. Doesn't she look lovely?' Milly turned to Brian and then to Jack. Sofia flushed furiously.

'She does indeed,' said Jack, his eyes holding Sofia's.

'Right then, shall we go before I have to file a workplace harassment claim?' She bit her tongue. That was certainly not professional or civil, and she'd said it in front of the guests.

Milly burst out laughing. 'Oh I like her. You tell him, girl!' She squealed and clapped her hands girlishly. 'This is going to fun, isn't it, boys?'

Brian grunted his assent and Sofia climbed into the boat, strapping up her life vest.

'All aboard?' asked Jack as he started the engine.

Milly settled herself on the lounger seat at the bow of the boat, in front of where Jack was driving. Brian sat near the stern staring out at the wake. Sofia sat behind Jack.

It was surprisingly spacious, and with the sun shining as they motored through sea spray, Sofia felt like she was on holiday.

They zoomed towards the coast, and then alongside it. The water was breathtakingly blue, a deep turquoise and clear as glass. The shore was jagged with castles of cliff, topped with green. Milly could not stop taking photos.

'Could you stop here a moment, Jack?' she shouted over the sound of the engine.

'We're on a bit of a tight schedule,' he replied.

She was crossing her arms sulkily when Brian interjected, 'Surely a minute or two can't hurt?' It was kind of romantic really, thought Sofia, how well he knew her, and how willing he was to step in to make sure she was having the best time.

Jack seemed a little irritated, but he hid it with a showman's smile. 'Of course, not a problem.' He cut the engine.

Brian knew the drill. When he got up to walk to Milly she was already holding out her phone for him to take it.

'So I think one with those hills in the background. If I lean like this can you see the water behind me as well?'

'Tilt your head back a bit. Your necklaces are in shadow.'

She obliged, and Sofia marvelled at them. For the next few minutes they were utterly focused on the task at hand.

'Try one with your hands under your head. Yep that's it, you look great, baby. Now sit up, try a laugh, shoulder back. No, the other one. Perfect.'

Sofia looked over at Jack, who was getting agitated. 'Are we almost done?'

*This is their job,* Sofia thought. She could tell that Jack thought it was all frivolous, but Milly and Brian were professionals making a living just like they were.

'OK,' said Brian, snapping another few photos. 'All done, thanks, man.' Brian leant down to hand Milly back her phone and give her a kiss. Sofia found herself transfixed by the tenderness in it, the way they looked at each other, and then she felt like she was intruding and busied herself trying to find the champagne.

As she rummaged under seats to find the fridge, she realised with a punch of dread that the hamper was not there. Her mind raced, reversing through the last hour. She had not brought it onto the boat with her. Sofia briefly considered throwing herself overboard, then she collected herself.

'All good, Harlow? I need you to take a seat, really, before we set off. Don't want to send you flying.' He winked at her. 'Well not yet.'

'Jack, I need a quick word,' she said in a stage whisper, jerking her head to the side to indicate that he should follow her to the other end of the boat. There was hardly very much privacy, but Brian and Milly seemed distracted enough for the moment.

'Um I don't really know how to say this.' She couldn't even look at him.

His patience was running low and they were already behind schedule. 'Spit it out, Harlow.'

'The hamper is not here?' She tried to soften the blow by phrasing it as a question.

'What?' Sofia flinched. He was angry. He was shaking his head. 'I knew this was a bad idea,' he muttered to himself. 'So what you're telling me is that you forgot the hamper. It didn't magically disappear, did it?' His tone was scathing.

Sofia had always loathed being told off. At school she would have to fight back tears if a teacher scolded her in class. She hated that her body would betray her like this, at the worst possible moment, and it was happening again. She quickly wiped away a hot tear from her cheek.

'Don't cry.' His voice was so soft, she barely heard him. She looked up and was met by something akin to compassion. 'It's OK, we can make do. These things happen.' Sofia was taken aback. She had expected gloating.

She scrubbed away another stray tear. 'I'm really sorry.' It was strange to speak to him so sincerely.

'I've got an idea,' he said suddenly, and marched back over to the bow. 'Hey, guys, Sofia's just had a great idea. There's a citrus grove just down the coast a bit. Instead of having a picnic on the boat, I think we should moor up and go grapefruit picking?'

Brian and Milly exchanged looks, unsure.

'It'll look great on your insta grid as well!' Sofia piped up. That was all the convincing they needed.

'Sounds good to me. Thanks, guys, what an adventure. Good thing I brought my Balenciagas,' Milly enthused.

This time when Jack glanced over and winked, Sofia

rolled her eyes but there was a grin on her face.

They cruised along until they arrived at a tiny, secluded cove.

'Here we are,' announced Jack, and Milly peered warily over the side of the boat. They would need to get wet.

'Um, I might just stay here, guys,' she said.

'Don't be silly, you can't miss out on the adventure.' Brian had gotten himself excited for the detour. Sofia wondered if it was because of the fruit picking or the photo opportunities. 'I'll carry you if you're worried about getting your trainers wet.'

'I mean she can just carry them in her hands.' Sofia shot Jack a look. Had he not heard of 'the customer is always right'? Luckily neither of them seemed to have heard him. Brian was already in the water, up to the middle of his calves and holding out his arms. Milly slipped into them effortlessly, planting a kiss onto his cheek and giggling as he began to wade towards the shore.

Sofia and Jack secured the boat, and then Jack jumped into the water. Sofia began unlacing her shoes.

'You don't want a lift as well?'

She looked over to find him with his arms outstretched and a smirk on his face.

'No, thank you, I'll be fine, and besides I can just carry them in my hands, right?'

'But then who will carry the bottle of champagne and my shoes?'

She stared at him in disbelief. 'Are you being serious?'

'It just makes more sense for me to carry you and you

to carry that basket with all the supplies, well *some* of the supplies, and our shoes, to save us having to do two trips,' he paused, and his expression turned to one of impatience. 'And we are already behind schedule.'

Sofia wasn't really sure what to think, apart from that she was grateful that Petra was in charge of packing refreshments, so at least they would have something to serve the guests to drink alongside their makeshift picnic. She didn't want to get into an argument, not with Milly and Brian waiting, and not after Jack had sort of saved her arse.

'Whatever, OK.' She awkwardly lowered herself into his arms and cradled the basket in her lap, refusing to meet his eyes but feeling the glow of smugness radiating off him all the same. She was distinctly aware of where his fingers rested against the sliver of exposed skin between the top of her waistband and the bottom of her T-shirt. He waded through the water, panting slightly from the effort, and Sofia was mildly horrified to find herself thinking that his breath smelt really good. She turned her face away and tried to get her rabid thoughts in order.

As they approached the shore Milly called out, 'OMG, you two make such a cute couple!' She snapped a picture, and Sofia wanted to die of embarrassment. This was not what she had in mind when it came to 'professional and civil'.

The moment they were on dry land she hopped down hurriedly, rearranging herself and trying not to look as flustered as she felt. Jack seemed unfazed as he laced up his boots. He rummaged through the basket until he found what he was looking for: a compass.

'Old-school!' said Brian. 'Cool!'

'It's not a long walk, as far as I can remember; but I don't want us getting lost.' Jack set the compass and the four of them found a narrow track up from the beach.

The walk was mostly pleasant, although on a few occasions they had to drop into a single file to avoid being attacked from either side by the overgrown and surprisingly prickly shrubbery lining the 'path'.

Sofia could feel Milly and Brian losing patience with the whole idea. They had been walking in the midday sun for about forty minutes. Jack was striding up ahead, and Sofia was beginning to worry that this plan was a terrible one. She imagined them wandering around in the heat for hours, running out of water and becoming so weak that they would have to be rescued. When the search party finally tracked them down she would have to admit that she had left the hamper on the *Lady Shelly* and that they were in search of a citrus grove. It sounded delusional.

Just as Sofia was about to suggest they abandon the escapade altogether, Jack called out, 'It's just here!'

'Thank Christ for that.' Milly was fanning herself with her hands, her foundation running in sweaty streaks down her neck. 'I'm going to need some blotting papers Brian.' She had barely finished her sentence before he was standing right beside her handing her a small envelope that looked like a packet of tissues. *She had this man extraordinarily well trained,* thought Sofia.

The citrus grove was an oasis. The dappled light and the smell of citrus in the air gave the place a surreal quality. There was nobody around. The trees were laden with fruit, bright yellow orbs nestled in bunches among the waxy leaves. Milly and Brian were in their element.

'Oh, babe, that bikini looks so great; it was meant to be.' Brian was in photographer mode. It was true, the pictures would be worth the trek. Milly was leaning against the trunk, her butter-coloured gingham bikini top and matching shorts contrasting against the dark foliage and picking up the yellow of the grapefruits hanging just above her shock of bright red hair. The streaks of sunlight would give the photos a startlingly dramatic quality, which some of Milly's 3.2 million followers would spend the rest of the summer trying to recreate.

Sofia laid down the wicker basket, which housed two bottles of decidedly warm champagne, two glasses and a picnic blanket.

Jack was halfway up a tree, with a grapefruit already in hand, and he yelled down to her: 'Sofia, I need you and that basket.'

She stood below him as he dropped the fruit down. With his trousers rolled up, Sofia found herself face to face with his calves. She was not in the habit of staring at men's legs but she decided that, of the ones she had paid attention to, these were some of the nicest. She had to admit that he was a good-looking guy and there was something about the ease with which he existed in his body. As if it was an instrument he had perfected, tuned and toned to play any symphony he put his mind to. He steered a boat as naturally as he climbed a tree or followed a compass. Sofia was envious of his surety about his place in the world. Maybe that was why she had taken against him so instantly?

'Harlow,' he called, 'think fast,' and just as she looked up, a grapefruit whistled past her ear. Instantaneously all the goodwill she had just cultivated was gone.

'Can you please watch out,' she yelled back.

'Damn I just missed you.' Sofia wondered if this was his idea of flirtation, a schoolboy's technique, pulling on her ponytail until she agreed to kiss him under the slide.

'Please, Jack, I'm tired and grumpy, and I think we have enough grapefruit now.' He slid down the trunk and landed firmly on his feet, a wide grin across his face.

'What on earth have you got to be grumpy about? Look around!' There was nothing that made Sofia less cheery than being told to cheer up. She scowled at him and began laying out the picnic blanket.

'I don't know if anyone's ever told you this before, and I'm only saying this because you don't have a drink in your hand,' he continued even after she shot him a look, 'but you can be kind of uptight, Sofia.' They had never discussed that evening at the bar, and Sofia was thrown by his sudden candidness. He was pushing his luck, but something about his boyish enthusiasm was infectious. Despite herself she let out a giggle.

'Now that's an unexpected reaction.' He seemed genuinely taken aback.

'I do have a sense of humour, Jack, I just don't enjoy being hit on by men who are simultaneously hitting on every other woman in the vicinity.'

'Ohhh, so you were just jealous?' He was standing with his hands on his hips, and he raised a single eyebrow.

'If that's what you want to tell yourself, go ahead!'

He shook his head with a chuckle and busied himself opening a bottle. It was the first time they had managed to joke with each other without one of them having a tantrum. Sofia was relieved.

After the four of them had gorged themselves on grapefruits, and Milly had finished off the champagne, they made their way back to the cove.

'If everyone isn't too tired, I think we should try and get to the caves before we head back.'

Everybody looked at Milly, who was swaying slightly from side to side, scrolling through pictures on her phone.

'What do you think, babe?' Brian prompted.

Milly looked up, blinking slowly. 'Whatever, babe – sounds good!'

Brian dropped his voice as Sofia and Jack turned away to pack up and take their shoes off. 'Maybe you could take a couple of shots of me, babe? I looked this place up and it looks really good. I need something from this trip for my grid.'

Sofia glanced over her shoulder to catch a moment of tenderness that seemed unwarranted for the subject of the conversation.

Milly placed her palms on either side of Brian's cheeks,

bringing him towards her so they were standing nose to nose. 'It'd be my pleasure,' she purred before diving in for a drunken kiss. Sofia quickly looked away.

'Right, ready to board.' Jack held out his arms to Sofia.

'Oh you're talking about yourself, not the boat?' He laughed and raised an eyebrow. 'On this occasion I think I can manage myself, thank you, Captain Carter,' said Sofia as she waded into the water towards the tender.

'If you lovebirds are ready,' Jack called.

Milly giggled and Brian lifted her into his arms. Sofia caught herself staring at them with a mixture of fascination and incredulity. Surely it couldn't be that easy? Maybe she had got it wrong all these years, and the only thing standing between her and true love was a willingness to giggle and bat her eyelashes. Maybe she'd been too dismissive, and Milly had it all figured out. Soon they were back on the boat motoring along to their next stop.

# Chapter Fourteen

The 'Grotta Azzurra', which Jack translated – quite unnecessarily, thought Sofia – as the 'Blue Grotto' was fairly unassuming from the outside, a craggy archway in a wall of cliff. Jack slowed the boat to a steady chug and manoeuvred through the opening. Suddenly everything was blue. The water seemed iridescent as the daylight lit up the sea from below, a bright bulb backlighting a brilliant azure.

Jack cut the engine and the boat floated into the centre of the cave. None of them said a word. Once Sofia had had a moment of awe she glanced over at Jack and found him watching her. Their eyes met for a moment and then he quickly looked away. Were those reddening cheeks she had spotted? It was hard to tell in the lagoon light.

'This place is insane.' Brian had finally recovered himself and was already fiddling with the setting on his iPhone camera. 'Can I, like, get in?' He peered over the side of the boat.

'Um yeah you can. It's a bit trickier to get back out though. I think we have a ladder somewhere, or we can try and use—' Jack was interrupted by a loud splash. Brian had stripped down to his disturbingly leather-look speedos in a matter of moments.

'Oh, man, it is fresh!' he exclaimed fervently, limbs trying to splash away the cold. 'Let me know where looks good, Milly?'

'Yep, I'm on it, babe.' Sofia leant over and delicately removed the phone from Milly's loose grip, rotating it the right way up and handing it back to her. 'You're a lifesaver.' Milly was still swaying from the champagne and for a terrible second Sofia thought she might topple into the water.

Milly snapped away from a variety of seemingly random angles, crouching down and then balancing on the tips of her toes.

'What do you think?' Milly was holding out the phone to Sofia.

'Me?'

'Yes, course you.'

Sofia peered at the pictures. They were not good. The basic components were there, the bright cyan against Brian's jet of dark hair and those very small trunks, but it was blurry and the left side of Brian's body was out of shot.

'I'll have a go,' offered Sofia.

Milly nodded dopily and sat back down with a thud, giggling drunkenly as she went. Sofia positioned herself at the edge of the stern and soon realised that she was not much better. She couldn't seem to capture Brian when he wasn't blinking and the pictures were too dark.

'How are they looking?' he shouted up, floundering again to keep warm.

'Umm . . .' He wasn't satisfied with that response and began clambering back onto the boat.

'Let me have a look,' he said, his wet hand swiping the phone from Sofia's. 'OK, I've reset the exposure. That should be better, and a higher angle please.' It was clear that Brian was the budding photographer of the pair, which Sofia supposed made sense, if Milly was usually the subject.

Brian dove back into the water. Sofia took more photos. Jack nervously checked his watch. Milly lay back on the white leather seating and closed her eyes. Twenty minutes later, Brian had been in and out of the water several times, hauling himself over the side of the boat, art director, photographer and model all rolled into one. Sofia had to remind herself that his actual job was kicking a ball around. It seemed a waste of his talents. Finally she felt that she might have taken a good photo, just as the last of Jack's patience was ebbing away.

'Right, I think we have enough photos, don't you, Brian?' Jack was already fiddling with the control panel, checking the GPS on his phone and pointedly looking at the time again.

'I'm going to try and get onto those rocks. One last pic and then you can come collect me. My arms are knackered anyway – don't think I could get myself back up again.'

Jack tried, and failed, to conceal his irritation. Sofia recognised the edge of mocking to his Brit-ish 'yep, all right, mate,' as he steered the boat to the edge of the cave. Sofia herself wasn't sure how much longer she could handle being a glorified selfie stick. They had already taken over one hundred photos.

'I'm just going to climb up here, so if you could do a lower angle from . . .' Brian trailed off and let out a grunt of concentration as he manoeuvred himself onto a rocky ledge.

All was quiet for a moment and then seemingly from every direction, a blood-curdling scream pierced the air. Milly sat up with a start, Jack cut the engine, Sofia dropped the phone in her hands. A splash, and Brian was back in the water. Sofia had barely managed to understand where the scream had come from, before Jack had stripped off his shirt and shoes and dived into the water, a surprisingly fast form frothing towards where Brian was gasping and spluttering for air.

Soon he had reached the ledge and was swimming back towards the boat with Brian in tow. Between strokes he shouted, 'Get the ladder.' Neither Milly nor Sofia moved. 'Sofia, Goddammit, ladder. Now!'

Sofia snapped into action. The ladder was located under the seats at the front of the boat, as Jack had showed her that morning. How long ago that felt now. She clipped it to the stern and dropped it into the water. Milly, who seemed to have sobered up instantaneously, had begun to wail. 'Is he OK?' She was shaking Sofia's shoulders.

'Milly, I'm going to need your help getting Brian onto the boat. Can you do that?' It was Sofia's turn to lay her hands firmly on Milly's shoulders. She nodded gravely and together they grabbed his arms and legs whilst Jack pushed him from below, and managed to roll him onto the deck of the boat.

Sofia was relieved that she could not see any blood, but was slightly concerned that she still found the time to admire the sight in front of her. Jack was on his knees, bent over Brian, inspecting for damage. The water had teased out loose curls and soaked his hair a glistening ebony. Rivulets ran down his arms, shoulders and back, finding tracks between the outline of muscle and sinew. She was wondering if she had ever noticed how dark and thick his eyelashes were, when she was dragged back into the present moment by the flash of green that suddenly appeared between them, looking back at her. 'Sofia, can you help me turn him over.'

Brian was wailing now as well, joining Milly in a duet of distress. Jack was impressively calm. The two of them turned Brian onto his side and Jack scanned his body for a sign of injury. When he met Sofia's eyes again he looked more bemused than concerned.

'Brian, can you tell me where it hurts?'

'My foot, man, my foot kills!' Milly was kneeling now as well, grasping Brian's hand.

'It's going to be OK, baby. We're going to take you to hospital; you're going to be fine.' She sounded like she was reassuring herself as much as him.

Jack inspected Brian's foot and then tried to conceal a smirk. 'I think, Brian, that you've stepped on a sea urchin.' Sofia leant in, and when she squinted she could just make out a smattering of deep purple spots. One seemed to have a thin spike sticking out of it.

Brian was panting from the pain. 'Are you sure, man? I swear it feels like I stepped on a needle or something.'

'That'll be the spines,' Jack said coolly, as he reached under a seat for the first-aid box. 'Can you keep her calm please,' he said more quietly. This was directed at Sofia. 'I need some space.'

Sofia put her arms around Milly and led her to the seat, rubbing her back as she let out sporadic sobs. Jack's composure was infectious though, Brian lay back quietly as Jack took tweezers out of the box, and Sofia was sure he was feeling the same thing as her: a sense that everything was under control. She watched Jack work, delicately extracting three spines from the sole of Brian's foot. She felt a pang of something unfamiliar, something akin to pride.

'We need to soak it in hot water, which we don't have, so it's going to be warm water for now and I'll get us back to the *Lady Shelly* as quickly as I can,' Jack said decisively. Sofia had to admit that the 'Jack to the rescue' look was a good one for him.

'He's in good hands with Jack, don't worry,' she found herself saying to Milly. He shot her a bemused look over Milly's shoulder and she felt herself blush. 'Um, I mean Officer Carter,' she fumbled. 'He's trained in first aid, as you can see.' Milly wasn't listening to her anyway.

Jack filled up a wine cooler with fresh water and instructed Brian to soak his foot. 'Now lie back and think of England. We'll have you back on the boat with a drink in hand before you know it.'

Brian managed an unconvincing chuckle and lay back on the deck. Milly rushed over and put a folded towel under his head. 'I think we should go to the hospital,' she said, not looking up, and stroking Brian's wet hair off his forehead.

'I'm not sure that's necessary . . .' Jack started.

'We're going to the hospital.' Milly looked up then, and her expression was uncharacteristically steely, her voice steady and cold. Jack and Sofia were momentarily stunned into silence.

'OK, it'll take a little longer, but I'll go as fast as I can,' Jack stuttered. Milly gave him a sharp nod and then turned her attention back to Brian.

# *Chapter Fifteen*

Sofia would remember the next hour as a sort of fever dream. There was Milly, crouched over Brian on the deck, red hair flying as Jack sped the boat through turquoise waves. When they arrived in Capri, Sofia had to talk Milly down from calling an ambulance.

'We'll need a stretcher to get him off the boat.' The tiny woman was strangely formidable. Once Jack had helped Brian to his feet, though, it became clear that he was still pretty mobile. He managed to hobble off the boat and onto the marina with only Jack's shoulder to hold on to, to steady himself. As he limped along the dock, Sofia sensed that he was beginning to feel embarrassed by the fuss that Milly was making.

'Maybe we should just go back to the boat,' he muttered weakly as he was lowered into the back of a waiting taxi.

'No way, I'm having a specialist take a look at that foot,' Milly said already tapping away furiously on her phone and Sofia wondered who she might know that could recommend a sea urchin sting specialist in Capri. 'We're probably going to spend the night at the hospital,' she said, turning to Sofia, 'or we'll go to the villa if he gets discharged, so I'll text you guys tomorrow when we want to come back to the boat.' She was all business. There was no doubt who was staff and who was in charge now.

'Yes of course, just let us know.' And then, after reminding herself that 'the customer is always right' she added, 'I hope he finds the care he needs.'

Milly gave her a look she couldn't quite decipher and Sofia worried she had sounded sarcastic. 'Thanks,' was all Milly said. Then she was in the taxi and the pair of them were sped away.

Sofia stood for a moment in a daze and jumped when she felt a hand on her shoulder. Jack chuckled. 'What a day.'

'That's an understatement.' She found herself laughing as well, trying not to think about the weight of his hand on her shoulder. 'I don't think anything else could have gone wrong if we tried. Talk about a series of unfortunate events.'

'Welcome to the yachtie life – always unpredictable, never dull.'

'This is why I'm supposed to stay locked up below deck, in my hole of a kitchen where I belong.'

'Oh but it's so nice out here above ground. The sunlight suits you.'

She laughed and it felt like she was releasing all the tension she'd collected throughout the day. She laughed like she meant it and Jack smiled, flushing a little. 'You have a lovely laugh,' he said quietly.

For some reason that made her laugh more. How

absurd it all was. After the day they'd had, he still could find the time for some inappropriate flirting.

'You never take the day off, do you? Always ready with the corny chat-up lines?' She had meant it teasingly, but he appeared surprisingly dismayed, looking down suddenly.

'And *you* never give a guy a break, do you?'

She slapped him playfully on the shoulder, annoyed with herself for dampening what had been a carefree moment. 'Not my style,' she said.

She was relieved when he rolled his eyes good-humouredly. 'Yes, Chef!'

'Now, Captain Carter, how the hell are we getting back to the *Lady Shelly*?'

'Right this way.' They walked back to the tender and he held out his hand to help her onto the boat. 'God, I am dying for a drink. You looking forward to your first crew night out?'

'Oh God that's tonight! I was actually thinking about how much I was looking forward to going to bed.'

'Well that simply won't do, Chef Harlow. You're going to have to pull yourself together and learn to loosen up.' He winked at her.

'Hmm, we'll see. I am famously very uptight.'

When he laughed, his eyes sparkled. His hair was still a little wet from earlier and the tousled curls framed his face perfectly. Sofia became uncomfortably aware of how handsome he looked, almost exactly as he had when she had first spotted him in that bar. She reminded herself of what she had deduced back then – that he knew exactly how good he looked – and resolved anew not to give him the satisfaction of her admiration.

'Well, we'd better go then,' she said, busying herself, picking up the soaking towel on the deck that had acted as Brian's operating table.

Jack checked his watch. 'Oh God, yeah we really better. We're so late, the captain will be wondering where the hell we've got to.'

It dawned on Sofia that they would have to explain the day to Captain Mary and she felt a pang of dread. Her first excursion and she had completely messed up. Would this scupper her chance at becoming permanent crew? And if Jack hadn't been there to save the day, she was sure she would have had no idea what to do with Brian's foot.


Declan and Petra were waiting for them as they pulled in, up beside the main boat.

'Where the hell are the guests?' Petra shouted over the motor.

'It's a very long story,' Jack shouted back. 'Dec, can you give me a hand here?' The pair of them manoeuvred the tender back into place, as Sofia tried to keep herself out of the way. Petra got stuck in, manning one of the pulleys.

Once they were all back on deck, with the boat safely secured, Petra turned to them. 'So?'

'OK, so don't freak out. It sounds way worse than it is, but they've both gone to the hospital in Capri.' Jack shrugged, offering a boyish grimace.

Petra was decidedly unimpressed and trying to conceal her growing agitation. 'What!?'

Sofia chimed in: 'Brian got stung by a sea urchin in the um, the blue cave?' she looked over to Jack.

'Grotta Azzurra,' he corrected.

There was that perfect Italian accent again. She had to remember to ask him about that, but right now she was getting distracted, and Petra wanted answers, so she continued: 'And then Milly freaked out and then we went to Capri, and then they went to the hospital.'

Sofia took a deep breath, wincing in anticipation of Petra's reply. To her surprise, she began to laugh. Declan, who had been watching the exchange anxiously, joined in, tentatively at first, but soon enough all four of them were doubled over.

Petra wiped away a tear from the corner of her eye. 'Right, OK, OK, let me get this straight, Brian has gone to the hospital, with a sea urchin sting?'

'That is correct,' replied Jack.

'Wow, and there was me thinking that these guests weren't precious at all. Did you tell him he probably just needed to soak it in warm water?'

'He did,' Sofia confirmed, glancing at Jack, who seemed unperturbed by Petra's questioning of his methods.

'Well I guess that just gives us more time to get ready for this evening then. You looking forward to your first crew night out, newbies?' It was phrased as a question, but Sofia felt sure there was only one right answer.

111

Declan had it. 'Absolutely psyched,' he said, nodding enthusiastically.

'Sure, it's been a long day but I'll come for a couple of drinks.' Sofia's response was met by a raised eyebrow from Petra and Jack, who exchanged a look.

'Sure, a couple of drinks. You got it, honey.' Petra's eyes sparkled mischievously. 'OK so let's get this lovely lady into port and then we can start driiiinking!'

Whilst Jack and Declan went to find the captain to coordinate the docking, Sofia and Petra headed back below deck.

'Hey, Petra, I'm really nervous about what the captain will think about all this. Do we have to have a debrief or something?'

'Oh don't worry about that. Jack will tell her all about it, and it'll be best coming from him,' Petra reassured her. They were ambling down the stairs, taking the scenic route to accommodate their very own debrief.

'Right, yeah.' She paused a moment, wondering if she should confess to her picnic fiasco. She guessed that Jack would tell the captain and everyone would find out anyway. 'I also left the food for lunch on the boat when we left,' she admitted quietly.

'Oh damn, so it was a whole day of drama then. What did you guys eat?' Petra seemed to be finding it all amusing, which was reassuring for Sofia.

'We went to a citrus grove place – kind of random. Jack took us there.'

'Oh really? Jack took you? I wonder if that's his

grandmother's place . . .' Petra trailed off, deep in thought.

'Grandmother?' Sofia was puzzling the pieces together slowly. That would explain the Italian.

'Yeah, I remember him saying something about that once. His mum's mum has lived on Capri on and off for years. He used to spend summers on the island when he was a kid.' Petra peered out of the side of her eye as they walked along the narrow corridor together. 'So you two managed to get along today then?' There was an edge of conspiracy to her tone, and she gave Sofia a playful nudge.

Sofia had a lot more questions she wanted to ask, but she knew that that would only give Petra more of the wrong idea.

'It's not like that, Petra,' Sofia said a little too defensively, 'but if you must know, yes, it was quite nice actually. He's not so bad once you get past all the . . .' Sofia mimed running her hand through her hair, and turned to give Petra a big Jack-esque grin.

Petra giggled right on cue. 'Oh yeah sure, the Prince Charming act is a lot,' Petra conceded, 'but he's a sweet boy really, and he's saved your arse twice now.'

'Twice?'

'Well today and then the other day when he made those burgers for Milly and Brian.' It took Sofia a moment to register what Petra was saying.

'Wait, when, you mean after you . . .' Sofia was embarrassed remembering that evening '. . . put me to bed.'

Petra nodded. 'You didn't think it was me or Declan

113

who cooked for them, did you? I can barely fry an egg and I don't think Declan would even know how to crack one.'

Maybe the Prince Charming act was not just a performance. He seemed to be making a habit of saving the day.

'Oh, I didn't know that,' she said slowly.

Petra wagged her finger playfully. 'You should never judge a book by its chiselled cheekbones, Sofia.'

'Apparently not . . . anyway, this is me.' They were standing outside her room.

'Don't get too comfortable. You have one hour and then we need to eat before we go out.' Petra marched off down the corridor.

Sofia sat down on her bed. That morning felt like a million years ago. She peeled off her stewardess uniform and lay down, not meaning to fall asleep but only to rest her eyes for a moment or two.

# Chapter Sixteen

Sofia woke up with a start, lying on top of her covers in her bra and pants. She checked her watch – only twenty minutes to make dinner. This job was relentless. She pulled on her chef's whites and went to inspect her fridge. And there it was, the picnic hamper, sitting on the shelf, mocking her. Except, she thought, she could repurpose it for the crew's dinner.

She had made far too much for two people anyway.

As everyone wandered into the mess and sat around the table, Sofia realised just how hungry she was. It was a quintessential British picnic spread, pork pies, finger sandwiches, sausage rolls, quiche, fruit salad, chocolate strawberries, all freshly made that very morning.

'This looks amazing, as usual.' Stuart began loading up his plate. 'Are those Scotch eggs? What a treat.'

Sofia laughed as Petra picked one up and eyed it suspiciously.

'It's a boiled egg cased in sausage meat,' Stuart explained.

'You Brits are disgusting,' she said, opting for a slice of quiche instead.

'Agreed.' Jack took a seat. 'Thank goodness I didn't have to force one down in front of our guests at lunchtime.' He smirked at Sofia.

'Am I missing something?' Declan was loading his plate high.

'This is the lunch that Sofia did not pack for the picnic today,' Petra clarified.

'Oh damn, it was an eventful day huh?' Declan chuckled.

Sofia was embarrassed. It wasn't like her to drop the ball like that at work; she prided herself on being a professional. 'I hope Captain Mary wasn't too disappointed about it.' She looked over at Jack.

'What she doesn't know won't hurt her.' He grinned. Sofia felt a flood of relief, and then gratitude, which was almost as uncomfortable a feeling to sit with as the anxiety she'd been harbouring before.

'Oh, you didn't . . . ? Thanks, Jack.' She didn't know what else to say, but it sounded so half-hearted, she blushed with yet more embarrassment.

Jack seemed unfazed. 'What happens on the tender, stays on the tender, eh?'

'Nobody else is doing anything dodgy on the tender apart from you, Jack.' Petra gave him a playful smack around the back of the head. 'Enough work chat anyway. Where are we going tonight?'

A few suggestions were thrown around 'Fernandos', 'Ballare', 'Oceana Azzurra'. Sofia was preoccupied thinking about whether or not she was going to drink. She was regretting having already said she might. She hadn't, since she'd left Nakachwa. It was part of her fresh start.

116

Everything had gotten so complicated and so many lines had gotten blurred when there was alcohol involved. But she didn't want to miss out on the 'yachtie' experience and she wasn't naive; she knew that there was a big drinking culture, and the others had already started to comment on her abstinence; maybe one night of drinking would keep any probing questions at bay.

'Sofia?' It was Petra. 'Let the boys clear up; we need some girls' time to get ready.'

It wasn't easy to 'get ready' together in the tiny cabins, and the bathroom was even smaller. Sofia had barely bothered with makeup since she got on the boat, partly because the lighting was so bad in her room and partly because she would invariably sweat it all off in the kitchen. Petra seemed to have a system, mascara, eyeliner, brow brush all precariously balanced on various ledges and nooks around the tiny mirror.

Sofia was wondering what to do with her hair. Up until now she'd had it mostly tied up. She let it down and used her afro pick to loosen up the curls that had stagnated in a bun for the past seven days.

'Wow, your hair is beautiful, Sofia. You should wear it down more often.' Petra had the starry-eyed look of wonder that Sofia had often encountered on the face of white women. They seemed mesmerised by her hair's defiance of gravity.

'Doesn't go well with kitchen grease, unfortunately.' Sofia shrugged. 'And I don't think Captain Mary would be best pleased to find a strand of it in her dinner'.

For a tense moment Sofia feared Petra might ask to touch it, but instead she said, 'I have a headscarf that would be great on you.' That was pretty much the last thing Sofia had expected her to say. Petra riffled through her washbag and pulled out a red and white gingham silk scarf.

'You know what, I have a really cute red top that might go with this.' Sofia had planned to wear a black camisole, but she had packed an off-the-shoulder red crop top at the last minute 'just in case'. It had seen her through dozens of summer nights out in London, and it was always a good look.

Sofia pulled on a pair of black jeans and slipped into the top, self-consciously turning her back to Petra as she wriggled into the tight fabric.

'OK, I see, you've come to play!' Petra gave a chef's kiss. 'I fear you're going to stop poor young Declan's heart in that outfit.'

'Oh no,' Sofia groaned, heart sinking. 'It's that obvious?'

Petra laughed. 'Don't worry, it's just puppy love. He'll get over it.' She went back to applying mascara, her face close to the glass. 'He has to anyway. Captain Mary is not messing around with her "no crew relationships" rule, even if you were interested.'

'Her what?'

'Captain Mary doesn't hire couples, or like if you hook up with another crew member, one of you is getting the chop. She says it complicates "boating dynamics".'

Petra leant back and admired her handiwork. 'I think it's written somewhere in the crew pack, but honestly it's like right at the end. I didn't even get to it.'

'Well, that makes sense to me.' And it did, though she'd hardly registered it when she'd first read the pack. But with such small quarters, romantic politics would be a nightmare. 'Well famously Declan didn't even know who the guests were so I suspect he definitely hasn't got to that bit.'

'You're not interested then?' Petra flashed an inquisitive raised eyebrow in her direction through the mirror.

'Oh no, God no. He's sweet, but not my type, and he's so young.'

Petra nodded, and Sofia seized on the moment of girlish intimacy to do some probing of her own.

'And what's the deal with you and Stuart?'

Petra snorted. 'Stuart? Are you joking?'

Sofia wasn't giving up that easily. 'Oh come on, he's obviously super into you. I've never seen anyone blush that hard.'

'I think that's just the Scottish genes.'

'If you say so. I think he's really lovely.'

Brow pencil down, Petra had produced a curling wand from somewhere and was sectioning out a length of blonde hair. 'He is really lovely; sadly that's also not my type.'

The two of them giggled, and Sofia once again felt a warming glow of budding friendship.

'Are you seriously done?' Petra was looking Sofia up

and down. 'How do you look that good? You just changed and let your hair down. If only you had some glasses to take off, we'd have ourselves a classic rom-com makeover scene.' Petra stood up, half her hair curled, and tied the scarf around Sofia's head, turning her around to tie a tight knot at the nape of her neck.

'Just a little bit of this.' She flipped her back around, so they were facing each other, lipstick in hand. 'There you go.'

Sofia focused on the frown of concentration on Petra's face as she applied. It had been a long time since she'd gotten dressed up. It felt nice.

'Voila, makeover complete.' Sofia turned to look in the small mirror. The startle of red lipstick suited her, she thought. She hadn't seen herself like this for months. 'You like?'

'I look hot.' Sofia beamed at Petra. 'Thanks, fairy godmother.'

Sofia sat on the bunk as Petra finished her extensive routine. Once the hair was curled and the face made up there were outfit options to consider. The turquoise top? The green dress? The denim shorts or the black mini skirt? All had to be given equal consideration. Finally the lucky winner was a low-slung black satin skirt and cropped white blouse.

'I think it's kind of classy actually,' Petra said and Sofia nodded enthusiastically. At this stage Sofia would have said anything to get them both out of the cramped cabin.

'Absolutely,' Sofia agreed.

Petra seemed satisfied and the two of them made their way back to the mess. Music was already blaring, and inside the smell of men's aftershave was slightly overwhelming.

'You boys really went heavy on the spray tonight.' Petra grabbed a bottle of beer from the fridge and held one out for Sofia. In that split second her mind was made. With four pairs of eyes on her, she took the bottle.

'Glad to see you joining us tonight, Chef.' Stuart handed her a bottle opener. She smiled shyly, opened the beer and took a swig. She had to admit that she'd missed it. She knew it was associative, but even after that one sip she could feel a warm cloak of comforting haze envelop her.

'You girls look great.' This came from Jack, who seemed to be drinking something stronger, either that or it was a glass of soda water.

Petra blew him a kiss. 'The mothers of Capri better lock away their sons tonight.'

It was only 9 p.m. and the five of them drank like there was lost time to catch up on. Around 11 p.m. Petra decided it was time for them all to leave. It seemed that the head stewardess role extended beyond the working day. All of them dutifully filed off the boat, with Declan coming stressfully close to toppling into the water as they staggered along the marina towards the taxi rank.

Sofia realised she was drunk. Her months of sobriety had wrecked her tolerance and she had to concentrate on walking and talking at the same time.

'I really feel like I've been here before,' she said to nobody in particular.

Jack started laughing.

'Why are you always laughing at me?!' She could hear the petulance in her voice, but she couldn't work out what to do about it.

'This is where we dropped off Brian this afternoon.' Jack put his arm around her shoulder and she was grateful for the support.

She giggled. 'Oh yeaaah, I remember now. Man, what a day.' She nuzzled closer into Jack's shoulder and surreptitiously inhaled, vying for a hit of that intoxicating blend of musk and sea salt.

Petra hailed a taxi and next thing she knew Sofia was bundled in the back and then bundled out. 'Oceana Azzurra' flashed in pink neon above her head. Sofia was pretty sure she'd been to an 'Oceana' before, somewhere near Portsmouth.

Petra leant in and whispered in her ear. 'This is where all the Italian stallions hang out.'

Stamps, shots, Euro pop. Sofia had no idea how long she was swaying in the crowd but she suddenly felt like all she wanted was fresh air. She stumbled out into the cool night, smokers standing around chatting, and a little further down the decking, a couple making out on a daybed.

She felt grit between her toes, and looking down she was surprised to see sand. She really was very drunk. They were at a beach bar; she was on the beach. She found herself wandering towards the sea, the crowd thinning as she went. The moon was mesmerisingly bright, a porcelain plate on an inky tablecloth. Sofia sunk down into the sand, lying on her back and then falling further, letting the wave of drunkenness wash over her. She couldn't know how long she lay there. In the distance the music kept playing and the waves kept lapping.

# Chapter Seventeen

'I thought that was you.' Sofia opened her eyes. She figured she must have fallen asleep. All of a sudden she was deliciously aware of the breeze on her skin. A layer of the cloak had lifted. She looked up to see Jack standing over her.

'Petra has been looking everywhere for you.' Jack sat down in the sand next to her.

'Oh, I'm sorry, I just needed a minute.'

Sofia sat up. They didn't speak for a moment. Two pairs of knees staring out to sea.

'I thought you didn't drink,' he said eventually.

'At my old job, I drank a lot and it wasn't very good for me. I got myself into situations where I never really knew how much I was in control.' She was surprised by her own candidness.

'That makes sense to me.' Jack paused but something about being surrounded by night and sitting side by side compelled a confessional. 'My brother is an alcoholic.'

Sofia was alarmed, she hated the 'a' word. She stiffened beside him.

'I don't think that you're an alcoholic, Sofia,' he continued. 'I think that being able to recognise that in

yourself and stop probably means you definitely aren't.'
He took a deep breath.

'I just meant that it makes sense to me that my brother never knows if he's in control. It becomes so hard to differentiate the person from the drink, and it becomes so easy to blame all the behaviour on a "loss of control" but you're right, the issue is not that you never have control, it's that you can no longer tell when you do.' Jack shrugged his shoulders and Sofia felt an urge to put her arm around him, but she didn't.

'Says the drunken man having a drunken 3 a.m. chat with the drunken woman on the beach.' It was easier to make a joke.

'Oh yes I forgot, you Brits have no capacity for sincerity – and it's only two.' His words were snarky, but he was chuckling.

Suddenly Sofia remembered she had something to say. 'I wanted to thank you for saving the day, and not just with the picnic, Petra told me about the other night.'

Now it was Jack who didn't know what to say. 'How's that for sincerity?' Sofia nudged him playfully.

'You're always keeping me on my toes, Chef Harlow.' He looked away, eyes scanning the water. 'But you're welcome. I know we haven't got off on the best foot, but I do know how hard your first charter is, and you're definitely a natural, and a great cook of course, but everyone needs a helping hand when they start out.' He turned his head to look at her. She couldn't bring herself to meet his gaze, so she stared at her hands instead.

'Captain Mary taught me that, so you shouldn't worry too much. You don't need to be perfect – everyone makes mistakes – you just have to learn from them.'

She looked up at him, eyebrows raised. 'Got it. Thank you, Mr Yachting Guru.'

'This emotional whiplash is intense, Harlow.' He groaned, and she felt him leaning back on his hands.

Sofia shrugged. 'What can I say, it is the British way. We have to follow anything heartfelt with a joke or else we spontaneously combust.'

'OK so I'll do the heartfelt and you do the joke?'

Sofia laughed. 'Deal,' she said.

He stared out at the moon-soaked sea as he spoke. 'OK, here we go, the thing about yachting is that everyone is running away from something. Petra always says it's like the circus.' As he continued, Sofia wondered how many drunken chats Jack and Petra must have had in the past. 'I don't know what you're running away from, Harlow, but my only advice would be to do what you're doing now: remember to take rest stops and smell the proverbial roses. It's far too easy to miss them when you're busy sprinting.'

'That's deep, man.' She was trying to deflect. Jack shot her an amused look out the corner of his eye.

Sofia felt emboldened by the alcohol. 'So what are you running from?' she asked.

'Oh I don't know, a life where every day looks like the last? My father? The choking grip of Waspy-American ambition?' His words were sarcastic, but there was a tinge

126

of bitterness in his voice.

Sofia couldn't think of a joke; instead she laid a tentative hand on his shoulder. 'I know this is going to sound sarcastic coming from me, but I actually think that the crush of ambition is one of the hardest things to climb out from under.'

He turned his head and this time she let herself take a dip in the green. 'Like I said, you just gotta learn to live a little.' His eyes finally sparkled again and Sofia couldn't help but giggle.

'Oh, so you're taking a turn at being the joker huh?'

'I think it suits me actually.' He pulled her into a rough embrace and Sofia felt her heart jump, but when he ruffled her hair, it resolutely fell back down with a thud. 'We should be getting back.' Jack was clearing the sand from his lap. 'Petra will be worried . . . She'll think I'm having my wicked way with you.' He stood up and held out his hand for her to take. She rolled her eyes and got up without his help.

'I got this, thanks, Prince Charming.' He chuckled and they wandered back across the beach towards the bar.

'There you two are!' Petra ran towards Sofia with her arms open and pulled her into a drunken hug. 'I just pashed Stuart,' she stage-whispered into Sofia's ear, before bursting into a fit of giggles. Sofia wasn't familiar with Australian slang, but she could deduce what Petra was confessing to.

'I knew it!' she whispered back as Petra dragged her back to the dance floor. Jack disappeared into the crowd.

It was about 4 a.m. when Sofia decided she needed to go to bed, and, after much convincing, Petra, Stuart and Declan were persuaded to head back to the boat. Nobody knew where Jack had gone.

'He's a big boy, he'll be fine,' Petra said as the four of them squeezed into the taxi. 'He's probably just found a local delicacy to savour.' The edge of mischief in her voice had the boys laughing. Sofia joined in but she couldn't quite ignore the strange feeling in the pit of her stomach. With a jolt she realised it was envy.

Back on the boat, Petra was determined to carry on the party, but Sofia could no longer ignore the pull of her bunk. Lulled by the drunken shrieking still coming from the mess down the hall, she fell into a deep and dizzying sleep.

# *Chapter Eighteen*

Sofia had been thrilled to get the job at Nakachwa. On her first day she turned up thirty minutes early because she had convinced herself that the buses would get stuck in traffic. Of course they didn't and she had stood outside in the cold January morning for fifteen minutes that felt much longer until Joy arrived. Even in a dream state she could still feel the electricity, the buzz of anticipation as she waited. Joy was everything she wanted to be one day: a restaurant owner, a great chef, a mother, a visionary.

Joy and Peter had opened Nakachwa before anyone in the culinary world had really considered that 'African' food was anything worth thinking about, years before the craze for Ethiopian food swept across gentrifying swathes of London. The restaurant had been open for fifteen years and had had a Michelin star for five of those by the time Sofia stepped through the door. They were a couple, and their baby also had the name Nakachwa. Joy was in charge of the kitchen and Peter was in charge of everything else, including service.

'You're here early,' said Joy, with an endearing inflection of a worn-down Ugandan accent. 'I like early – too many of these youngsters who think that blackness absolves them from timekeeping. Not in my house.' She stood back and motioned for Sofia to pass.

The L-shaped dining room was set up for around one hundred covers. All the tables were circular, highly polished, ethically sourced teak. From where she was standing in the doorway, it looked like a forest of trees, each felled to dining height. The walls were painted in various shades of warm earth tones: terracotta, ochre and mahogany. The length of the back wall, where the kitchen could be spied over the top of the serving counter, was a dreamy mauve, like the colour of the horizon as the sun dips out of view. Overhead large wicker lamp shades pooled each table with light. The pictures she'd seen online, and glimpses she'd spied behind Joy's head during her rushed and furtive Zoom interview, hadn't done it justice.

'It's beautiful,' said Sofia. She wasn't being hyperbolic; she thought it might be the most enchanting space she had ever seen.

'Thank you,' said Joy. 'It reminds me of home. That's all I have ever tried to do really – bring a slice of home to this grey city.' She chuckled. 'Peter never believes me when I say I'm a proud Ugandan, but this is my homage.' They stood in silence for a moment, and then Joy collected herself from her daydream. 'Anyway, I'm sure what you really want to see is the kitchen.'

'Yes please.' She could hardly contain her excitement.

Joy led the way. The kitchen was just as breath-taking. For Sofia – who had been a lowly commis on the bottom rung, and cornered into the windowless depths of one of Lochland's kitchens – it was a revelation. It was 8 a.m., an hour before the first prep shift started, and the sun was just rising. Along half of the back wall of the kitchen, which was gilded with large windows, the first rays of light flooded in.

That first day passed in a daze. At 9 a.m. the other cooks started arriving. She spent most of the day mesmerised watching Joy work. She was calm but authoritative, and came over to Sofia's station on a couple of occasions to compliment her work, as she did with the others in the kitchen. It was a revolutionary approach. No shouting, no swearing, no threats.

Over the next couple of months Sofia settled into her new life. A few friends from back home in Portsmouth had been in London for a while and soon enough she had infiltrated a couple of groups. She knew just the right number of people to keep things interesting without feeling like she had to frequently bail on plans because of her unsociable hours.

At work too, she found herself a little group that had begun to solidify into friendship. Tony, Erica and Simon – the four of them would go for an ill-advised round or two or three after work in a nearby pub. There was a lot of drinking. Sofia often found herself commuting through a fog of dehydration, the proximity of other bodies bumping against her on a tube carriage prompting hair-raising waves of nausea.

Tony was a chef de partie like Sofia. Her full name

was Antonia, although she hated it for 'outing her as the Sloane Ranger' she tried so hard to conceal with her cropped blue-black mullet and pierced eyebrow. Erica and Simon were front of house. Among the rest of the restaurant staff there was a divide between the two 'camps' but their little gang enjoyed bridging that gap. Erica was a little shy, but breathtakingly efficient, and a stickler for details. She had a lilting French accent that endeared her to customers – that and her infectious smile.

Simon was Peter's second in command, and not immediately likeable. Sofia's first impressions of him had been that he was quite reductive: a posh, white, public-school boy who'd never had a knack for academia but had enough connections to land a job in a Michelin-starred restaurant straight out of school. He was the kind of man who was always simultaneously gagging to let you know that he knows better, and absolutely mortified that he can't help himself from telling you that. Something about private schools in this country bred that kind of bizarre combination of arrogance and self-loathing. She found that as time wore on, she began to find it strangely endearing, the rawness with which he understood the contradiction.

On this particular evening they were at Erica's, crammed around a small table in the kitchen of her shared flat. Erica was the worst cook, but, predictably, the best hostess. Your glass was never empty at Erica's house. It was a wonder she could even afford her rent alongside her drink-induced generosity. 'I'll go get another few bottles,' she said. They had finished the lasagne, which Sofia reckoned was shop-bought and transferred to a baking tray just before their arrival. The four bottles of red wine on the table were already empty.

'I'll come with,' offered Tony. The pair of them swayed around the room in search of a tote bag and then stumbled out the front door.

'So how would you rate your time at Naka so far?' Simon had a habit of trying to catch her gaze when he started a sentence and then breaking eye contact about halfway through. It was all part of his self-deprecation schtick and Sofia had gotten used to it, although it took some time to shake off first the irritation and then the pity it had inspired in her. Recently she had begun to find it sort of charming.

By now she was firmly in the category of drunk, the tipsy giggles making way for earnestness. 'I honestly love it, and it's not just that the kitchen is amazing, it's the team. We all just work so well together. It's a unit, and everyone is, like, friends.' This wasn't quite true, but having come from a kitchen where everyone seemed to be trying to get ahead by any means possible, it felt something akin to homely.

Simon nodded thoughtfully. 'Yeah, it's a good vibe,' he said, 'but you've got to watch out for number one. Do you think you're going to go for the sous position?'

The sous chef, Mark, was leaving at the end of the month to set up his own pop-up in one of those shipping containers turned overpriced watering holes in East

London. That meant the position was up for grabs.

'I've only been here six months, Simon, and I've only been a chef de partie for a year total. I've got to pay my dues.'

'But you're the best.' This time he didn't look away, and Sofia blushed at the sincerity of it. She'd never really thought about the fact that he was sort of good-looking. Not her usual type, but then again she wasn't really sure she even had a usual type.

Her dating history was limited to a two-week boyfriend in secondary school, a couple of flings at culinary college, and one more serious year-and-a-half stint with a perfectly nice, but perfectly boring guy named Ethan in Oxford. A sweet boy, but after he had revealed that he thought the Black Panthers were an American football team, she'd known that they were just treading water until she left the city. She had to admit, rather shamefully, that she hadn't thought about him at all since she'd arrived in London.

Simon was darkly funny, a cynic and a pessimist, but she often found his company refreshing. He was honest, she thought, about himself and about other things too, so she knew he wouldn't be giving her a compliment like that for the sake of it.

'Well I mean, has Peter mentioned anything to you?' Sofia asked.

He smiled slyly. 'Oh so you want some insider knowledge?'

Sofia was embarrassed but also enjoying the playful tension that was blooming between them. 'No, no forget

134

I asked. That's not fair on you and I don't want to go behind Joy's back.'

He laughed. 'You're such a goody two-shoes. Between you and me, he said that Joy has her eye on you, and that's a direct quote.'

Just then Tony and Erica giggled their way back into the room, and Sofia, realising that she had leant forward over the table towards Simon, quickly sat back in her chair. She didn't know why she felt like they were doing something illicit, but when Simon smiled at her, she felt a thrill of conspiracy.

For the next couple of weeks, Sofia and Simon found moments throughout the day to laugh at each other's jokes, moan about their hangovers, and evaluate how the restaurant was running that day. Among the four of them Sofia began to feel self-conscious about how often she said things that were only meant for him to hear. Not flirty things particularly, but pick-ups from their other conversations or variations on an in-joke they shared.

She also started to notice Erica, and the way that she interacted with Simon. When she caught sight of them over the top of the chef's counter, giggling together, she was troubled by the wave of envy that surged through her. She didn't like to admit it to herself but she had thought she was one of the only people who could really make Simon laugh. Watching them made her feel angry because it exposed that delusion.

It was an unremarkable Tuesday lunchtime shift, until Joy came in. She didn't usually work Tuesdays, and there was always a sense of substitute teacher mischief on those days. Sofia felt the mood shift before she noticed Joy striding across the dining room, her fine dreadlocks architecturally spiralled atop her head. Out of her chef's whites she looked regal. A thick cuff encircled her upper arm, her ears dripped with gold, and she was wearing a long loose tunic the colour of blood. The guests couldn't help staring as she walked past – the queen of her kingdom, Joy owned the space she was taking up. She leant over the chef's counter.

'Sorry to barge in like this. Hello, everyone.' Her brown eyes twinkled.

'Hello, Chef,' came the response in chorus.

'Sofia, could I talk to you in the back office please?' Sofia felt a dozen pairs of eyes fix on the back of her head.

'Yes, Chef.'

The back office was claustrophobic – having utilised the windows for the kitchen and dining space, there weren't enough to go around, so the room was dimly lit, and with only enough space for a desk and a chair facing it.

'Take a seat, Sofia.' It felt oddly formal, except Joy had to perch on the corner of the table, and Sofia had to scoot the chair up against the wall for them to maintain eye contact.

'I guess you might have an idea of what I want to talk to you about?'

Sofia didn't know what the right answer was. 'I think I might,' seemed appropriately non-committal.

Joy held her gaze, seemed to start saying something and then thought better of it. 'I want to offer you the sous chef job,' she said matter-of-factly.

And there it was, the thing that she had not let herself believe that she wanted, in her more sober moments, but had hung over her ever since Mark announced he was leaving. The first person she wanted to tell was Simon.

Sofia realised that she had not said anything and that Joy was looking at her expectedly.

'Um, Joy, I don't know what to say. I'm honoured. Are you sure?' She was welling up. She willed herself not to cry.

'I've thought about it a lot, and obviously it's important to take experience and well, politics, into consideration, but I for one cannot sit back and ignore raw talent. And that is what you have, Sofia. It would be a waste not to make use of it in my kitchen.'

'I really don't know what to say.' She lost the fight and swiped aggressively at her wet cheek.

'Say yes.' Joy held out her hand. Sofia shook it.

'Yes.'

No one asked her what the meeting with Joy was about. She'd just gone quietly back to her station. Tony had raised an eyebrow as she walked past. *'Pub later,'* Sofia mouthed back. That night the four of them met outside the Black Bull and Sofia could hardly contain her excitement.

'I got the job!' she blurted as soon as they were all standing within earshot.

'Oh my God, amazing.' Erica was all hugs and pats on the back.

'Knew you would.' When Simon hugged her she thought she could feel him linger just a beat too long.

Tony was quiet. Once Sofia turned to face her, she felt her ecstasy draining.

'You good, Tony?' Simon probed tentatively.

'Sure, just finding it a little hard to understand why you've been promoted to sous after six months and I have been in that kitchen for two years, and others have been there even longer.'

There was a heavy silence. Sofia felt numb. She had been naive to think that this wouldn't happen. Joy had essentially warned her, when she talked about the 'politics' of her decision.

Tony looked at the floor, unsure of what to say or do next. 'I think I'm going to head home, guys.'

The three of them watched her leave. Erica was the first to break the silence. 'So what's everyone drinking?'

For Sofia it was red wine. Soon her teeth were stained and her discomfort and guilt had dissipated. She wouldn't be able to remember much the next day. She remembered that she soon lost count of whose round it was. She remembered that they had been laughing so loudly that people kept looking over disapprovingly. She remembered that after closing they had tried to find somewhere else to drink. But in the hungover grogginess of the next morning, when she woke up in bed naked next to Simon, that was all she remembered.

After an awkward 'good morning' and a feeble excuse from Sofia about needing to 'get to a gym class' she was out of his flat and on her way home. She felt a little embarrassed on her 'walk of shame' but also triumphant. She had not misread the signals, and even though the exact progression of their evening still eluded her there was something about an unexpected falling into bed that felt exciting and cosmopolitan. She had never done anything like it before and she couldn't help grinning to herself for the rest of the day, basking in the glow of a conquered crush.

Over the next few days, flashes of that night would come back to her. Some of them clarifying, others mortifying. Snogging outside the pub, pawing at each other in the back of a taxi, discarding pieces of her clothing in his hallway, but the 'main event', she still had no recollection of.

Back at work, Tony was no longer talking to her. When Joy announced that Sofia would be taking the sous chef role at Friday dinner service, the reception was muted, met with a perfunctory round of applause. Sofia plastered on a smile and tried to ignore the reluctant tone of everyone's 'congratulations'. Tony had been right. There was bitterness towards her in the kitchen; Joy had misjudged how strong the reaction would be.

Simon and Erica at least were genuinely happy for her, and she retreated out of the kitchen and into the dining room whenever she got the opportunity.

'They'll get over it,' Erica reassured her. 'Just give it some time, and I'll try and talk to Tony.'

'It's hard for people, you know, to see someone else just be more talented than them.' Sofia playfully smacked Simon's arm and felt a thrill when he grinned at her.

'Keep your voice down,' she scolded, although she was giggling. 'The last thing I need is for any of the cooks hearing you say something like that.' Her hand was still on his arm and when he looked down at it and smirked, Sofia quickly pulled it away and blushed. They still hadn't talked about that night, but nothing had really changed at work. Sofia sought out his company as a welcome balm to the hostility in the kitchen, and knowing that he wanted her was the perfect antidote.

'Are you guys going to Mark's leaving party on Sunday?' It was Erica, who seemed oblivious to what felt to Sofia like palpable sexual tension between them.

'Yeah I think so,' said Simon nonchalantly, and then whilst holding Sofia's gaze intently, 'unless any other, more interesting plans come up.'

She blushed, looking away.

'I think I'll go.' She knew it would be badly received for her not to, now that she had to consider the politics of everything.


Sofia decided that she wanted to make an effort that night. She didn't want to admit to herself that it had anything to do with seeing Simon, but it crossed her mind a few times, as she discarded outfit after outfit onto her bedroom floor. She settled on a deep red halter-neck top but skipped the matching lipstick with half a mind that she might be kissing a certain someone. Black jeans, boots, hair piled on top of her head with curls cascading down over her forehead, and in ringlets down her neck, she was ready to go. She looked good, sexy even, and despite the anxiety of navigating the tension with her colleagues, she was excited.

On the bus, she texted Simon to tell him she was on her way, and then she texted Erica. Neither of them had replied by the time she was standing at the top of the three-storey walk-up in Camden. She could hear music thumping on the other side of the door, and the chatter of a drunken crowd. She took a deep breath, resigning herself to the solo entrance she had been hoping to avoid.

A few drinks in and Sofia was dancing with the other guests and actually enjoying herself. She had spotted Tony, but the way she quickly looked away suggested to Sofia that they were not ready for a reconciliation just yet.

'I need to cool down,' Sofia shouted at Mark over the music.

'If you go out through the door at the end of the hallway, you can get up to the roof. It's where the smokers congregate.' She gave him a thumbs up and stumbled out into the hallway.

The roof was bigger than Sofia expected. People were clumped in small groups sharing cigarettes and passing around rolling papers. Sofia checked her phone. *We're on our tray*. Erica had sent that about an hour ago. Sofia deduced that 'tray' was a drunken attempt at 'way' but was still confused by the 'we'; perhaps Erica was bringing her housemate. Sofia took a few deep breaths, leaning into the euphoria of a cool breeze brushing against her dance-tired, drunk body. She decided to circle the perimeter of the roof before heading back downstairs and it was as she walked past the first chimney stack that she saw them.

In the moonlight, it was a romantic scene, Erica's head of blonde curls tilted back with her hands entangled in Simon's shaggy dark mop. They were so engrossed in their embrace that she felt confident standing in the shadows, unnoticed, if morbidly voyeuristic. A freeze of shock, and then a bolt of anger, Sofia let the emotions course through her before settling into a state of embarrassment and shame. Had she really thought that she was special? That Simon was in love with her or something? Clearly, she thought, she had been a drunken mistake for him, and she had completely misread the signals. What she had interpreted as flirty was just him being friendly, perhaps not wanting to shut her down, to spare both their embarrassment.

Quietly she took herself away, down the stairs, into the party to say goodbye to Mark and then out into the city. That night, wandering the streets alone, was the first time Sofia began dreading going to work.

The restaurant was closed on Mondays, so Sofia had a whole day to sit with her anxiety, which by that evening had reached a fever pitch. The next day she called in sick, and the day after that. She whiled away the hours, bingeing bad TV and ordering expensive takeaways. On the Thursday she received a text that made her heart stop. It was from Simon. **Are you OK? Hope you haven't got that nasty bug going around.** She contemplated throwing her phone out the window. The sight of his name made her actually feel sick.

In the evening she got a call from Joy.

'I really need you. I know you can't help being sick but it's your first week as sous and I think it would be good to have you in, even for a half-day, to get you up to speed.' Sofia felt a stab of guilt. 'It's been a tough week, what with Erica off as well. We're a bit short-staffed.' Joy sounded stressed.

'I'll be in tomorrow,' said Sofia, trying to push down the panic rising in her throat at the thought of facing Simon.

'See you then,' was all Joy said before hanging up. This is what people meant about not shitting where you eat, thought Sofia. It made even more sense not to shit where you cook. She needed to try and be a grown-up about this. She drafted a text to Simon. *Back to work tomorrow. Could we meet before the dinner shift for a chat?* She hit send, her heart pounding. Now she had to work out what to say to him. She decided she would not be 'overly emotional'. She would simply lay down the facts and voice her disappointment and suggest they try and 'remain professional' from now on. Her reaction to

143

the whole affair had made it pretty clear to her that she wasn't the sharing type, at least when it came to romance.

The conversation did not go well. Simon already seemed agitated before they began speaking. He offered Sofia a brisk hug, which she reluctantly accepted.

'How have you been?' he asked, reverting to his old habit of avoiding eye contact, and instead staring straight ahead as they stood side by side outside the restaurant.

'I'm fine,' she replied, sensing his discomfort and taking courage in it. 'I wanted to talk about the other night, last week.' He stared blankly, as if Sofia hadn't said anything at all. 'I just wanted to clear the air, or you know, just clarify a few things.' She felt irritated that he was acting as if she was boring him. He stayed silent.

'I saw you and Erica at the party the other night and I wanted to let you know how I felt about it.' That caught his attention. He snapped his head round to look her in the eyes, and she felt a chill when she saw the mixture of panic and menace in his stare.

'What did you hear?' he asked in a strained tone, trying to feign indifference and failing miserably. He wasn't really listening to her.

'What do you mean? I didn't hear anything. I just said I saw you guys getting together and well, I think it hurt my feelings. I don't know, I guess I thought maybe . . .' She was tripping over her words and she couldn't think straight. She was picking at her thumbnail as she spoke. 'I thought that maybe you and me were, getting to know each other or whatever.'

He let out mocking laugh. Her stomach dropped. She dared to meet his eyes. They were cold and vacant.

'Listen, Sofia, I think you're a lovely girl, but that night was just a bit of fun. I thought we'd both agreed to that.' Sofia burned with shame. She couldn't remember if she had; she couldn't remember most of that night. 'I don't really have time for this shit right now. I'm sorry you were hurt by the Erica thing but to be honest I am actually allowed to sleep with whoever I want.'

There was a silence, as Sofia contemplated how naive she had been.

'Let's try and be cool at work though, yeah? And it may be best if we keep the whole situation to ourselves.'

Sofia nodded meekly, looking down at her feet. She felt a perfunctory pat on her shoulder and then watched his boots stride back into the restaurant.

The next week was a slog. She had a lot to learn as Joy's sous, which at least kept her from having time to mull over her situation during working hours. She stayed late and arrived early, determined to surpass Joy's expectations. When she had to put her dishes on the counter for Simon to serve, she would look down or stare blankly ahead as she flatly said, 'Service,' and dinged the bell.

She stopped seeing her other friends, and stayed in bed until the sun went down on her days off. On her commutes home she stared out the window and tallied up how many people hated her. Simon, Tony, pretty much all the cooks. Erica had been off work since the party, which was over a month ago, and Sofia hadn't heard from her. If she was being honest with herself, she had also avoided getting in touch. Sofia was concerned about the unwelcome sense of envy and anger she was feeling towards Erica, and how it might manifest.

Her dream life had come crashing down, mutating into a monstrous distortion of what it had been just a few weeks before.

It was her Monday off when she got a call from Erica. Sofia was so surprised she took a moment to stare at the call ID before she answered tentatively, 'Hello?'

'Hey, Sofia.' She let out a deep sigh. 'It's good to hear your voice.'

Sofia was awash with relief. 'You have no idea how much it means to me for you to say that.' Her eyes stung hot with tears of gratitude. 'I've not been in a great place recently.'

'That makes two of us.' Erica let out a dry chuckle. 'Are you around today? I'd really like to talk to you in person.'

Sofia looked down at herself. It was four in the afternoon and she was still in her pyjamas. 'Sure, I can be ready in an hour. Shall we meet at the Hope and Anchor?' she suggested.

'Um, I'm trying not to drink at the moment. Maybe Bert's café next door?' Sofia was sure she'd get the full story soon enough. 'See you soon.'

Both women looked tired and resolutely pale as they took a small table by the window. Erica clutched a mug in her hands, and stared at the cooling coffee as she spoke. 'I've quit Nakachwa,' she burst out suddenly, like a confession. Sofia didn't say anything, sensing that Erica needed space for what she wanted to say. She took a deep breath. 'It's about Simon.'

Erica's story was the same as Sofia's save for a few key details. Both had been very drunk, neither could remember a lot of what happened. But when Erica woke up in Simon's bed, she was not embarrassed but somewhat triumphant; she was scared and confused.

'I'm not really into him like that. I thought we were friends, and it terrifies me that I don't know how I got there.' Sofia slowly began to grasp what Erica was saying.

'I saw you at Mark's party,' she said quietly, feeling embarrassed that her first instinct was to think of Erica as competition for Simon's affections.

'I don't remember being there,' Erica admitted. Sofia's heart sank.

Suddenly the scene no longer seemed romantic at all, recast in this disturbing light. Sofia imagined his arms wrapped around her waist were holding her up, rather than holding her close.

Sofia reached her hand across the table and took Erica's hand in hers. They didn't need to say the words 'assault' or 'consent' to understand each other.

'Have you spoken to him since?' Sofia asked.

'I rang him a few days after. It didn't go well, really. I told him how I felt and he just dismissed me, said I had been drinking too much and it wasn't his fault I couldn't remember anything.' She wiped away a hot tear running down her cheek. 'Anyway I've told Peter and Joy I'm not coming back. I can't.'

Outside Sofia gave Erica a big hug. She hadn't told her about her own night with Simon. This was not the time. After hearing Erica's story, she didn't really know how to feel about it anyway. Unlike Erica she knew that she *had* 'wanted it', but now she couldn't for the life of her remember why.

Sofia went back to work the next day. Every time she caught sight of Simon over the counter she felt some combination of confusion, shame and anger. So she began to simply never look at him. He seemed to understand this unspoken agreement instinctively. He made no effort to speak to her. They orbited around each other seamlessly.

With Erica gone and Tony resolutely ignoring her, her world began to quieten further, until she minimised talking to anyone at work to direct orders in the kitchen. When her shift was over she was the first out of the door. She politely declined any increasingly rare offers to go to drinks or parties.

For six months she lived like this, or rather existed like it, not knowing how to feel and eventually forgetting to feel at all.

It was a friend from home who snapped her out of it. She was back in Portsmouth for Christmas and managed to drag herself to the pub on Christmas Eve. She hadn't seen this friend, Isla, since school.

'So yeah, basically it's split over two seasons, May to

October and then November to April. You get a bit of time off if you don't do back-to-back charters but it's pretty full on.'

Sofia was only half listening, as she had grown accustomed to doing.

'Sofia, you should totally look into it. I've just done a season with Captain Mary and she's been looking for a decent chef for ages.'

'Oh yeah, I mean I'm working in London at the moment.' She gave an unconvincing smile.

Isla gave her a mildly patronising rub on the shoulder. She hesitated before speaking. 'Are you, like, happy there though? You look a bit . . . grey. And you've always loved the sea. I'll send you the link to the Facebook page anyway.'

Sofia nodded weakly, deciding not to engage with the look of pity staring back at her. 'Sure – thanks, Isla.'

It took Sofia another three months to accept that she was depressed, that her dream had turned into a monotonous nightmare. She found the link, clicked through to 'Yachties of the Med' and almost immediately spotted a post from Captain Mary.

# Chapter Nineteen

The day after the crew's night out in Capri, Sofia woke up with a headache that made the back of her eyes sting. She checked the time: 8 a.m. She must have had about three hours of sleep but it was time to make breakfast. As she sat up, the room began to spin and she thought for a horrifying moment that she might vomit, but the nausea passed. She chugged a large glass of water, took a quick shower and scraped her hair back into a bun, chastising herself lightly for so indulgently letting her hair down.

Breakfast would have to be eggs. The wooliness of Sofia's brain was not conducive to cooking up anything more imaginative. Once she was done poaching and toasting, she radioed for backup. When Petra walked into the kitchen, Sofia had to stifle a laugh. It was alarming to see Petra, usually so put together, with her hair in a matted mess and her mascara smeared under her eyes.

'Please don't say anything,' she said irritably, as if reading Sofia's mind. 'My sense of self is too fragile this morning.' Sofia dragged her thumb and forefinger across her sealed lips and picked up two plates. Petra followed suit.

Sofia was surprised to see the captain at the mess table. She rarely joined them for breakfast.

In response to Sofia's quizzical expression Captain Mary said, 'Oh don't mind me, I'm just here out of morbid curiosity. I like to see how everyone is faring after their trip to solid land.' The normally inscrutable captain was trying to hide a mischievous smile.

'I didn't make enough eggs, I'm sorry.'

'I'll have Jack's portion. I suspect he's not on board this morning?' This last question was directed at Petra.

'You have deduced correctly, Captain. Our Jacky boy must have found himself a bed for the night.'

Sofia was taken aback at the ease with which they were discussing Jack's sex life – his boss and a colleague. Sofia would be mortified. She was also, she had to admit, contending with that kernel of jealousy that had nestled in her stomach the night before. She didn't really want to think about what it meant, so she decided she would ignore it, and chalk it up to some bizarre manifestation of her hangxiety. She knew better than most that no good could come of her harbouring any romantic feelings towards Jack.

For now she sat back and listened to Declan regale the captain with the sordid details of the night before. Sofia noticed that he did not mention Petra and Stuart's kiss. Had he not been a witness or had Petra got to him in time to emphasise the need for discretion? Sofia also noted that Stuart had not said a word and was resolutely avoiding eye contact with anyone, especially Petra. It was yet further confirmation that a workplace fling was a doomed endeavour.

'At one point Petra bought flaming shots and then this um . . .' Declan was blushing, although you couldn't tell '. . . a very nice lady asked me if I wanted to take it out of her belly button.' The captain seemed to find this story hilarious and Declan looked relieved. He had faltered halfway through the anecdote, perhaps coming to the realisation that it was not entirely work-appropriate.

'To be young again—' the captain sighed '—if I took a body shot off a "very nice lady" I certainly would not be able to come to work the next day.' She winked at Declan, and he laughed nervously. Captain Mary had finished her breakfast and she laid her cutlery down emphatically.

'Not to interrupt this lovely chat with logistics but I'd like to go through the next couple of days with everyone. Well, almost everyone – Officer Carter will have to be brought up to speed at a later date.' That was met by a muffled chuckle from around the table.

'As I'm sure you all know by now, our guests went to the hospital yesterday, but you will all be pleased to know they were quickly discharged and spent the night in the villa on the island as planned.'

'He didn't need his foot amputated then?' Petra said dryly.

'Now, now, Petra, you must remember that some of our guests have very . . . delicate sensibilities.'

'Ever the diplomat, Captain.' It was clear Petra was not in a patient mood, and Sofia nudged her foot under the table. *Be quiet,* she thought, willing Petra to tune in to her telepathy.

'So in that sense the plan has not really changed. We'll be onboarding more supplies today and, drumroll please . . .' everyone seemed too dazed to take the command on board and there was silence until Declan obliged, tapping on the table rhythmically.

'Thank you, Declan, I am glad to see one of you is awake today. We will be welcoming a new crew member, a replacement for poor Tabitha. He is called Patricio and he'll be answering to Petra as our new steward.'

'Huh, so it'll be a mixed bunk?' Petra did not seem thrilled at the prospect.

'Actually, I was thinking maybe you and Stuart could swap, so Petra would bunk with me and Stuart and Patricio can share a bunk. Obviously that's only if that is OK with you, Stuart?' The captain phrased it as a question, but it was clear the plan had already been well thought out.

There was the crimson flare-up again. 'Of course, if that's more comfortable for you, Petra?' He glanced over at her quickly as he said her name and Sofia saw that Petra seemed determined not to meet his eyes.

'That works for me, thank you, Stuart.' She said this flatly, looking at the captain the whole time.

'Right then, that's settled. He's joining us this evening so let's do the swap during the day, preferably before our guests are back, which should be around four o'clock. We'll be lifting the anchor tonight and our next stop is in three days at the Isola d'Ischia, but remember we can't get any more supplies until we dock at Gaeta

153

in two whole weeks, so we really have to be organised today.'

It was not what Sofia wanted to hear today. She could barely concentrate on getting her fork from her plate to her mouth without missing, let alone plan for the next two weeks of meals with ever-diminishing fresh produce. Looking around the table at the glum faces, she wondered who had decided that it was a good idea for yachties to drink to excess. Wasn't there some famous rule about impaired motor function and heavy machinery not being a great mix?

'Right, thanks, everyone. Let's get to work.' Captain Mary clapped her hands together and Petra flinched. 'Might I recommend some strong coffee,' she added, as she strolled out the room.

Petra sunk her head into her hands '*Why?*' she moaned. 'Why do I never learn?'

Declan gave her a reassuring rub on the back. 'At least you'll have another pair of hands soon to help out,' he said optimistically.

Petra shot him a look. 'Oh yeah great, another green-gilled teenager to train up.' Declan looked dejected, and Petra bit her lip. 'Sorry, Dec, I'm in a foul mood. It's nothing personal.'

'I guess I better get to planning this menu. Hopefully Jack will have appeared by the time I need to get my supplies.' She hadn't meant it to sound as accusatory as it did.

'Don't worry, Sofia. I can help.'

Sofia eyed Declan suspiciously. 'How are you so perky this morning?'

Declan broke into a cheeky grin. 'Well if you must know, I was only drinking lemonade yesterday. After you had to step in for me on the boat trip, I thought I better get my act together. You inspired me actually.'

'Huh, I'm not feeling much like an inspiration today.' Sofia's temples had begun to throb ominously. 'But good for you, kid.'

Declan frowned for a moment and then recovered himself. 'Just let me know when you need me.' He bounded to his feet and left the room, leaving Sofia, Petra and Stuart. The atmosphere immediately became tinged with something loaded. Sofia didn't have the stomach for whatever it was – awkwardness or sexual tension. She made her excuses and a swift exit.

'I'll leave you two to clear if that's OK?' Petra shot her a dirty look but she was already out the door.

# Chapter Twenty

On her way back to the cabin, she bumped into Jack. He was rushing down the hall, staring at his phone, and he came towards her so quickly that despite trying to stand to the side, his shoulder crashed into her.

'Watch it.' She felt irritated by him not noticing her.

'Sorry, Harlow, I'm in a bit of a rush.' He tried to push past her but she blocked his way. She felt like picking a fight.

'Where have you been then?' She didn't try to hide the accusatory tone from her voice this time. There was something about the arrogance of his being late and everyone simply laughing it off that rubbed her up the wrong way.

'Christ, Harlow, is this an interrogation? If you must know, I bumped into an old family friend last night – Luchiano. He used to work for my grandmother when we were younger.' He stopped abruptly. 'Not that it's really any of your business.'

Sofia kicked herself. Why had she made assumptions? And why had she taken it so personally that Jack might have spent the night with someone anyway? Her anger turned inwards and darkened into shame.

She dropped her head. Any amicable advances they may have made yesterday, she had dashed in a moment. 'Oh, I'm sorry I didn't realise. It's just that Petra and the captain were making all these jokes and . . .'

'And you thought you could come out here and accuse me of something, something that I am well within my rights to do anyway, might I add.' It was his turn to be angry. 'I don't really know what I have to do, Sofia, to convince you that I am not some horrible monster of a man, and to be honest I'm a little bored of trying.'

'I'm really sorry, Jack, I don't think you're a monster. I think I'm just in a horrible mood today.' Sofia felt awful. She had not included 'grovelling apology' in the list of tedious chores she had to do that day, and it was draining an already low reserve of self-worth. This, she noted, was just one of the reasons she had stopped drinking in the first place.

Jack sighed heavily. 'It's OK, Sofia, I'm just . . . It's been an intense couple of days. Capri it's . . . There's some family stuff that always comes up whenever I'm here and . . .' He trailed off and ran his hand through his hair exasperatedly. 'Apology accepted. I don't really have time for this right now, Sofia, but it's fine, we're cool.' He was not very convincing, but Sofia was more than happy to let the conversation end there.

'OK, sorry again. I'll radio you when I need help with the supplies later?'

'Sure,' he said coolly and then he looked down at his watch. 'Until then.' He strode off.

It was a stark realisation to consider that men like Jack had 'baggage' of their own, inner lives and family drama that sat somewhere below the charm. Sofia wasn't sure she was enjoying the revelation. It was far easier to think of Jack as purely two-dimensional. She stood alone in the corridor, fretting anxiously about her tendency to mess up her work relationships. She resolved to be friendly from here on out. He might be infuriating at times, but he had also really looked out for her and saved her from some tight scrapes. His personal life was none of her business, and now that she thought about it she wasn't sure how she'd convinced herself otherwise.

'Sofia, Sofia.' Declan's voice cracked through the radio. 'We're going to get supplies now, so if there are any last-minute changes to the menu speak now or forever hold your peace.' Damn, she didn't have time for contemplation. She had a whole new ingredients list to write up; mussels needed to be swapped out for chicken fillets, lobsters for steaks.

'Give me ten minutes, Dec. I'll bring the new list up to you.' She marched towards the kitchen.

'Copy that.'

Something about the need to distract herself from her run-in with Jack turbo-charged her ailing brain into gear. When Petra wandered into the kitchen, she didn't even notice; she was scribbling away on her notepad so furiously.

Petra stood quietly, and when Sofia looked up, she jumped. She was making a habit of it – things on this boat always seemed to be creeping up on her.

'Damn, Petra, you can't creep up on me like that. I'm in a delicate state today.'

'Tell me about it.' Petra did not look like herself. She was pale and she seemed jumpy. 'I'm really stressed about this Stuart situation,' she blurted.

Sofia put down her pen. 'Have you guys talked about it?'

'God no, I'd rather die. Did you see the vibes at breakfast? Abominable!' So it had been good old-fashioned tension Sofia had felt, and not the sexual variety. She felt a pang of pity for Stuart.

'Well to be honest I think it's best to just shut it down. He obviously likes you, but workplace stuff – it's always complicated and everything will be much simpler if you just try and stay friends.' Sofia was talking to Petra, but she was also talking to herself. It all sounded so reasonable when she said it out loud and part of her wished she'd had someone say this to her at Nakachwa, before everything went wrong.

Then again, she probably wouldn't have listened.

Petra looked deflated. 'I guess you're right. It's not like . . . I like him or anything, but he's so sweet and the idea of blowing him off seems so cruel, like kicking a puppy.'

'It's got to be done, Petra, before he gets the wrong idea.' She had been the puppy once, and although she knew it wasn't nice being kicked, she hoped Petra might have a bit more tact. 'Sorry, Petra, I have to get this list to Declan.' Sofia put a steady hand on her shoulder and

159

waited until Petra looked up. 'You got this.'

Petra rolled her eyes, 'Yeah OK, I'm not going to war, just gotta kick a puppy.' Petra took a deep breath and the two of them split off in opposite directions, geared up for the tasks at hand.


Sofia found Declan standing outside the captain's quarters on the top deck. The pair were laughing. Declan didn't seem to have any problem making friends on board. When he spotted her he waved and walked over. She handed him the list.

'Oh no, you're not getting away with it that easy. I'll be needing some guidance; I don't know what half this stuff is.'

Sofia was not impressed. She was functioning on very little sleep and she had to start thinking about dinner. 'You don't know what . . .' she glanced down at the list '. . . an onion is?'

Declan laughed. 'Nah that's not fair – I obviously know what an onion is but, man, I don't know the difference between—' he pointed '—a sirloin and a bavette steak.'

'Well can't you just ask?'

'Don't speak Italian, mate,' he said. Sofia was finding his wide grin more and more irritating. 'I was going to go with Jack but he's got some family stuff or something to sort out. I'm not really sure what, so it's you and me. At least you'll know what this stuff looks like, then we can just point.'

It was clear to Sofia that she was doomed to have ever more tedious chores to do that day. She had resolved to be a helpful and friendly team player, and she sort of owed Jack one.

'OK fine, but we need to keep it moving. I have to be back in time to get dinner ready.'

# Chapter Twenty-One

Most of the supplies had been ordered beforehand, but since Sofia had had to change her menu considerably, there were some things that had to be bought at the market. Sofia was tired and grumpy and trying to hide it. In the taxi Declan was chatting idly, and Sofia was glad that he seemed to be quite happy soliloquising with very little input from her.

In her head she had envisioned a quaint collection of stalls, piled with fresh produce and a cacophony of vendors selling their wares. When they pulled up at what looked like the Amalfi Coast's answer to a trading estate she was confused. The squat sprawling building in front of her was steel grey.

Declan leant forward and asked the taxi driver if he was sure that this was the address. His response suggested that he had little patience for Brits, especially ones who questioned his sense of direction on an island that measured no more than four square miles. They got out of the car and wandered towards what looked like a ticket office in the side of the building.

'*Ricezione*, that's gotta be reception right?' Who needed Jack's Italian anyway? Sofia thought.

'*Hola,*' said Declan brightly to the woman behind the glass. She might have been the sort of person who always looked resolutely unimpressed, but the Spanish didn't help.

Sofia shot Declan a look. 'Sorry, he means, ummm *ciao.*'

'Dammit, yeah that's the one.'

The woman sighed audibly. '*Inglesi?*'

'*Si!*' Sofia held out hope that she could retire her guidebook Italian.

'*Hai una lista?*' The woman was no longer looking at them, but typing lazily on her computer.

'List! Yes we do, um, here you go.' She fumbled in her pockets and pulled out the crumpled list, flattening it hastily between her palms before sliding it under the glass. The woman sighed again, tearing her eyes away from the screen to look down at the yellowing notepad sheet.

'*Trenta minuti.*' Sofia and Declan looked at her blankly. 'Thirty minutes,' she said in near-perfect English. Sofia felt that they were being tested, and they had both failed miserably. She held two thumbs up.

'*Grazie!*' Declan and Sofia wandered over to a low wall in the shade and sat down side by side.

'So now they just, like, get all the food?'

'Honestly, Dec, I have no idea. I feel like this job is just one steep-as-hell learning curve, I'm trying to learn to ride the wave.' Sofia smiled, as a flash of the conversation with Jack on the beach came back to her. 'Learn to live a little, you know?'

163

When she looked up Declan was staring at her intently. There was a sudden heaviness between them. She felt her stomach drop, racking her brains for something else to say before he filled the silence. He opened his mouth, and she knew she'd lost the battle.

'Sofia, listen, there's something I feel like I need to say.' He looked down at his hands, and she felt for him, his sparse stubble barely struggling over his chin. 'I like you, man, like I really like you.' When he looked back up his eyes were soft and warm. She felt the urge to pinch his cheek.

'Dec . . . I think you're great, really, but I don't feel that way about you. I'm sorry.' The words hung between them, his gushing, hers tender, both a little clichéd.

Declan seemed to be doing some mental gymnastics, his brow furrowed. Finally, he said, with a cheeriness that was almost imperceptibly forced, 'That's OK. I just wanted to get it off my chest, better out than in as they say.' Another eternity ticked past. Sofia reached out her hand and laid it over Declan's. She tried to give it a squeeze but he gently pulled it away.

Sofia remembered how mortified she had felt in his position, standing beside Simon in the cold. Although the rejection she had faced had been far more brutal, she knew how much courage it took to put yourself out there. She also knew that sometimes being shot down was a necessarily battle-hardening part of falling for people. She hoped that she had been as gracious as she could be and treated him with the kindness she would have once appreciated. Sofia understood that he would need time to lick his wounds. It was just a shame that the first twenty minutes of that time would be sitting next to her in this hot car park.

She decided to take advantage of the time, and signal, to check on Milly's Instagram page. Judging by the last post, which included a snap of the infamous leather Speedos and aquamarine cave pool, and the hashtag #blessed and #livingladulcevida, she assumed that Brian and his foot were in good health.

Sofia checked the time, silently stood up and walked to the window in the wall. The woman looked up briefly and then cranked her head to the left. At another hole in the wall a few yards away, a man who looked like he was barely out of his teens was standing with a trolley loaded with sealed Styrofoam crates.

'Declan!' They had to communicate at some point. 'I'm going to need a hand.' She tried what she thought was a friendly but firm tone.

He ambled over and they waited for their lift back to the marina. Sofia tried to think of something to say, but she'd never been good at filling awkward silences, so she went back to her phone. The day was steadily sliding from bad to worse. As they sat in the back of the car, Sofia was glad for the cheery Italian radio host, and when they got out and Declan began wheeling the trolley wordlessly toward the boat, she missed him.

\* \* \*

On board, they continued their wordless caravan to the kitchen. Sofia couldn't stand it anymore, and as they unloaded the boxes she blurted out, 'I mean it's not like even if I did think of you that way anything could happen – the captain has that rule about no couples.'

Declan was startled for a moment by the sudden abandonment of their wordless pact, and then he just looked confused. 'What rule? That doesn't make any sense. I thought . . .' He trailed off nervously.

'You thought what?' Sofia was reaching the end of her patience.

'Well Jack and Petra hooked up last charter and they're both still here so . . .' His tone had descended into petulance and Sofia was reminded how young he was.

After that first thought came a second, more unpleasant one – that Petra had lied to her. Admittedly through omission, but still she thought they were getting close. On top of that it was Jack.

Suddenly Petra's teasing about Sofia and Jack was retrospectively thrown under a different light. Was Petra jealous about some misperceived dynamic between her and Jack? Or was she just playing with Sofia, indulging in some high school scheming to get Sofia to think she had a chance, only for it to be revealed that Petra herself and Jack were an item all along? And then all those comments about what a 'sweet guy' he was. Sofia felt bewildered.

Declan cleared his throat emphatically. Sofia had been standing in a stupor for just a couple of moments too long.

Cautiously, he asked, 'Are you good, Sofia?' His voice

166

broke her through the surface, out of the sea of choppy thoughts.

She shook her head instinctively, and then caught herself. 'Yeah, I'm fine,' she mumbled unconvincingly.

Declan looked awkward, like he knew what he had said had hit a nerve but wasn't sure which, or why. 'I'm going to head out. Will you be OK with all this?'

She didn't know if he was talking about the half dozen crates or the unexpected flood of feeling, both of which would need to be unpacked.

'Yes,' she said firmly and hoped it was true.

Alone in the kitchen, Sofia unloaded the crates and arranged her fridge in a frenzy. Something about organising the fresh produce calmed her frazzled mind. She took time to focus on the depth of the colour of an aubergine, stroke the fronds of a fennel bulb, and smell the stalk of a ripe tomato. Focusing on flavour for a moment helped her reconnect with her senses. She stood up and leant against the counter, taking a deep breath. She would not let herself fall into panic.

What had happened at Nakachwa was not somehow doomed to happen again; she had learnt from that experience. This time she would go directly to Petra, talk it out. She knew now that bottling things up only fermented them into something toxic. She would not let a man be the reason she messed up her friendships, or her career – not this time.

# Chapter Twenty-Two

Sofia resolved to find Petra after dinner. Brian and Milly were due back any minute and she and Petra would both be busy until food had been served and eaten. Sofia couldn't let herself think about how tired she was. She had known that she was signing up for an intense job but she had to admit that she hadn't been worked this hard in a Michelin-star restaurant. She prepped and cooked and plated, radioing in for service and holding her breath in anticipation of Petra's arrival. She was trying out her best 'everything is normal' smile when the door swung open to reveal a strikingly pretty man wearing the steward uniform. He was slight, olive-skinned, with thick dark curly hair that was perfectly styled. Sofia noticed that his fingernails were painted with clear polish when he picked up the plates.

'Hi, I'm Patricio, sorry for the rushed introduction. I promise I will say hello properly after service.' Sofia was pretty sure she could detect a trace of an Italian accent, but only just. When he flashed her a smile on the way out, his teeth were startlingly white.

The whole meeting was so quick that Sofia barely had time to say, 'Sofia, it's a pleasure,' before the kitchen door swung closed. He was certainly efficient. Petra and Patricio seemed destined to make a great team.

She set about making the main course, sirloin steaks cooked to a blasphemous 'well done' and chips. Since she had devised the new menu she had come to realise that the chef in her would need to coexist with the cook if she was going to make it in yachting. Being a cook was about comforting people, occasionally expanding their palettes, but ultimately it was caregiving, feeding people who wanted to eat rather than savour or 'experience' food.

That being said, she would be sure to triple-fry the chips and sneak some anchovy paste into the garlic butter sauce. If they were going for meat and two veg, she was going to make sure it was the tastiest version of it they'd ever tried.

Patricio was back, and then after a well-choreographed exchange he was gone again. Two clean plates where two full plates had just been. One more round for dessert and then they were done. Sofia was wiping down her countertops when Patricio came back with the bowls where the raspberry cheesecake had sat.

'*Mama mia!*' he exclaimed, wiping his forehead with the back of his hand. Before Sofia had a chance to verbalise what she was thinking, he answered her question. 'No don't worry I'm not *that* Italian.' Sofia laughed. She was grateful to be having a conversation that was not loaded with some sort of hangover-induced tension.

'What a shame, I could do with some practice,' Sofia

said jokingly, although Patricio seemed to have missed the edge of humour.

'*Ah, stai imparando l'italiano?*' he replied, and his cheerful earnestness reminded her of Declan, before she had broken his heart.

She blushed, embarrassed by just how little she understood of what he was saying. 'Oh no I, I was joking. My Italian is terrible.'

'*Terribile!*' he corrected.

'*Terribile,*' Sofia repeated awkwardly. 'Well anyway, we are very glad to have you. You certainly know what you're doing. Have you been yachting for a long time?'

'No, it is my first time on a boat. I'm a virgin, in that sense at least.' He gave her a theatrical wink and she giggled. 'I used to work for the Alexandrea. It's the fancy hotel just down on the south coast of Capri.'

'Ah, so that's where you get your impeccable waitering skills. Petra will be thrilled.' For a man who seemed so comfortable in his own skin, she was surprised by how awkwardly he received the compliment.

'Thank you, Sofia,' he said softly, looking down at his hands and smiling to himself.

'Well I'm afraid I am the one who has to rush off now. I need to speak with someone. I will see you for crew dinner in an hour?'

'Looking forward to meeting everyone properly,' he said eagerly.

Sofia smiled. 'Yes they're quite a bunch of characters.'

She headed back to her cabin and tried to radio Petra,

170

but the walkie-talkie came back with only a white-noise buzz. Sofia was afraid that if she lost her nerve she might end up not saying anything and holding on to the kernel of resentment until it flowered into something even uglier.

She wandered around the boat for the next half an hour, poking her head into cupboards, utility rooms, even the top deck, but Petra was nowhere to be found. She came across Milly who was sitting in the main saloon drinking a cup of tea and, to nobody's surprise, scrolling through her Instagram.

'Oh sorry to disturb,' Sofia said apologetically. Milly was so in the zone that she hadn't noticed Sofia come in but when she looked up she offered a weary smile.

'That's OK, I'm not really up to much anyway.' She seemed deflated, and Sofia fought the urge to ask what was wrong. She didn't have time for this, but Milly seemed to be willing her to ask.

'How are you doing? Has Brian recovered?' Milly sat up and patted the space next to her. Slightly reluctantly, Sofia took a seat.

'He's gone to bed early. I think the past two days have been pretty exhausting.'

Sofia couldn't agree more, she had never longed to 'go to bed early' more than she did at that moment.

'It was scary, seeing him hurt like that.' That steely look Milly had had on the boat flashed across her face quickly and then her expression melted into something softer. When she looked over at Sofia, she had tears in her eyes. 'But, like, in a way, it was nice to feel close to him.

Is it weird to say that the evening in the hospital was one of my favourite of the trip so far?'

Sofia looked around the room, at the excess of luxury adorning every visible surface. She chuckled warmly. 'A little,' she said.

Milly looked embarrassed. 'Oh no I mean you guys have been great . . . well most of you. I just meant like it was nice to have some proper time alone. Obviously I'm super blessed to be able to be here.' The influencer sheen of unrelenting optimism had returned to her voice as she said this last part, culminating in a bright but slightly unconvincing smile.

But Sofia couldn't let one thing slip. 'Most of us?' She tried to keep her tone light and curious.

Milly rolled her eyes, leaning in conspiratorially, whispering as if they might be overheard in the large and empty room they were sitting in.

'I actually had to have a word with the captain this evening. Usually she has to serve the food as well, but tonight she was just on drinks and it was unbearable. The way she drools over Brian, it's totally unacceptable!' Milly's voice had built resolutely out of a whisper. 'Honestly if that's what she's like when I'm in the room, I'd hate to imagine what goes on when I'm not there to keep an eye on things.'

Sofia had had just about enough of *sinking feelings* for one day, but here was another wave. 'You're talking about Petra, right?' she asked reticently.

Milly huffed, arms folded. 'Who else?'

'I don't think you need to worry. I've seen the way Brian looks at you.' It wasn't a lie; she had indeed seen Brian look at Milly, but if she was being totally honest, he was not the most expressive person.

Mostly, Sofia felt the need to defend her friend in a way that wasn't too obvious. Petra could be a bit of a flirt, but she was also a professional. Sofia knew she wouldn't cross that line. Then again after what she had learnt earlier, maybe Petra wasn't as infallible as Sofia had first thought. Right now though the fault lines were clear, and she wasn't about to be caught bad-mouthing Petra to the guests.

'I mean look at you, how could he not be madly in love?' Sofia cringed at herself internally but to her surprise it seemed to have the desired effect on Milly.

She beamed, dropping her head coyly and smiling into her lap. 'Do you really think so?'

Sofia swallowed her dignity. 'Of course, you're an absolute stunner. Any guy would be lucky to have you.'

Milly pounced and, before Sofia could react, she had been pulled into a too-tight hug.

'Oh, Sofia, you don't know how much I needed to hear that. You're always there for me!' Milly effused into the crook of Sofia's neck.

For someone who spent most of the day reviewing reams of affirmation from millions of strangers, Sofia was shocked by how fragile Milly's self-esteem was. She rubbed Milly's shoulder awkwardly and then extracted herself from the embrace. Both women sensed that the moment of shared intimacy had been a little performative.

'I'd better start getting the crew's dinner ready.' Sofia was eager to get back below deck.

'Of course. Thanks again, I know you're probably thinking "silly little insecure influencer getting upset about her sham relationship".' Milly tried a laugh to make her self-deprecation more light-hearted, but it sounded hard and forced.

'Not at all,' replied Sofia with a sympathetic smile, although she wasn't sure what she thought quite yet.

Milly waved her away. 'Anyway, you better be going. I've kept you here long enough.' Another smile, a little wave and Sofia was retreating down the stairs, a little more hurriedly than she usually would.

One last circuit around the boat, a knock on Petra's door and still no sign. It was time to get the crew dinner ready anyway, so she got to work: a borlotti bean and fennel sausage stew. Patricio helped her bring the plates in and Sofia scanned the table for Petra.

Jack, Declan, Stuart and Captain Mary sat around in what had presumably been a comfortable silence that turned a little sour when Sofia walked in. She tried to ignore it, and the creeping sense of déjà-vu.

'No Petra tonight?' she asked. She was aiming for a nonchalant tone.

'She's feeling a little . . . under the weather,' said Captain Mary in a way that sounded a little euphemistic.

Everybody looked even worse for wear than they had

174

that morning, everybody apart from Patricio, who was chatting away, masking the rest of the table's general lack of lustre. Sofia had a hard time appearing like she was listening to the conversation when her mind was racing, thinking about what had happened to Petra, how easily Milly had turned against her, how the last thing she needed was a pile-on about Jack. On top of that she was avidly avoiding eye contact with both Declan and Jack.

When they were done, Sofia cleared the plates, grateful for a quick exit, hastily wishing everyone a good night.


In bed, she tossed and turned, her brain running through the day over and over. From Jack to Declan to Petra, she felt like she had woken up that morning with a sense of where she stood with them all. Now she was going to sleep with all three relationships in turmoil. In the life of a yachtie, and in the words of her mother's favourite singer, what a difference a day makes.

# Chapter Twenty-Three

Sofia woke up bleary-eyed and, if not totally refreshed, then at least more clear-headed. She needed to talk to Petra; that was today's goal. Petra, to her relief, was there at breakfast. It had to be said that she still wasn't looking all that well. She had a dazed look on her face and Sofia had to stand right in front of her to catch her eye.

'Glad to see you feeling better, Petra,' Sofia said, spooning scrambled eggs onto her plate.

'Mhmm, yep, thanks.' She pulled on a half-hearted smile. It was an answer that signalled to Sofia that she should not ask any more questions, at least not here, and she turned away to watch the crew devouring their breakfast. Jack was sat at the end of table, quietly listening to Patricio, a faint smile tugging at his lips. It was hard to tell if he was hanging on Patricio's every word or actively avoiding looking over at her, thought Sofia. Probably both.

Declan was turned to face Patricio, leaning on one hand and shovelling eggs into his mouth with the other.

'So you were actually born in Capri?' He seemed genuinely enthralled.

'Yes, and it's a funny story, because my mother had

planned to go to the mainland to give birth but she went out orange picking one day and her waters broke. She was miles from anywhere, with no mobile phone of course, and so she gave birth to me right there in the middle of the trees.' Patricio was animated as he told the story. 'My middle name is actually Aranciano, you know like *arancia*!' He was met with mostly blank looks.

'It means orange,' Jack pipped up.

'*Exacto!* Mama's little orange blossom – that's what she called me.' Patricio grinned.

'That's crazy, wow, and like you've lived there your whole life?' Declan asked.

'Yes, pretty much, actually my whole family, they never leave the island, mostly.' Sofia noticed Patricio glancing over at Jack. 'We have been Capreses for generations.'

'Well not anymore – you're going to travel the world now.' Declan spoke through a mouthful of food. It seemed he had met his match. They couldn't get through the conversation quickly enough. The back and forth was breathless.

'Well not quite, up the coast to Anzio is hardly that far from home.'

'For now sure, but that's just this charter. Who knows what the future holds!'

'If you keep up with the early morning laundry duty, I will personally see that no one ever lets you off this boat,' Petra interjected dryly. Patricio giggled, giddy on the appreciation of new company.

After everyone was done eating, Sofia decided it was

time to make her move. 'Petra, could you help me clear?'

Petra nodded wearily and began collecting the plates. Back in the privacy of the kitchen, Sofia was running through the remit of conversation starters.

'I know what you're going to ask.' Petra sounded a little accusatory, but mostly she sounded sort of sad. Petra let out a big sigh, and from the way her eyes glistened, Sofia braced herself for tears.

'I'm guessing you heard about my chat with the captain.' She looked defeated, picking at her fingernails anxiously. 'I'm so embarrassed, Sofia, honestly. I thought I would combust from the shame, and I don't even know how to defend myself. We barely even looked at each other; he just thanked me for the Moscow mule I made him, for God's sake.' Then the tears fell.

Sofia pulled her into a hug. They stood there for a moment, Petra sniffing softly into Sofia's shoulder. When she pulled back her eyes were red.

'I spoke to Milly yesterday and she seemed pretty upset. It is clearly a them problem, not a you problem. I think she's just young and a bit insecure about their relationship,' Sofia said cautiously. The sudden flare in Petra's expression suggested she had ruffled feathers, rather than smoothed them over as she had intended.

'Well to be honest I don't really give a damn about her insecurities. She's put my career on the line for what? Because she's scared her boyfriend is going to run off with the staff?' she scoffed. Her anger was palpable, having burnt off any residual self-pity.

'She's only young, Petra, what like twenty-one? She's basically a teenager.' Sofia wasn't really sure why she suddenly felt so defensive of Milly – maybe she could sympathise with how small it could make you feel when you don't know where you stand with someone. She could only imagine how that must be amplified when you brought fame into the mix.

Petra didn't say anything and Sofia was worried that she'd just severed the last decent relationship she had on the boat. A range of feelings filtered across Petra's face. When the anger passed, there was confusion, resignation, and then, finally – thankfully – empathy.

'Twenty-one?' She nodded thoughtfully. 'You're right. I didn't even know my left and right when I was twenty-one.' Petra laughed wryly, and Sofia smiled. 'It doesn't make Captain Mary telling me to keep it in my pants any less mortifying though.' Sofia couldn't help but giggle.

'Honestly, I'm impressed you made it to breakfast. I think I would have thrown myself into the sea.'

'I thought about it.' Petra was giggling too now.

'What did she say?'

'Oh I don't know, I've blocked it from my memory.' Petra covered her face with her hands. 'Something like: "We have a duty to our guests; it's nice to be friendly but there is a line that cannot be crossed".'

'Oh, that is bad,' Sofia teased.

'The way she said "friendly" I felt like a common harlot.' Petra dropped her hands, looking at Sofia with a grimace, and then they both burst out laughing.

179

When they had wheezed and wiped the tears from their eyes, Sofia didn't want to ruin the moment by bringing up the 'Jack issue'. Instead she got on with making the guests' breakfast, whilst Petra leant against the counter analysing every detail of her conversation with the captain and subsequent evening of self-reflection.

'I guess it just really brought home to me that I'm single, I'm thirty-two and I still don't know how to pick a man, or rather I do, but they're always the wrong man,' she mused. 'When I was sitting there and she was trying not to call me a slag it just hit me – I'm always looking for a fun time but I can't seem to look past that, you know? Like after the shag, after the honeymoon period, I'm always left with something I didn't really ask for. And when I say that I mean, I actually didn't ask for it. I only asked for that hit of male validation, I never consider what comes after, you know what I mean?'

Petra had been throwing around a generous number of rhetorical questions, so it was never entirely obvious when Sofia needed to provide a response. The pause suggested that this was one such moment.

'Mmhmm I know what you mean,' she said absent-mindedly as she whisked the pancake batter.

'I mean even when it comes to Jack, who I really rate, I never considered that it could be more than a fling. I just never seem to be in the headspace to make informed decisions when it comes to men.'

Sofia froze for a second and then, for fear of stemming the flow of information that Petra was willingly spewing, she continued cooking, feigning indifference.

'You and Jack?' Sofia didn't look up as she asked the question she had been burning to ask for the last twenty-four hours.

'Oh God, did I never tell you about that?' Petra seemed genuinely surprised. 'I guess it probably wasn't my finest moment.' She shrugged. 'It was last charter and we were both wasted, and like I said I hadn't realised about the captain's rule. When she found out she was livid, well as livid as Captain Mary can be, and so we agreed to be mates.' Petra paused contemplatively. 'I think probably for the best. He's a great guy but he is quite . . . moody, lots going on in that pretty head of his. He's a bit too much of "a thinker" for me.'

Sofia was relieved. There was no dark ulterior motive to Petra's teasing about her and Jack. Maybe Petra thought Sofia might be better equipped to deal with 'a thinker'. To the contrary, Sofia had found the suggestion of Jack's complex inner life affronting rather than intriguing.

'From what I can remember though, he's dynamite in bed.' Sofia looked up at this comment, Petra winked and they both giggled.

'Isn't it awkward now, working with him?' Sofia thought back to those painful encounters with Simon.

'I mean, not really. When the captain had a word, he broke it off straight away but honestly we both just knew that the job was more important than whatever it was we had going on, so that was that.'

Sofia felt a stab of envy towards Petra for her tendency

towards level-headed thinking. How nice it would be to have a brain that didn't make life harder for you.

Petra checked her watch. 'I've really been slacking this morning. I can't tell you how nice it is to finally have a decent steward – Patricio is a godsend.'

'Do you think he's got a friend who could be my sous?' Sofia asked wryly as she plated up the pancakes and poured the berry coulis into a small pot.

'You don't need a sous. Look at you, you're the full package all on your own.'

Sofia scoffed at Petra's cheerleading, and handed her the dishes. 'It's over to you, and try not to hump Brian as you serve him his breakfast, yeah?' Petra laughed, in spite of herself.

'Too soon! Damn it, Sofia, too soon.' But she was shaking her head and chuckling as she walked out of the kitchen.

The rest of that day passed without incident. Jack and Declan took a newly recovered Brian out diving and Milly dedicated herself to the tricky task of tanning without burning, not an easy feat for a redhead. There were no tense conversations, no near-death experiences and no declarations of love, and Sofia was grateful for it. At the crew's dinner, the mood was jovial. Declan even complimented the food. Sofia was hopeful that his heart was well on the way to being mended. His new-found fascination with Patricio certainly seemed to have helped him along.

When it came time to go to bed, Sofia could hardly get undressed quickly enough. She brushed her teeth in a frenzy, the siren call of her pillow buzzing in her ears.

# Chapter Twenty-Four

He was coming towards her with hunger in his eyes, and when he circled her waist with his arms she felt a weight in the pit of her stomach start to throb. His lips brushed the top of her ear and then settled in the nape of her neck. Her breathing ran hot and his was laced with low moans. She threw her head back as his teeth grazed her collarbone and his fingers slipped the strap of her dress off her shoulder. Suddenly she was naked, the light fabric pooling at her feet, her nipples dark and hard. He stood back and admired the sweeps of her body, the swell of her breasts, the arch of her back, the curve of her belly. She stepped forward and gazed at him, swimming in the pools of green as she slowly unbuttoned his shirt, unbuckled his belt, unzipped his jeans. Now they were both panting skin, leaving trails of goose bumps wherever they touched.

When she begged him to kiss her, he obliged, and the taste of him made her gasp. She was ravenous now and her hands could not hold enough of him. Nails leaving tracks across his broad shoulders. Fingers tangled in his hair, pulling, trying to get more of him, trying to get closer. Their tongues fighting for space, jousting, and she was burning now. Between her legs, the slickness of anticipation was taking over, the need to be entered was all she could think about.

He lowered himself to his knees, and she whimpered as he parted her legs, hoisting one over his shoulder. She felt his stubble brush against her inner thigh, and she held her breath. His lips, his tongue teasing her, dancing around, making her brain fuzz. When his mouth finally found her, she sighed with pleasure, but also relief. His hands were grasping at her arse, pulling her onto his face, burying himself in her. The metronome of her desire began to quicken. With each pass and flicker of his tongue, she felt her insides tense, in expectation of the release. She was moaning loudly now, glancing down to see the mop of dark brown waves, bobbing in time with her. She knew she was close. The summit was in sight, and as he slid his fingers inside her, she readied herself for the plummet.

A loud knock on the door jolted Sofia awake.

'Sofia, it's 7.30, honey, breakfast needs to be on the table in T-minus . . .' a pause '. . . twenty-nine minutes.'

'Right, thanks, Petra – alarm malfunction!' she replied breathlessly, although she could already hear the footsteps retreating down the hallway.

Sofia collapsed back into her pillow, staring at the bottom of the bunk above her. Tentatively she reached down into her pyjama shorts, the rude awakening bringing her senses into a sharp focus. She was definitely wet. She giggled to herself; she hadn't had a sex dream since she was a teenager. She considered finishing the job herself.

185

She closed her eyes and tried to find herself back where she had left off. It was only in that moment, when her brain relocated itself, and she peered down once more, that it hit her.

The face staring up at her had been Jack's.

Sofia quickly threw back her covers, sitting up in bed and staring at the door. She felt flustered, in a panicky sort of way, and resolved to get on with her day and not overthink things. Even as she was giving herself a talking-to she knew it was pointless. Her anxious brain was already whirring, flip-flopping between worst-case scenarios and a more reassuring refrain that 'sex dreams don't mean anything'. She'd had one about her history teacher, Mrs Hilder, when she was thirteen and she wasn't even attracted to women, let alone grey-haired ones.

It must just be her subconscious working through the conversation with Petra. That was the party line and she was sticking with it.

At breakfast with the crew, Sofia found herself trying not to stare at Jack. There was no getting around the fact that he was handsome. The colours of his face were perfectly complementary, like someone had carefully selected each tone to go with the rest. The pale sage of his eyes, the rich chocolate of his hair, streaked with strands that looked either blue black or coppery depending on the light. His complexion, a testament to good genes and sunshine, tanned and smooth, save for the shadow of dark stubble curving around his blush-coloured lips. The colour scheme might work quite well in a luxury country club, Sofia thought. He could hardly look more like money.

Her toast was unpleasantly cold and brittle by the time she took a bite. She had to get a grip. There were so many reasons why it would not be a good thing for her to fancy Jack. There wasn't even one that she could think of on the 'pros' side of things.

Apart, of course, from the thrill she got when she allowed her mind to wander back to the night before, his hands gripping her waist, the graze of his stubble on her thigh, the sound of him moaning against her . . .

'Did you want to come on the hike around Vivara then, Sofia?' It was Declan's voice, wrenching her out of her daydream.

'Huh?' She had not been listening.

'Well Brian and Milly are going to Isola di Vivara, today. It's a national park and they want to hike around it. I really want to go and so does Petra. Patricio used to go there as a kid sometimes so he's keen to see it again, but there isn't really enough room for all of us to go . . .' Declan trailed off. He looked sheepish.

'To be honest, I'm kind of exhausted so I'm happy to stay on board. You guys go and enjoy yourselves.' Declan looked at Patricio and the pair of them grinned at each other. 'I can make some food for the trip, and you guys can actually remember to bring it.' She glanced over at Jack and was quietly pleased to see him chuckle.

'Cool. Sounds like a plan. Thanks, Sofia.' The joke seemed to have gone over Declan's head. He began to excitedly plan the itinerary for the day with Patricio and a few helpful interjections from Petra. The heartbreak was a distant memory, thought Sofia. It seemed everyone apart from her was more than capable of casting off romantic rejection – maybe it was something about the transitory life of a yachtie, or maybe Declan and Petra were just far more well-adjusted.

While the others got the tender ready, Sofia served the guests breakfast and prepared everyone's picnic lunch. There was a buzz of excitement on board as preparations were made. Sofia waved them off, alongside Stuart and the captain, who were also staying behind.

'Didn't fancy a hike then?' she asked Stuart as they stood waving at the retreating dinghy.

'With my asthma and beer belly? You've got to be kidding.'

Sofia giggled, already mapping out the day ahead.

# Chapter Twenty-Five

Sofia lay back, feeling like she was finally living the life she had naively imagined for herself back in London when she'd first messaged Captain Mary. She was on the top deck, lounging on a recliner with a glass of homemade lemonade. Sunglasses, headphones, and bikini on. She was listening to one of her favourite podcasts, *The Last Supper*, where famous chefs talked about their favourite foods to eat and chatted about their upbringing. Sofia hadn't had a moment to relax since she'd stepped on the boat, and she was grateful that she wasn't having to hike under the midday sun. Stuart had gone to read inside, far from the heat, and Captain Mary was holed away doing whatever it was she did all day. Sofia felt like she had free rein.

Ali Kamar was whispering in her ear about his love affair with saffron, when she felt a hand on her shoulder and jumped, spilling the lemonade she was holding. She yanked her headphones off and turned to see Jack, standing there with a smirk on his face.

'You scared me to death,' she protested, still breathless from the shock.

He sat down on the recliner next to hers and chuckled.

'And here was me thinking you'd finally learnt how to relax.'

She suddenly felt very self-conscious about how few clothes she was wearing. The bright scarlet of her halter-neck bikini now seeming overly ostentatious, and she crossed her arms over her chest. 'I wasn't expecting company,' she said defensively. 'I thought you were taking them to the island.' She looked around uneasily, worried that the trip had been cancelled and she would hurriedly have to get back below deck and into her chef's whites.

'Relax, Sofia, it's just me. You can't park the tender there, so I brought it back. I'll go pick them up later.' He casually began unbuttoning his shirt, and Sofia's heart quickened. She looked away.

'You don't mind, do you?' he asked, although he had already tossed it to the side.

'Not at all,' she said, hoping it wasn't totally obvious she was lying.

He reclined into the lounger, hands behind his head. 'Good, I've been meaning to find an opportunity to top up my tan.'

They lay side by side in silence. Sofia assumed that he wasn't feeling as uncomfortable with the new set-up as she was. She pressed play, but she could no longer concentrate on Ali Kamar's dulcet tones; she kept having to rewind and listen again every time she caught her mind wandering off.

She was acutely aware of his body next to hers, and she had an irrational flash of fear that he could hear her restless thoughts. She hadn't felt like that since she was at school. Except she wasn't a pubescent teen anymore, so really what excuse did she have for the sweat on her palms and her overly frequent need to swallow?

'I'm sorry about our run-in the other morning. I was in a bad mood,' he said suddenly.

Sofia was surprised. She was pretty sure she had been the one at fault, overly judgemental and unfoundedly accusatory, as she remembered it.

'Don't be silly, it was my bad. I don't know what got into me. Let's blame it on the hangover eh?'

'Agreed,' he said. She looked over at him. His eyes were closed as he basked in the sun, his torso heaving softly. Her gaze trailed from the smattering of dark curls on his chest down to his belly button where the path was abruptly cut off by the white trousers of his officer's uniform. She felt feral.

'So,' she started cautiously, 'I know it's probably none of my business, but what was all that stuff about a family friend?'

Jack let out a deep sigh. He opened his eyes and turned his head to the side to look at her. She pulled her sunglasses off, feeling like he was about to let her in on a secret.

'Luchiano, he used to work for my grandmother.' He paused. 'And he knew my mother.' Sofia noted the past tense, and the weight with which he said 'mother'.

'I'm sorry,' she said, instinctively sitting up and reaching out her hand. Jack looked down at it, and then back up at the sky. Sofia awkwardly laid it on her lap.

'I hate that look,' he said evenly, staring ahead, a distant expression clouding his face. 'The pity. I think I prefer it when you look at me like I'm a jerk.'

'Really? Oh well that can be arranged. I think I have it saved somewhere.' She frowned in faux concentration and then fixed her face into a look of derision, eyebrow raised and lip curled.

He laughed and she smiled. She liked the sound of it, warm and a little raspy. 'I can always rely on you to not take me seriously, Harlow.'

'But I am sorry, Jack. Losing a parent, I can't imagine how horrible that is.' He held her gaze, and she felt her heart ache at the sadness in his eyes.

'You close with your folks?' he asked.

Sofia had to look away. She couldn't handle the intensity of it anymore. 'Yeah, I'm an only child so me and my parents have always been close. I guess you could say I was spoiled with a deeply functional and happy upbringing. How to explain the neurosis then, I hear you ask?' She had meant it to be self-deprecating, but as soon as the words were out she realised how callous she sounded.

'Shit, I'm sorry, that came out wrong. I didn't mean . . .' She scrambled for the right words.

He held up his hand and shook his head. 'It's OK, Sofia. I asked. It's not a competition; I'm not trying to win some kind of tragic backstory Olympics. Besides you mustn't forget my silver-spoon, multi-generational wealth is nothing to be sniffed at.' He was self-aware too. Sofia wondered where she had got her terrible first impression from. She had thought him all too eager to trip her up but here he was offering her a gentlemanly hand out of the hole she'd dug herself.

'So tell me more about this life of unimaginable wealth then.' Sofia had recovered herself, and she was still curious.

'I don't think I said unimaginable, did I?' He chuckled, and then looked thoughtful. 'My dad's family, I'm pretty sure they were on the *Mayflower* or whatever, so the money goes way back.' He paused, looking a bit uncomfortable. 'I think that a fair of amount of it was . . . you know, from slavery.' He looked so embarrassed that Sofia had the urge to laugh.

Instead she said, evenly, 'I mean, that makes sense. It's kind of the backbone of American capitalism.'

'God will take care of the poor trampled slave, but where will the slaveholder be when eternity begins?' Jack recited this absent-mindedly, as if to himself, and then caught himself. 'Oh God sorry, that is the most obnoxious white-man thing I have ever said.' He looked so nervous.

Sofia raised an eyebrow approvingly. 'I'm impressed. I like a man who knows his Sojourner Truth,' she said.

He grinned at her, clearly relieved. 'So you like me now huh?'

Sofia didn't take the bait. 'So you're woke then?' she said teasingly.

'Oh stop it. I'm so embarrassed, I haven't even read most

of that stuff since my undergrad. It's all just contextless quotes floating around my head, waiting for the perfect moment to mansplain them to some poor passer-by.' Sofia had never seen him like this. He was self-conscious.

'What did you study?'

'My dad's in publishing so literature, of course, but I minored in sociology, which was actually way more interesting.'

'My mum teaches sociology, at the local secondary school. That's the only reason I know about Sojourner Truth. I never went to university – my heart was set on the kitchen,' Sofia explained.

'I really envy people who have always known what they want to do. I think I spent a long time just trying to do what other people wanted me to do, and then trying to do what they didn't want me to do.' He was lying back again, sunglasses on, speaking to the sky. '*People*, I keep saying, as if it's not just my dad.' He scoffed at himself.

'It's a bit of a cliché, no? Rich boy rebelling against the life his parents always had planned for him.' Sofia was feeling empowered to dig deeper. She was the bikini-clad therapist, sat up, legs crossed, hands clasped, with her elbows resting on her knees. He was her patient, tanned chest glistening.

'Oh for sure, it makes the whole thing so unsatisfactory, to know that running away from that high-powered publishing job to spite my father isn't even original.' His tone was light before he stopped. 'I think my dad found it more amusing than anything else, unlike the situation with my brother. I think that's what really broke his heart.' It felt like they had tiptoed to the edge of the abyss. Sofia wasn't sure she had the stomach to peer down.

She leant back and let out a pent-up sigh. 'That's a lot, Jack.' She wasn't trying to shut down the conversation but Jack seemed to take it as an admission of defeat on her part.

He looked over at her with a smirk. 'Don't worry. Harlow, I've already got a shrink; your work here is done.' He was putting on a brave face but his tone was not quite convincing. A tinge of sadness clung to his voice.

'Thank goodness for that.' She smiled, deciding that the inquisition could wait for now. They lay side by side for some time, a comfortable silence hanging between them.

Sofia settled into a sun-soaked doze, and time became elastic. She was right on the outskirts of sleep when she heard Jack gently say something about 'getting the tender ready'. She nodded, eyes firmly shut behind her sunglasses, and she fell into sleep to the sound of his chuckle as he walked away.

# Chapter Twenty-Six

When she awoke, she could feel a throbbing on her side. The pain was confusing in her sleepy daze until she looked down. Her skin was taut and alarmingly pink. She had fallen asleep in the sun. *What else did you expect?* she berated herself. It had been years since she'd gotten burnt. She'd ended up lying on her side, so she was horrified to find the burn resolutely set into the shape of a triangle on her left side and back where the shade had vanished as the sun moved.

She gingerly pressed her fingers against it, wincing as they left three distinct white shadows in their wake.

'Damn,' she muttered under her breath.

Then she checked the time, and muttered a much more anxious '*damn*'. The guests would be back in half an hour and she hadn't even started meal prepping yet. She gathered her things hastily and trotted across the deck to see Jack zipping into the distance, a vision of blazing white among the cerulean waves.

In the kitchen she was on autopilot, chopping and whisking at double speed, but her mind was firmly stuck on the deck, turning over the conversation with Jack. She was worried. Hating him, finding him insufferable, that was challenging; but liking him, that might be its own kind of trouble. She had chastised her lurid brain for spending the night with him, because she couldn't quite convince her body that it hadn't happened. Up on the deck, she had felt drawn to him, and when he had told her about his mother, she had felt compelled to hold him.

No good would come of this. She could not keep making the same mistakes. This was a new start; that was the plan. Maybe if she repeated these things to herself, she could override whatever it was she was starting to feel about him.

'Sofia! How are ya?' She was startled out of her thoughts by Declan, bounding into the kitchen with the energy of a puppy.

'Great,' she lied. 'How was the trip?' She looked down and realised the batter she was mixing had begun to separate.

'It was amazing, honestly. You missed out, although I think there's something weird going on between Petra and Milly,' he mused, aimlessly pacing around the small square of floorspace. It wasn't helping with Sofia's nerves. 'And Patricio, honestly, he's like a genius or something. He knew the name of, like, every plant. It's crazy.'

Sofia was glad at least to see that any residual awkwardness between them had evaporated.

'Sounds cool.' She was distracted, adding more flour with one hand as the mixture stiffened into something far too dough-like. 'I'm a bit behind, Dec, so if you could give me, like, an hour to get the dinner ready, I'll be all ears.'

'Course course, did you know that Patricio and Jack already know each other? Such a small world eh?'

'Really, how come?' Now Sofia was interested. She couldn't seem to get enough of knowing about Jack.

'They're family friends or something. They go way back, but basically Jack got him the job.'

It wasn't really a big deal, but Sofia wondered why nobody had mentioned it to her, especially Jack. She wasn't sure why she felt like she'd been left out of something.

'Interesting,' she said, busying herself with a new batter. She hoped that Declan hadn't clocked the edge of bitterness in her tone.

'Anyway, I'll leave you to it,' he said cheerily. He turned to leave then stopped suddenly and spun back around looking like he wanted to say something else.

'Yes?' Sofia's patience was running thin.

'I hate to be the bearer of bad news, but Milly mentioned earlier that she thinks she's a bit bloated, so she'd rather avoid anything too heavy for the next few days.' He shrugged apologetically, eyeing the bowl in her hands.

Sofia had to take a deep breath. This job was certainly keeping her on her toes. 'So I'm guessing no deep-fried tempura then?' she said through gritted teeth.

'I mean, you're the chef but I'm guessing probably not.' He flashed her a grin and raced out of the kitchen before she could shoot the messenger.

Sofia dumped the bowl in the sink and slumped against

the counter, remembering too late the burn on her back and letting out a yelp. She was really being tested.

After a flick through her notebook and a review of the vegetables she'd already prepped she landed on ratatouille. Brian and Milly would have to make do with a slightly later dinner – she wasn't a miracle worker.

In the end, dinner was only seven minutes behind schedule, and Sofia felt a little triumphant as she radioed Patricio for service. She wanted to pick his brains about his mysterious shared past with Jack but she knew that he was all business when it came to dinnertime so she waited until he brought back the dessert plates.

As he put them on the side she noticed, with a mixture of relief and annoyance, that they had been scraped clean. Banoffee pie evidently didn't fall under the category of 'heavy' in Milly's mind.

'So,' she began, 'a little birdie told me that you and Jack are old friends?' She had intended for it to sound casually inquisitive; instead it came out probing.

Patricio blushed and looked embarrassed. 'Um, yeah, our parents knew each other, but I mean I have the experience as well. I had an interview with Captain Mary and everything.' He was defensive, and Sofia was confused.

'It's OK, I didn't mean it to sound judgemental.' Now she was the one being defensive. 'I'm just being nosy.' She chuckled anxiously.

'Oh, it's OK, it's just that Jack warned me that . . .' he paused, looking for the right word '. . . people might think I only got the job through . . . um . . .' again the cogs whirred '. . . *nepotismo*? I don't know the English word.'

'Nepotism,' Sofia offered, realising that the 'people' he was referring to must be her. Sofia was mortified that she was getting a reputation for being judgy. Worst of all it was Jack going around telling people that she couldn't be trusted. She was angry, and – she had to admit – a little hurt.

'Don't worry, Patricio, I can see that you're more than qualified, better than most of the waiters I used to work with in London, in fact.'

Patricio grinned at the compliment. 'Ah well, a little misunderstanding then. Yes Jack has known me since I was a *bambino*. His mother, God rest her soul, she was good friends with my father. She was Caprese too, you know?'

It all clicked into place. If Jack's mum had been from the island, it explained the Italian, and his uncanny ability to navigate around the place. She wondered how she hadn't managed to put it all together earlier.

'I didn't know, I knew his grandmother lived there, but he never mentioned he was half Italian. I thought he was American born and bred.'

Patricio shook his head. 'No, surely you can tell! He is the prime example of what you Brits call an "Italian Stallion", no?' Sofia laughed and Patricio joined in.

'Oh I don't know, I hadn't noticed,' she said coyly. Patricio laughed at her and flounced out of the door.

Sofia was left with a collection of revelations and yet more questions. It seemed she could never get to the bottom of it all. Each new detail only confused her opinion of him. One thing was clear: as friendly as he was now being towards her, he didn't think much of her. He thought so little of her that he felt compelled to warn off others, lest they invite the same judgement she had made of him.

She realised that the fantasy she had been in for the past twenty-four hours was just that, a fantasy. He had not been in her bed that night. She had imagined it; it was all her. She felt like a fool for talking herself into a 'connection' that was now so evidently one-sided. At least she didn't need to worry about breaking any of Captain Mary's rules. It takes two to tango, she thought, and she was waltzing with an imaginary friend.

# Chapter Twenty-Seven

When she walked into the crew mess with their dinner plates in hand, there was a commotion. Nobody was sitting and Captain Mary was standing with her hands on her hips.

'So how many rooms are infected then?' Petra was asking, her voice slightly strained with annoyance. Sofia set the plates on the table and joined the huddle. It was a tight squeeze with the seven of them in the room.

'Well, so far it's only in the main guest room and in the cabin next door,' Stuart replied, his voice soothingly calm.

Sofia chimed in, 'What are we talking about?'

'Mould,' said Declan, Petra, and Patricio in unison.

'That doesn't sound good.' Sofia grimaced.

'It's not.' Petra was getting more agitated. 'We're going to have to do some juggling. I've already moved Milly and Brian to the secondary suite. Honestly the way Milly was acting you'd think I'd crept in in the middle of the night and hidden a cobra in her bed or something.' Everyone ignored the dig and Petra continued, 'But the crew set-up is going to be more complicated. We're a bed short.'

Nobody said anything for a moment and Petra put her head in her hands and groaned. 'Honestly, just when you think everything is going smoothly . . .'

'I'll bed down in the captain's quarters.' It was Stuart again. 'I don't mind. We have a camp bed somewhere and I wake up early anyway so the light won't bother me.'

When Petra looked up, it seemed she might cry with gratitude. 'Are you sure, Stuart? It'll only be until we dock in a few days; then we can get someone on board to sort it out.'

'No problem.'

'You're a lifesaver.' When she lunged to pull him into a hug, everyone was a bit startled, including Stuart.

'It's really no bother,' he said, awkwardly rubbing her back and flushing his characteristic shade of crimson.

Petra composed herself, also a little embarrassed by her sudden outpouring of affection. 'Right well that means, there's only Jack left to bed.' Again she blushed, realising too late her questionable choice of words. 'I mean, to um, find you a bed.'

'Well, he can just stay with Sofia, right? She's got a spare bunk in her cabin, no?' It was Patricio, and Sofia glared at him. The last thing she needed was to have to share a room with Jack.

When Patricio raised his eyebrows cheekily, it occurred to her that he probably thought he was wing-manning her, and she kicked herself for her throwaway joke in the kitchen earlier.

She looked over at Jack. He wouldn't meet her gaze and shifted from foot to foot. Obviously he wasn't enthused by the idea either, but after Stuart's heroics how could she protest? Petra was finally beginning to look like herself again, the aura of panic melting away.

'If that's easiest I guess . . .' she began as Jack spoke over her.

'If there's no other . . .' They both stopped, exchanging a nervous chuckle, a tension settling in the space between them.

'I'll take that enthusiastic response as a "yes" shall I?' Petra seemed to find the whole thing amusing.

'Yes,' said Jack and Sofia in unison.

'So, Declan and Patricio, you two are good to share then?' At this point the question was only a formality. Petra's tone suggested she had little patience for any more negotiation.

From the look that shot between Declan and Patricio, Sofia suspected that Patricio's eagerness to have Jack stay in her cabin was less of a selfless act of matchmaking than she had first thought.

'OK well Jack and Stuart if you could clear your rooms ASAP, then we can all eat.' The matter was closed. There were clear winners and losers, and when Sofia saw the dread she was feeling reflected back at her in Jack's face she knew they were both the latter.

Dinner was cheery. Despite the upheaval, Petra was happy to report that the guests seemed to prefer their new room. Sofia said very little. She was imagining the walk back to her cabin. It was once a haven for her to unwind and escape the stresses of the day. Now it was to become the *most* stressful part of her day.

How would they navigate such a small space? It was barely big enough to accommodate two bodies let alone house the bizarre tension that seemed to follow them around like a bad smell. Now that she knew the extent of his ambivalence towards her, she wasn't sure how well she could keep up with her friendly and civil strategy.

'I'm going to go to bed,' she said quietly once she had finished eating. She had barely touched the apricot tart she had laboured over. All of a sudden the rosemary glaze tasted overly medicinal and she couldn't stop thinking that the arsenic tang of the stones had seeped into the fruit's flesh.

'Night, Sofia, thanks for being a champ about the room swap.' Petra gave her a grateful smile.

'No problemo,' she said chirpily, cringing at herself as she grabbed her plate.

'Try not to be startled by the strange man coming into your bedroom after dark.' It was Jack and she assumed he was trying to engage in some 'roommate banter'. It fell flat and the polite titters died into silence.

'As long as you're not startled by my night terrors, we should be fine.' Sofia was pleased that her retort got a better reception. Jack laughed along half-heartedly and Sofia slipped out of the room.

In her cabin she got undressed and into her pyjamas quickly, anticipating an imminent intrusion. She decided to move to the top bunk. Something about Jack clambering up the narrow ladder over her made the whole situation seem even more undignified.

She lay staring at the ceiling, replaying the day, as she had made a habit of doing. Only three nights, and then they would dock at Gaeta and Jack would move back to his old room. She reasoned that it wasn't so bad; she'd had the flu for longer than that.

# Chapter Twenty-Eight

Sofia woke up with a start. She checked her phone: 5.16 a.m. She tried to go back to sleep, but it was hopeless. She tiptoed down the ladder and out the door. If she couldn't be alone in her cabin, she would have to go and find solitude elsewhere.

Up on the deck the expanse of mauve sky was streaked with peach, the water liquid silver. The moment she saw the figure at the bow of the boat, she knew it was Jack. They seemed doomed to play each other's shadows.

She didn't want to spook him, but she also wanted to watch the sunrise.

'Room for one more?' she called softly. He turned, surprised by the crack in serenity. *She* was surprised to be met by a smile.

'Harlow, are you following me?' His tone was light-hearted.

'Yes, that tracker I slipped into your pocket is mighty accurate.' In the soft mist, with the waves lapping in her ears, she couldn't quite convince herself this wasn't a dream.

'We must stop meeting like this.'

'I was actually looking for some solitude.'

'Ah, yes well, me too. I was trying to get away from this pain in the ass that I'm having to roomie with.' She knew he was teasing but after what she had heard yesterday, she thought of the old saying about grains of truth in every joke.

She must have looked visibly dismayed. He quickly added, 'I'm kidding, Harlow. I come out here every morning, and let me tell you it's a relief not to have to put up with Stuart's snoring.'

She rolled her eyes. 'Poor Stuart, valiantly falling on his sword so you could have a bed, and here you are disparaging his good name!' Sofia quipped. Humour could be a decent armour as well.

Jack scoffed. 'You expect me to believe that Stuart did that for me?'

The question hung in the air a moment and then they both said, 'Petra,' as if on cue.

'He should know better.' Jack shook his head. 'He saw what happened with me and her last charter. Captain Mary won't stand for it.'

'To be honest, Stuart's not the one who Petra is after on this boat anyway.' Sofia bit her tongue, immediately feeling guilty for betraying her friend's confidence.

'It's OK, Sofia, I already know about the Brian catastrophe.' Jack chuckled. 'It's crazy really that she would risk her job like that, for some random guy. You only get so many warning shots.'

'Yeah, I will not be making that mistake again, letting someone come between me and my career. It's so completely not worth it.' Sofia was forgetting herself; Jack didn't want to hear all this.

'I can't imagine there will ever be room in my life for another love.' Jack was looking out at sea, his voice steady but dreamlike. 'You're going to say that this sounds corny, but the ocean, she has my heart.'

'You're right, that does sound corny.' Sofia couldn't help herself. Granted, she had been the one who had pulled the conversation into earnestness, but she could never bear to stay too long. Jack rolled his eyes.

'No but I get you. I guess for me it's food, or rather flavour, the kind of buzz I get when I discover some fantastic new combination – there's nothing like it, puts an orgasm to shame.' She blushed, remembering in an intrusive flash Jack's tongue lapping at her, his eyes looking up from between her legs.

'I don't know about that.' He smiled wickedly. 'Maybe you're not doing it right?'

She blushed harder, thankful to the low light of dawn for masking her unease.

'Oh you would say that. Don't tell me that you've ever even looked at a woman with the same longing in your eyes that I've seen when you're racing through the waves on that tender of yours,' she retorted.

He cracked a grin. 'So you've been watching as well as following huh?'

'Well what would be the point otherwise?' Sofia was blagging her way through, hoping that he couldn't tell she was swimming out of her depth.

There was silence for a moment. Just as Sofia was thinking of something to say, Jack piped up. 'This time of day always makes me think of my mother.'

Sofia studied his profile, the strong line of his nose, and those eyes of his, suddenly something like amber in the light, and deep with sorrow.

'Something about the dawn, between the night and the day, I can feel her in the air. She always loved to get up with the sun,' he continued softly. 'I guess in that way it's not really alone time I'm looking for.' He turned and looked straight at Sofia. A shiver fizzed down her spine. 'Maybe I'm looking for company.'

There it was, that urge to reach out, to take him in her arms. Then she remembered, she was probably the last person he would want to be comforted by. She stood with her arms clamped to her sides, waiting for the impulse to die down.

'Well I'll leave you to it. Three's a crowd as they say.' It was a pathetic response really but she needed to get out of there. It was all too intense. He looked back out to the waves. She was finding it hard to understand what role she could play in the theatre of his grief. She felt like whatever she said, she was messing up her lines.

'I'm sorry.' She tried to look sympathetic and then worried that she was giving him the look of pity he so hated, but he wasn't paying attention to her anyway.

'Thanks. I'll see you at breakfast,' he said absent-mindedly, cycling through a well-worn script of his own.

She gave him a limp pat on the shoulder and he smiled

weakly. As she walked back to the cabin she wondered if he was in the habit of opening up to people who he found 'judgemental'. Every conversation she had with him left her feeling more confused about how he felt about her.


The rest of the day went smoothly, or as smoothly as any day on this boat could go. There was only one crisis to be averted, when Milly misplaced her Fendi sunglasses.

'I need them for a promo post.' She wailed as Sofia served up an afternoon snack: an elaborate fruit medley, piled high on a tiered crystal stand. Petra was topping up their wine glasses with yet more champagne. They were all on the second deck.

'They won't pay me unless I have them on my grid by the end of the day.' It was directed at Brian, but he seemed engrossed in his book, a crime novel by the looks of the dark grey and black cover, embossed with the silhouette of a gun.

'Brian, are you even listening?' She was pouting, a child demanding a parent's attention.

Brian put down the book with a sigh. 'I have no idea, baby, maybe Petra will have seen them, when she was clearing out the old room?' He looked over at Petra who was standing to attention holding the bottle, with a white tea towel draped over her arm.

Sofia knew that Petra had been avoiding talking directly to Brian. After her close call with the captain she didn't want to give Milly any reason to tell on her again.

She avoided looking at Brian as she said, 'I'm sorry, I haven't seen them, but I will go and have a look if you'd like?' This was directed at Milly.

'Sure, that'd be great. I doubt you'll be able to find them though.' Milly was scowling as she said this. Sofia was glad to retreat alongside Petra as they left the couple on deck. The mood was far from friendly.

'What is that bitch's problem?' Petra fumed as they trotted down the stairs.

'Easy, tiger, that Fendi endorsement might be our tip. It's in everyone's interest that they are located immediately,' Sofia teased.

Petra grimaced. 'Somehow I doubt she'll be leaving me anything. She'll probably ask the captain to dock my wages at this rate.'

It turned out that Milly's bad feelings towards Petra could be fixed as quickly and inexplicably as they were prompted. On presenting her with the missing Fendi glasses, which had been 'hidden' on the bedside table, Milly beamed and gave Petra a big hug.

'It was completely bizarre,' Petra recounted as Sofia prepped for dinner that evening. 'And then she started asking me about my skin routine! I don't know what happens to people on reality TV shows, but it must be messing up some kind of brain chemistry right? Being watched and judged all the time must make you paranoid that everyone is out to get you, I reckon.'

Sofia shrugged. 'Honestly, who knows – as far as I'm concerned everyone on this boat is crazy.'

Petra raised an eyebrow. 'So how is it going with Captain Jack then?'

Sofia wasn't sure she was ready to reveal the depths of her inner turmoil. 'Fine, we barely cross paths really. He comes in after I go to sleep and he's up before I wake up . . . well so far anyway. Let's see.'

Petra wasn't satisfied by the diplomatic response but she let it go. 'Mmmhhmm,' was all she said.

After guests and crew had eaten, and after Captain Mary had excused herself, Stuart passed the whisky around. Sofia needed to unwind so she accepted a glass.

'You seem to have an endless supply of this stuff,' Jack noted. Stuart tapped the side of his nose.

'A sailor never reveals his sources.' He chuckled.

Just then Jack's phone rang. He checked the number, excusing himself hurriedly. He looked flustered, like he had that morning after Capri. Sofia found herself desperate to know who was calling. Why was she so curious to know what was going on with him?

After an hour or so she decided it was time for bed. As she walked out she noticed that Petra had slid into the seat closer to Stuart, and Declan and Patricio were also looking cosy. Maybe it was Captain's Mary's rule working its magic; people always seemed to want what they knew they couldn't have.

As she approached the cabin door she could hear Jack's voice. He sounded anxious.

'Listen, Danny, it's OK. Just speak to Dad – I'm sure he can sort it. He knows people. He'll get you a lawyer or whatever.' A pause as an inaudible mumble came through the phone. 'Well yeah, he'll be mad, but not as mad as if you don't call him.'

Sofia didn't want to be caught eavesdropping, as much as she wanted to keep doing it. She knocked lightly on the door.

'Just a minute,' Jack called, and then, in a loud whisper: 'Just call him. Please, Danny, for me.' Another pause. 'Yeah, exactly, exactly, love you.' Jack opened the door gingerly. 'Sorry about that, it was . . .' he seemed to be weighing up whether to tell her the whole truth '. . . it was my brother.'

'No problem,' Sofia said brightly, before noticing that Jack was shirtless. She willed her eyes not to wander, but when he turned she settled on the muscles straddling his spine. It wasn't the first time she'd found herself wondering what they might feel like under her fingers. She needed to get a grip. She followed him into the small cabin as he sat down on the lower bunk, typing on his phone, and running his hands through his hair. It occurred to Sofia that maybe it was an anxious tick, rather than a flirting technique.

She took her pyjamas into the bathroom and changed. When she came out he was still there, typing with his chest bare. Sofia didn't know where to look. She clambered inelegantly up the ladder and lay staring at the ceiling. Jack sighed loudly.

214

'You all good down there?' she asked tentatively.

'Honestly?' He sounded tired.

'Yeah.'

'Not really. Danny, my brother, he got done for a DUI, and now he's in jail for assaulting an officer.'

'Shit.' She didn't know what else to say.

'He'll get out – I'm not worried about that. My dad, he knows people or whatever. What I'm worried about is that he's going to hurt himself, maybe that's what he . . .' Jack stopped abruptly, as if realising he'd said too much.

'It's OK. Whatever you might think of me, I'm not going to judge you.' Sofia hadn't meant for it to sound accusatory, but her hurt was obvious in the barb of her words.

'What do you mean? Why would I think that?'

Sofia grimaced. She was just adding to his load. His voice was hoarse and weary.

Something about not having to look at him empowered her to go on. 'It's just something Patricio said. You warned him that I was judgemental, that he shouldn't tell me about you getting him the job.' She held her breath for his response – another loud sigh.

'It wasn't aimed at you, Sofia. Everyone on this boat can be judgemental. It took years for anyone to respect me for the actual work I was doing, instead of assuming that I was some rich layabout who got handed the job because of family connections. He wasn't supposed to tell anyone.'

Sofia breathed out. Part relieved, part embarrassed for once again assuming the worst; maybe she *was* the person

215

he hadn't accused her of being.

After a beat he added, 'And for the record, I told him not to tell anyone, not you particularly. I'm assuming he couldn't help but tell Declan though?'

Of course, he hadn't only told Sofia, he had also told Declan. Those two were becoming thick as thieves.

'Bingo,' she said, trying to laugh off the matter.

'For what it's worth, I actually find it surprisingly, maybe even worryingly, easy to talk to you, Sofia.' The hard edge had melted from his tone and she found herself warmed by it.

'I'm sorry about your brother. It's nice that you're there for him.'

'Not as much as I'd like . . . I feel bad sometimes, for abandoning him, to live the life I never could, under the thumb of our dad.' He was speaking so softly, Sofia had to strain to hear him.

'You can't blame yourself for going and living your life. He's an adult. I expect he's probably proud of you, if a little envious, for finding what you love and going after it.'

There was silence, and Sofia imagined he might be crying. 'All good down there?' she tried again.

'Yeah,' he said, gruffly. 'I think I really needed to hear that.' His voice broke on the last word and Sofia held her tongue. She didn't want to tip him over the edge.

More silence, and then: 'You're a good friend, Sofia.' It was almost a whisper.

'Thanks.' It was her turn for gratitude. 'I think *I* really needed to hear that.'

They lay in the quiet, the distant sound of the sea lulling them both into drowsiness.

'Night, Sofia,' he said finally, turning off the light.

'Night,' she whispered into the darkness.

# Chapter Twenty-Nine

The next morning, Sofia was surprised to see that Jack was still fast asleep when she came down from her bunk. He looked peaceful, his eyelashes casting long shadows down his cheeks in the low light.

She got dressed in the bathroom again. She didn't want him to wake up to her naked – and now softly peeling – body. The burn had started to itch. She spent the morning in the kitchen, rubbing her lower back against the counter occasionally when her hands were full, like a cartoon bear.

Petra came in looking a little worse for wear. 'I was up until three with Stuart and his whisky in the captain's quarters,' she explained. At the look on Sofia's face, she clarified. 'Oh not like that! Just chatting. Did you know his dad was a marine biologist? Spent years out at sea looking for whales to tag.' She sounded genuinely fascinated.

'Random,' said Sofia, only half listening and slicing up a grapefruit, the smell transporting her back to the afternoon in the citrus grove and bringing a smile to her face.

'And after spending his whole childhood resenting his

father for being away, here he is doing the same thing,' Petra continued.

'Men and their fathers, eh.'

Petra latched on to her throwaway comment straight away. 'So Jack's been telling you all about his daddy issues then?' There was that tone again, the one that wasn't really asking about the *conversations* she was having with Jack.

'It's not like that!' Sofia parroted, noting with a tang of something like jealousy that Jack must have opened up to Petra as well.

'If you say so, Sofia,' Petra chimed with a devilish twinkle in her eyes. 'But I have found myself wondering how that whole bunk-sharing situation is playing out.'

'Well, I'm sorry to disappoint, Petra, but it's mainly stilted pleasantries and sleeping.' Sofia kept her eyes fixed on the knife in her hand, fearful that Petra might pick up on something in her expression. It was ridiculous really; she was telling the truth, mostly.

'Hmmm, how boring.'

Sofia could feel Petra's gaze burning into the back of her head. For a moment the only sound was that of blade on chopping board.

'I better get on.' Sofia threw Petra what she hoped was an easy smile, which seemed to do the trick of bringing the interrogation to an end.

'OK, I'll leave you to it.' But Petra didn't leave immediately; instead she examined Sofia's face suspiciously. Eventually she broke into a grin, deciding to bide her time. 'See you at dinner then!'

Sofia responded with a half-hearted 'see you' as the door swung shut. It was never a good sign when she felt like she was hiding things from a friend, but then again Jack was her friend now too, and there was something to be said for roommate confidentiality.

Another day passed, another three meals and a crew meeting over dinner about the plan for Gaeta. They would dock, sort the mould, get more supplies, and there was the chance of another night out, as Brian and Milly were once again spending the night on land. Sofia dreaded the thought – she had barely recovered from their last excursion.

She hadn't seen Jack all day, and when he walked in and sat down, Sofia was aware that he was looking everywhere apart from at her. She felt dismayed. Hadn't they made some real progress last night? Maybe it had just been the whisky talking.

By the time she'd finished eating, the itching on her back had become almost unbearable, and she could think of nothing else. She excused herself and half walked, half ran back to the cabin, bending her arm at awkward angles to try and get a good scratch.

When she peeled off her T-shirt in the bathroom, the redness had flared into an angry foam of peeling skin. She was peering over her shoulder, tentatively picking at it, when Jack opened the door.

'Excuse me!' she protested.

He quickly shut it again. 'Damn, sorry! I didn't realise

you were in there,' he said from the other side of the laminated wood. There was a pause, but Sofia didn't hear retreating footsteps.

'That burn looks pretty bad,' he said softly through the door.

'It's fine, I just need to moisturise it.' She wasn't convincing even herself.

'I have some aloe vera somewhere – I think that'd help. What kind of chef doesn't come prepared for burns?' He was teasing, but there was fondness to his tone.

She looked at the patch of skin. 'He's the first-aider on board, Sofia. Why must you always make life more difficult for yourself?' she muttered sternly at her reflection.

'What was that?' he called.

'Nothing!' She pulled her T-shirt back on and opened the door. She was face to face with Jack, barely a breath between them in the tiny room. He stepped back awkwardly and they both made a point of looking in different directions. 'Aloe vera sounds great, thanks,' she said quickly.

'Sure yep, I'll grab it,' he said equally quickly before dropping to his knees to pull his suitcase from underneath the bunk. The cabin was so small there was barely enough room for them both to stand, let alone rummage through a bag. She sat down on his bunk gingerly, as he looked for the bottle.

'Here we go.' He stood up holding the green bottle triumphantly up in the air. He looked down at her, motioning for her to move over with a jerk of his head. She did as she was told.

He sat down next to her and angled her shoulder away from him so she was facing the wall and he was behind her.

'Do you mind?' It was almost a whisper.

His hands were gentle, his palms laying warm and heavy on her shoulder, and so she said 'not at all' before she had a chance to register how heavy the air had suddenly got. He lifted her top away from her back and she felt her body tense at the anticipation of his touch. The gel was cool and soothing. She let out an involuntary sigh at the relief. His hand stilled, fingertips grazing her waist tenderly, and she could hear his breath in her ears, ragged.

She was not really surprised when she felt his lips, soft and parted, against her neck. She *was* surprised by how easily she melted into him, her head falling to the side to give him better access. He groaned and she knew that there was no turning back. It was a siren call and her body responded eagerly.

She turned to face him, his gaze dragging slowly from where they were trained on her neck until their eyes met. She could see her own want reflected back at her in those pools of clouded green. He slowly, deliberately raised his palm to her cheek, their breathing matching pace. His fingers curled around the back of her head, thumb stroking jaw. The seconds seemed to crawl. His mouth felt agonisingly far. She couldn't bear it anymore and just as it occurred to her that this was definitely a bad idea, they crashed into each other, the tension between them suddenly igniting.

He tasted divine. She could not get enough of him in her mouth. She was grabbing him, his shoulders, his hair, and she could hear herself, panting like an animal. She was not quite able to orientate herself, but she noted that there was movement and then she was on her back, pulling the weight of him on top of her.

He pulled away suddenly, hovering over her, his brow furrowed. 'Sofia, I'm sorry, I couldn't help . . .' His voice trailed off as she reached up and guided his face back to hers. She heard a whimper as their lips met again, then realised it was from her.

'I want this,' she breathed into his ear, and he moaned into her neck. Her mind was fuzzing, drifting in and out of sensations all over her body. His tongue hot on her neck, his hands grasping at her hips, his pressing hardness against her. She was aware of the twinge in the pit of her stomach, telling her she was hungry, that she was ready, that she wanted to be full. *We are wearing too many clothes,* she thought, with a flash of urgent clarity. She pulled at his shirt, fumbling with the buttons, and he pulled himself away, kneeling over her. He smiled softly as he tossed his shirt to the side and pulled hers over her head, laying a soft kiss on her shoulder. He left goose bumps and a pang of something else, the tenderness knocking the breath out of her momentarily.

She was up on her elbows admiring him, more freely than she already had, allowing her eyes to linger on the lines of his shoulders, the ridges of his toned stomach, and then dropping to the bulge of his trousers, the twinge turning to something more like a throbbing. When she looked back up at him, he smiled again, but there was something more carnal in it this time. He deftly snaked his hand around her back and unclasped her bra. Firmly he pushed her shoulder back down into the mattress and slipped the straps down her arms, the black lace going the same way as his shirt.

He sighed in appreciation, casting his eyes over her as she had, and then his hands followed. Her breath caught in her throat as his thumb brushed over her nipples, and he bit his lip as he watched her respond to his touch.

'You really are something else,' he breathed, lowering himself down to take the hard tip he had summoned with his hand into his mouth. She could only moan in response, pleasure washing over her. She didn't think she had ever had her body react this way to somebody before; she felt as if he was all over her, smothered in him.

When he began trailing kisses down her stomach, she was worried she might forget how to breathe. He let out a soft sigh of appreciation as he slid her pyjama shorts down her legs to find she wasn't wearing anything underneath, then glanced up at her, a question marred with want in his eyes. She nodded, a silent pact of desire.

He took his time, caressing the inside of her thighs, placing soft kisses everywhere apart from where the aching was: her belly button, her pelvic bones, the crease at the top of her leg. She arched her back, partly in protest, partly in desperation. Finally, his tongue found her and she gasped. He groaned into her, the vibrations concentrating all her focus to the point of her, his teeth gently enclosing and tugging, his tongue dancing until her vision began to blur. She could hear her heart in her ears, faster and faster as he tapped into the rhythm of her quickening breaths. Momentarily she was aware of his hands creeping up to her breasts, and the feel of her fingernails clawing at the back of his head, and then she was falling into the darkness in the back of her eyelids. The room went silent as she reached the very lightest ends of herself and then collapsed into the warmest depths.

Slowly she floated back to the surface, opening her eyes. She was surprised by how light the room was. He was grinning at her when she could finally focus on his face again. Her breathing still felt laboured. 'Did you enjoy yourself?' Sofia still wasn't in possession of all of her faculties, so she nodded lazily. She pulled him in for a kiss, tasting herself on his mouth. She was still feeling hungry.

She pushed him back and he looked confused. She found herself relishing her power takeover as she looked him dead in the eye and said evenly, 'It's my turn now.'

He looked a little taken aback, and then his eyes twinkled devilishly. 'You're the boss, Harlow.'

She rolled on top of him and began to unbuckle his belt. His eyes were trained on her hands as she pulled down his boxers and took him in her palm. He was rock hard and heavy. He threw his head back as she stroked him, slowly. She was in charge now. When he looked up at her, she thought she might come again just from the want in his eyes.

'Ride me,' he said. It was meant to be an order, but it sounded more like a plea. She smiled coyly as she ignored him and continued her work, keeping her pace torturously steady. He let out a low moan, and she could feel it reverberating through her, setting off something primal, which shattered her momentary composure. She needed him inside her. When she lowered herself onto his stiffness, she was submerged once more. The thrumming of her desire overriding her senses until it was just him, the sound of him, the smell of him, the feel of him sliding in and out of her.

The crescendo started again as he grabbed her arse, thrusting up into her, hard. The build was relentless. Each second she came closer to the release without reaching it, she worried she couldn't handle any more. And then, the walls of her mind came crashing down again and she was sure she wasn't alone in the ecstatic darkness. She forced herself to open her eyes and caught him, eyes shut, brow furrowed in euphoria, his lips parted in a silent prayer. He looked beautiful, she thought.

# Chapter Thirty

## Jack

When she collapsed on top of him, they lay panting for some time, wrapped up in each other. He stroked her hair and was struck by how comfortable he felt, lying there naked with her, like he had done it a thousand times before. If he was being honest with himself, he knew deep down that they were indulging in a fantasy, but right now he couldn't quite make a dent in the bliss he was feeling.

'We could have done that ages ago, if you'd let me,' Jack said softly.

'Oh yeah? Jumped my bones after I caught you raiding my fridge?' She looked up at him playfully. 'To be honest, even through my strawberry rage those eyes of yours might have persuaded me to do some very unsanitary things in my kitchen.'

'Oh I was taken long before that – the moment I spotted you across the bar in Amalfi.' He paused, unsure of whether he wanted to reveal himself. 'I thought, I'm going to buy that girl a drink, and she's going to wake up in my bed tomorrow.'

'Well that kind of thinking is exactly why I didn't.'

He chuckled, thinking she was teasing him. But when he looked down her expression was sombre, her eyes glossy with something like sadness. He was taken aback and chastised himself for ruining the moment. His concerned look prompted an explanation. Sofia looked away, and he fought the urge to take her by the chin to force her to look at him. She sighed as if gearing up for an unpleasant chore.

'At the restaurant, there was this guy I worked with.' There was silence and he felt she needed encouragement.

'I'm listening,' he said, apprehensive of what she was going to say next. Did she have a boyfriend she'd never mentioned? He realised he'd never even asked her. He tried to get a handle on the unexpected rush of panic he felt.

'I slept with him. It was after a night out and I don't really remember much of it. It wasn't, like, dodgy.' She didn't sound completely convinced, thought Jack. 'Like, I wanted it to happen, but then he did the same thing with someone else at work, and I'm not so sure that she did.' Sofia seemed to be wrestling with something. Jack waited, hoping the silence would draw her out. 'That's when the drinking was quite bad, and for a while afterwards. That's part of the reason I stopped.'

Jack felt the weight of the words hang in the air, not just a confession, but an origin story, a piece of history that explained some of her. He realised that he hardly knew anything about her really. How many times had they talked? And she knew about his mother, his brother, his father; he hadn't wanted to let her become a full person.

A full person you could fall in love with. He preferred his conquests to be acquaintances, friendly ones at most, women with beautiful faces and minimal biographies. All of a sudden, the panic was back.

'I'm sorry,' was all he could muster, aware of how many times those words had seemed empty to him. But he wasn't sure he could handle any more exceptionalism for one night. He had already broken his usual routine of being drunk, and his rule about postcoital cuddling, and now here he was engaging in inquisitive pillow talk. On top of that, she was crew, and that wasn't his rule to discretionarily break, it was Mary's.

After Petra, she had given him a stern talking-to, which he hadn't been expecting. There were lots of rules on the boat, and a lot of them were met with a don't ask, don't tell policy. Mary had worked on boats most of her life and she knew what went on. She was wise enough to know that sometimes it was better to let people blow off steam, than to tempt a pressure cooker explosion.

'It's just really difficult to find good people, Jack,' she had said in a steely tone he rarely heard. She usually called him Jacky in private. 'A lot of hard work has gone into you rising up the ranks, yours certainly, but also mine. You're about to become first officer, and Petra's on track for head stewardess. I can't afford to have a lovers' tiff on my hands.'

It hadn't been hard to cut things off with Petra. She'd seemed more inconvenienced than hurt when he told her. They had both been drinking and although he liked her company, it had felt perfectly natural for them both to stumble back to their respective bunks when the act was done. He had not felt compelled to smell her hair or stroke her back, or kiss her earlobe as he was doing with Sofia. The most affectionate relationship he had ever had with a woman was probably with Mary, he thought.

She had been the one who had held him when he wept for his mother, when his father seemed to always be away, and his brother refused to talk about her. At least he'd learnt that it made people uncomfortable to talk about the dead, that as much as his days were flooded with memories of her face and her voice, he had to keep it to himself. No one liked morbid talk. She was gone and it was best that everyone just moved on.

'What was your mother like?' He had thought Sofia had drifted to sleep, so calm and regular was her breathing. He found himself wondering if she could read his thoughts.

'Well, as much as it sounds like a reductive thing to say, she was beautiful.' The back of his throat burned, his voice hoarse. It was an unfamiliar feeling, fighting the urge to cry, and here he'd had to try two nights in a row. What was it about this woman in his arms that made him feel like a boy again? 'She was also a bit wild. She loved travelling, something about being trapped on the island all her childhood, call it cabin fever.' He chuckled weakly at his own lame attempt at lightening the mood.

Sofia said nothing, just looked up at him with those

almond eyes of hers. Before he could stop himself, he reached for her face, stroking her cheek softly. Her eyelids fluttered closed and she let out an almost inaudible sigh. He was a fool to think he could have stopped all this from happening. It all felt so inevitable.

'She married my dad when she was twenty-two. He was thirty-five, and like all the great works of art he finds, he wanted to bind her, keep her neatly tucked away on his bookshelf.' Jack couldn't seem to stop himself. 'They split up when I was about thirteen and I didn't see her for years. It was only when she got the diagnosis that my dad let us come back to Capri.' His voice cracked. He had lost the battle against his tears, and his cheeks flushed hot as one rolled down his face. Sofia's eyes flashed open and he was surprised to see his own sorrow reflected back at him. She raised her hands and gently wiped the wayward drop away with her thumb.

'I think my dad was scared that we would inherit her bohemian ways. Don't get me wrong, she was an incredibly hard worker, but she was never interested in money really. She was only ever looking for adventure.'

Sofia smiled up at him and Jack could feel his heart beating a little faster. 'So it didn't work then,' she said.

Jack laughed, the whole tragic story suddenly seeming so ludicrous. 'No, it didn't work; well, not for me.' He thought of Danny, getting up at the start of each day to put on a well-pressed suit, and then falling asleep in it at the end of that same day, probably on his sofa, passed out drunk.

'What did she do, your mum?' Jack was a little overwhelmed by her curiosity, alien as it was.

'She was one of those, I guess you would say "multi-hyphenates". She met my dad at an exhibition of her photography – I think it must have been her student show, but later she was a poet, a painter, the whole shebang.'

'She sounds amazing, and then two kids on the side. I don't know how people do it.'

Jack was touched by the awe in her voice. 'She was amazing. I think she was lonely though. Mary was her only real friend in New York, I think, and then she went away . . .'

'Captain Mary?'

'The very one. I owe her a lot – she got me out.'

'Of New York?'

'Of New York yeah, of the life my dad had set for me, of everything really.' They lay in silence. They were both avoiding the topic of their transgression. Jack wanted to stay in this moment a little longer, before he had to face the fact that he would have to choose between these two women. The one who had given him a life and the one who made him feel so excited, if a little terrified, of living it.

'I feel like we only ever talk about me. What's your story, Harlow?' Jack wanted to move on from the subject of Captain Mary.

'Me? Nothing half as exciting. My parents met in London, moved down south, had me. That's it really.' He couldn't quite work out if she was deflecting, but as someone who often thought of his own backstory in suffocatingly ambivalent terms, he found the simplicity of her answer refreshing.

'Sounds idyllic,' Jack mused.

'I guess it kind of was, but I think in a weird way having everything my way, being free to do whatever I wanted, I was the one who had to put the pressure on myself. I had to become my own taskmaster, and I was so sure that I needed to be successful, to be a Michelin chef, that I never stopped to think if I wanted to be?' Sofia sounded uncertain, like she was wading through those thoughts for the first time. 'In London, I was right on track to achieve everything I had worked for, and then . . .' She stopped, looking embarrassed.

'And then it didn't make you happy?' Jack offered.

'Exactly, and I thought it must be something to do with me, some sort of self-sabotage or retribution for the charmed life I'd had.'

'I don't think it works like that, and anyway, it's pretty impressive stuff, to cook in a place like that at your age.'

Sofia rolled her eyes, bursting the delicate bubble of sincerity they had been building for themselves. 'Ease up on the old "when I was your age" stuff. You're only like five years older,' she scolded, but there was humour in her tone.

'Six,' Jack corrected. 'But I mean it, you don't get to be a sous chef at a place like Nakachwa by twenty-seven without being pretty exceptional.'

Sofia looked up at him, eyebrow raised. 'So you've

been doing your homework huh?'

He blushed, caught out. 'I may have read your CV, and done some light internet stalking before you started. I wanted to know who this "magnificently overqualified" chef that Mary kept going on about was.'

Sofia looked bashful. 'She really said that?'

'That was the least complimentary thing she said, but I don't want to go inflating your ego too much.' When she grinned at him, his heart soared, and he let himself enjoy it, rather than chastising himself as he had been doing.

# Chapter Thirty-One

## Jack

He thought back to that first day, when he had seen her walk into the mess. The girl from the bar, the one he had thought about all evening, even as he laughed and joked with his friends from back home. They had teased him as he returned to the table with an Aperol-tinted stain down his shirt, but he couldn't stop berating himself for not having asked her name. When she had walked out of the bar, amber-tinted curls flying in the wind, he had resisted the urge to run after her.

He couldn't remember now if he had just wanted to sleep with her, this lovely woman with long, smooth brown limbs, but she had certainly played on his mind. Then there she was, introducing herself politely in front of the rest of the crew, avoiding his gaze as he watched her, running through the funniest lines he could pull out to defuse the tension between them and maybe even get her to smile. He had failed miserably, of course, when she had finally looked at him with that expression of derision and he had made his weak joke about the spilled water, and she had been deeply unimpressed.

With Captain Mary watching on he'd had to remind himself what he was here for – his on-land antics would have to be put to one side. She had finally entrusted him with a first officer role and he wasn't about to mess that up for some pretty girl with hazel eyes.

She had introduced herself as 'Chef Harlow'. It seemed clear to him that she had no interest in his banter. She was there for the same reason as him: to work. He had resolved that he would try and suppress this little infatuation. He barely knew the woman anyway, and there were plenty of other pretty girls out there.

'I thought you hated me.' Sofia's voice broke through, suddenly clearing away the fog of his reminiscing. He looked down to marvel at her face, and brushed a strand of hair away from her eyes.

'Well, that was only because you hated me. You literally threw a drink over me the first time we met.'

Sofia slapped at his bare chest playfully. 'You look quite charming in orange I think, and anyway, that was only because you were very rude.'

'I thought that Brits loved a bit of banter.' He was aiming for cockney, but it came out sounding more Australian.

'Not with strange Americans I've only just met who push in at the bar.' Sofia giggled.

Jack feigned a shocked expression, covering his mouth with his hand.

'No you're right, it was all very improper.' His British accent was terrible, and he always enjoyed how much it seemed to rile her. This time she did not take the bait.

'No but for real, you always seemed to want to get away from me, when you weren't raiding my fridge.'

He smirked at that, thinking of how he had planned to apologise for his weirdly macho behaviour earlier that day, when he had told her she wouldn't be able to help load the boat up, even though he had, of course, been right. He had been nosing around, trying to piece together clues about this strange, mesmerising woman. The shelves in the fridge had been beautifully, if a little neurotically, organised. Fruits and vegetables piled high, and making up every colour of the rainbow.

The punnet of strawberries made him think of early summer in his grandmother's house. He and his mum would go out into the garden, when he was only as tall as her knee, and spy the bursts of scarlet among the bright green leaves. Each time he found one, he would hand it over, stretching all the way up to reach the box in her hands. It wasn't until the punnet was full that they would sit in the grass and gorge on the sweet fruit.

The taste of them brought him so clearly back to that moment, that he hadn't noticed Sofia come in until it was too late. Behind the fridge door her eyes were full of rage. The plump red berry in his hand might as well have been a grenade. The ensuing explosion was almost as destructive.

'I think you might have overreacted with the strawberries.' He was amused to see a flash of anger pass across her face. 'You're still angry about that now?'

Sofia seemed embarrassed for a moment, and then defiant. 'I am actually – it was my first day and I wanted everything to be perfect, how would you feel if you found me messing with some of your—' she reached for the right word '—ropes?'

'I would not mind you messing with my ropes one bit.' It was a lame joke really but it made her giggle. He was struck by how joyous it made him, to see her laugh. 'And to clarify, I never hated you, Sofia. I just always got the impression that I made you . . . I don't know, uncomfortable in some way. I could never quite say the right thing.'

It was the truth, but not the whole truth. He didn't want to admit that he was the one who often felt uncomfortable in her presence, that he could never quite understand the tension that festered between them. What's more he suspected that he hadn't wanted to understand it, better for them to clash occasionally and then avoid each other, than to give that 'tension' its proper name. The pact to stick to their half of the boat had given him some welcome respite, to actually concentrate on his job.

The morning on the deck, when he had seen a figure standing in the fog, his brain delirious from sleep, had convinced him it was his mother. The dark curls fluttering in the wind drew him closer. For a moment, after Sofia had turned round, he was frozen with shock. It was the stuff of dreams, and he wasn't entirely sure he was awake.

It was his domain – dawn on the deck – and there she was, radiant but also, as usual, very unhappy to see him. When she had taken a jab at him, he heard himself sounding like a petulant child, reminding her that this was *his* part of the boat, and for the rest of the day he felt embarrassed about it. He never lost his cool like that. He was exactly the privileged sulky man-child that she had accused him of being.

Petra had come to him in a state of despair. 'One stewardess down, a green deckhand and now our chef is having a panic attack about the menu,' she gushed breathlessly. He had thought she was exaggerating. Petra shook her head. 'No really, she's having a lie-down. I thought she was going to faint or something. That poor girl's perfectionism will be the death of her, I swear.'

He had stepped in, cooked up his 'signature' beef burgers, the only thing that his mother had ever taught him to cook, and incidentally, the only thing she actually could cook. He told himself he was doing it for Captain Mary, that he didn't want her to bear the brunt of the guests' displeasure, but if he was being totally honest with himself, he really didn't like the idea of Sofia getting in trouble either. Maybe this good deed would atone for his spiteful words that morning.

'I only just clocked the other day, after talking to Patricio, that that citrus grove you took us to, it's basically yours right?' Sofia had been trailing her fingers over his arms and chest, eyes closed, when the question rose from their contemplative silence.

'I mean, it's my grandmother's for the moment, but I guess one day it'll be mine.' She repositioned herself so she was facing away from him, taking his arm with her and remodelling him into the big spoon. 'But yeah, I wasn't worried about being arrested for trespassing or anything,' he murmured into the back of her head.

She sighed contentedly. 'I'll think of that day every time I cut into a grapefruit for the rest of my life,' she whispered. He smiled into her hair.

Declan had been a mess that morning. Jack smelled him before he saw him, a nauseating mix of body odour and vomit.

'There's absolutely no way you can come on the excursion today,' Jack had said sternly, as Declan groaned over the toilet bowl. They were a steward down, so Petra was already doing double the work and Stuart had to remain on board, which meant there was only one person he could ask to sub. Since their terse exchange on the deck they had successfully managed to only see each other at meal times, and he was going to have to propose a truce, at least for the day.

He had felt nervous going into the kitchen, his palms sweaty on the door handle, like some sort of teenage boy. In the end it had been much easier than he expected to convince her to come; perhaps she wanted to quash the bad blood as well, he thought.

He was a little ashamed to say that his first thought when Sofia stepped onto the tender was how good she looked in the stewardess uniform. The burgundy, which he had been certain up until that moment didn't suit anybody, somehow looked tasteful against her tanned, brown limbs. He suspected she had borrowed the uniform from waif-like Tabitha, because it was a little too tight and a little too short, but in all the right places. Jack had had to give himself a bit of a talking-to. It was one thing to admire women out in the world, but they were supposed to be working. He had to fight his pervy compulsion to steal a glance at her whenever she was bent over or looking in the other direction.

It was not entirely her fault then that the picnic box was left behind; he too had been preoccupied. She had looked so panicked when she realised her mistake, and Jack recognised that feeling, from his first few charters. When he had everything to prove and everything to lose, and it felt like there might be a parade of people waiting for you back home, all eager to remind you that they had 'told you so', that running away to sea would only end in disaster. He had done what he would have done for any member of the crew, but he was aware that her gratitude felt particularly bracing.

The citrus grove was the first time he knew, for certain, that he was in trouble. He had brought her into his world, even if she didn't know it. The grapefruits she ate were from the same trees he had picked as a boy. Her present rubbed up intimately with his past, and he had enjoyed it, to accompany this new person in this old world of his.

After the debacle with Brian and the sea urchin,

when they sat in the moonlight, toes soaked in sand, when the darkness and the alcohol had emboldened them to speak frankly, Jack felt a deep sense of calm. The sea, the sky and Sofia, everything seemed exactly as it should be – maybe that was what peace felt like, he'd thought. Nevertheless, if he wanted to keep his life, perfect as it now felt, the only place for Sofia would have to be as his friend. In the past he might have belittled the idea of the 'friend zone' as an acceptable place to end up, but with Sofia, it didn't feel like a consolation prize.

'Shall I turn the light off?' Jack breathed into Sofia's ear now. She stirred, blinking lazily, and turned her head to look at him out the side of her eye.

'I like it like this. It feels like the day isn't quite over yet,' she said, although she was closing her eyes again.

'At some point we're going to have to work out what to do about . . . everyone.' Jack dared to say what they had both been avoiding. Sofia just shook her head calmly and then brought his hand up to her mouth and planted a soft kiss on his palm.

*'Not tonight,'* she mouthed.

He stroked her cheek, mesmerised by her deepening breaths as she fell into sleep. Tomorrow they would have to work out a plan. He tallied up a list of people he was dreading having to tell.

He had felt envious of Declan's puppy love for Sofia, not because he wanted Sofia for himself, but because it was so joyfully uncomplicated. The way Declan spoke about her, and his adoration of her reminded Jack that for some people it wasn't so hard, to open themselves up like that. To Jack it seemed suicidal to wear your heart on your sleeve – you were just asking for someone to skewer it.

He had confided in Declan about Petra in a bid to warn him that no good would come of trying to start something with Sofia. He was also worried about his own feelings about Sofia, and sometimes when Declan would wax lyrical about her beauty or her food, Jack would find himself agreeing with him. In that way, telling Declan about his and Petra's tryst was also a way of throwing him off the scent. It was pretty clear from the off that Declan was a hopeless gossip, as well as a man in love. It was best for everyone that he not suspect for a moment that Jack had any feelings other than friendly disinterest and mild irritation towards Sofia.

When Declan recounted his sorry tale of rejection though, Jack had to admit to himself that he was relieved. He hated to see Declan's tender heart broken, but he had begun to understand the nature of his feelings enough to know that his own heart would have been bruised to see them together.

Jack reached over and turned off the light. Sofia was by now fast asleep. How strange it was to have her in his arms. Never mind his own mixed-up feelings, he had also had to convince himself that she felt nothing for him, and certainly not romantically. But up on the deck, when the others were on their day trip and it was just the two of them, he thought he had spied something like admiration in her eyes when she looked at him, or at least his bare chest. And then yesterday morning, in the dawn, when she had left him with his mother, he felt sure that she had wanted to stay and to hold him. When she was gone, he had missed her too.

# Chapter Thirty-Two

## Jack

Jack woke up in the dark, momentarily disorientated by the weight of Sofia's body at his side. He got out of bed slowly, so as not to disturb her, and closed the bathroom door behind him before he turned on the light. He stared at his reflection, dissociating as he scrutinised his own face. He thought that he looked different. He wondered how he could go about his day as if nothing had happened, how he could face Captain Mary without her seeing his transgression written plain across his face.

He splashed cold water over himself, and ran his hands through his hair, that tick of his that everyone seemed to find so infuriating. He remembered how his father had once slapped his hand away from his head, how it had only made him want to do it more often.

He took a deep breath. He would wake Sofia up and they would have to talk about what to do next, before the rest of the boat woke up. When he turned on the light, she was gone, the sheets crumpled into a pile. Maybe she had gone out to the deck, as had become their strange joint ritual, but out in the morning mist, there was no dreamy figure waiting for him by the railings.

The sun was beginning to come up and Jack was growing concerned that she was avoiding him, but also that they were running out of time to get their story straight. He searched the boat, starting in the kitchen. He could see the light was on and was so expecting to see her behind the door that he called, 'There you are, Harlow,' before it swung open to reveal the empty room.

The top deck, the large deck, the saloons, nothing. As he came back down the stairs to check the cabin again, he bumped into Captain Mary.

'Morning, Jack, I see you're up with the early birds as usual,' she said, seeming a little distracted.

He felt a flash of panic. He hadn't expected to have to face Captain Mary before he and Sofia had agreed on how to handle 'the situation'. He was convinced that Mary would be able to smell the guilt he felt was radiating off of him.

'Morning, Mary,' he said a little stiffly.

'Sofia's up and about as well. I just bumped into her.'

Jack's heart began to beat loudly in his chest. He tried to compose himself. 'Oh really?' He impressed himself with how nonchalant he sounded.

'Yes, she seemed a bit agitated.' Captain Mary paused, taking the time to mull over what to say next. 'She kept apologising to me – I'm not sure why. She said she was really enjoying her work, but that she kept "messing things up".' Captain Mary looked directly at Jack, her grey eyes probing. 'I know you two have been sharing a room. Is there anything you think I should know about?' The question hung in the air, heavy with implication, and Jack knew that he had to come clean.

'We slept together last night.' Jack hung his head in shame, missing the look of surprise that flashed across Captain Mary's face.

'It won't happen again. It was a mistake, and we both regret it.' As he said the words, he willed them to be true. Even if he didn't fully believe them now, he could come to.

Sofia had obviously come to the sensible conclusion, the one he had been too infatuated to come to. As much as there might be something between them, the job was what they were here for, and what was the point in sabotaging that, especially when they were both adamant they wanted to do the full season? Both of them had taken such big risks to choose this life. If they had wanted a happily ever after, the white picket fence, neither of them would even be on the boat.

'I'm so sorry, Mary, I know there's no excuse, but I promise that it's just sex, one stupid night. After we dock today, we'll be back in separate rooms and I will barely see her.' Jack spoke with a calm certainty that he did not feel.

'Well.' Captain Mary was momentarily lost for words. 'I wasn't expecting that.'

Jack's heart sank. He'd thought she already knew. He had shot himself in the foot, his own guilt exposing him as he had thought it would. He kept his expression placid.

'I'm going to have to think about all this, Jacky. You've

already had a warning, and I don't like the idea of this becoming some sort of pattern.' Captain Mary frowned at the thought, and Jack could see the disappointment in her face.

'I'll need to have a word with Sofia too of course.' She sighed heavily. 'It's a shame, she has such promise.'

'Please, Mary, it wasn't her fault. She probably hasn't even read the small print about crew relations. You gave me and Petra a caution; she deserves one too,' Jack pleaded.

Captain Mary nodded curtly. 'You make a good point, Jack, but this is my boat and I will run it at my own discretion. It would do you well to remember that, on this vessel, I am foremost your captain. Please address me as such.' Her tone had taken on a steely edge.

'Yes, Captain.' Jack stood up straight, staring straight ahead, an impervious expression on his face. As she walked away he tried to untangle the chaotic jumble of thoughts in his head. Striding back to the cabin in his officer's uniform, he gave off an air of composure, a swan whose legs were kicking furiously under the surface.

# Chapter Thirty-Three

When Sofia woke up in the bottom bunk, the sheets beside her still warm from Jack's body, she smiled into the darkness. It usually took her body some time to feel comfortable enough to sleep through the night with a man in her bed, perhaps it was an instinct to be on guard. With Jack she had slept soundly; in fact it was his absence that had stirred her. She figured he must be on deck. She slipped on her shoes and a jumper and left the cabin.

Out in the mist she couldn't see him. She did a circuit of both decks and then decided to head to the kitchen to make coffee; perhaps he had already come back inside by now, or popped to the bathroom.

She made coffee for two, in a Bialetti on the stove, the smell reminding her of home. Thinking about sharing her pre-dawn morning with him in the bunk made her heart beat a little faster. She was impatient for the water to boil.

Holding the two mugs, she skipped down the corridor. As she turned the corner she almost spilt both down the front of Captain's Mary's uniform.

'A close call there.' Captain Mary chuckled. Sofia burned with embarrassment. She felt flustered, caught out in her pyjamas, the two cups in her hand a telltale clue as to her indiscretions.

'Oh sorry, I wasn't looking where I was going!' she babbled. 'I thought I might as well make one for Jack, as I was in the kitchen anyway. Not sure where he's gone but I'm sure he'll be back any moment.' The words tumbled out.

'I'm sure he will. He likes the dawn, as I'm sure you've noticed. How is the room sharing going anyway?' Captain Mary seemed politely curious. Sofia blushed.

'It's going well,' she said brightly. 'He's umm, very knowledgeable about the boat and everything, so we've had some good chats about the yachtie life.' Half true, she thought.

'He's a great boatsman,' Captain Mary said. Sofia could hear the pride in her voice. 'And a hard worker. He can be a bit shy though, as unlikely as it seems, so it's nice he's been opening up to you.'

Sofia looked down; she couldn't meet the captain's eyes. 'Yes, he's been . . . very welcoming,' she enthused.

'And how are you finding your time on the boat so far? You seem to have taken to the lifestyle like a duck to water, pardon the pun.'

'I mean, it's been amazing. Thanks again for the opportunity. I know I have messed up a lot but everyone has been so helpful, and I'm learning.' She laughed anxiously. 'I won't be making the same mistakes again.'

The captain seemed taken aback. 'Messed up? I have only heard glowing reviews from the guests and crew alike. I think maybe you need to stop being so hard on yourself, Sofia.' The captain laid a gentle hand on her shoulder. 'Learn to live a little, as they say.' Her tone was sincere but Sofia let out an involuntary snort.

'Sorry, I don't know where that came from. It's just . . . that's not the first time I've heard that. Jack said it to me a little while ago.'

There was that proud smile again. 'Yes, well he does sometimes provide a few kernels of wisdom. You could say he's learnt from the best.' The captain smiled broadly at her before walking off.

Sofia stood still for a moment, running through the conversation. She'd slipped up by admitting to messing up, remembering too late that the others, especially Jack, had covered for her. Overall though she'd played it pretty well, she thought. Back in the cabin, Jack was still nowhere to be found, although the bathroom light was on, so he must have been there sometime this morning. She sat on the bunk and sipped her coffee.

She knew they had to talk to the captain, but she was feeling optimistic. It was clear to her that Jack loved his job, and he understood how much her career meant to her, so maybe they could prove to the captain that being together wouldn't affect their work. With his established relationship with the captain, she felt that together they could come up with a plan. This didn't have to be the doomed ending she'd feared.

As if she had willed them from her thoughts, she heard both their voices, from somewhere on the other side of the cabin door. Her first instinct was to go out and join them, but as she opened the door, she overheard a snippet of their conversation.

'I promise that it's just sex, one stupid night,' Jack was saying, his voice hard and unfeeling. 'After we dock today, we'll be back in separate rooms and I will barely see her.'

Sofia's blood ran cold, and she shut the door quietly. She sat back down on the bunk, staring at the full coffee cup, and waited for the tears to fall, but her eyes were dry.

A light knock on the door. 'Sofia, may I come in?' she scoffed to herself quietly. Just hours before he had been inside her, and now here he was performing as 'the gentleman'.

'Give me a moment,' she said flatly, quickly changing into her chef's whites and pulling her hair back into a tight bun. She would shower later. For now she just wanted to get away from him as fast as possible.

She opened the door to find him leaning against the opposite wall. He smiled at her gingerly. 'Are you off to cook breakfast already?' he asked sheepishly. His arms were crossed and he couldn't quite meet her eyes. She stomached a wave of disgust. How could he just stand there, as if last night had never happened?

'Yes,' she said stonily. She hoped he might say something else, but he just stared at his feet. She took it as her cue to leave and marched to the kitchen.

# Chapter Thirty-Four

Over the course of the morning, Sofia experienced a range of emotions. When the disgust had subsided, it was replaced by a blinding anger. She could hardly concentrate on making breakfast. Her scrambled eggs were overcooked and oversalted. When Petra walked into the kitchen she tried to put on a brave face.

She handed over the plates. Petra eyed them, and then Sofia, suspiciously.

'I've never seen you overcook an egg before.' Petra put the plates down and her hands on her hips. 'What's wrong?'

That's when the tears came. Petra enveloped her in a hug. 'Tell me what happened, Sofia. It's OK.' But hearing the care in her voice only made Sofia cry harder. It reminded her of how cared for she had felt, in Jack's arms, only hours ago.

As the tears dried hot and her cries turned to shaky breaths, Petra leant back, examining Sofia's face, her own steeped in worry. 'Please tell me,' she begged.

Sofia took a ragged breath. 'I slept with Jack.'

Petra's arms dropped to her sides in shock. 'Oh,' was all she said.

'I don't really know what came over me, but it was a mistake.' Now Sofia was feeling angry again, with herself. How had she let this happen? Hearing the words come from her own mouth, it seemed so obvious that Jack was right – it was a mistake, a slip-up, and it could never happen again.

Petra was clearly absorbing what she had just been told. Cautiously she said, 'What does he think about it?'

'He also thinks it's a mistake. I heard him telling Captain Mary this morning.' Sofia's voice broke and more tears started streaming down her cheeks.

'Oh, honey.' Petra pulled her in again. 'It's probably for the best. He's a lot of things, but boyfriend material is not one of them, and anyway you wouldn't both be able to keep working here if anything else happened, and I don't want to lose either of you!' Petra was trying to lighten the mood and Sofia smiled weakly.

'Sorry, I know this must be awkward for you, what with Jack . . .'

'Don't be silly.' Petra batted away Sofia's apology. 'That stuff is ancient history. I'm more worried about these eggs.' Sofia giggled half-heartedly. 'There you go, that wasn't so hard.' Petra took Sofia by the chin and levelled it with her own. 'Listen, Sofia, I know that this is going to feel like some awful case of history repeating itself, but it's not. These things happen and the best course of action you can take now is to buck up, laugh it off, and fake it till you make it.' Sofia nodded – maybe she could manage that?

'Now, for the love of God make me some more eggs. I can't possibly serve these up as they are.' They both chuckled. Sofia wiped her eyes and resolved that, unlike last time, she wouldn't let a man get the better of her and her work.

The second time around the eggs were silky, bright with fresh yolk and flecked with smoked salmon. 'Now there's the Chef Harlow I know,' Petra said appreciatively, blowing Sofia a kiss as she walked out the kitchen. In a way it had been exactly what she had needed, to redirect her pride into her cooking, forget about workplace romance, and concentrate on being the best she could be. That was the point of all this.

Afterwards she sent out the crew breakfast. 'Just tell them I'm not hungry.' She hoped Petra would deliver the line convincingly. She couldn't quite face up to sitting across from Jack yet.

Instead she decided to slave over a spectacular lunch – four courses, Milly's calorie counting be damned. She was determined to try and send their palettes on at least an excursion if not a full-on adventure. For the first course, an orange, radicchio and fennel salad with an anchovy dressing, which they had enjoyed the last time she'd snuck it into a dish. For the second course, a gorgonzola and pear risotto, with candied orange peel. After that she would serve a duck confit. She thought back to her days at Lochland Fleet's, his clipped, precise orders ringing out through the kitchen. Duck confit had been one of his signature dishes, one that had taken him years to perfect in Paris, where he had trained.

The key, he said, was the marinade. It had to be left to sit for at least twenty-four hours. In her time under Lochland's tutelage, Sofia had discovered a different method. It involved less time, but she would have to massage the duck, in its marinade, at least every hour. It was more labour-intensive. The duck would essentially need her attention for the whole day. Today, she couldn't think of anything better than clearing her mind of errant thoughts with a fixation on a duck leg.

At first Lochland had been unimpressed, bordering on incensed by the idea. He had scolded her, every time she broke rank and scuttled to the fridge to tenderise the duck. When it came time for tasting, Sofia had been a bundle of nerves, imagining what form his derision might take. She had never forgotten the feeling she had gotten when he put the fork to his lips, chewed and then smiled. It was pure elation.

The other students in her class grumbled when he sang her praises, complaining that he had told them how to prepare the duck the best way and weren't they there to learn from him? From the best?

'Indeed you can learn from the best but that does not mean you can learn to *be* the best,' he had said calmly, and then motioning towards Sofia. 'True greatness, in the kitchen, as in life, comes from knowing, instinctually, when to follow the rules, and when to break them.' It was the first time in her life that Sofia had been sure she was on the right path. Maybe it was the last time as well, she thought now, as she dug the heels of her palms into the flesh.

For dessert, she would keep it simple, but continue her orange flavour theme. The crème brûlée too would be flecked with zest. Sofia didn't leave the kitchen all morning. In the steam, the sizzle, and the smells she could lose herself, laser her focus onto a singular slice of fennel, or spoonful of browning butter.

It was Patricio who came to collect the first dish. His eyes widened when he came in and he saw every inch of the counter space littered with utensils, bowls, chopping boards.

'Whoa, Mama is making a feast today!' he exclaimed. 'It smells magnificent in here.' Sofia grinned, the pride swelling in her chest and driving away that persistent pearl of shame in the pit of her stomach.

'I just thought I'd send them off with their bellies full.' They would be docking in Gaeta that afternoon and Brian and Milly would not be eating dinner on the boat.

'Miss Amelia is a little concerned about the four courses, but Mr Brian looks thrilled I must say.' Patricio picked up the plates. The segments of orange intertwined with the charred fennel, topped with pomegranate seeds that caught the light like gems. '*Bellissimo,*' he said, almost to himself.

The next three courses went out in quick succession, each replacing the pristinely clean plate that Patricio returned. Sofia was buzzing. When the crème brûlée went out and she set to cleaning up manically, she found herself worrying about the crash that was surely just around the corner. As if on cue, Petra burst through the door, a single shot glass in hand.

'I wanted to wait until you were done. The food today, Sofia, was beautiful. They both loved it.' Petra was also glowing with pride; Sofia was touched. 'And now I think you deserve one of these, after the past twenty-four hours you've had.' Petra handed her the glass. The vodka burned, but Sofia welcomed the numbing haze.

'OK, we'll have them off the boat in about an hour, and you better be ready to party. We are going hard tonight.' Sofia remembered her earlier resignation about going out again.

Maybe it was the alcohol, or maybe it was Petra's infectious enthusiasm, but suddenly she couldn't think of anything better than whiling away the night dancing to Europop. Jack would be there of course, but she supposed she would have to face him sooner or later, and a little Dutch courage might smooth the process.

Sofia headed back to the cabin and when she saw that Jack's things were gone she was, above all, relieved. The mould expert must have come straight onto the boat as soon as it had docked. As she undressed she tried to ignore the niggling undercurrent of longing. Despite everything there was a tiny, delusional part of her that mourned his absence.

She finally had a shower. The scalding water washed

away the last traces of the night before from her body. Next the sheets, which smelled of him, went into the laundry, and then her pyjamas, the ones she had worn when he offered to tend to her burn, were sent off to be boiled too. The only thing left to erase were her still-vivid memories. She had a plan for those, a plan that involved more of Petra's vodka.

Sofia went on the hunt. When she saw Captain Mary at the top of the stairs she considered throwing herself into the nearest cupboard to avoid whatever hellish conversation she would surely have to have. But the captain spotted her, waving for her to come. Sofia was expecting a telling-off right there and then but the interaction was far more unsettling. The captain gave her a shallow smile, the type that didn't reach her eyes.

'It's not really the time now, but could you come and find me in the morning, Sofia? I would like to get some things straight.' Both women knew exactly what was being spoken about, but the polite ambiguity had the effect of sending a shiver down Sofia's spine.

'Of course, I'll come up to your quarters about midday?' Sofia matched the captain's civil tone, throwing in a superficial smile of her own.

'Perfect.' A curt nod and Captain Mary was gone. *If this is to be my last night on board, I better make it one to remember, or forget,* she thought wryly.

# Chapter Thirty-Five

As the crew piled into the mess, Sofia noticed that Jack was not there, something she was both grateful for and keenly aware of. Every time someone came in or out of the room, she found herself unable to relax until she checked who it was.

Petra leant in close. 'Don't worry, I don't think he's coming.'

Sofia wanted to know why, but instead she said dryly, 'I'm not worried. I'm over it, remember.'

Petra whooped, drawing attention to what had been a discreet aside. 'That's the spirit, girl!'

'What are you two bambinos chattering about?' Patricio, like Declan, was a bloodhound for gossip and the two of them crowded around the girls, leaving Stuart to sip his whisky alone at the table. He was looking a little dejected tonight, Sofia thought.

Petra gave Sofia a look, a look that begged, *Can I tell them?* Sofia knew it was probably a bad idea to expose her ill-advised personal life to her colleagues, but the drinking was already holding her better judgement hostage. She shrugged and then nodded.

Petra beamed. The cat who's got the cream, or very

salacious gossip. 'Sofia, well she hooked up with Jack.'

Patricio trilled his tongue, slapping Sofia on the back with a force that left her momentarily fearing she might lose balance.

Declan was quiet, and then softly he asked, 'Really?' He was looking straight at Sofia. If she had thought that his feelings towards her had completely dissipated, the hurt in his eyes told another story.

She felt awful, and heard herself repeating the words that had cut her so deeply that very morning: 'It was just sex, it didn't mean anything.'

Declan just nodded, looking away. Sofia felt like she'd broken his heart all over again.

Noticing that the air had grown heavy, Patricio valiantly tried to recover the mood. 'Just the sex? OK, honey, tell us all about it. Is he as good as all the ladies say?'

Sofia couldn't help herself, dryly asking, 'All the ladies?'

Patricio laughed, a little uneasily, his attempt at repairing some levity falling flat. 'Well, you know, when he came back to Capri, there was always some commotion. It's a very small island . . .'

Sofia wasn't surprised. She'd heard before that Jack had a reputation. Why then did it feel like a punch in the stomach hearing Patricio talk about Jack's salacious past?

Sofia wanted to change the subject. 'So where are we going out tonight then?'

Patricio too seemed relieved that they were talking

about something else. 'I have a friend who owns a bar just down from the marina. It is just a small place but she says we can drink for free, so . . .'

'So it's perfect!' interrupted Petra. She had stayed silent amid the exchange of strange tensions, swaying slightly from side to side, but now she was back in the room.

'I think we should head out before eleven,' Petra announced, gesturing over at Stuart. 'What do you think, Mr Keep to Yourself, over there?'

Stuart shrugged. 'Whatever you want, Petra.'

Sofia wondered what had gone on between them. In the midst of her own drama she had neglected to check in. She thought about her old friends back in London, how she had placed herself at the centre of a story that turned out to be about Erica's pain, and felt a pang of shame. She seemed to lose her ability to be a good friend in direct correlation with the romantic turmoil in her own life. She needed to work on that.

Despite herself, Sofia looked back at the boat one last time as they stumbled across the dock, half expecting to see Jack running to catch up. As Petra had predicted, he had never shown up. Sofia tried to ignore what she feared was a sense of disappointment and determined that tonight would be about her friends.

When they arrived at the bar, they were all drunk, Patricio and Petra merrily so, the other three in varying degrees of ennui. Sofia was trying her best to have a good time, but Declan and Stuart were doing a less convincing job. Both were sullen, throwing back drinks but refusing to dance.

Petra went out to steal a cigarette off someone. As Sofia danced with Patricio, his arms tight against her waist as he dipped her dramatically, she spotted Stuart suddenly looking animated, stood by the bar, chatting with a pretty, dark-haired woman who seemed to be laughing a little too hard at whatever he was saying.

When Petra came back in to join them, she pointed over at the pair as soon as she saw them. 'Who is that Stuart is talking to?' she shouted over the music, right into Sofia's ear.

'No idea, but they're looking a bit cosy right?' Sofia shouted back.

Petra frowned. They kept dancing but Sofia could see Petra straining to keep an eye on the activity at the bar. Sofia was facing away from it when Petra stopped suddenly in her tracks, as if the music had been cut off in a game of musical chairs. Sofia swung around in time to see Stuart locked into a passionate kiss with the woman he'd been talking to.

Sofia wasn't sure how Petra would react. She suspected that her friend had feelings for Stuart, but she had always denied them, and maybe they really were just friends. Something about her expression in that moment, though, told Sofia that even if Petra herself hadn't realised it until just then, she could no longer pretend that there was nothing between them.

As Patricio spotted the scene, whopping and clapping encouragingly, Stuart leant back, the lipstick smeared across his chin matching the rising blush creeping up his neck. In the commotion, Petra rushed for the door and Sofia glanced over to see Stuart's face drop as his eyes followed her out the bar.

Outside, Petra had procured herself another cigarette. She was sitting on the kerb when Sofia found her. Petra offered her a drag as Sofia settled down beside her. Sofia shook her head.

'Talk to me,' Sofia said gently.

Petra sighed. 'What is there to say really? If I were giving myself advice, it would be the same that I gave you this very morning . . . Let it go.'

'I didn't think you liked him like that,' Sofia probed, and Petra gave her a bemused look.

'Didn't you?' She smirked.

'Well,' Sofia conceded, 'I suspected of course, but when you said you were just friends, I don't know . . . that also made sense to me.' She thought back to those precious moments with Jack where she had thought they might be friends. In retrospect, maybe that's what she should have held on to, instead of making everything so difficult and tense by giving in to a crush.

'I just didn't want to make the same mistake all over again. The captain made it clear that she wouldn't tolerate any kind of relationships on board.' Petra's voice pulled back Sofia out of her own thoughts. 'It was fine with Jack because there were no real feelings there . . . but Stuart.' She stopped as if afraid that saying it out loud might make it too painful to bear.

'We've only had that one drunken kiss, so I guess this is all a complete over-reaction from me. He obviously moves fast—' she gestured vaguely at the bar behind them '—so it's probably all in my head, whatever I thought was going on.'

Sofia thought about how many times she had had this exact conversation with the women in her life, and many more times she would have it in the future. It was a sort of universal phenomenon that when they were left feeling hurt and confused, the blame would be turned inwards. It was their fault for 'misinterpreting the signs' or for 'expecting too much'.

'For what it's worth, Petra, you're not delusional. The way he looks at you, I've seen it. You're not imagining anything.'

Petra had a go at a smile, her eyes welling. 'We really must stop all this crying,' she said sternly, shaking her head and swiping her finger under her eye to fix up her running mascara.

Sofia stood up and held out her hand, pulling Petra to her feet. 'Fake it till you make it,' she said as she fixed Petra's fringe. When they went back inside, Petra danced even harder than before, with her back to Stuart.


It was only when it came time to leave that anyone realised that Declan had disappeared. While Stuart had been otherwise occupied at the bar and the other three had been dancing the night away, Declan had slipped away from his quiet spot in the corner.

'I thought you two were together.' Patricio was looking around anxiously, but talking to Stuart.

'He was otherwise occupied, I believe,' Petra interjected, a bitter edge to her voice.

Stuart looked agitated. 'I swear he was right there. I only looked away for . . . for a bit.' He faltered, stuffing his hands in his pockets and looking defeated. 'I'm sorry, everyone.' It was hard to tell if he was apologising for losing sight of Declan, or something else.

Sofia felt sorry for him. 'It's not your fault, Stuart; you're not his babysitter. He can't have gone too far. Anybody got his number?'

They all checked their phones.

'How do I not have his number?' Patricio exclaimed, frustrated.

'We all live together all the time. It's one of those weird quirks of yachting – it never seems the right time to exchange contact details,' Petra said as she scrolled through her contact list. 'Jack might have his number?' She glanced over apologetically at Sofia as she said this. 'I'm going to give him a call and see.'

As the phone rang they stood outside in silence, waiting for the pick-up. Eventually Jack's voice rattled through. 'It's three o'clock in the morning, Petra. What's going on?'

Petra got straight to the point. 'We've lost Dec. Do you have his number?' Rustling on the other end and then a sigh.

'I'm coming to find you guys. Where are you?'

'There's no need, Jack. We don't need a knight in shining armour; we just need his number.' Petra raised her eyebrows at Sofia knowingly as she spoke.

'I'll send it over to Stuart now. Stay on the line with me. I want to see if he picks up.' Even in absentia, Jack was taking control of the situation. Stuart's phone pinged, and he dutifully dialled. All Sofia could hear was their steady breathing and the continuous ring. Declan didn't pick up before it went to voicemail.

'OK, I'm on my way. Send me your location.' Jack hung up before Petra had the chance to respond. She did as she was told.

'What if he's hurt?' Patricio asked, his voice full of genuine worry. 'Declan! Declan!' he yelled up and down the street.

Petra put a comforting hand on his shoulder 'I'm sure he's fine.'

It was hard to believe her. If his phone was off and he was drunk and wandering back towards the marina alone . . . Sofia shook the thought from her head.

Everyone was restless, and having to wait for Jack felt like a waste of precious time. 'I'm going to go look for him,' Patricio declared, marching off.

'Wait . . .' Petra tried to call after him, but it was useless. 'Great now we're two down.' She checked her phone again. 'Where is he, dammit?' she muttered under her breath.

Her phone rang just then and the three of them

jumped. Petra checked the caller ID, waving Stuart and Sofia away as they peered over her shoulder. 'It's just Jack.'

'I've found him,' Jack said simply. They all let out a sigh of relief. 'But you better come meet me. He keeps saying he doesn't want to talk to me.'

'Where are you?' asked Petra.

'Literally just by *Lady Shelly*. He's sat right here, legs swinging off the pontoon, no idea where he got a bottle of vodka from . . .' Jack tailed off.

In the background of the call, Sofia could faintly hear Declan yelling, 'You betrayed me, man. You lied to me!'

'What's he talking about?' Petra was hearing it too.

'I don't know.' Jack's tone was defensive, clipped. 'Can you just come and help me out with him?'

'On our way, Captain Jack.' Petra hung up. 'Now where the hell is Patricio?'

Earlier it had seemed like such a long way, but sobered by the events of the evening, Sofia noted that the walk was only about fifteen minutes.

When they got to the boat, Declan was wailing incomprehensibly into the dark, bottle in hand, legs swinging over the water. Jack stood to one side a few feet behind him, talking furtively with Patricio, who'd found his own way back to the harbour. As Sofia, Petra, and Stuart approached, Jack and Patricio stopped talking abruptly, both crossing their arms. Side by side like this, Sofia's drunk brain thought that Patricio looked like Jack in miniature.

'There you are, Patricio. We thought we'd have to send out another search party!' Petra exclaimed.

Jack caught Sofia's attention and she searched his eyes for any sign of the tenderness they had held the night before. But the green was frosted and he looked away quickly, addressing Stuart. 'We can't let the captain see him. Can you help me get him on board?' Jack was all business.

Stuart and Jack flanked Declan, each bending to grab an arm. Declan flailed like a wild animal. 'Get off me, man. I mean it.' The venom directed at Jack took everyone by surprise.

'He's only trying to help,' Sofia said, her voice barely more than a whisper.

Declan sniggered, but there was a meanness in it. 'Oh of course, the two lovebirds sticking together. What a surprise.'

Jack stepped away from Declan, clearly taken aback. No one spoke for a moment.

It was Patricio who braved the silence. 'I'm going to head back on board.'

Stuart jumped on the life raft. 'Me too,' he said, jogging after Patricio.

Petra turned to Sofia. 'Do you want me to leave you?'

Sofia knew that this was her mess to sort out. She nodded. Petra shot Jack a look.

'Let's try and remember that it takes two to tango, Jacky. If there is to be any blame, you can't lay it all at Sofia's door.' When Jack didn't respond, she waited, hands on her hips.

'Yeah OK, sure,' he muttered finally. Petra didn't look satisfied by the response but she took it, running to catch up with the others.

Sofia was left with Declan and Jack. *How had it come to this?* she wondered.

Jack didn't even look at Sofia when he said stonily, 'I see you took it upon yourself to tell everyone about . . .' He paused and she held her breath. She wanted to know more than anything what exactly he thought last night had been. 'Us,' he concluded, and she let out the breath, none the wiser.

'Well, after you took it upon yourself to tell the captain, it seemed only fair that everyone else should know too.' She felt defiant; maybe it was the shots still coursing through her blood. She wasn't going to just lie back and take it.

Jack scoffed, 'Oh right, like I was the one who ran away?'

'I went to make us coffee, Jack.' Sofia was indignant. Jack's expression flickered, the stony mask slipping for a moment, and Sofia thought she spotted something like surprise, or maybe regret.

Their exchange was interrupted by a loud sob coming from Declan. 'I want to talk to Sofia.' He sounded like a toddler having a tantrum.

Sofia took one last look at Jack. He didn't say anything, just ran his hand through his hair exasperatedly. It was up to her to fix this mess, it seemed. She sat down tentatively next to Declan. He wrapped his arms around her, the bottle falling into the water below with a loud splash. Declan buried his head in the nape of her neck and started crying softly. Sofia pulled him closer.

'I'll leave you two to it.'

'OK.' She didn't turn around as Jack walked off.

# Chapter Thirty-Six

Sofia waited until Declan's cries had quietened. She wondered if all charters were this dramatic. Something about the close quarters and proximity to so much water seemed to bring everyone closer to tears. She pulled away so that she could turn to look at him.

'Tell me what's going on, Declan.'

He sniffed, scrubbing at his eyes and nose. 'I don't really know, Sofia. I'm so confused. Everything is so . . . intense.'

'Preaching to the choir,' she said dryly.

'I don't know what's going on with you and Jack, but I really liked you, Sofia, and I thought I was over it or whatever but . . .' He hung his head.

'I wasn't thinking, Declan. I'm sorry. I was so wrapped up with it – I mean, I'm probably as confused as you.' Sofia didn't know what else so say. She felt overwhelmed by the seesawing. Every relationship she had on this boat seemed to be in constant flux; it was hard to know where you stood.

'I've never liked a girl like that before,' Declan said quietly. Sofia's heart heaved. 'If I tell you something, can you promise to keep it a secret?'

It was the least she could do. 'Of course,' she said.

Declan looked scared for a moment and then determined. 'Usually, I like boys.' He searched her face as if expecting a certain reaction. 'I've never said that out loud to anyone before.'

Sofia smiled encouragingly. 'That's OK, Declan, thanks for telling me.'

'Except it's not really OK. I can't tell my parents, or my sisters. They always say that "all that stuff is for white people".' It might not have been completely appropriate but Sofia couldn't help but let out a yelp of laughter. She was grateful to see Declan crack a smile.

'You might be surprised, you know. Parents say all sorts of stuff about other people, but when it's their own kids, it's usually a different story.'

'Maybe.' He shrugged. 'I think part of me was really relieved that I finally fancied a girl.' He looked suddenly bashful. 'Sorry, a woman.' Sofia reached out and squeezed his hand.

'When you rejected me, it felt like my chance at living a normal life was over.'

'You call this a normal life?' Sofia gestured around. There they were, sitting on the edge of harbour, legs swinging over the inky ocean at 4 a.m., under the glow of the moon and the holiday yachts of the super-rich.

'Fair point,' Declan conceded wryly. They sat in a peaceful silence and then Declan got another wind.

'I'm also pissed at Jack though. He was all like: "You should tell her how you feel; I'm rooting for you, man."

273

What a load of rubbish.'

Sofia had never seen Declan angry. It didn't suit him at all. It was strange to think of them talking about her like that, but if Declan thought she had any insight into Jack's motivations, he was about to be sorely disappointed.

'To be honest with you, I have no idea what's going inside that man's head. Last night he was so . . .' She caught sight of Declan's expression and cut herself off short. 'Never mind. The point is, he's all mixed up. You could drive yourself crazy trying to figure him out – take it from me.'

'Men.' Declan rolled his eyes, and then they both burst into a fit of giggles.

'I'm no expert, but it sounds to me like you like boys *and* girls. Also, you're twenty-two, so you've got time to work it all out.' Sofia wanted to ask about Patricio, but she thought better of it. There was only so much soul searching a person could do in one night. Even for the relentless drama mill that was the *Lady Shelly*, this had been a full-on day.

'I think we should probably go to bed.' Declan stood up suddenly, and Sofia grabbed onto his leg as he swayed precariously.

'Easy now, let's take it slow shall we?' Sofia draped his arm around her shoulder and they made their way back to the boat. When they reached Declan's cabin, Patricio opened the door before they got to the handle.

'Oh thank goodness, I was sick with worry.' Patricio took over from Sofia, fussing over Declan. Sofia smiled sadly to herself as she walked back to her cabin. Declan was better off without her. Love was supposed to be simple and everything she touched seemed to become more complicated.

Back in her cabin, she paused at the sight of the bottom bunk, stripped and empty. She felt silly as she climbed up the ladder, but it would have been strangely sacrilegious to go to sleep where they had been together. She needed to preserve some proof that it hadn't just been another dream.

# Chapter Thirty-Seven

Sofia slept in, a rare privilege afforded to her by the absence of Milly and Brian that morning. The longer she stayed in bed though, the more terrifying leaving the protection of her cabin felt. She had to face the captain at some point. As the clock neared twelve, she had already run through a dozen ways their conversation might go.

She hauled herself out of bed and into the shower, channelling her anxious energy into the long put off task of detangling her hair. She stood in front of the mirror and let the worst-case scenario play out in her mind. Sometimes the exercise calmed her, but today the image of her wheeling her case off the boat brought her close to hyperventilating.

She took a deep breath and ventured into the corridor. She was glad not to bump into anyone on her way upstairs. Tentatively she knocked on the door of the office. When the captain opened the door, she was smiling.

'Come in, Sofia, take a seat.' If the friendly tone was supposed to ease her nerves, it wasn't working at all. There were two armchairs on one side of the desk and she stood awkwardly for a moment, paralysed by the choice. Captain Mary sat down and pointed to the chair on the left. Sofia was grateful.

'Now, Sofia, I'm assuming you know what I would like to talk about today?'

Sofia's palms were sweaty. 'I think so,' she said cautiously.

'Officer Carter informed me yesterday about your . . . relations.' The formality of it all made her feel like the naughty schoolgirl, sent to the principal's office.

'I am also assuming that you *have* read my rules and you are aware that we have a no-fraternisation policy when it comes to staff relationships. The only people that are allowed to umm . . .' Sofia realised that the captain was probably just as uncomfortable as she was '. . . have sex on this boat, are the guests, and exclusively with each other. Do you understand that?'

'I do.'

'Now Officer Carter has told me that it was a one-time occurrence and that you have no plans to repeat your mistakes.' Sofia flinched at that last word, but she nodded effusively.

'I think that's wise,' the captain continued, 'and I also think it best that you both exercise your discretion and keep the matter between yourselves.' Sofia looked down at her hands, visibly ashamed. She heard the captain sigh softly.

'That is, unless it is too late for that?'

'I'm so sorry, Captain, I don't know what came over me. I wasn't . . . thinking straight.'

The captain raised an eyebrow. She was unimpressed

to say the least.

'Might I hazard a guess that this lapse in "thinking" was last night?'

Somehow it was going even worse than her overanxious brain could have fathomed. 'Yes,' she said, unable to meet the captain's gaze.

'Well in that case, I really will have to think about your future on this boat.' And there they were, the words that Sofia had been waiting, with dread, to hear. 'If the rest of the crew knows about this dalliance, it really does make it hard for me not to be seen to take action.' The captain seemed a little exasperated. It was unsettling to see her lose even a fraction of her cool.

'It's just such a shame, Sofia, because you really are a great chef. I would have loved to keep you on permanently, but it will be very difficult to have the both of you on board.' Sofia had a sickening flash of déjà-vu. She had already been in this position, only a couple of months before, with Joy sitting opposite her.

'Please, Captain, I know what I did was wrong, but you gave me a chance once when I really needed one, and I'm begging you for just one more. I won't let you down again.'

Sofia wasn't just fighting for her job, she was fighting for herself, like she hadn't done last time. 'I've loved my time in your kitchen, and I'm just asking for one more shot to prove to you that that *is* what I'm here for. Jack . . .' She stumbled over her words. 'I mean Officer Carter – he's not why I'm here. I'm not looking for a love story; I'm here to be the best chef I can be, and if that means I never talk to Officer Carter again, I can do that.' She sat up a little straighter, looking defiant.

Captain Mary leant back in her chair, taking her time to consider her options. 'OK, Sofia,' she said after a long pause. 'You have one more chance. Consider the rest of this charter your opportunity to impress me, and I'll think about the permanent role.'

Sofia wanted to kiss the captain's feet. 'Thank you, thank you so much. I won't let you down.'

The captain held up her hand, cutting her off. 'As for Officer Carter, I'm afraid you simply won't be able to completely avoid each other, but might I suggest you try and keep your interactions civil and . . . professional.'

'Of course.' Sofia thought she might cry with relief.

'I see a lot of myself in you, Sofia. Don't disappoint me.' The captain's tone was stern but Sofia thought she spied a fleck of sympathy in her eyes. Sofia scrambled to her feet as the captain opened the door for her.

'See you at dinner.' And with that, the door swung closed, and Sofia was left standing in the corridor.


As she walked down the stairs, she spotted Jack through a window. He and Declan were kneeling in front of what looked like a vent. They were both concentrating, but they seemed comfortable enough around each other. Sofia wondered if they had discussed what happened last night, or swept it all under the rug.

Sometimes she envied the ease of male friendships; other times she felt resentful that it always seemed to fall on the women present to get to the bottom of the things they were trying to leave unsaid.

She automatically headed for the kitchen and then realised she didn't really have anything to do before dinner. It was so rare that she wasn't rushed off her feet that Sofia was at a loss. She decided to go and find Petra.

The laundry room was stuffy and humid, but there was something so cosy about the smell of freshly ironed linens that it made her homesick. In London her small studio hadn't been big enough for a washing machine so she would often spend her Mondays off at the laundrette, watching a film on her phone as people literally aired their dirty laundry in public. The rhythm of life was so different on board. It was strange not to have those moments of private domesticity.

Petra's ironing was mesmerisingly efficient. Sofia began folding towels and sheets from the dryer.

'Not those, I'm going to iron those.' Petra thrust her chin in the direction of the lace-scalloped pillowcase in Sofia's hand.

'That's true luxury. I don't think I've ever ironed my bed sheets.' Sofia said it offhandedly. She wasn't expecting the look of horror that flashed across Petra's face.

'I'm sorry, I just didn't realise I was in the presence of a teenage boy,' Petra scolded.

Sofia couldn't help but laugh. 'Wait, do you?'

'Of course! It's about the little things, you know. I'm

very house proud.' All the hours they had spent gossiping and baring their souls, and Sofia had never asked about Petra's home life, what it was she had left behind. She didn't even really know where she was from.

'Where is home for you, anyway?' Now Sofia was curious.

'Well, I was born just outside Melbourne but I was working in Sydney before I left.' Petra chuckled to herself. 'I was supposed to go to Europe for six months, but six years later and here I still am.'

'And where do you go in the off-season?' Sofia somehow couldn't really imagine Petra doing things like food shopping or paying council tax.

'I have a tiny flat in Brighton that I rent out when I'm away, and then I spend the first week back cleaning it compulsively from top to bottom.' Petra was huffing over a persistent crease.

She put down the iron and looked up at the ceiling thoughtfully. 'I actually bought it last year, never imagined I'd be able to afford it. I promised myself once I had that stability I would find a "normal job" and settle down.'

'What happened?'

'Oh you know, I got the call from Captain Mary and the call of the high seas was too much to resist.' Her sarcastic tone made it hard to tell how much truth was buried in the humour. Sofia waited, hoping the silence might draw her out. It worked.

'Maybe part of me is scared? That if I stop moving I might just look around and realise there's no one around me.' Petra hurriedly went back to her ironing. 'I don't know, just your run-of-the-mill, mid-thirty-something paranoia about dying alone.'

'Nah, you'll always have Captain Mary.' Sofia tried to lighten the mood, but Petra's polite smile was a sad one.

For a few minutes the room was only filled with the sounds of hissing steam and the thudding of the dryer. Sofia needed to scramble onto safer conversational ground, but every topic she thought of seemed fraught with controversy.

'Well last night was interesting.' She hoped the statement was vague enough that Petra would feel comfortable guiding it in whichever direction she wanted.

'That's putting it mildly. I think this boat is cursed. The moment the captain made that rule, Cupid's evil twin has been running rampant.' She counted off on her fingers. 'On this charter alone we've had you and Jack, you and Declan, me and Brian . . .' She blushed as she said this but Sofia couldn't help but interject.

'You and Stuart!'

'Well I'm not counting unrequited, undeclared crushes,' Petra said firmly, as if the rules were obvious.

'Well you're counting Declan's unrequited crush and I'm not sure you can dismiss a drunken kiss as "undeclared" anything, so . . .' Sofia smiled devilishly, and Petra rolled her eyes.

'Fine, Stuart and I,' she conceded, with another finger. 'I don't know what your read is, but honestly whatever is going on with Patricio and Declan, that's at least a half strike.' She thrust her hand in the air emphatically. 'Almost five infractions, and we're only just over halfway through the charter.'

Sofia reflected on how little time had actually passed since she had met everyone, thirteen days to be precise, but already they felt like family, the dysfunctional sort that you argue with, sure, but also people she felt she could rely on.

Patricio popped his head round the door. 'Petra, I'm just finishing up the guests' suite and I'm a little worried. I think I've found more . . .' He stopped short when he saw Sofia, and she was surprised to see his eyes turn cold.

'Oh, hello, Sofia. I didn't realise you were here.' There was a definite hardness to his voice, which was all the more disconcerting coming from him.

'I'm just killing some time until dinner – nothing to do with the guests out for lunch!' she said cheerily.

Patricio pursed his lips. 'Nothing to do for *you* perhaps,' he said snootily, before flouncing out of the room.

Sofia turned to Petra, whose eyebrows were as raised as Sofia's own.

'Well, that was . . .' Petra began.

'. . . passive-aggressive to the extreme? OK I'm glad I'm not imagining it.' Sofia was baffled.

'Well that just confirms my suspicions,' Petra said with a knowing look.

Sofia was a beat behind.

'Isn't it obvious?' Petra continued, but Sofia looked

blank. 'He's jealous. He's obviously mad about Declan, and after last night he knows that you're his love rival.'

'Love rival? Isn't that a little overly dramatic?' Sofia wasn't convinced.

'Have you met Patricio?'

'Just when I put out one fire,' Sofia huffed, exasperated, 'ten more pop up to replace it.'

'Funny that! It's almost like somebody should make a rule to avoid all this unnecessary competition and tension.'

Sofia had to laugh. It was all so absurd, but if she didn't laugh, she might cry. 'So do you think I'll have to challenge him to a duel or something, to restore his honour?' Sofia was joking, but at this point it didn't even feel completely out of the realms of possibility; maybe it was a yachtie tradition she just hadn't heard of yet.

'I reckon a couple of sweet treats and the passing of time will do the trick,' Petra mused.

'Yes, because that worked so well with Declan,' Sofia muttered under her breath. 'Anyway I better go. It's about time to start prepping, and I can leave you to your perfectly pressed pillowcases.'

'See you later.' Petra blew Sofia a kiss as she walked out.

# Chapter Thirty-Eight

Sofia was in the kitchen, slicing wafer-thin lengths of courgette when her radio cracked to life. She jumped, as she was prone to doing, and the knife slipped into her finger. The pain was instant and sharp. She instinctively brought it to her mouth, swearing quietly out of the corner of her lips. She found a plaster and grabbed the radio.

'Chef Harlow? Emergency meeting in the mess now, over.' It was Jack's voice, but unfamiliar, distant and steely, like it had been on that first day when he had withdrawn into himself.

'On my way, over,' she said stonily. Two could play at that game.

She wondered when she might have an uneventful day on this boat. How could they be facing yet another 'emergency'. Patricio was in full swing when she walked in.

'It is not just in the wardrobe. When I pulled the bed back this morning, well firstly it was clear it had not been cleaned back there for a long time.' He shot a look at Petra as he said it. He seemed to be in a generally bitchy mood then, thought Sofia. Petra's diagnosis of this morning's incident might not be as accurate as she feared.

285

'And secondly, the wall, it was covered in mould. *Dios mio*, I tried to tell Petra as soon as I could but she was distracted.' He clutched at his chest and Sofia had to suppress the urge to scoff out loud.

'So our mould guy didn't do a very thorough inspection then?' Petra said defensively.

'There is little use in doling out blame now. I will give him a call and see if he can come back before our guests return.' Nothing could flap Captain Mary. She pulled out her phone and dialled, addressing the man on the other end in what sounded to Sofia like fluent Italian.

'*Quindi non potete venire fino a domani?*' Sofia had picked up just enough to know that *domani* meant tomorrow.

The captain hung up and put the phone back in her pocket.

'So we'll have to stay an extra night in Gaeta then? I can contact the port authorities now to ask for clearance.' Jack had understood the entire exchange, already a couple of steps ahead of everyone else in the room.

'Thank you, Jack, that would be much appreciated.' There was that maternal-like tinge of pride in her voice again. Sofia felt bitter that his transgressions were not met with the same disapproval as everyone else's.

'And I will need another favour from you,' the captain continued, addressing Jack.

'Of course.'

'The guests will need to be taken out on another day trip. I think that Cala Fonte might be nice? Perhaps with

286

the scuba-diving equipment?'

Sofia couldn't imagine Milly in the water, let alone swimming among the fishes with an oxygen tank strapped to her back. After this morning though she was not about to publicly contradict the captain.

Jack nodded. *Obedient foot soldier that he is,* thought Sofia. 'I'll see if I can organise that and let you know, Captain.'

With that, they were all dismissed and Sofia headed back to the kitchen, making sure to catch Declan's eye on the way out and offer up a smile. He returned it, a little shyly. Sofia was happy that that was one fire that had been, if only momentarily, extinguished.

As the afternoon wore on, Sofia settled into a peaceful rhythm in the kitchen. Intermittently she would hear someone scuttle hurriedly up or down the hall. Getting the guests back on board was always hectic and Sofia was glad to be away from the chaos.

When Patricio came to collect the starters, it became clear that he had switched tactics and was now opting for the silent treatment.

'Thanks very much,' she called after him cheerfully as he huffed out the door. She would kill him with kindness. That was her counter-offensive.

When the dessert plates were brought back, he seemed physically pained to have to speak to her, but he managed the words: 'Miss Amelia would like to speak to you in the dining room.' It was hard not to find the whole thing funny – his haughty tone, his narrowed eyes – but Sofia knew that laughing at him would set back the reconciliation time catastrophically.

'Thanks for letting me know, Patricio. I will be up in just a moment.' He gave her a curt nod, laid down the plates and was gone.

Up in the dining room, Milly wailed with delight at the sight of Sofia, as though they were old friends who had been separated for years.

'Sofiiiiiaaa, honey, how are you? Sit, sit.' Milly patted the seat beside her and as Sofia sat down she spotted Petra was standing behind the bar, trying to conceal her amused expression.

Sofia knew that Milly meant well, but the blurring of the line between staff and friend only made Sofia uncomfortable. It was all the deference of the former with all the emotional labour of the latter and nothing in return.

'I was wondering, if you would come with us tomorrow? We're going to . . .' She looked across at Brian, who was dressed like a moody teenager, grey hood pulled over his head, slouched deep into the chair and apparently playing some sort of game on his phone.

Brian just grunted.

'What's it called again?' Milly persisted, her tone growing more shrill.

Brian looked up then. 'Cala Fonte, innit?'

'Cala Fonte, that's it. Thanks, baby.' Milly turned back

288

to Sofia and Brian turned back to his puzzle. 'We had such fun the last time, with you and Captain Jack, we were hoping you might come along again!'

Sofia's stomach dropped, remembering the day out with Jack, the citrus grove, the cave, the race to the hospital. It all felt so long ago, although it had actually only been just under two weeks. In her mind it appeared like a movie she had watched, enthralled in the drama in a way that was hard to relive once you knew the ending.

'I'm not sure, Milly. I think that usually it's the steward who goes, or even the deckhand. I only went last time to cover for someone.'

Milly pouted, her pale freckled forehead contracting into a deep frown. 'I don't really know the new steward though, and I want you.'

It occurred to Sofia that Milly was probably lonely, in that way that famous people so often seemed to be. Famous people and trophy wives. Milly was on her way to being both.

'I'll have to ask the captain.' Sofia was pinning her hopes on the captain vetoing the pair of them spending the day together. She had warned Sofia to stay away after all.

'I already did!' Milly squealed. Sofia tried to stop her disappointment from playing out on her face. 'She told me to ask you, but she's fine with it.'

Sofia wished she could feel even a fraction of Milly's excitement. 'Brilliant,' she said, trying to mirror Milly's tone.

A burst of sound from the corner of the room, and

Sofia looked up just in time to see Petra trying to conceal a giggle with a coughing fit.

Milly was unperturbed. 'Perfect, we're setting off at about ten tomorrow, just after breakfast, so I'll see you then.' Milly gave Sofia an enthusiastic hug before she was able to excuse herself.

'I'm afraid I need to get the crew dinner ready, but I'll see you tomorrow.'

Back in the safety of her kitchen, Sofia groaned loudly. She couldn't catch a break. If she was doomed to spend the day with Jack, again, she would have to try and break the ice this evening. She doubted that Milly and Brian would want to endure the arctic level of frostiness that was currently blustering between them.

# Chapter Thirty-Nine

It was moules-frites for dinner, a people-pleaser, and also simple to make. Sofia could switch into autopilot and have a think about what she might say to Jack. The problem with trying to predict their conversations was that she never knew which version of him she would be confronted with.

He could be kind, thoughtful and witty, or he could be cold, distant and irritable. The strategy for talking to each Jack would have to be different. Either she would appeal to his human side and try and revive something like the friendship they had before or she could present him with a rational outline of how they could fake good relations for the day.

Everyone thoroughly enjoyed the huge pot of steaming mussels; even Patricio conceded that they were '*gustoso*'. The chatter, however, was stilted. After all there was a fair amount of unresolved conflict festering around the table. Stuart and Petra were still not really talking, Declan was unusually quiet, Patricio and Jack were resolutely trying to ignore Sofia, and the captain was clearly feeling uncomfortable about having changed the travel schedule so last minute.

Petra and Patricio cleared the plates, and Sofia took the opportunity to go over to Jack, her heart beating in her chest.

'Jack,' she started timidly. He was standing with his back to her, talking to Declan. 'Jack,' she tried a little louder. He spun around, looking as though he had been ambushed. 'Can I have a word?'

'Sure,' he said, looking uneasy. 'Can you give me a second, Dec?'

'I'll leave you two to it.' Declan seemed eager to extricate himself from whatever was about to happen. He followed the captain out of the room. Now they were alone, Sofia felt her resolve falter. All of a sudden she was lost for words.

Jack waited for her to speak and when she didn't he began tentatively, 'I'm guessing you want to talk about the other night?'

Her cheeks flushed hot. She realised too late that she hadn't prepared for *that* conversation. She thought they had made an unspoken pact to just move on. She was wanting to discuss fall-out strategies, not analyse the disaster itself.

'Not really, I just wanted to clear the air, before tomorrow, if we're going to be together all day.' She stumbled over her words, trying to read his expression. 'Well you know not together, well with Brian and Milly and . . .' Finally he came to her rescue as she flailed from one unfinished sentence to the next.

'Yes of course, that makes sense,' he said calmly.

A silence hung between them, heavy with unutterable thoughts.

'I know it's all a bit messed up, but I spoke to the captain this morning and I think we should try being . . . friends?' Sofia lost her nerve and the last word came out like a question.

She studied his face, and thought that she saw a shadow of the tenderness from that night, then the shutters came down once more.

'Friends.' He spoke as if testing how the word sounded out loud. 'That works for me, Harlow.' A smile, but a cool one. Sofia felt a fool for building up in her head what was turning out to be a pretty undramatic exchange.

'I really love this job—' She had an urge to explain herself, but Jack cut her off.

'So do I,' he interrupted. He obviously wanted to end this conversation, and who was Sofia to be the one to drag it out unnecessarily?

'So we understand each other?' She found herself holding out her hand, as if to seal the deal.

'Perfectly.' He shook hers firmly and Sofia decided to ignore the fizz that travelled up her arm when they touched.

'Well, I'm going to head to bed then. See you tomorrow.'

He nodded. As she turned to go though, he reached out almost absentmindedly, noticing the plaster on her finger. He caught himself suddenly, settling his hand at the back of his head instead.

'Was there something else?' Her heart began to beat a little faster as she peered up at him, suddenly shy.

'No . . . I . . .' He sighed heavily, and Sofia wondered, not for the first time, what was going on inside that head of his. When he finally caught her eye, that vacant look that she so hated was still there. 'I was just going to remind you not to forget the picnic this time.' He smiled, but it was unconvincing.

'Right, yep, got it.' She felt deflated. She had known it would be trying to be 'friends' but she hadn't prepared herself for the bitter pang of rejection she would have to stomach every time he spoke to her as if they were nothing more than two colleagues having to put up with each other's company. As she walked away she could feel his eyes following her, but this time he didn't try and stop her.

# Chapter Forty

She was in the citrus grove again, but it was night-time and the trees were laden with fluorescent fruit. Every time she set her sights on one and began to climb, the branches would get longer and longer, the grapefruit further and further away. Eventually she made a leap for it, lunging and snatching one from the cluster of leaves just before it grew out of reach. She landed on her back, staring up at the inky sky, the only light the glowing yellow orbs above her. As she peeled back the skin, she saw that the pith was black and smelled like sea water. It stung her fingers as she picked at it. When she bit into a plump segment, the fruit was rotten, even though the flesh looked perfectly fresh. When she spat it out her teeth came with it, bright white pearls amidst the frothy pulp, and her mouth was awash with the coppery taste of blood.

Sofia woke with a start, the cold sweat on her back prickling at her burn and the cut on her finger bleeding onto the white sheets. She checked the time: 5.06 a.m. For a moment she longed to go up on deck and then she remembered that it was Jack's time. She couldn't face him in that strange dreamlike realm of dawn, not today.

She got up to find another plaster. In the bathroom she

spotted the bottle of aloe vera, carefully placed inside the mirrored cabinet. He must have left it for her, she realised as she held it in her hand, popping the lid and sniffing at the gel. She shook her head, chastising herself. He had probably just forgotten it.

She put it back, even though her back itched, and wound a plaster around her finger. Cabinet closed, she looked at herself in the mirror. Half-moons of mauve had begun to nestle under her eyes, and her skin was dry. She needed to get more sleep. She needed to stop drinking again.

She knew she wasn't going to go back to sleep, and she didn't fancy another trip to the nightmarish citrus grove anyway. Maybe she could channel some of her restless energy into her recipe cards. She showered and changed and headed up to the main saloon. She was sure the guests wouldn't be up for at least another couple of hours and she had the time before she needed to get breakfast ready.

She settled into a green velvet daybed, legs crossed, recipe cards fanned out and notebook in her lap. She lost herself in the food, imagining new combinations that clicked into place as she shuffled the cards around, a rotating kaleidoscope of tastes.

When she heard footsteps she panicked. There were a lot of people she didn't want to see right now. When she spotted the mop of blonde hair coming up the stairs she sighed with relief. Stuart was not one of them.

'Morning,' she said. He seemed startled to find that the room was not empty.

'Oh hi, Sofia, I wasn't expecting anyone to be in here. I can leave you . . .' He started to turn.

'No, don't worry, it's fine. I'm just here with my imaginary friends,' she joked, splaying her hand over the cards in front of her.

Stuart looked bewildered. 'Like Tarot or . . . ?'

Sofia laughed. She was in that giddy state of exhaustion, and she couldn't stop for a moment. Stuart joined in with a tentative chuckle.

'No.' She wiped tears from her eyes. 'Excuse me, I'm in a weird place.' She pointed at her head. 'Mentally,' she explained. 'They're recipe cards.'

'Oh, right.' Stuart looked genuinely relieved, which made her laugh even more. When the giggles had died down, Stuart was still standing awkwardly, hands thrust into his pockets.

'Take a seat,' Sofia managed finally. She cleared the cards and Stuart sat down, at the furthest end of the sofa. 'Why are you up so early anyway?'

Stuart huffed. 'Well it's hard not to be disturbed when Officer Carter is up with the early birds, and then the light is so bright.'

Sofia wasn't following. 'You mean in the cabin?'

Stuart cocked his head to one side, obviously calculating something. 'I'm guessing that you didn't know that he's camping out in the captain's quarters with me? There was more mould in our cabin as well. The guy should be coming to fend off the last of it today though.' He yawned. 'Thank goodness.'

Sofia didn't know whether to feel grateful that he had saved them both from an unimaginably awkward night together, or hurt that he would rather sleep on the floor with Stuart than face her. Had he been that eager to get away after his 'mistake'?

She noticed Stuart was still scrutinising her. 'I know it's probably not my place to say anything, but I think it's best you two leave it alone. He's not been himself since you came on board.' Stuart said this matter-of-factly. Sofia knew he didn't mean it to sound harsh, but she felt bruised.

'When he was gunning for first officer, he was so focused, even after the thing with Petra.' Stuart looked down at his lap, unable to hide the effect that saying her name always had on him. 'He shut it down immediately when he realised it might jeopardise his chances. He was single-minded.' Sofia hoped Stuart would stop. He didn't. 'But now, I don't know, it's like he's lost his focus. He forgets things, makes mistakes.'

He looked up at Sofia again. 'This thing between you, it's messing with his head.'

It was Sofia's turn to hang her head. 'We've decided to be friends now, so . . . it's over, whatever it was.' Sofia's voice was meek. For the second day in a row, she was starting her day with a scolding.

Stuart scoffed and Sofia was surprised by how much it stung. 'Friends? Yes, I've heard that one before, believe me. That won't stop him from turning everything over and over and over in his head. If anything it just makes everything even more confusing.'

It dawned on Sofia then, that he was no longer talking about Jack, and maybe he never had been. There was too much emotion in his voice, too much involvement. 'Is that how you feel about Petra?' Sofia asked so quietly, it was barely a whisper. She dared to glance up at him.

He was taken aback. It amused Sofia to think about how subtle men often believed they were being.

'Petra?' he spluttered. Sofia nodded. 'What, has she said something to you?' Now she was the one with the valuable insight.

'I mean, she's told me that you two are . . . good friends,' Sofia said coyly. Stuart blushed, and she was emboldened to say more.

'I think she was a little . . .' Sofia chose her words tactfully; she didn't want to betray her friend's trust, but sometimes it was important to share the facts with the relevant parties '. . . disappointed, when you were chatting with that girl all night in Gaeta.'

Sofia watched as the cogs began to whir behind Stuart's eyes. 'I didn't think . . .' he muttered to himself and then seemed to remember he had company.

'If I'm correctly inferring what you're trying to say, Sofia, then I guess I'm in trouble as well.' His face was placid as he said this. Sofia marvelled at his ability to keep everything below the surface. No wonder it had taken Petra so long to peel back the layers.

'There's no room for romance on this boat.' His voice cracked as he said 'romance', so he wasn't completely immune to the force of emotion.

'Honestly, as I get older, I wonder what I'm still doing here. If I want *that* kind of life for myself, a life with love and family, I need to stop clinging on to a young man's dream.' He sighed, sounding weary.

Sofia realised she had no idea how old Stuart was. His full head of startlingly blonde hair made his age hard to place. He could have been thirty or nearing fifty. There seemed to be nothing else to say, and so neither of them spoke. Sofia wondered what Stuart might do with the information she had passed on. She suddenly felt stressed that Petra might have to face down a declaration of love of her own. From her recent experience, she wouldn't wish it on her worst enemy.

'Maybe you're right,' Sofia said at last, 'maybe it's best not to complicate things.' She hoped she might dissuade Stuart from doing anything dramatic, although he didn't seem like the dramatic type.

'Best not to complicate things,' he repeated back at her, like a man committing himself to a mantra.

She checked the time. She probably didn't need to start breakfast for another half an hour, but she was beginning to feel like she needed an out. 'I'm going to head down to prep,' she said brightly, to which Stuart only nodded vacantly in agreement. She left him there, the sun rising into the sky behind him, lost in his thoughts. She wished him a pleasant journey and that he might find his way back with a little clarity.

\* \* \*

Back in the kitchen, she tried something new – French toast with mascarpone and a cherry compote. It took her a little longer than expected and when Patricio came in to collect the food, she was only just plating it up.

He stood with his arms folded. She could feel disdain radiating off him – it was putting her off.

'Everything OK today, Patricio?' she asked, carefully spooning a blob of deep crimson stewed cherry on top of the creamy cheese.

'Perfectly OK, thank you,' he said, his voice clipped. 'The guests are just very hungry.' Sofia tried to keep her cool. She wasn't enjoying the attitude but she had no energy for a fight. She was trying to preserve it for the day ahead.

She leant back, pushing the plates across the counter. 'All ready for you.'

'*Grazie*,' he said as the door swung shut behind him.

Sofia fought the urge to stick her tongue out, and then decided to do it anyway. Something about the release of that childish impulse calmed her. She chuckled to, and at, herself as she went about getting the crew breakfast ready, which would be left behind. Next it was onto the picnic lunch, which she immediately took up to the deck, placing it by the tender. She doubted Jack would surprise her with his forgiveness a second time around.

Back in her cabin, Petra had left a neatly ironed stewardess uniform. Sofia had hoped she might get away with just wearing casuals today, but this was a clear sign that that was not an option.

301

This one at least was not that awful shade of maroon; instead it was a chocolate brown, with a white trim around the bottom of the skort and around the arms. At the last minute she remembered to slip on a plain black bikini underneath, just in case she managed to muster up the courage to dive in herself. She let her hair down and thought it looked quite nice, for a day-three wash. She clipped back the front to keep it out of her eyes. Eyeing herself in the mirror she had that same thought that she looked like she was about to play in a school sports team. She was not, however, about to lump Petra with another ironing job.

She fiddled with her hair for a while, becoming aware that she was trying to stall. There was only one way to get through the day and that was to get on with it. She tried on her best 'hello, friend and colleague' smile. She was no great actress but it was convincing enough. She might have spent most of her life in the kitchen but she had always understood the tenets of the service industry: absolutely no one you are serving is interested in how miserable your life is. It is your job to make them forget you even have a life.

# Chapter Forty-One

Sofia saw Jack before he saw her, and somehow she felt like that gave her a head start. He would be the one caught off guard, and so she might be able to set the tone.

'Aye aye, Captain, reporting for duty.' She found herself saluting, the cringe registering both too soon for her to pull off the levity, and too late to stop. Her hand drifted back down to her side awkwardly. 'I'm not sure why I said that,' she said flatly. Jack's look of bemusement irritated her slightly, but then again how else could he be expected to respond to the mortifying display he had just witnessed?

'Well that makes two of us.' He smirked at her, but she also caught a flash of him eyeing her up. 'I see you remembered lunch this time and I have the scuba gear, so hopefully we can keep the improvisation to a minimum.'

It was strange. Sofia felt like she had stepped back in time. He was speaking to her with that same patronising tone he had used the first time they had been out together. It was as if that night had never happened.

She had to remind herself that that was *her* plan. 'Friends,' she had said. She supposed that the last day out must have been the closest they had ever come to 'friends' just before it had tipped over into *something else*, for her at least.

'Well that is a shame isn't it. You do so like to save the day – it's hard when everything goes to plan.' Sofia's tone dripped with sarcasm.

Jack smiled, genuinely this time. 'Ah yes, that's more like it,' he said with a level of enthusiasm that felt mocking. 'Come on, Harlow, I need a hand getting her in the water.' He handed her a rope and she held it limply.

'I don't really do this kind of boat stuff. What am I supposed to do with it?' She held it up gingerly, looking bewildered.

'Harlow, you can't be caught saying things like "I don't do boats" out loud. If the captain hears you, she'll have you walk the plank. She's a big believer in "all hands on deck" being literal.'

He started gathering the length of rope in his hand, winding it deftly around his elbow and forearm. He looked good, with his sleeves rolled up and the tendons pulsing in time with the looping of the rope. He was in his element. A flashback in her mind's eye of those same arms clutching at her hips as he lost himself inside her. Sofia dragged herself back into the present. Turned out he was his hottest at the two extremes, completely in control and completely helpless. This was not the time for those kinds of thoughts. She looked down at her own arms and began to mimic Jack's movements.

'There you go. It's easy once you get the hang of it,' Jack said in what he must have thought was a genuinely

304

encouraging voice.

Sofia rolled her eyes. 'Yep, I think I can just about manage winding rope.'

'Well, we're pulleying her into the water next, so don't get too cocky.' Jack seemed to be enjoying himself. Compared to the placid, meek man she had tried to talk to at dinner last night, he was transformed. So much for *her* setting the tone.

She changed the subject. She was bored of the teacher-pupil dynamic he was trying to forge with all this rope business. 'So are you actually imagining that Milly is going to go scuba diving?'

Jack had dropped the bundle of rope and was now fiddling with something that looked like a carabiner. Sofia did the same.

'I mean, she said she wanted to . . .' he paused, and let out a loud grunt as he pulled at something that looked like a clamp '. . . try it out . . .' a snap and the rope around the pulley slackened suddenly '. . . on her preference sheet.' Jack was panting ever so slightly from the effort.

Sofia scoffed. 'Her preference sheet? I've been burned that way before.'

Jack looked up at her, his eyebrow raised and a hand resting on his hip. 'You think you've got it all figured out, Harlow. A couple of weeks on a boat and you're an expert in VIP neuroses?'

'Not neuroses, just wishful thinking. Milly is a woman who has very strong ideas of the type of person she wants to be. They just don't necessarily match up with who she

305

actually is, or what she actually likes doing.' Jack seemed to be listening intently; it was a bit unnerving.

'She likes the idea of liking seafood, she likes the idea of going scuba diving, she also likes the aesthetics of it, but I'll bet you . . .' Sofia wasn't sure what she wanted from Jack, but she suddenly felt the need to exhibit some of what made her a good yachtie, just as he had. Suddenly it came to her. 'I'll bet you a morning a week of dawn.' She smiled triumphantly and held out her hand.

'Only one a week?' He was hesitant, his hand firmly in his pocket.

Sofia looked away, realising too late that she had walked herself into a trap. 'I still want you to have time with your mum,' she said quietly. She didn't dare look at him. She had transgressed on the very terms she was trying to establish. This was not in the remit of 'friendly and professional' – it was a thing shared in an intimate past, and that's where it should have stayed. They were supposed to be moving on.

They were both silent and then Jack cleared his throat. 'Right, OK deal,' was all he said, thrusting out his hand. Sofia shook it, and vowed silently to be more careful in future.

'Everything is ready, so could you go and collect the guests? They were supposed to be here about ten minutes ago.' Jack was all business again, checking his watch with a frown on his face.

'Of course.' She was grateful to leave that awkward exchange behind her. She trotted across the deck and was walking down the stairs when she heard furtive whispering. She stopped before she rounded the corner. It was Brian and Milly.

Milly sounded upset. 'I just don't think I can do it. It doesn't seem right to be under the water like that, and then there's all the fish.' Her voice was agitated.

Sofia had to really strain to hear Brian's response. His voice was measured but sympathetic, soft and comforting.

'Babe, I know you, and I know that it seems scary right now, but I also know how pumped you'll feel after, how bummed you'll be if you miss out *and* how proud of yourself you'll be.'

Milly sniffed in response. Sofia couldn't see them but she imagined that he was holding her face in his hands, maybe stroking her cheek.

'Will you hold my hand?' She sounded like a little girl.

'When I can, baby, I will always hold your hand.' A rustle that sounded like a hug and then Brian's voice was muffled, as if he was speaking into her hair. 'But, like, from what I can remember with scuba, I might need my hands to control the oxygen or whatever.'

'You mean I'm not as important to you as oxygen?' Milly sounded petulant and then she giggled. Sofia had been taken for a ride, just as it sounded like Brian had been.

He joined in laughing. 'I thought you were serious then.'

A light-sounding slap, most probably on the chest or arm, thought Sofia. 'As if!' Milly exclaimed and then after a moment of silence, maybe they were hugging again.

'I love you,' Brian said tenderly.

'I love you more,' Milly responded playfully.

'Now we don't have time for that game, Mills. We're already late.' Sofia scuttled up the stairs just in time to turn and appear as if she was just coming down as they began climbing them. Milly was wearing a Lara-Croft-esque one-piece swimsuit made of silver scuba. Her jet of red hair wound into a tight bun at the nape of her neck. Brian was at the point of recycling outfits, so it was the leather flip-flops and Speedos paired with a black mesh shirt he wore undone.

'There you two are. Are you ready for the trip?' She smiled, hoping that there was nothing close to guilt hiding in her expression.

'Sorry we're a bit late.' Milly looked embarrassed. Brian reached out his hand and took Milly's.

'I'm sure it's no bother, right, Sofia?' He looked up at Sofia, protective and stern.

'Not at all. Right this way,' she said brightly, leading them over to the tender.

Jack was looking resolutely grumpy when as they made their way over, the tender was already in the water. 'Are we finally ready?'

Sofia wondered, not for the first time, where this obsession with timekeeping came from.

It was her turn to give a stern look. They didn't want a distressed Milly on their hands for the day.

'That was my fault,' Brian piped up, and Sofia spied

the look of gratitude Milly shot up at him.

'Right, well we better get a move on.' Jack ushered them all onto the boat, handing around the life jackets. 'So have either of you scuba dived before?' he asked brashly.

'I have,' Brian said, and then putting his arm around Milly he added, 'And Mills has tried in a pool once.'

Jack raised an eyebrow and Sofia understood why he had never made it as front of house. Not expressing disdain and irritation with your guests was probably lesson number one.

'Well that's a great start,' Sofia interjected before Jack could say something dismissive. 'I've never been before, so it's nice to have a few people with experience around me.'

Milly and Brian both beamed and Sofia hoped she was making up for Jack's raincloud. She did, after all, feel partly responsible. The reminder of his dawn trips to visit his dead mother had been ill-timed, at best.

'Well, Sofia, I might need you to stay on the boat honestly, but let's see.' He hadn't understood her strategy for making Milly feel more at ease. It only then occurred to her that her strategy was also going to lose her that stupid bet.

Jack started the engine and they glided across the waves. Once again Sofia was reminded how much she loved being out on the water. Something about the spray and the motor imitating white noise made her feel totally free without feeling alone.

* * *

After about half an hour on the water, they began running parallel with the jagged cliff face. The pale grey stone protruded from the sea in bulbous clumps, like coral coming up for air and dotted with parasol shoots and beach towels in every colour.

Jack slowed the boat as they came to an opening in the rock. From where they were, it seemed impossible that he could drive through it. As they approached at an angle the facade gave way to an alcove of shallower, crystal-clear water. It was a popular local spot by the looks of it, children splashing in the rock pools at one end, teenagers jumping off ledges into the deeper waters at the other.

Jack manoeuvred the boat and jumped out onto a craggy ridge, seamlessly pushing the bow of the boat with his foot to stop it crashing, and pulling the rope tight to tie it around a hook hammered into the rock face.

'Anything I can do?' Sofia was standing helplessly in the middle of the boat, awaiting instruction.

'Just sit there and look pretty,' Jack replied, distracted as he hopped back onto the boat and fiddled with the controls. Sofia flopped back into her seat.

Milly clapped her hands together gracefully. 'You two are so cute. Today is going to be so much fun.' Sofia just smiled. She wasn't really in a position to explain to Milly that there was, in fact, nothing cute going on between her and Jack. It was anything but cute; it was ugly and complicated and threatened both their livelihoods, not to mention wreaking havoc on her nerves.

\* \* \*

When he was done parking, Jack turned to face them. 'So who wants to go first?' He didn't seem as bad-tempered as earlier but Sofia could see that the mask he sometimes wore, the one that gave his eyes that vacant expression, was on.

Brian raised his hand eagerly.

'Right, let's get you into the kit then, and then Milly maybe you can join us for a bit? If there's time at the end, Sofia, we can do some basic breathing exercises in the shallows.' Jack rattled off the plan robotically, as if reciting from a memorised script. Sofia supposed this was how colleagues might usually interact, but she felt a little stung by how impersonal it all was. No more knowing looks and in-jokes, just the matter at hand.

Sofia had to avert her eyes as Jack removed his shirt and trousers. Underneath he wore simple navy swimming trunks. She was looking down and caught herself staring at his calves again. They were tanned and toned, just like the rest of him. Both men shrugged into the scuba harnesses and tested their oxygen. Once they had pulled on their flippers and goggles, Sofia trusted herself enough to look directly at them.

Jack looked goofy, sure, his dark hair pushed up and away from his forehead by the mask and the harness clipped across his nipples, but it also felt tantalising to see his body so exposed in the full light of day. That night she had felt her way around, more than she had looked, and it was only now that the two senses were calibrating that she could fully understand just how beautiful he was.

Milly went over to where Brian was sitting on the edge of the boat and removed the breathing equipment from his mouth, replacing it with her lips and tongue. Both Sofia and Jack looked away.

'Have fun, baby. Come back in one piece,' Milly whispered into his ear. He pecked her on the cheek and pulled down his goggles. The men fell backwards into the water, leaving Milly and Sofia on the boat.

'I hope they're going to be OK.' Milly was already fretting. Just then Jack came to the surface with a thumbs up.

'Jack knows what he's doing.' *At least when it comes to scuba diving,* thought Sofia.

Milly looked over at her, perhaps sensing there was something left unsaid. 'Am I allowed to ask what the deal is with you two? Compared to last time, something seems a bit . . . off.' Milly came over and sat a little too close to Sofia.

Sofia blushed. She looked straight ahead as she spoke. 'You're allowed to ask, but I'm not allowed to say.'

Milly cocked her head to one side, considering whether to probe further. She apparently decided against it.

Instead she said, 'Well, whatever it is, I think you should try and sort it out. I kept telling Brian after our last trip that I was convinced you two were in love, even if you didn't know it yet.' Milly sounded so matter-of-fact, as if she hadn't just said the unsayable, as if she hadn't trampled all over Sofia's pact with herself to not even think about the L-word.

Sofia laughed nervously. 'Oh I don't know about all that – surely you can't tell that sort of thing from just one day.' Sofia wanted this conversation to end.

'Well with Brian I remember it was the same.' Milly paused, pulling a strand of her hair out of her bun and twiddling it around her finger. 'Well, not the *same* – we were on national television – but the point is that it was everyone else who saw what me and Bri had before I did.' She peeked over at Sofia, seeming to steel herself for what she was about to say next.

'I never really expected to find love on there. Sure, it's called *The True Course of Love*, but let's be real I was there for Instagram followers and a BabyDoll line.' She mused for a moment. 'And, like, obviously I got those things too, but Brian . . .' She sighed.

'Brian was so much more than I signed up for and for ages I didn't really know how to handle that. It was one of the other girls – you remember Angie?' She looked over expectantly and Sofia shook her head. 'Well anyway, this girl Angie, she was kind of my bestie on the show, *she* was the one that was like, "Babe, you love him," because I just refused to accept it. I mean it's ridiculous, to fall in love with someone in like two weeks right? But then you're with them twenty-four hours a day, and it's all so intense and you really get to see what someone is made of, how they act under pressure.'

She looked over at Sofia again, who was in a sort of daze. 'And I knew that Brian was the one, because he made me fearless, still does, like he makes me feel like it's OK to fail, because even if I do he'll still be there. It's really amazing what you can do once you're not afraid to fail anymore.' Milly tucked the strand back into her bun.

'You know I always assumed that I would have to choose between a great career or a great love, that it was impossible to juggle both, but I think we've actually made each other more successful, and not just like on Instagram or whatever, but like that kind of support, it makes you braver.'

Sofia didn't know how to respond. She was aware that Milly couldn't possibly know how relevant her situation with Brian felt to what was going on with Jack, and so something about it felt fated.

In a rare moment of earnestness Sofia looked over at Milly and said, 'It's really beautiful that you two have found each other.'

Milly beamed, her eyes welling. 'I just hope I don't mess it up. It feels like a lot of pressure sometimes, what with him going off to play his games abroad and me trying to set up my own makeup brand. 'And with that the relatability evaporated. Sofia patted Milly on the shoulder sympathetically.

A splash caught Milly's attention and she rushed across the boat to see Brian and Jack coming up.

'It's beautiful down there, baby. You've just gotta see it!' Sofia didn't think she'd heard Brian sound so enthused since the urchin-sabotaged photo shoot.

'OK, I'm going to do it.' Milly sounded determined. That must be the bravery she was talking about, Sofia thought.

Jack lithely climbed up the ladder, drops of water dripping from his body onto the deck.

'Let me give you a hand with the kit,' he offered, grabbing another harness and tank from under the seat and slipping it over Milly's shoulders. Sofia remembered what it was like to have his fingers caress *her* shoulders and felt an unexpected bite of jealousy.

'It's very heavy,' Milly said, concern echoing through her voice.

'Once you're in the water, it'll feel more comfortable – don't worry.' Jack's voice was reassuring and calm. He could be empathetic when he wanted to be.

Milly had a couple of trial goes with the breathing equipment and then she was ready, or rather: 'I guess as ready as I'll ever be.' A squeal and a splash and she was in, bobbing in the turquoise water with a smile on her face.

Sofia watched as Brian coaxed her into taking more and more breaths underwater until eventually, with a flick of the flipper she was gone. On the boat alone, Sofia couldn't stop thinking about what Milly had said. It sounded cheesy to talk about love giving you courage, but she'd seen it so clearly today that it felt like a morality tale from the universe.

For the first time she dared explore the possibility that she might love Jack. It seemed preposterous on the face of it. She had only known the man a couple of weeks after all, but then again, from the moment they had met there had been *something* between them.

At the start she had thought it was disdain, and then hatred, then tension turned to chemistry. For one brief moment there was friendship, and for another there was passion. But all of it was visceral and charged. There had never been apathy or disinterest. From the moment they had met she had thirsted after details of him, even in the beach bar she had found herself imagining the sort of person he was, repulsed by his bravado but also fascinated.

She sat as the boat swayed lightly, marvelling at her surroundings, the sound of children's laughter ricocheting through the cove. It didn't feel so terrifying here, to consider that she was in love.

She tried to employ a bit of rationality, if she was indeed in love what would that mean?

It would mean that trying to 'just be friends' was a hopeless endeavour and she'd only be torturing herself. Secondly it meant that what she would want more than anything would be for him to be happy, and what made him happy was boating. Sofia thought back to her conversation with Stuart, how he'd said that Jack had lost his focus with her around. It dawned on her that if she *did* love him, she would probably have to do that most sacrificial of acts and let him go.

An interruption to her mulling came in the form of three bobbing heads yelling from the water. Sofia leant over the railing to throw the long ladder down. Milly spluttered. Sofia rushed into action, almost hitting Brian in the head in her haste.

The three of them scrambled up the ladder and collapsed onto the deck. Sofia held her breath, concerned, before they all burst out laughing.

'We made it!' Brian said as he pulled off his mask.

'What the hell happened?' Sofia had her hands on her hips, feeling a little left out of the joke.

'Milly saw a shark, but we're pretty sure it was just a dogfish,' Jack chimed in.

'No way, I reckon it was a great white!' Milly sounded indignant, but she was grinning. 'OK, maybe just a baby one.'

'We were swimming along and then Milly did the hand signal for a shark, or danger or whatever, and we all panicked, when we came up Jack explained it was harmless, but once she'd got it into her head . . .' Brian was teasing, and Milly rose to the bait.

'Wait wait, there was definitely a moment there where you were scared too!' she objected.

'Call it group hysteria.' Jack rolled his eyes dismissively but even he looked a little shaken up.

'Well, after the shock you've all had, I think it's the perfect time for a spot of lunch.' Sofia helped Milly up and headed to the cool box.

'Which we are lucky enough to have had lovingly prepared, and remembered, by our one and only Chef Harlow.' It was Jack, in hushed tones, but when Sofia turned round to give him a scathing look she was caught off guard by the good-humoured twinkle in his eye.

'Yes, this time around we won't have to scavenge for

our food,' she retorted, and then catching Jack's eye, she added, 'As enchanting as that little detour was.' He smiled at her and she felt her heart skip. She blushed slightly at the radiance of his face.

She set up the tender's small collapsible table, grunting a little at the effort of tightening the bolts into the deck. She could feel Jack's bemusement as he watched her, arms resolutely folded.

'You're not going to help then?' she puffed.

'You're doing a fine job as is it, Harlow. Wouldn't want to interfere,' he said with his face fixed in a smirk.

Sofia laid out the picnic on a gingham blanket. She'd thought it might look good on an Instagram story when she'd chosen it, and then felt silly for taking that into consideration. Now that Milly was getting her phone out and rearranging the strawberries and slices of cheeses to better sit in the frame, she was glad that she did.

'What are those?' Milly pointed at a small jar.

'They're preserved mussels. They're delicious with a bit of crusty bread.' Sofia broke off a chunk and handed it to Milly, who wrinkled her nose.

'Come on now, you can't knock them until you've tried them, babe.' It was Brian, softly berating.

Milly took the bread from Sofia's hand and then picked up the jar of mussels, eyeing them suspiciously. 'I simply can't eat that. They have, like, little beards on!'

Brian took the jar, opened it and then spooned a single mussel onto a corner of bread. Sofia and Jack were mesmerised by the scene in front of them. It was familiar and strange, performative and intimate. Brian reached forward and using two fingers lowered Milly's eyelids, a mortician arranging his dead. As he did so, she opened her mouth and he fed her the snack in his hands. They all held their breath as she chewed contemplatively.

'That's actually super tasty,' she said, clearly surprising herself. She opened her eyes and smiled at Brian. Then she turned to Sofia. 'He's always getting me to try new things like that. If it wasn't for him I never would have tried that weird risotto. Turns out blue cheese and pear actually works!'

So it was Brian that Sofia had to thank for being able to expand her repertoire. When she caught his eye, he looked down bashfully. 'It just seemed a waste to not get her to at least try all your wonderful food.'

Sofia was touched. Brian was so full of surprises, a football player with a heart of gold, a penchant for photography and an adventurous palette.

Sofia thought back to when she had met them, how Milly had seemed to be the one in charge, the one with the vision. Now she realised that they were a pair, each bringing their own strengths and skills to the union, and pushing each other to be better.

# Chapter Forty-Two

After they had gorged themselves and washed it down with a couple of glasses of champagne, Brian and Milly dozed on the loungers at the bow of the boat. Jack and Sofia cleared away lunch.

'So, I lost the bet then,' Sofia said, for want of something to fill the slightly awkward silence they had been manoeuvring around all day.

'Oh hands down, she had a whale of a time.' He looked at her expectantly. She didn't want to give him the satisfaction of laughing at such a lame pun, but it was the lameness of it that tickled her.

'I didn't take you for the dad joke sort.' She was trying not to look at him too much, instead concentrating on the plates in her hands.

'You, Sofia Harlow, are famously a terrible judge of character, so I'm not surprised by that at all.' He nudged his shoulder against hers playfully, and she almost lost her balance, squatting as she was with her hands full.

'Careful!' she squealed.

He raised a finger to his lips. 'Shhhh, you'll wake the kids.' He gestured towards the front of the boat where Brian could be heard snoring softly and Milly's Prada sunglasses had slipped halfway down her face.

'All that excitement always wipes them out.' Sofia shook her head, raising her eyebrows in the universal sign language for 'what are they like!'

Jack chuckled, and then there was the silence again and only the sound of cutlery scraping against crockery.

After clearing his throat, Jack began speaking, but it came out strangled and unintelligible. Sofia giggled. 'What was that?' She had never seen him be anything other than in control of himself, and she was even more surprised to see him blush afterwards.

'I don't know, maybe you make me nervous, Harlow,' he muttered and then added, 'I never know when you're about to throw a drink over me next.'

'That was one time!' She wasn't ready to engage with the first half of that sentence; she was much more comfortable falling back on that tired joke of theirs.

'I was trying to ask if you wanted to try the scuba kit? We could just swim over to that beach over there and have a go in the shallows?' His expression was earnest.

'Do you think we'll have time?' Sofia didn't want to deal with grumpy guests or a grumpy Jack when the sacred schedule would need to be pushed back.

'Yeah, they're sleeping like babies.' Jack winked at her. She was a little apprehensive about trying scuba diving. If she was being honest with herself, she had probably projected a lot of that onto Milly. Suddenly though, knowing she would have Jack to guide her through it, she felt fearless. As she slipped on the kit and pulled on the flippers, it wasn't the thought of diving down that was tying a knot in her stomach, it was a niggling feeling that the thing she had been trying to ignore for so long was finally coming to the surface.

They tumbled into the water and swam towards the shallower end of the cove. Once Sofia could touch the bottom, Jack stopped them.

'OK so first I'm going to teach you the signs, then I'm going to show you how to breathe.' He was in instructor mode again, but now that they were doing something exciting, Sofia found she didn't mind.

'OK!' she said and then realising she was getting ahead of herself, added, 'sorry what do you mean by signs?'

'Signs we do with our hands under the water to communicate, seeing as we can't speak.' She was finding it hard to take him seriously with his goggles on. He started making shapes with his hands. 'So this means "danger".' He held his fist out straight in front of him. 'This means "help".' He waved his arm up and down at his side. Another couple of gestures. 'This one is "I'm OK"; this one is "Are you OK?" This one is "going up" and then this is "I'm going down".'

Sofia was nodding along, but if she was being honest she was a little distracted. They had moved closer to the beach and now most of his chest was out of the water. The smattering of curls on his torso beaded with droplets of seawater were catching the light, and her attention. She willed herself to concentrate.

'This is "hold hands".' He clasped his hands together in front of him, his expression earnest.

'And why would we need that one?' Sofia asked coyly.

Jack shot her a look. 'Don't be getting any ideas, Harlow. It's only if you're in distress and then I can lead you to safety.'

'You do so enjoy the white knight role. I'll see what I can do.' She pouted her lips and batted her eyelashes. She was joking of course, but there was also something a little dangerous about how close she was stepping to 'the line' that thrilled her.

He pulled up his goggles and gave her a stern look. 'Sofia, you have to listen – this is important.'

'OK, OK! Sorry, Captain, do go on.' She planted a serious expression on her face and he rolled his eyes.

'This one is "you lead, I follow".' He pointed with both his index fingers to the left. She was on top of him, teasing him with her hands and devouring him with her eyes. She shook her head slightly. What was up with these intrusive dirty thoughts? She felt like a horny teenager.

'Everything OK?' Jack had seen her glaze over.

'Yep!' she said brightly.

'OK last one, and this is the most important one really, so I'm going to get you to repeat it.' He held his hand in front of his chest, flat, palm down, and moved it back and forth, as if polishing his chin. It all felt so absurd, Sofia snorted.

'It's no laughing matter, Sofia. That means "I've run

out of air".' He seemed genuinely put out, but that just made it funnier. Jack waited for her giggles to subside, hands on hips.

'Sorry, sorry,' she said catching her breath. She stood up straight and mimicked the movement.

'Good,' he conceded, 'ready to breathe?' He reached behind her to grab the air hose. His cheek grazed her ear and her breath caught in her throat. There it was, that energy between them, so tangible that she had to scratch at the place where they had touched when he leant back. She noticed that his cheeks had reddened slightly.

'This is the octo, short for octopus.' He held up the mouthpiece, not looking her straight in the eye. For a moment she thought he might actually put it in her mouth. The idea of it felt overwhelming, but he placed it in her hand instead. She wrapped her lips around it, feeling it settle around her gums.

'OK when you feel comfortable, take a big breath in, and then take it out to breathe out.' She did as instructed.

'Good,' he said encouragingly. 'One more time.' This time he held her gaze, and as she breathed out, he let out a sympathetic sigh.

Goggles on, they repeated the exercise a few times under water. Sofia was impatient to get going, but Jack insisted on running through the signs once again.

'We're going to take it really slow, and stay where we can stand for a bit.' Jack's tone was stern. Sofia considered they were decent words to live by, but she was always eager to swim right into the deep end of things.

After some time paddling around, Sofia was itching to go further out. She signalled for them to go up. As they broke the surface she removed her goggles. 'I can literally only see sand, Jack, surely we can go a little deeper?'

He was hesitant. 'Usually people do about five days of prep before going out into the sea.'

'Well I'm pretty sure Milly didn't, and anyway, I'm a quick learner.' She was determined to actually see something.

'OK, fine, if you're going to keep nagging, but stay close.' Jack seemed to know he was destined to lose this battle.

Sofia beamed, pulled her goggles on and dived down. Under the water she turned her head to see Jack gliding along beside her. He gave her a thumbs up and she followed suit. Below her a school of tiny silver fish darted around erratically. As they approached the base of the cliff face she spotted a starfish, and then, to her mild horror, an eel.

She kept bashing Jack in the arm and pointing frantically at every new creature she saw.

At a certain point she began to feel like she had to drag a little harder on the octo. In the distance she could see what looked like a ray, and she was determined to reach it. She swam harder, and huffed harder. As she drew nearer, it occurred to her in a flash of panic, that she was probably running out of air.

Suddenly the peacefulness of the silent underwater world she had been enjoying morphed into something suffocating. Her mind went blank. She couldn't remember any of the signals. Then it came to her, chin rub. She turned herself around and gestured as she had been shown. Jack didn't react – maybe he hadn't seen her. She tried again, but the energy of it was using up more oxygen. Her brain was telling her to go up, to get air, but now she couldn't seem to remember which way that was, or move her limbs in the right way to get there.

Her vision blurred, and a strange weightlessness spread over her. Everything was getting darker.

# Chapter Forty-Three

She came to with Italian all around her, but the sound of concern was the same in any language. She opened her eyes and, as her surroundings came into focus, she saw Jack's face, etched with a deep frown, leaning over her.

'Christ, Harlow, you had me worried,' he said, his voice dripping with relief. Sofia tried to sit up and spluttered sea water. She realised, with growing mortification, that almost everyone on the beach was crowded around her in a big circle.

'What happened?' she leant in to whisper to Jack, trying to hide her face from the prying audience around them.

'You passed out in the water.' Jack spoke softly. 'I think you ran out of air.' Sofia's head was spinning. She tried to piece together the last of what she could remember, but it was mostly starfish and silver scales. She felt exhausted.

'I want to go, Jack.' Her eyes were wide and brimming with fear.

'Of course,' he said, 'do you think you can stand?' He sounded distressed, and he kept running his hand through his hair. Sofia felt the need to soothe him.

'It's OK, Jack. I'm just a little disorientated – maybe

some water would help?'

He immediately turned to the crowd. '*Acqua, qualcuno ha dell'acqua?*' he called, his voice raspy.

A young woman stepped forward with a bottle of water and Sofia guzzled it gratefully. '*Grazie,*' she said feebly, and the woman smiled and then said something to Jack in Italian.

'What did she say?' Sofia asked as the woman stepped back into the crowd.

Jack seemed embarrassed. 'You don't want to know,' he muttered.

'Go on,' Sofia was reassured that she was feeling energised enough to be nosy again.

'She said that a beautiful girl like you is lucky to have a brave man like me to save her.' His tone was flat as if he was reading from a teleprompter.

Sofia laughed, and then spluttered, and then coughed. Jack handed her another bottle of water. She took a sip.

'Well it's good to see you've maintained your sense of humour,' Jack said dryly.

'I told you I'd give you your shot at being my knight in shining armour.' Sofia was teasing, but then she thought about the fact that he had probably saved her life. Before she could stop herself, she reached for his cheek, turning his face to hers.

'Thank you,' she breathed. They were so close, she could feel the heat radiating off him. She stared into his eyes, noticing the flecks of amber amidst the green. His lips were tantalisingly close. Their breathing slowed and his gaze darted down to her mouth.

'*Baciarla!*' a call from the crowd brought them back down to earth. They both turned away, remembering that they were far from alone.

'There's an ambulance on the way' Jack said sheepishly, looking away and busying himself with gathering up the scuba kit sprawled around them. She must have looked panicked because he added quickly 'it's only a precaution' and then almost as if to himself 'it's a miracle you're already up and talking to be honest'.

The next hour was a blur, Sofia was finding it hard to concentre on anything the paramedics were asking her and the language barrier wasn't helping, all she wanted was to go to bed. They poked and prodded her in the back of the ambulance, listened to her heartbeat, shone a light in both her eyes. From where she was sitting, facing out towards the beach, she could see Jack pacing anxiously back and forth. Occasionally he was interrupted by a concerned bystander, eager to get a first hand account of the dramatic rescue. Far from basking in the praise, that even Sofia with her non-existent Italian could tell was being lavished on him, Jack was jittery, irritable, even rude, as he waved them away.

Finally the paramedic, a young, tanned woman with piercing blue eyes and an unfathomably neat French braid, summoned him over. Sofia was too tried to even try and decipher the exchange. She was relieved when Jack knelt in front of her and smiled reassuringly. 'You've got the all clear, plenty of rest and you should be fine'

Sofia let out a wry chuckle 'Rest? On that boat? Chance would be a fine thing.'

Jack didn't laugh, that look of concern still cemented on his face. 'I should get you back,' was all he said, helping her down from the ambulance. She felt a little unsteady on her feet. The brightness of the sun, the smell of the sea, even the grit underfoot felt disorientating. She walked a few steps and then had to sit down, finding a perch on a large boulder protruding from the sand.

The reality of what had just happened came crashing down on Sofia then. She had left her guests stranded on a boat whilst she went off on a jolly and persuaded her colleague to let her skip training and rush to the deep end. This was the result: her almost drowning, Jack having to come to her rescue and no doubt smacking the schedule with a fatal blow.

'I'm just going to get the tender a little closer to shore, are you going to be OK here?' Jack said, his brow furrowed. She nodded stoically and he jogged off towards the surf.

While she sat on the beach, Jack swam out to the boat, drove it in closer and then jumped back into the water to come and collect her. He helped her to her feet, and draped her arm around his shoulders to support her. The adrenaline had turned her legs to jelly. She looked over at him – he was wearing a steely expression and staring straight ahead.

Sofia could see two figures standing. How long had poor Brian and Milly been waiting for them on that boat?

Sofia had no idea how long they'd been gone.

With the help of Brian and Jack, Sofia made it onto the deck, where Milly was standing with a towel, ready to drape around Sofia's shoulders.

She was aware that looks were exchanged around her. 'I ran out of air,' she said to no one in particular. It was obviously the question Milly and Brian were burning to ask.

'Oh my God, Sofia, are you OK? That's so scary you could have died.' Milly suddenly became frantic, and Sofia regretted having said anything. She lay a hand on her arm. 'It's OK. Jack saved the day, the paramedics said I'll be fine. I'm OK.'

Milly threw herself on Jack, pulling him into a hug. 'Oh my God, did you swim with her all the way to the beach? That is SO romantic – you saved her life!' Milly was verging on the hysterical and Jack seemed overwhelmed.

'I just . . . I just did what I could, but it was my fault she was out there in the first place really.' He hung his head and Sofia's heart ached to look at him.

'It wasn't your fault, Jack,' she said quietly. All three sets of eyes were on her. 'I was being super pushy. I made him take me out deeper.'

'You mustn't blame yourself!' Milly flitted back over to Sofia, wrapping her arms around her. Brian was stood awkwardly, obviously unrehearsed in the female art of comforting.

Jack headed over to the helm. 'We should get back,' he said steadily, with his back to everyone. He radioed the main boat and Sofia could only catch the odd word as he murmured furtively into the mouthpiece. 'Petra is waiting for us now,' was all he said before he started the engine. Soon they were back out in the open seas, Sofia coddled in Milly's unrelenting embrace, and Brian staring out at the waves.

# Chapter Forty-Four

When they got back to the *Lady Shelly*, two hours behind schedule, Petra was standing on the deck with her hands on her hips. Once she saw Sofia in Milly's arms, her expression melted from agitation to worry.

'Is everyone OK?' she shouted over as Jack attached the pulleys to each side of the tender.

'We had another accident!' Milly shouted back. 'But Jack saved Sofia's life so yes, now everyone is OK.'

Petra shot Jack a look, which Sofia couldn't translate, but it was adjacent to scolding.

'Yes I heard,' Petra said flatly, reaching out to help Sofia off the tender. 'Let's get you all on board. The captain has been wondering where you all are. I've just told her you were held up, until we can get to the bottom of everything.' Petra, always thinking one step ahead. Sofia was grateful to have a friend who was always willing to cover for her. What would they tell the captain? That was just not something she could think about at that moment.

Once they were all safely on deck Petra held Sofia at arm's length, examining her. Before Petra could ask her if she was okay, Sofia reassured her with an 'I'll be fine', giving her the sort of look that says: *I'll tell you all about it later.*

Petra seemed satisfied with that answer for now and began to lead Brian and Milly back to their suite, but not before Milly lunged for one last rib-crushing hug. 'He's a keeper,' she whispered into Sofia's ear. Sofia waved at them limply as they walked down into the boat.

Left alone, Sofia felt she had to say something meaningful to Jack; she just wasn't sure what. In the end it was him who broke the silence. He seemed agitated. Sofia had never seen him look so nervous.

'I'm just going to come out with it, because I don't know how else to say it.'

Sofia held her breath. The possibilities were sending her thoughts into a spin.

'It was my fault that you ran out of air. I should have checked the gauge before we went deeper, and I didn't. You could have . . .' he stammered, full of contrition, 'you could have died.' His eyes were glossy and Sofia could hardly bear to look at the anguish on his face.

'Jack,' she said softly. From her lips the word sounded like a prayer. She stepped towards him and then couldn't remember what she had planned to do. She folded her arms across her chest. 'Please don't blame yourself. It was my own stupid cavalier attitude towards the whole thing that got us into this mess.' She sighed. 'Sometimes I don't like to be told.'

She detected a faint smile and it rallied her. 'We both were fully aware that we shouldn't go deeper and

I pushed it,' she said calmly. 'We swam right up to the limit and then we crossed the line and then we reaped the consequences.' As she spoke they broke eye contact. Suddenly it felt like they were talking about something else.

'At least no one got too badly hurt.' It was almost a whisper from Jack.

'Speak for yourself.' The words were out before Sofia had time to think. She needed to get away from him, before she said more things she'd regret. When she looked up, he seemed visibly pained, like he had something else to add. She waited a beat, but he said nothing.

'Anyway, thank you, Captain Jack, for the heroics. I better be off back to my dungeon. All this time you thought I was the princess, but I'm actually the troll,' she remarked dryly. Her attempt at levity fell flat. He just nodded absent-mindedly and then turned away.

'Take care of yourself, Sofia,' he said with his back to her. Something about that phrase sounded so final. She presumed it was his way of reaffirming their pact to keep their distance.

She had planned to walk to the kitchen, but as she passed her cabin door, she suddenly felt shattered. Just ten minutes of shut-eye wouldn't hurt she thought, as she collapsed on her bunk and closed her eyes.

# Chapter Forty-Five

Sofia was awakened by a loud knock on the door.

'Sofia, are you planning on cooking dinner tonight?' It was Patricio sounding shrill and a little smug. Sofia checked her watch and groaned. She had been asleep for half an hour, and twenty of those precious minutes had been stolen from her prep time.

'Yes, Patricio, I'm coming.' She was still in her stewardess uniform, and her voice was muffled by the fabric as she frantically pulled it over her head. She heard a huff from the corridor and then retreating footsteps. She was definitely going to have to confront Patricio at some point soon. The situation was getting out of hand.

She pulled on her chef's whites and trailed dutifully to the kitchen. She was so tired she could barely think straight, but somehow she managed to pull together a full meal, discounting the fruit salad, which she had to admit was a cop-out dessert.

Patricio was giving her absolutely no sympathy, even as she winced and wheezed around the kitchen. Her bloodied finger throbbing, burn itching and oesophagus burning. The consequence of oxygen deprivation and swallowing vast quantities of sea water, she assumed.

'What happened to you?' was as close as he got to acknowledging her plight, and even then it was delivered with an edge of disgust rather than concern.

'It's a long story,' she said wearily, plating up a pyramid of spaghetti, 'maybe you should ask Jack about it.'

His expression soured, which Sofia hadn't thought was possible. 'I think it might be better if we just leave Jack out of this, don't you?'

Was he still upset about Declan? Sofia couldn't work it out. She was using all her energy to cook and stay upright. 'Sure.' She sighed. 'Service.' She pushed the plates towards Patricio.

For the crew Sofia served up the same spaghetti, a Cajun take on a puttanesca, but she was too tired to eat it herself. As soon as Petra took the plates away she slinked back to her bed, and fell asleep almost instantaneously.

After a dreamless night, Sofia woke up early. The light was grey and she knew that her body was urging her to find him. Dawn was their time and she found herself pulling on a jumper and walking up to the deck in a trancelike state.

It was raining slightly, and the fog was thicker than usual. She had to walk all the way up to the railing to be sure that he wasn't there. She was disappointed and she couldn't ignore the ache in her heart any longer. In that instant she knew it would be impossible to ignore the pull. That almost innate force that had her searching for him in the liminal space between days.

Then, as if she had willed him, he was in front of her, hair tousled and damp from the drizzle, but eyes radiant.

'I thought I might find you here,' he said simply, and she wasn't entirely sure she wasn't dreaming.

'Me too,' she replied, 'although I know I am breaking the terms of our little bet.' She wanted to reach out, but she didn't.

'I think the bet died when I almost killed you. You can have the dawns, Sofia.' He looked sad, she thought.

'You didn't almost kill me, Jack. I'm fine, but I'll take the dawns if you're offering.' She smiled at him, but the one he returned didn't reach his eyes.

He turned out to sea, leaning on the rail, and she joined him. They stood silently side by side for a while.

'I think she likes you,' he whispered, looking straight ahead.

'What do you mean?'

'My mum – I think I feel her more when you're here anyway, if you were worried about that.' He sounded like a boy, and Sofia felt the sting of tears pricking her eyes.

'Did she like the sea?'

He glanced at Sofia with a look of sorrow, defiance and love. 'She *is* the sea now.' He closed his eyes and turned his face into the spray. 'An island girl at heart – it was the only place she could ever rest.'

Sofia gazed at him, this beautiful, brave, funny, sad man in front of her, who sailed the high seas to keep his mother company, and she knew for certain that she loved him. The realisation almost made her want to laugh out loud. How ludicrous it seemed to her now that she had imagined she could run away from it, bury it somehow. She reached out her hand and laid it over his. He squeezed it lightly. As they stood, facing the iron-coloured waves, she also knew that she would give this all up for him. He could have the dawns, the sea, the boat, the job. She could not be the thing that tore them away from him. If she stayed, they would only slip up, and the captain had already given him a second chance. She was not a woman who was in the habit of handing out a third.

They stayed until the sun pierced the horizon and floated into the sky, and Sofia found herself resenting it for rising too quickly. The rain stopped and the hairs on her head began to bounce into coils as the rays dried them both off. She didn't want this time to end but the daylight had a way of illuminating reality. She slipped her hand from his.

'I'd better go.' She guessed he thought she meant to prepare breakfast, but as she said the words, they rang poignantly true. He nodded, almost imperceptibly, without turning his head and she found herself longing for one more swim in those green pools, before walking away.

She passed by her cabin, taking her time to shower and get dressed, suddenly feeling pre-emptive nostalgia for her cramped quarters. She made breakfast for the guests, huevos rancheros with the green salsa on the side, although she was hoping that Milly might continue her adventurous streak. When Petra came to collect the plates she seemed distracted. Sofia had been expecting an inquisition about the day before, but instead Petra just said, 'Looks delicious, Sofia,' absent-mindedly and took the food away.

When she came back with the empties, Sofia's curiosity got the better of her. 'Everything good with you?'

Petra looked like she'd been caught out, a deer in the headlights. 'Yes, everything's fine. Why do you ask?' She rushed through her words defensively.

Sofia held up her hands in surrender. 'No reason, you just seem a bit . . . out of it this morning, and you haven't even asked for the details of yesterday's fiasco.'

'Not everything's about you, Sofia.' Petra had spoken teasingly but Sofia was stung, probably because she recognised the truth in it. She had come to rely on Petra as a sounding board, a confidante, but it was often only in moments of crisis that Sofia actually asked Petra about what was going on with her.

'Ouch, noted.' Sofia was embarrassed.

'Oh sorry, I didn't mean it – I was only joking. Obviously I want to know all about it.' Petra leant over the counter and lifted Sofia's cheek to look her in the eye. 'Go on, spill,' she said cheekily.

Sofia felt a little self-conscious now, but she had to play along, after she'd made such a fuss. 'Oh it was nothing really. We just went scuba diving when the guests were asleep and then I ran out of oxygen in the water and passed out and he rescued me and swam me back to the beach.' Sofia was wiping the countertop and delivered the news nonchalantly but she couldn't resist peeking up to catch Petra's reaction.

'You WHAT?' Petra seemed lost for words. 'I'm sorry but what the hell? You two think you're in a romance novel or something? That is beyond dramatic.' Petra seemed to still be processing.

'So what does this mean for your . . . situation?' And there it was: the crux of the matter.

All of sudden Sofia felt shy. She worried that if she revealed her plan, Petra might try and talk her out of it.

'I don't really know,' she said dismissively. Now she suddenly wanted to reverse the line of questioning. 'So what did you get up to last night?'

'Nothing,' Petra said, a little too quickly.

Sofia narrowed her eyes. 'OK, if you say so.' It was a role reversal. Petra had once met Sofia's evasions with exactly the same response.

Petra countered her suspicion with a bright smile. 'Anyway, got places to be! See you later.' And she was gone.

# Chapter Forty-Six

Sofia had put it off long enough, she had to follow through. It was the only way. She was going to speak to the captain. As she made her way up the stairs to her office, she passed Stuart, who was grinning from ear to ear.

'Hey, Stuart, you're looking like the cat that's got the cream today.' She couldn't help but comment on it. His usual expression would best be described as glumly uninterested.

'You could say that,' he chirped as they passed each other, but he didn't stop to expand and so Sofia went on her way.

Outside the door she took a deep breath to steady herself. Had it really only been two days since she was last here begging to keep her job? So much had changed since then. Or maybe not. In a way everything was the same as it had always been; it was only that now she recognised *it* for what *it* was.

She knocked. She waited. When Captain Mary answered the door, she looked surprisingly flustered. Sofia was momentarily taken aback and they stood and stared at each other for a moment.

'How can I help you, Sofia?' the captain said finally.

'May I come in?' Her voice was croaky.

'Sure.' The captain sounded weary. 'Take a seat.'

Once she was sat down Sofia realised that perhaps for the first time in her life, she hadn't prepared anything to say. The captain raised her eyebrows and planted her elbow on the table in front of her emphatically.

'I don't mean to rush you, but I'm having quite a busy morning and I have some things to sort out, so if you would care to tell me what you came here to say, that would be much appreciated.'

The inflection of irritation in the captain's voice jolted Sofia out of her stupor.

'I have come to say that as much as I am really, really grateful for you giving me another chance, I don't think I can keep working on this boat.' Sofia surprised herself with how calm and considered she sounded. In her chest her heart was pounding wildly.

The captain looked shocked for a second and then recovered herself. 'I see,' she said evenly, leaning back in her chair. 'And may I ask what has led you to take this decision?'

Another deep breath. 'May I be candid?' The stress of the situation seemed to be turning her into a Victorian lady.

'Please do.' The captain was growing impatient.

'I lied to you, Captain, when I told you that I did not have feelings for Jack . . . I mean Officer Carter . . . That wasn't . . . isn't true and I don't want to jeopardise his career. He loves working here, on this boat, with you, and it wouldn't be fair for me to take that away from him because we . . . I can't maintain a purely professional relationship with him.' Her panic had subsided, replaced by a calm sense of knowing. She was doing the right thing. 'So, if you'll have me, I would still like to finish the charter, but I won't be vying for the permanent position after that.'

'I see.' The captain seemed to be deep in thought. 'Have you spoken to Officer Carter about your decision?'

'No,' Sofia said firmly, 'this is my choice, and I stand by it.'

'All right.' The captain stood up and reached her hand across the table. 'If you have made your choice, I can only thank you for coming to me and letting me know. I will have a think about the best course of action in terms of this charter but, may I just say, we'll be sad to lose you.'

Sofia shook the captain's hand. 'Thank you, for everything. I have learnt so much and really enjoyed myself. You cannot know how much I needed that.'

Sentimentality was obviously not the captain's forte. She nodded curtly and led Sofia to the door. 'Good day,' she said as she left Sofia in the corridor.

She didn't know what she had expected but it had ended up feeling anticlimactic, especially as it was already time to get started on lunch. She made her way back to the kitchen. Ever a slave to the meal schedule, she began dutifully chopping.

\* \* \*

When Patricio came to collect the dishes, Sofia didn't even flinch when he noted that the Spanish omelette looked a little underdone, she just slid it back into the pan for a minute and then replated it. Once he had flounced out of the room, she resolved to confront him when he returned. She had nothing left to lose after all. They would only be colleagues for another couple of weeks, maybe less, if the captain decided to kick her out at the next port stop.

When he laid the empties on the counter, he turned to leave without saying a word. Sofia had already faced a difficult conversation that morning. What was one more?

'Patricio, can I have a word?' He spun on his heel, hands on hips, smirking. She could hardly remember the old Patricio, so sweet and conscientious, so dramatic was his personality transplant.

'Yes?'

'I was just hoping we could clear the air.' Sofia tried to sound breezy. She felt like giving the situation too much gravitas would play into Patricio's melodrama. 'I've noticed that you've been a bit short with me recently.'

Patricio responded by curling his lip.

'What did I do?' She had slipped into exasperation. 'Is it because of Declan?'

Patricio sniffed.

'Please, just tell me.' Now she was begging.

Patricio indulged in the tension, taking his time before replying. 'OK, Sofia, you want to know the truth?'

Sofia nodded.

'Obviously I feel sorry for my friend Declan. It is clear

that he feels very strongly for you, and he is hurting because now he knows that you do not feel the same way about him.' He spoke slowly and deliberately. 'But the person I am hurting for, whom you have wronged, that is Jack.'

Sofia blinked, confused.

Patricio seemed to find her reaction infuriating. 'I am angry because you have treated them both like they are disposable. Declan is young and he will get over it, but Jack, I have never seen him open up like this with anyone. He is . . . well not so young, and it takes a lot for him to let down his . . .' he was shouting and waving his arms around, frustrated to be at a loss for vocabulary '. . . how do you say? Walls? His defences, his barriers!

'That night when you told me that you had been together, I was so happy. Finally I thought he might have a chance at love. He might start to believe that it was possible for him, but then you . . .' He trailed off, and shot her a look she could only describe as one of revulsion. He sighed theatrically and crossed his arms. 'You broke his heart, left him alone in that room and ran away. When he tried to talk to you, you dismissed him. You made it clear that it had meant nothing to you. That is what I cannot forgive you for.'

Sofia was in a state of shock. She didn't know where to begin. She had so many questions, and she started with the most pressing. 'What has this got to do with you exactly, Patricio?'

He huffed, 'Me? We are brothers, Sofia. His blood is

346

my blood, and family is everything. There is some truth in *that* Italian stereotype.' He was catching his breath, climbing down for the adrenaline high of his rage.

Brothers, of course. But why hadn't Jack told her? The burning next question popped into her brain. 'Does he know?' she asked quietly.

Patricio's face drained of colour, and she had her answer. He had overstepped, thrown down all his cards in anger and now it was Sofia who held them. She didn't want them.

'Patricio,' she said softly, as if calming a wild animal, 'that is not how it happened.'

'Jack was the one who left in the morning. I went to find him, but I couldn't and then I overheard him telling the captain it was all . . .' She paused. Even now the words stuck in her throat painfully. 'It was all a mistake. I assumed he meant it and . . .' She considered whether to reveal herself. It seemed only fair. 'And let's just say that it is not the first time that a man has said that about me, so I wasn't going to wait around and be made a fool of.'

She searched his face and was relieved to see a trickle of empathy.

'He didn't mean that, Sofia,' Patricio said hesitantly, 'or maybe he thought he did when he said it, but he doesn't really. Surely you must know what men are like?'

Sofia snorted in bemusement. 'Apparently not.'

Patricio looked deep into her eyes. 'They so often do not know their own hearts; they think only with their minds.'

'I think maybe I am guilty of that too,' she admitted.

Patricio suddenly looked hopeful. 'And what do you feel in your heart?'

'That I love him.' The words tumbled out before Sofia could stop them. Patricio pulled her into a tight hug.

'I knew it,' he whispered into her ear. 'I am certain that he feels the same. You must tell each other immediately.' Patricio pulled away, a bundle of excitement, his demeanour transformed. Sofia did not know how to tell him that she would never do that, that she would rather leave and let Jack have the life he had always dreamed of.

'You have to tell him too, Patricio.' She thought of the little boy grieving for his mother all alone. 'He is always looking for her and she is a part of you, so he has been looking for you too.' Patricio blinked tears and this time it was Sofia who pulled him into a hug. He sobbed softly against her shoulder.

'None of them were ever supposed to know,' he began, his words muffled by her hair. 'The Americans,' he clarified. He leant back, scrubbing at his eyes with the backs of his hands. 'She got pregnant with me almost as soon as she returned to Capri, and she was still married then so it was very shameful.' He hung his head, as though he was to blame. 'My father worked for the family and when I was born I went to live with him and my grandmother. He tells me that she would often come to visit me,' he sniffed, holding back more tears, 'but I was not even three years old when she passed.'

Looking at him standing here in front of her, Sofia

could not believe that she had not clocked the connection the moment they met. The angular jaw and full lips, the dark hair – even their build was similar, although Jack was taller. And in those same green eyes, that same deep sorrow she had seen that very morning on the deck.

'I never even knew her.' The tears cascaded down his cheeks.

'She was amazing.' Sofia smiled, wiping away the drops as they fell. 'And Jack would love nothing more than to tell you all about her.' Patricio nodded, gulping. Sofia rubbed his back gently until his breathing slowed.

# Chapter Forty-Seven

The crackle from the radio made Sofia and Patricio both jump, so long and comfortably they had stood together in the quiet kitchen.

'All crew report to the main saloon, immediately.' It was Captain Mary's voice, and they did as they were told. Sofia felt uneasy as she climbed the stairs. Usually crew matters were conducted in the mess, away from prying eyes. It felt disconcertingly formal to have a meeting above sea level.

The mood was tense when they walked in. Jack, Petra, Stuart and Declan were already sitting in a semicircle.

Sofia noticed that Petra and Stuart were sitting especially close, the sides of their legs conspicuously touching.

'Thank you all for convening so swiftly.' Captain Mary was standing and gestured for Sofia and Patricio to take a seat. They slid in beside Declan. Sofia wasn't sure she could bear to be so close to Jack, knowing the decision she had just made to take herself far away.

'I've had . . .' the captain stopped to consider the most appropriate phrasing '. . . an interesting morning.' Sideways glances were exchanged. Between Petra and

Stuart a sly smile. Between Patricio and Declan a raised eyebrow. Sofia looked over at Jack to see him staring straight ahead.

'Over the course of the past four hours, four of you have handed in your notice,' the captain said evenly. This time the reaction was universal: shock.

'What? Four? Who?' It was Declan, voicing the questions on everyone's mind.

'First thing I had a visit from our dear Petra, and then from Stuart. They have both informed me that after this season, they wish to step down from their roles.' Sofia looked over to see Petra reach for Stuart's hand. When she spoke she was gazing at him.

'We've decided to . . .' she stammered, smiling into her lap and then recovered herself '. . . to try out life on land, together.'

Sofia must have been the single person in the room for whom this was not a total surprise and still she was struck silent by shock.

'I'm sorry, what?' Jack looked completely stunned. 'I didn't even realise you two. I . . .' Sofia realised that she'd never quite pieced together how long they had all known each other, but to have made it to the top of their respective career ladders, she supposed that Jack, Stuart and Petra must go a long way back.

Stuart blushed. 'It wasn't an easy decision to come to, and I know it seems all very sudden, but Petra and I had a long talk and we realised that it's something we both want.' He looked up at the captain apologetically. 'To try this thing out properly, and give it a real shot, away from this . . .' everyone was being careful with their words it seemed '. . . hectic lifestyle.'

'So you two are leaving yachting?' Declan again.

'For now, yes. I have loved the past decade at sea.' She laughed self-consciously. 'God, has it really been a decade? But I've given the entirety of my twenties to this life and I need a fresh start.' She smiled at Stuart, who nodded encouragingly.

Sofia let the news sink in. In front of her were two people, clearly in love and so confidently choosing each other. She was happy for Petra, but there was a part of her, the cynic, who worried. How could they be so sure? How could they be so willing to give up on the life they had built for themselves in pursuit of something that, as far as Sofia knew, they had only managed to verbalise to each other last night?

Then it struck her – it was basically what she was doing. Except she hadn't even had the courage to verbalise it. She wasn't even left with a chance of happily ever after. She was still trying to protect her heart, even as she tore it in two.

'And who else?' Patricio was growing impatient.

Sofia braced herself for what she knew the captain would announce next.

'Well, after Stuart and Petra, I was visited by our very own Captain Carter.' It took Sofia a moment to register what was being said, so sure had she been that she was about to hear her own name.

'Jack?' She didn't realise she'd said it out loud until the captain looked her straight in the eye. 'Yes, Sofia.'

Her thoughts were racing. She ran through the gamut of explanations of why Jack would resign. Maybe something had happened to his brother Danny and he had to go back to New York; or maybe he was taking a better job on another boat; maybe he had finally had enough of their incessant hot-and-cold and just needed to get away from her.

Unlike Stuart and Petra, Jack was not a man who felt the need to explain himself. He simply nodded curtly at the captain. 'It's been a pleasure and an honour working with you, Captain Mary.' Sofia willed him to meet her eyes, but his expression was steadfast and fixed on the horizon.

'And finally, after only a brief stint on board, Sofia too has decided to leave.' The full force of all the eyes in the room bore down on her. She had known her time would come around but she had hoped that when it did she would suddenly know what to say.

She stared at her hands as she spoke. 'Yes, um, I . . .' She could not tell the entire crew the things she could not even say to the one person who might need to hear it. She glanced up and locked on to the only pair of eyes that mattered, those green pools so perplexed.

She took a deep breath, and looked at the captain as she spoke. 'I no longer think that I can confidently fulfil my duties on board, in line with your . . . regulations.' It sounded pathetic really, to boil down the enormity of her feelings into such a paltry sentence.

Even the captain was unimpressed. 'Hmmm,' she said, turning back to address everyone. 'In light of this, I have been thinking about the best way forward, and I would ask that the four people who have resigned might stay back and allow me to propose a plan.'

Nobody moved for a second, and then the penny dropped, and Patricio nudged Declan to stand. Reluctantly Declan followed Patricio out of the room, throwing one last longing look over his shoulder as he closed the door. Knowing those two, Sofia felt sure that they would not be too far away on the other side.

The captain pulled out a chair and dragged it closer to face the remaining four. 'Now, what I have witnessed today has been quite something. In all of my thirty years, I have never had one, let alone two . . . *couples*—' the word seemed to stick in her throat, and she cleared it emphatically '—two couples resign in order to pursue a relationship, and in a single day!' Captain Mary shook her head in bemused disbelief.

It dawned on Sofia that the captain thought that she and Jack were doing the same thing as Petra and Stuart, but that they had just chosen to be more deceitful about it. Maybe the captain had concluded that she and Jack had conspired to hide the real reason they were both leaving together. That they had carried on their relationship illicitly even after they had been found out.

'Stuart and Petra, I am going to put an offer on the table. If I were to strike off the ban on onboard relations from the rule book, could you be convinced to reconsider?' The captain was leaning forward, her hands steepled in front of her face.

Still clutching hands, Petra and Stuart exchanged a meaningful look, each nodding faintly as they reached the end of their telepathic huddle.

'That is a very generous offer, Captain, but this isn't just about the rule. I made a pact with myself that I could not grow old on this boat.' Petra stopped, worried that her words were pointed. 'I mean no disrespect by that, but ever since I was little, I have always dreamed of the white picket fence, of being a mother . . . as clichéd as that sounds.'

'Not at all, Petra, it is a gift to be blessed with the clarity of what one wants in life, and it is each of our responsibility to be brave enough to pursue that.'

Petra's eyes glistened, and now she reached for the captain's hand. Maybe she did do sentimentality after all, thought Sofia.

As Petra clasped her hand, the two women seemed to be having an unspoken conversation of their own. The captain had chosen her path, even if it meant giving up on a family life. She seemed not to begrudge Petra for making the inverse choice.

The captain turned to Stuart. 'And you, Stuart?'

Evidently uncomfortable talking about his feelings, Stuart picked at his thumbnail. 'I guess sort of the same. I didn't really have a stable base growing up and I think that if . . .' He glanced at Petra who smiled encouragingly.

'If I ever had a family, I'd like to be, you know, around.'

The captain nodded. 'Very well, thank you both, for your honesty.' Now *that* felt pointed. Sofia was bursting to defend herself, but how?

'Would you mind leaving me with Jack and Sofia alone?' Unlike Declan, Petra and Stuart were all too keen to be out of the room as quickly as possible, Stuart ploughing into the door frame in his haste.

Jack and Sofia were left on either end of the large curved sofa. They could not have been sitting further apart. The captain looked from one to the other and motioned for them to shuffle into the middle. It was a deeply undignified manoeuvre and by the end of it, Sofia felt they were sitting far too close.

She started with Jack. 'Now, I would be tempted to offer you both the same deal, but to be honest, Jack, I am disappointed that you didn't feel able to tell me the truth.'

Jack hung his head. 'I'm sorry. Mary.' His voice was meek, like a child's.

'You told me that you wanted to resign because you felt like you had reached the end of your career development here, and that hurt me.' Sofia had never seen the captain look so emotional. She almost felt like she should look away, like this moment between them deserved privacy.

'I really advocated for you, Jacky. In the beginning I put my neck on the line recommending you. I was only a first officer then, but I saw how much you needed a helping hand and I was happy to support you.' The captain looked down. 'And then when you came to me this morning, I felt

356

so confused, so guilty that I had neglected you recently.' She shook her head, and when she spoke again her voice had a steely edge. 'And then when Sofia came to my office I realised what was going on, that you must have been carrying on with your fling and now you were going to give all this up for it.'

Her words hung in the air, pregnant with betrayal and shared history. Jack took a moment to collect himself before he replied.

'Mary, I am so sorry, I hate lying to you, and I was a coward to do it today but the truth is . . .' he looked over at Sofia and smiled sadly '. . . the truth is I only wanted to leave so that she could stay. This thing between us, I'm not sure what it is, but it isn't "a fling". We haven't even . . .' he blushed, and cleared his throat '. . . since that night.'

A deep breath, and now his voice was less shaky, more assertive. 'I have tried to keep it professional, I have tried to avoid her, I have tried to be her friend, but it is all futile, and I didn't want to disrespect you by carrying on behind your back. I didn't want Sofia to lose this job that I know she loves, because I couldn't keep *it* under wraps.' He sighed. 'God knows, I have had my fair share of adventures on this boat, but Sofia, she's got it all to come.'

Sofia didn't realise she was crying until a tear fell onto the hand curled in her lap. She wiped her eyes hurriedly, but not before the captain saw.

'So you didn't know that he was going to resign?' the captain asked Sofia, putting the pieces together.

'No, I quit . . .' she felt silly admitting it after his impassioned speech '. . . for pretty much the same reason.'

Jack's eyes widened. His face suddenly lit up with something like . . . hope?

'And you, Jack, you didn't know that Sofia was resigning?' The captain was determined to get the facts straight. Jack shook his head distractedly, not taking his eyes off Sofia.

'Jack . . .' she began, 'I had no idea. Why didn't you . . . ?'

'Why didn't you?' he interrupted, an amused look tugging at the corners of his mouth.

'Well, I must say, this is all a little Shakespearean, wouldn't you say? I didn't take you for indulging in these kinds of dramatics, Jacky.' The captain shook her head in disbelief. 'Who would have thought that one simple rule would cause such havoc,' she muttered to herself.

Sofia had stopped listening. She was still trying to process what Jack had said. She reached for his hand, clasping it tight, all sense of embarrassment momentarily suspended by the swell of joy coursing through her. 'I thought I was the only one who felt it,' she muttered in disbelief, as if to herself.

'You kids, call *it* what *it* is, for God's sake. You are clearly, madly in love.' They both looked at the captain, who was sitting across from them with her arms folded and an incredulous expression on her face. Suddenly the whole scene seemed outlandishly funny to Sofia, and she burst into a fit of giggles, Jack joined in and, after the surprise had passed, so did the captain.

Sofia was delirious by the time the laughter died down, but Jack had the presence of mind to dare to ask, 'So, Captain, can you forgive the lie, and bend the rules for two kids in love?' It felt jarring to Sofia to hear him throw the word around so cavalierly.

Captain Mary smiled. 'It brings me the greatest joy to see you so happy, Jacky, but you know me, ever erring on the side of caution. Here's my proposal.' Sofia squeezed Jack's hand as they waited to hear their fate.

'I would like to hire you both for the next charter. We can call it a test drive. Before Sofia came to me this morning I had been meaning to offer her the permanent position, but I will hold off, for now, and see how you two fare working together.'

They both agreed immediately and Sofia thought that Captain Mary seemed the most pleased with the outcome. Sofia supposed it would be a headache to replace a first officer *and* a chef before the next guests arrived.

# Chapter Forty-Eight

As the three of them left the room, Sofia was having a hard time understanding all that had just happened. For now she had *not* lost her job, of that she was sure, but in the whirlwind, everything else still felt up in the air. Miscommunication had gotten them into this mess and she wanted to be sure that this wasn't just another misguided strategy from Jack to keep their jobs.

The captain headed back upstairs, and Sofia looked up at Jack, lost for words. Where to start.

'Well, that's a first, Sofia Harlow rendered speechless,' Jack teased.

'Nah, I thought I'd leave all the talking to you from now on. That was quite the soliloquy in there, dragged on a little bit by the end though.' She grimaced playfully. As ever it was easier to make a joke than say what needed to be said.

She took a deep breath and watched Jack's expression turn sombre to match her own. 'Did you mean what you said in there?' She was surprised to hear her own voice trembling as she spoke. 'About . . .' She paused, plucking up the courage. 'About love . . . about loving me?'

He laid the palms of his hands flat against each cheek,

waiting until their eyes met before he replied, 'If you're asking me if I love you, Sofia, the answer is yes. Somehow after . . .' he frowned, calculating in his head '. . . fifteen days, I have found myself irrevocably, undeniably, some might say madly, in love with you.'

As Jack continued, Sofia fought back tears, unsuccessfully, and two firm thumbs wiped them as they fell. 'You're stubborn, sarcastic, completely incapable of having a serious conversation, but you're brilliant, Sofia, and I love you not in spite of any of those things, but because of them. Every day with you, every conversation, in fact, is an adventure where I don't know where I'm going to end up next. Being with you is like being with myself in a way I haven't been able to do in a very long time. It feels like being home and I like it, which is saying something from someone who has spent the past decade running away from that. The last two weeks have shown me that maybe I don't know myself as much as I thought I did, but this . . .' He shook her gently. 'This, I know. So yes, I meant it.'

Sofia found herself in the grips of some strange combination of a sniffle and a snigger, quite unable to handle the surge of contradictory feeling.

He pulled her into a hug, and waited for her to quieten. 'I knew for certain yesterday, on the deck,' he whispered into her ear. She pulled away, suddenly fortified.

'That's when I knew I loved you too,' she said simply, and he grinned. She was not the effusive type. She hoped in time she might be able to return the favour with her own romantic proclamation, but for today that would have to be enough.

They stood for a moment, the words settling between them, eyes searching eyes and finding certainty. All of a sudden, he picked her up and threw her over his shoulder. She found herself yelping, giddy with childlike delight.

'That's quite enough of that for now, Harlow, we're colleagues after all; we gotta keep things professional.' He marched across the deck with her legs dangling across his chest.

'Put me down!' she demanded, but she was laughing.

As they walked past the downstairs saloon, she spotted the guests lounging behind the glass.

'Jack! They're going to see!' But it was too late. Brian was prodding Milly and wolf whistling. Even through the glass, the shrill of Milly's squeal was piercing.

'Jack and Sofia for ever,' she called, clapping excitedly. Jack gave a salute and Sofia waved as she was carried past.

Outside the door to the mess, Jack put Sofia down. They were both breathless with excitement, but as they looked at each other, the world slowed. She smiled, he smiled, and then she couldn't stand it anymore – she grabbed his collar and pulled his lips to hers. Instantaneously the furnace was lit, burning ferociously in the pit of her stomach. It was going to be hard to keep her hands off him long enough to get food on the table. He groaned and grabbed at her waist, pulling her in to him. Just before the fuzz in her brain took over her better judgement, she pulled him away, panting softly.

'We can't do this here, we're on a test run, remember? We can save that—' she slapped his arse playfully '—for the bunk.' She winked at him, revelling in his look of horny bewilderment and swung open the door.

Patricio and Declan were sat together in one corner, and Petra and Stuart in another. The chatter died immediately as they stared expectantly.

'So, guys, we have a little announcement.' She was trying to be coy, but she couldn't stop grinning.

Patricio was not going to indulge her in the dramatic build-up. 'OMG! Yes, love it, love it!' he exclaimed before trilling his tongue.

'She hasn't even said anything yet!' Petra said impatiently. 'Go on!'

'We're both staying on the boat.' Jack took the reins, and Sofia was overwhelmed by the cheers. Next it was all hugs, a little perfunctory from Stuart and Declan, but longer and tighter from Petra and from Patricio, who had tears in his eyes as she leant back.

'And just to be clear, you two are . . . ?' Petra was not going to let them get away with any ambiguity.

'Together,' Sofia and Jack said at the same time.

'Now that's too much,' Petra said dryly before breaking out into a grin.

'One charter, two couples. Poor Captain Mary must be having to rethink that famous rule,' Declan chimed.

'Well if she will keep inviting people onto the *Lady Ixchel*, what does she expect?' Everybody turned to Stuart, confused. '*Lady Ixchel*? Ixchel, like the Mayan goddess of love?' His insightful observation was only met with shrugs and murmurs. 'Never mind,' he mumbled.

'Well it seems she's scrapping that rule now,' Petra interjected, coming to Stuart's aid. Sofia spotted Patricio glancing over at Declan.

'So, what now?' Declan wondered, ever full of questions.

'Well,' Petra took a moment to compile a list in her head. 'The top deck needs scrubbing.' She pointed at Declan. 'The beds need stripping.' She pointed at Patricio. 'Our next stop needs to be mapped out and our spot in the harbour reserved.' The finger spun to Stuart and then Jack. 'Dinner needs to be cooked.' Sofia's turn. 'And I have a pile of ironing sitting in the laundry room with my name on it.'

They all stood for a moment. 'Chop, chop, this isn't a holiday!' And with the clap of Petra's hands, they all scattered.

# Epilogue

## Six months later

Sofia woke up with the dawn, and immediately knew that Jack was not beside her. It was hard not to notice when you were sharing a single bunk with someone. She wondered if she should join him on deck but just as she'd psyched herself up to throw back the covers, he came through the door with two cups of coffee.

'Did I wake you?' Sofia had been surprised to find that Jack was very attentive, always wondering if she was comfortable or hungry or cold.

'Nope,' she said, stretching out a yawn, 'I was about to come and find you.'

'Well, here I am.' He set down the two mugs and Sofia grabbed him by the bottom of his T-shirt, pulling him towards her.

'Here you are, indeed.' She smiled devilishly as he leant over the bunk and placed a soft kiss on her lips. She pouted as he turned away. 'Is that it?' She sounded petulant, but when he turned back he looked amused.

'Oh, you want more?' he said, feigning surprise, but stepping out of his pyjama bottoms.

She bit her lip and nodded coyly. 'Just a little bit more please.' He pulled off his T-shirt and then his boxers. She feasted with her eyes and it only made her more ravenous.

'I have to say, it is so very lucky that we both wake up at dawn,' he murmured as he threw back the cover to reveal her naked body. He admired her quietly, the rise and fall of her belly quickening with each passing second.

He climbed on top of her, and she laced her arms around his neck. 'When else would we have time for all of this?' he whispered in her ear before taking the lobe between his teeth. She sighed deeply, her body awakened and fizzing wherever her skin touched his. He pulled her head back, his fingers tangled in her hair, and scattered kisses down her exposed neck. Already she was trembling beneath him. She could not seem to get used to his touch. Each time she was newly shocked by the singe it left in its wake. By now at least she had managed to control the urge to check for marks.

Against her leg she could feel the smooth hardness growing, and she reached for it. He whimpered against her throat as she handled him. Softly, teasingly at first, and then tightening her grip, rubbing herself against him as she stroked up and down. He rolled onto his side, and she spread her legs. It was a choreography they had become adept at. His hand traced spirals on her stomach and then thighs. He liked to wait until just before she thought she might have to beg for it. His fingers found her and the spike of pleasure frothed all the way to *her* fingertips, and as she let out a wail, his other hand collapsed around her mouth.

'You gotta keep it down. Some people don't like to be woken up before the sunrise,' he scolded her, but it only made her want to scream louder. He was quickening now, watching her intently for cues, fingernails grasping at the sheets, toes curling, legs shaking, back arching. Only then, and after he had kept her on the edge for an agonisingly unknowable amount of time, would he stretch inside of her and lull her off the cliff, to fall into rapturous oblivion.

In the darkness she clawed at him, bringing his face to hers – her guiding light out of herself. When he sunk into her, exhaling at the quenching of a savage thirst, she welcomed him into that liminal space. The space where there was only them and throbbing, and aching, and reaching, and release.

How many times since that first time had they been to that place together? She couldn't remember, but it always felt new, like they were discovering it together, pioneers of sex. He was grunting, and she was panting, and the white noise from her mind was trickling over her body. They were going to arrive together, and she grabbed for his hand as they tumbled. Moaning, bracing, wincing as they went.

Sofia often found it hard to orientate herself in the moments afterwards, she might have the impression that she was hanging upside down or that her body was hovering just above the mattress. It was the sensation of Jack's hands stroking her hair, or his voice that directed her back down to reality.

'Today's the day,' she said, as the weight of earthly

concerns nestled itself back into her brain. It was Petra and Stuart's last day, the end of the season, and perhaps an opportunity to meet the new recruits.

It felt like a lifetime ago that Sofia had stepped onto the boat for the first time.

'I'm going to miss Petra,' Jack mused. Sofia turned her head and shot him a look. She had also surprised herself at her tendency towards jealousy, something she had never experienced with her exes. Jack laughed.

'You can't be serious! Even now, even after that.' He snuggled his nose into the nape of Sofia's neck and she felt the tension evaporate from her body. 'Even after the proposal?' he teased.

Stuart had popped the question, to everyone's surprise, after the last guests had left two days ago. Petra had been in hysterics when she came down to the mess to show everyone the ring. Sofia had only been able to make out the words 'deck', 'sunset' and 'marry' but it was enough to come to an accurate conclusion.

Sofia might have once only pretended to be unquestioningly happy for Petra. There was a past version of Sofia – the grey, ambitious, slightly cynical version – that would have faced Petra with a smile but been wondering how long a marriage between two people who only started dating six months ago could possibly last. Now she was glowing with the sort of blinding faith in love that only came from being in the depths of it yourself. They had clasped at each other, and Sofia had found herself succumbing to the tears. 'I'm so happy for you,' she had said, blinking back the heat behind her eyes, and she had meant it.

'I wonder where the wedding will be?' Sofia mused out loud, her fingers wandering up and down Jack's back. She could feel the hotness of his breath against her chest and she found herself marvelling, as she did most days, at the overwhelming sense of wellbeing she felt. It was hard to describe an extreme feeling of contentment. Usually it was experienced in its well-known, milder form. With Jack, the groundedness felt both calming and ecstatic.

'I guess it'll be in the UK? That's where they're going to live, but then it might be a long journey for her family coming all the way from Australia,' Jack mumbled, his lips vibrating against her rib cage so she could feel the words more than hear them.

'You don't think they'll do it in Italy? Surely that's the most natural choice.'

Jack looked up at Sofia, two gems of green poking through dark lashes. 'Is that right?' he said, a small smile creeping across his face.

Sofia blushed, suddenly aware that they had stumbled into a conversation about marriage. 'Well I mean, it's terribly romantic, isn't it.'

'It is,' he agreed, pulling himself onto his elbow and planting a soft kiss on her lips. He looked down at her admiringly. 'I would offer them the use of my grandmother's villa; the citrus grove would be a perfect spot . . .' He trailed off. Sofia watched the green turn liquid, molten. 'But I'd rather save it for something special.'

He held her gaze for a second longer before looking away, chuckling to himself. 'One day,' he muttered.

Sofia wasn't ready to let go of the moment. She reached for his cheek and pulled him back to her, kissing him deeply. '*One day,*' she mouthed and Jack smiled shyly.

When they were together, the hours seemed to melt into minutes and soon they were both scrambling into their uniforms. There would be no guests until next season but both Petra and Stuart's replacements had made the effort to fly out to Cannes, where they were now docked, to meet the team before the next charter.

They stood side by side nudging each other out of the way of the slim wall-mounted mirror to check their reflections. Sofia watched Jack as he wrestled with a wayward curl and then tackled one of her own.

A lingering kiss in the doorway and then they went their separate ways, Sofia to the kitchen, Jack to meet the captain. Sofia was in charge of making a 'welcoming brunch' for the two newbies, whatever that was. She suspected it was just a ploy to make them feel a little less overwhelmed by the information dumping that the captain was planning to impart. It was obvious that Captain Mary was apprehensive about having to replace a head stewardess and the engineer at the same time.

Jack had been advocating for Patricio to take on more responsibility, and there had been an agreement that the role would be renamed 'senior steward' so as not to create an awkward situation whereby Patricio would be having to train up his own boss, only to be relegated back to his role as underling afterwards.

Sofia was preparing a full English breakfast for brunch and just as she began grating the potato for her homemade hash browns, Patricio walked in.

'*Ciao, bella.*' He grinned. Ever since their head-to-head in that very kitchen, Patricio had reverted to his old charming ways.

'*Ciao, come stai?*' Sofia had been practising.

'*Molto bene! Grazie,*' he responded approvingly. 'Your accent is really coming along nicely.'

Sofia blushed at the praise.

'I suppose you must be getting in a lot of out-of-hours practice,' Patricio said with a devilish smirk.

She didn't know if it was a European thing, but the ease with which Patricio seemed to be able to acknowledge, let alone joke about, his own brother's sex life was astonishing to Sofia. She was eager to change the subject.

'Are you looking forward to your break?' It seemed an innocent enough question, except for the fact that Patricio was travelling back to Capri with Jack, and he would be meeting his other brother and his grandmother for the very first time.

'Ayyy, I'm apprehensive, truth be told.' Patricio was wringing his hands, as expressive as ever. 'I'm looking forward to seeing my . . .' he paused, struck by the strangeness of what he was about to say '. . . my old family. Is that the right way to phrase it?' He chuckled nervously. 'But I am also, obviously, thinking a lot about meeting my "new" one.'

'I can't imagine what that feels like,' Sofia admitted. 'At least you'll have Jack with you.'

Patricio laughed. 'Oh, bella, are you jealous?' he teased.

She hadn't meant it to sound bitter, but if she was being honest with herself she was not looking forward to going back to England and spending two weeks with her parents and away from Jack.

She rolled her eyes and then said, 'Maybe a little . . .'

'You can have him back as soon as I'm done with him – don't worry.' Patricio rubbed her shoulder. She assumed he had meant it mockingly, but it was surprisingly comforting.

'I'm really going to miss everyone,' Sofia found herself saying.

'Oh, so sentimental! What has happened to you, Sofia? Love really has softened you.' They both giggled. 'We'll all be back, soon enough . . . well almost all of us . . .'

The mood had dampened, and Sofia decided that there was no point being nostalgic about something that wasn't, quite, over yet.

'No more wallowing. Today is about looking forward, not back,' she said, a little forcefully.

Patricio took a step back. 'Yes, Chef! T-minus twenty minutes until food to table.'

Sofia nodded, firing up the stove and dropping a hunk of butter into the large pan. 'See you in eighteen then,' Sofia called as Patricio slipped out of the kitchen.

\* \* \*

When the pair of them brought the food up to the deck, the others joined in to help lay the table. As Sofia looked around her heart thrummed with joy. Petra and Stuart could hardly keep their hands off each other long enough to put plates down, Declan and Patricio were giggling at some inside joke as usual, Jack was chatting animatedly to the captain. In the background the throng of Cannes bustled along merrily.

'They should be here any minute, I reckon,' the captain said as she eyed her watch. 'I have given her the name, length and docking number so if they can't find us they have fallen at the first hurdle.' Sofia couldn't help thinking back to her first day, dragging her case alongside Declan, so unsure of what she was walking into, and now here she was.

'Captain Mary?' called a voice. They all rushed to peer over onto the dock. Sure enough two young, and rather attractive, Sofia found herself noting, women were standing with cases of their own. Sofia checked herself, realising that she had been expecting the new engineer to be a man. She should have known better. There was nothing Captain Mary liked better than challenging the idea of 'gendered' crew roles.

'That's me,' the captain called back. 'Laura and Josephine I presume?'

'Reporting for duty,' said the shorter of the two, brushing her thick dark fringe out of her eyes as she looked up. 'You can call me Jose.'

'Shall we come up?' Laura was tall, lithe and very pale,

her auburn hair tied into a tight bun.

'Yes, do!' Declan chimed excitedly. 'We're all very excited to meet you!'

Sofia thought back to her first day, how she had thought that everyone was exaggerating about how chaotic life would be on board. Now she found herself chuckling, watching the two women wrestle their cases onto the gangway. 'Welcome to the madhouse,' she said, in all sincerity, as they walked onto the deck, smiling.